Winding Paths

by

Gertrude Page

Double 9
BOOKS

Winding Paths
by Gertrude Page

ISBN: 978-93-64288-02-6

Published by

DOUBLE 9 BOOKS

2/13-B, Ansari Road
Daryaganj, New Delhi – 110002
info@double9books.com
www.double9books.com
Tel. 011-40042856

ABOUT THE AUTHOR

Gertrude Page, born on December 19, 1865, in Oxford, England, was a prolific British novelist and writer known for her romantic and dramatic fiction. Her works often explored themes of love, personal growth, and social dynamics, reflecting the complexities of human relationships and societal expectations. Gertrude Page was renowned for her ability to craft engaging narratives with a focus on **romance** and **drama**. Her writing often involved detailed character development and explored the emotional and moral dilemmas faced by her characters. Some of her notable novels include: **"Winding Paths" (1912):** This novel explores themes of romance, conflict, and personal growth against the backdrop of Victorian society. **"The House of Dreams" (1913):** Another example of her work that delves into the complexities of relationships and societal constraints. **"The Iron Heel" (1912):** Not to be confused with Jack London's novel of the same name, this book also delves into themes of societal struggle and personal conflict. Gertrude Page's novels were well-received in her time, and her work contributed to the genre of romantic and dramatic fiction. Her ability to weave intricate stories with deep emotional resonance made her a notable author in early 20th-century literature. Gertrude Page's literary works continue to be appreciated for their insightful exploration of romance, social issues, and personal growth, leaving a lasting impact on the genre of early 20th-century fiction.

CONTENTS

"So many gods, so many creeds,
So many paths that wind and wind,
And just the art of being kind
Is all the sad world needs."

CHAPTER I

There were several interesting points about Hal Pritchard and Lorraine Vivian, but perhaps the most striking was their friendship for each other. From two wide-apart extremes they had somehow gravitated together, and commenced at boarding-school a friendship which only deepened and strengthened after their exit from the wise supervision of the Misses Walton, and their entrance as "finished" young women into the wide area of the world at large.

Lorraine went first. She was six years older than Hal, and under ordinary circumstances would hardly have been at school with her at all. As it was, she went at nineteen because she was not very strong, and sea air was considered good for her. She was a sort of parlour-boarder, sent to study languages and accomplishments while she inhaled the sea air of Eastgate. Why, among all the scholars, who for the most part regarded her as a resplendent, beautifully dressed being outside their sphere, she should have quickly developed an ardent affection for Hal, the rough-and-ready tomboy, remained a mystery; but far from being a passing fancy, it ripened steadily into a deep and lasting attachment.

When Hal was fifteen, Lorraine left; and it has to be admitted that the anxious, motherly hearts of the Misses Walton drew a deep breath of relief, and hoped the friendship would now cease, unfed by daily contact and daily mutual interests. But there they under-estimated the depth of affection already in the hearts of the girls, and their natural loyalty, which scorned a mere question of separation, and entered into one another's interests just as eagerly as when they were together.

Not that they, the Misses Walton, had anything actually against Lorraine, beyond the fact that she promised a degree of beauty likely, they felt, coupled as it was with a charming wit and a fascinating personality, to open out some striking career for her, and possibly become a snare and a temptation.

On the other hand, Hal was just a homely, nondescript, untidy, riotous type of schoolgirl, with a very strong capacity for affection, and an unmanageable predilection for scrapes and adventures, that made her more likely to fall under the sway of Lorraine, should it promise any chance of excitement.

And one had only to view Lorraine among the other "young ladies" of the seminary to fear the worst. Miss Emily Walton would never have admitted it; but even she, fondly clinging to the old tradition that the terms "girls" or "women" are less impressive than "young ladies", felt somehow that the orthodox nomenclature did not successfully fit her two most remarkable pupils. Of course they were ladies by birth and education, else they would certainly not have been admitted to so select a seminary; but whereas the rest of the pupils might be said more or less to study, and improve, and have their being in a milk and biscuit atmosphere, Hal and Lorraine were quite uncomfortably more like champagne and good, honest, frothing beer.

No amount of prunes and prism advice and surroundings seemed to dull the sparkle in Lorraine, nor daunt nor suppress fearless, outspoken, unmanageable Hal. In separate camps, with a nice little following each, to keep an even balance, they might merely have livened the free hours; but as a combination it soon became apparent they would waken up the embryo young ladies quite alarmingly, and initiate a new atmosphere of gaiety that might become beyond the restraining, select influence even of the Misses Walton.

The first scare came with the new French mistress, who had a perfect Parisian accent, but knew very little English. Of course Lorraine easily divined this, and, being something of a French scholar already, she soon won Mademoiselle's confidence by one or two charmingly expressed, lucid French explanations.

Then came the translation lesson, and choosing a fable that would specially lend itself, she started the class off translating it into an English fabrication that convulsed both pupils and mistress. Hal, of course, followed suit, and the merriment grew fast and furious after a few positively rowdy lessons.

Mademoiselle herself gave the fun away at the governesses' dinner, a very precise and formal meal, which took place at seven o'clock, to be followed at eight by the pupils' supper of bread-and-butter with occasional sardines. She related in broken English what an amusing book they had to read, repeating a few slang terms, that would certainly not, under any circumstances, have been allowed to pass the lips of the young ladies.

After that it was deemed advisable Lorraine should translate French alone, and Hal be severely admonished.

Then there was the dreadful affair of the Boys' College. It was not unusual for them to walk past the school on Sunday afternoons; but it was only after Lorraine came that a system was instituted by which, if the four front boys all blew their noses as they passed, it was a signal that a note, or possibly several, had been slipped under the loose brick at the school entrance.

Further, it was only Lorraine who could have sent the answers, because none of the other girls had an uncle often running down for a breath of sea air, when, of course, he needed his dear niece's company. He was certainly a very attentive uncle, and a very generous one too, judging by the Buszard's cakes and De Brei's chocolates, and Miss Walton could not help eyeing him a little askance.

But then, as Miss Emily said, he was such a very striking, distinguished-looking gentleman, people had already been interested to learn he had a niece at the Misses Walton's seminary. Besides, one could not reasonably object to a relative calling, and he had seemed so devoted to Lorraine's handsome mother when they had together brought her to school.

But of course, after the disgraceful episode of the notes that blew into the road, the windows had to be dulled at once, so that no one could see the boys pass. It was a mercy the thing had been discovered so soon.

Then shortly after came the breaking-up dances, one for the governesses, when the masters from the college were invited, and one the next night for the girls, when the remains of the same supper did duty again, and with reference to which Miss Walton gently told them she had not been able to ask any of the boys from the school, as she was afraid their parents would not approve; she hoped they were not disappointed, and that the big girls would dance with the little ones, as it pleased them so.

Lorraine immediately replied sweetly that none of them cared about dancing with boys, and some of the children would be much more amusing. She made herself spokeswoman, because Miss Walton had half-unconsciously glanced at her at the mere mention of the word boys, fondly believing that the other well-brought-up pupils would prefer their room to their company, whereas Lorraine might think the party very tame. Her answer was a pleasant surprise.

But then, who was to know that the night of the governesses' dance she had bribed the three girls in the small dormitory to silence, and after some half-dozen of them had gone to bed with their night-gowns over their dresses, had given the signal to arise directly the dance was in full swing. After that they adjourned to the small dormitory and spread out a repast of sweets and cakes, to which such of the younger masters as were brave enough to risk detection slipped away up the school staircase at intervals, to be more than rewarded by Lorraine's inimitable mimicry.

"There will be no boys for you to dance with, dear girls," she told them gently, "as your parents might not approve," then added, with roguish lights in her splendid eyes: "No boys, dear girls, only a few masters to supper in the small dormitory."

Hal's misdemeanours were of a less subtle kind. Neither boys nor masters interested her particularly as yet; but there were a thousand-and-one other ways of livening things up, and she tried them all, sometimes getting off scot free, and sometimes finding herself uncomfortably pilloried before the rest of the school, to be cross-questioned and severely admonished at great lenght before being "sent to Coventry" for a stated period.

But, had she only known it, there were many chicken-hearted girls who envied her even her disgrace, for the sake of the dauntless, shining spirit of her that nothing ever crushed. And as for being "sent to Coventry", well, Hal and Lorraine easily coped with that through the twopennyworth system.

If an offender was sent to Coventry, any other girl who spoke to her had to pay a fine of twopence, and if either of these two gay spirits found themselves doomed to silence, they persuaded such of the others as were "game" enough, to have occasional "twopennyworths".

Of the two, Hal was far the greater favourite; she was in fact the popular idol; for though the girls were full of admiration for Lorraine, and not a little proud of her, they were also a little afraid of a wit that could be sharp-edged, and perhaps resentful too of that nameless something about her striking personality that made them feel their inferiority.

Hal was quite different, and her unfailing spirits, her vigorous championing of the oppressed, or scathing denunciation of anything sneaky and mean, made them all look up to her, and love her, whether she knew or not.

Even the governess felt her compelling attraction, and would often, by a timely word, save her from the consequences of some forgetful moment.

At the same time, the one who warned Miss Walton against the possible ill results of the girl's growing love for Lorraine little understood the nature she had to deal with.

When Hal found herself in the private sanctum, being gently admonished concerning a friendship that was thought to be growing too strong, she was quick instantly to resent the slur on her chum. She had been sent for immediately after "evening prep.," and having, as usual, inked her fingers generously, and rubbed an ink-smudge across her face, to say nothing of really disgracefully tumbled hair, she looked a comical enough object standing before the impressive presence of the head mistress.

"Really, Hal," Miss Walton remonstrated, "can't you even keep tidy for an hour in the evening?"

"Not when it's German night," answered outspoken Hal; "where to put the verbs, and how to split them, makes my hair stand on end, and the ink squirm out of the pot."

Miss Walton tried to look severe, remarking: "Don't be frivolous here, my dear"; but, as Hal described it later, "she looked as if having so often to be sedate was beginning to make her tired."

But when she proceeded to explain to Hal that neither she nor her sister were easy in their minds about her growing devotion to Lorraine, Hal's expressive mouth began to look rather stern, and neither the ink-smudges nor the tousled hair could rob her of a certain naïve dignity as she asked, "Are you implying anything against Lorraine?"

"No, no, my dear, certainly not," Miss Walton replied, feeling slightly at a loss to express herself, "but I have never encouraged a violent friendship between two girls that is apt to make them hold aloof from the others, and be continually in one another's society. And in this instance, Lorraine being so much older than you, and of a temperament hardly likely to appeal to your brother, as a desirable one in your great friend—"

"I am not asking Dudley to make her his great friend—"

"Don't interrupt me, dear. I am only speaking of what I am perfectly aware are your brother's feeling concerning you; and seeing you have neither father nor mother, I feel my responsibility and his the greater."

"But what is the matter with Lorraine?" Hal cried, growing a little exasperated. "She is not nearly so frivolous as I am, and works far harder."

Miss Walton hesitated a little. "We feel she is naturally rather worldly-minded and ambitious, whereas you—" She paused.

"Whereas I am a simpleton," suggested Hal, with a mischievous light in her eyes. "Well, then, dear Miss Walton, how fortunate for me that some one clever and briljant is willing to give me her friendship and help to lift me out of my slough of simpletondom!"

Miss Walton looked up with a reproof on her lips, but it died away, and a new expression came into her eyes as she seemed to see something in this unruly pupil she had not before suspected. Hal still looked as if a smothered sense of injustice might presently explode into hot words; but in the meantime the air of dignity stood its ground in spite of smudges and untidiness.

Neither spoke for a moment, and then Miss Walton remarked: "You do not mean to be guided by me in this matter?"

"Lorraine is my friend," Hal answered. "I cannot let myself listen to anything that suggests a slur upon her."

"Not even if your brother expressed a wish on the subject?"

"I do not ask Dudley to let me choose his friends."

"That is quite a different matter. He is fifteen years your senior."

Hal was silent. She stood with her hands behind her, and her head held high, and her clear eyes very straight to the front; well-knit, well-built, with a promise of that vague something which is so much stronger a factor in the world than mere beauty.

Miss Walton, who necessarily saw much of the mediocre and commonplace in her life-work of turning growing girls into presentable young women, felt her feelings undergo a further change. She also had the tact to see an appeal would go farther than mere advice.

"I was only thinking of you, Hal," she said, a trifle tiredly. "I have nothing against Lorraine, except that she is dangerously attractive if she likes, and her love of admiration and excitement does not make her a very wise friend for a girl of your age. You are different, and your paths are likely to lead far apart in the future. It did not seem to me desirable you should grow too fond of each other."

Even as she spoke she found herself wondering what Hal would say, and in an unlooked-for way interested.

Hal answered promptly:

"I do not think our lives will lie apart. Both of us will have to be breadwinners at any rate, and that will be a bond."

Her mobile face seemed to change. "Miss Walton, I'm devoted to Lorraine. I always shall be. But you needn't be anxious. The stronger influence is not where you think. I can bend Lorraine's will, but she cannot bend mine. It will always be so. And nothing that you nor any one can say will make me change to her."

They said little more, but when she was alone the head mistress stood silently for some minutes looking into the dying embers of her fire. Then she uttered to herself an enigmatical sentence:

"Beauty will give to Lorraine the great career; but the greater woman will be Hal."

Shortly after that Lorraine departed, and about a year later embarked in the theatrical world.

No one was surprised, but very adverse opinions were expressed among the girls concerning her success or otherwise; those who were jealous, or who had felt slighted during her short reign as school beauty, condemning any possible likelihood of a hit.

Hal said very little. She was already reaching out tentacles to the wider world, where schoolgirl criticisms would be mere prattle; and it was far more serious to her to wonder what Brother Dudley would think of her having an actress for her greatest friend.

She foresaw rocks ahead, but smiled humorously to herself in spite of them.

"What a tussle there'll be!" was her thought, "and how in the world am I to convince Dudley that Lorraine does not represent a receptacle for all the deadly sins? Heigho! The mere fact of my disagreeing will persuade him I am already contaminated, and he will see us both heading, like fire-engines, for the nethermost hell."

CHAPTER II

If Dudley Pritchard's imagination did not actually picture the lurid and violent descent Hal suggested, it certainly did view with the utmost alarm his lively young sister's friendship with a fully fledged actress.

As a matter of fact, Miss Walton's prognostications concerning his attitude to Lorraine Vivian, even as a schoolgirl, had been instantly confirmed upon their first meeting.

For no particular reason he disapproved of her. That was rather typical of Dudley. He disapproved of a good many things without quite knowing why, or being at any particular pains to find out.

Not that it made him bigoted. He could in fact be fairly tolerant; but as Hal affectionately observed, Dudley was so apt to pat himself on the back for his toleration towards things that it would never have occured to most persons needed tolerating.

She knew perfectly well that he considered himself very tolerant towards much that was to be deprecated in her, but, far from resenting his attitude, she saw chiefly the humorous side, and managed to glean a good deal of quiet amusement from it.

Considering the fifteen years' difference in their ages, and the fact that Dudley was a hard-working architect in London, seeing life on all sides, while Hal was still a hoydenish schoolgirl, it was really remarkable how thoroughly she grasped and understood his character, and a great deal concerning the world in general, while he seemed to remain at his first decisions concerning her and most things.

It was just perhaps the difference between the book-student and the life-student. Dudley had always had a passion for books and for his profession. His clever brain was a well of knowledge concerning ancient architectures and relics of antiquity. He studied them because he loved them, and, before all things else, to him they seemed worth while.

He loved his sister also—he loved her better than any one, but it would never have occured to him that she should be studied, or that there was anything in her to study. To him she was quite an ordinary girl, rather nice-looking when she was neat, but with a most unfortunate lack of the sedate dignity and discretion that he considered essential to the typically admirable woman.

That there might be other traits in their place, equally admirable, did not occur to him. They ware not at any rate the traits he most admired.

Hal, on the other hand, was different in every respect. She loathed books, and learning, and what she called "dead old bones and rubbish." But she loved human nature, and studied it in every phase she could.

Left at a very tender age to Dudley's sole care and protection, she had to grow up without the enfolding, sympathetic love of a mother, or the gay companionship of brothers and sisters. Not in the least depressed, she started off at an early age in quest of adventure to see what the world was like outside the four walls of their home.

Brought back, sometimes by a policeman, with whom she had already become on the friendliest terms, sometimes in a cab in which some one else had placed her, sometimes by a kindly stranger, she would yet slip away again on the first opportunity, into the crush of mankind. Punishment and expostulation were alike useless; Hal was just as fascinated with people as Dudley was with books, and where her nature called she fearlessly followed.

Through this roving trait she picked up an amount of commonplace, everyday knowledge that would have dumbfoundered the clever young architect, had he been in the least able to comprehend it. But while he dipped enthusiastically into bygone ages, and won letters and honours in his profession, she asked questions about life in the present, and grappled with the problem of everyday existence and the peculiarities of human nature, in a way that made her largely his superior, despite his letters and honours.

And best of all was her complete understanding of him. Dudley fondly imagined he was fulfilling to the best possible endeavours his obligations of love and guardianship to his young sister. The young sister, with her tender, quizzical understanding, regarded him as a mere child, with a deliciously humorous way of always taking himself very seriously; a brilliant brain, an irritating fund of superiority, and something altogether apart that made him dearer than heaven and earth and all things therein to her.

Hal might be dearer than all else to Dudley, without finding herself loved in any way out of the ordinary, seeing how little he cared much about except his profession; but to be the beloved of all, to an eager, passionate, intense nature like hers, meant that in her heart she had placed him upon a pedestal, and, while fondly having her little smile over his shortcomings, yet loved him with an all-embracing love. He did not suspect it, and he would not have understood it if he had; being rather of the opinion that, considering all he had tried to be to her, she might have loved him enough in return to make a greater effort to please him.

Her obdurate resistance during the first stage of his disapproval of Lorraine Vivian increased this feeling considerably. He felt that if she really cared for him she should be willing to be guided by his judgment; and while perceiving, just as Miss Walton had done, that she meant to have her own way, he had less perspicacity to perceive also that nameless trait which, for want of a better word, we sometimes call grit, and which dimly proclaimed she might be trusted to follow her own strength of character.

When, later, his attitude of displeasure increased a thousandfold.

He was not told of it just at first. Hal was then in the throes of convincing him that her particular talents lay in the direction of secretarial work and journalism, rather than governessing or idleness, and persuading him to make arrangements at once for her to learn shorthand and typewriting with a view to becoming the private secretary of a well-known editor of one of the leading newspapers.

The editor in question was a distant connection, and quite willing to take her if she proved herself capable, recognising, through his skill at reading character, that she might eventually prove invaluable in other ways than mere letter-writing.

Dudley, seeing no farther than the fact of the City office, set his face resolutely against it as long as he could; but, of course, in the end Hal carried the day. Then came the shock of the knowledge that Lorraine had gone on the stage; and if, as had been said before, he did not actually picture the lurid exit to the lower regions Hal gave him credit for, he was sufficiently upset to have wakeful nights and many anxious, worried hours.

And to make it worse, Hal would not even be serious.

"Oh, don't look like that, Dudley!" she cried; "we really are not in any immediate danger of selling our souls to the Prince of Darkness. You dear old solemnsides! Just because Lorraine is going on the stage, I believe you already see me in spangles, jumping through a hoop. Or rather 'trying to', because it is a dead cert. I should miss the hoop, and do a sort of double somersault over the horse's tail."

Dudley shut his firm lips a little more tightly, and looked hard at his boots, without vouchsafing a reply.

"As a matter of fact," continued the incorrigible, "you ought to perceive how beautifully life balances things, by giving a dangerously attractive person like Lorraine a matter-of-fact, commonplace pal like myself to restrain her, and at the same time ward off possible dangers from various unoffending humans, who might fall hurtfully under her spell."

"It is only the danger to you that I have anything to do with."

"Oh fie, Dudley! as if I mattered half as much as Humanity with a capital H."

"To me, personally, you matter far more in this particular case."

"And yet, really, the chief danger to me is that I might unconsciously catch some reflection of Lorraine's charm and become dangerously attractive myself, instead of just an outspoken hobbledehoy no one takes seriously."

"I am not afraid of that," he said, evoking a peal of laughter of which he could not even see the point; "but since you are quite determined to go into the City as a secretary, instead of procuring a nice comfortable home as a companion, or staying quietly here to improve your mind, I naturally feel you will encounter quite enough dangers without getting mixed up in a theatrical set. Though, really," in a grumbling voice, "I can't see why you don't stay at home like any sensible girl. If I am not rich, I have at least enough for two."

"But if I stayed at home, and lived on you, Dudley, I should feel I had to improve my mind by way of making you some return; and you can't think how dreadfully my mind hates the idea of being improved. And if I went to some dear old lady as companion, she would be sure to die in an apoplectic fit in a month, and I should be charged with manslaughter. And I can't teach, because I don't know anything. The only serious danger I shall run as Mr. Elliott's secretary will be putting an occasional addition of my own to his letters, in a fit of exasperation, or driving his sub-editor mad; and he seems willing to risk that."

"You are likely to run greater dangers than that if you allow yourself to be drawn into a theatrical circle."

"What sort of dangers?... Oh, my dear, saintly episcopal architect, what foundations of darkness are you building upon now, out of a little old-fashioned, out-of-date prejudice which you might have dug up from some of your studies in antiquity books? There are just as many dangers outside the theatrical world as in it, for the sort of woman dangers are attractive to; and little Sunday-school teachers have come to grief, while famous actresses have won through unscathed."

Dudley's face expressed both surprise and distaste.

"I wonder what you know about it anyway. I think you are talking at random. Certainly no dangers would come near you if you listened to my wishes and settled down quietly at home. If you don't care about living in Bloomsbury, I will take a small house in the suburbs, and you can amuse yourself with the housekeeping, and tennis, and that sort of thing."

"And when you want to marry?"

"I shall not want to marry. I am wedded to my profession."

"O Dudley!... Dudley!..." She slipped off the table where she had been jauntily seated, and came and stood beside him, passing her arm through his. "Can't you see I'd just die of a little house in the suburbs, looking after the housekeeping: it's the most dreadful and awful thing on the face of the earth. I'm not a bit sorry for slaves, and prisoners, and shipwrecked sailors, and East-end starvelings; every bit of sympathy I've got is used up for the girls who've got to stay in hundrum homes, and be nothing, and do nothing, but just finished young ladies. Work is the finest thing in the world. It's just splendid to have something real to do, and be paid for it. Why, they can't even go to prison, or be hungry, or anything except possible wives for possible men who may or may not happen to want them."

"Of course you are talking arrant nonsense," Dudley replied frigidly. "I don't know where in the world you get all your queer ideas. Woman's sphere is most decidedly the home; you seem to—" but a small hand was clapped vigorously over his mouth, and eyes of feigned horror searching his.

"Do you know, I'm half afraid you've lived in your musty old books so long, Dudley," with mock seriousness, "that you've lost all count of time. It is about a thousand years since sane and sensible men believed all that drivel about women's only sphere being the home, and since women were content to be mere chattels, stuck in with the rest of the furniture, to look after the children. Nowadays the jolly, sensible woman that a man likes for wife or pal, is very often a busy worker."

"Let her work busily at home, then!"

"Why, you'll want me to crochet antimacassars next, or cross-stitch a sampler! Just imagine the thing if I tried! It would have dreadful results, because I should be sure to use bad language—I couldn't help it; and the article I should concoct would make people faint, or turn cross-eyed or colour-blind. I shan't do nearly so much harm in the end as a City secretary with an actress pal."

"One thing is quite certain: you mean, as usual, to have your own way, and my feelings go for nothing at all."

He turned away from her, and took up his hat to go out.

"Your protestations of affection, Hal, are apt to seem both insincere and out of place."

The tears came swiftly to her eyes, and she took a quick step towards him, but he had gone, and closed the door after him before she could speak. She watched his retreating figure, with the tears still lingering, and then suddenly she smiled.

"Anyhow, I haven't got to be sweet and gentle and housekeepy," was her comforting reflection. "I'm going to be a real worker, earning real money, and have Lorraine for my pal as well. Some day Dudley will see it is all right, and I'm only about half as black as he supposes, and that I love him better than anything else at heart. In the meantime, as I'm likely to get a biggish dose of dignified disapproval over this theatre business, I'd better ask Dick to come out to tea this afternoon to buck me up for what lies ahead. Goodness! what a boon a jolly cousin is when you happen to have been mated with your great-aunt for a brother."

CHAPTER III

For a few years after that particular disagreement nothing of special note happened. Hal got quickly through her course of shorthand and typewriting and became Mr. Elliott's private secretary and general factotum, which last included an occasional flight into journalism as a reporter. Naturally, since this sometimes took her to out-of-the-way places, and brought her in contact with human oddities, she loved it beyond all things, and was ever ready for a jaunt, no matter whither it took her.

Brother Dudley was discreetly left a little in the dark about it, because nothing in the world would ever have persuaded him that a girl of Hal's age could run promiscuously about London unmolested. Hal knew better. She was perfectly well able to acquire a stony stare that baffled the most dauntless of impertinent intruders; and she had, moreover, an upright, grenadier-like carriage, and an air of business-like energy that were safeguards in themselves.

A great deal of persuasive tact was necessary, however, to win Dudley's consent to a year in America, whither Mr. Elliott had to go on business; but on Mrs. Elliott calling upon him herself to explain that she also was going, and would take care of Hal, he reluctantly consented.

Curiously enough, it was that year in a great measure that changed the current of Lorraine's life. She came to the cross-roads, and took the wrong turn.

Perhaps Miss Walton, with her knowledge of girls, could have foretold it. She might have said, in that enigmatical way of hers, "If Lorraine comes to the cross-roads, where life offers a short cut to fame, instead of a long, wearisome drudgery, she will probably take it. Hal will score off her own bat, or not at all. Lorraine will only care about gaining her end."

Anyhow the cross-roads came, and Hal, the stronger, was not there. As a matter of fact, for some little time the two had not seen much of each other. Lorraine was touring in the provinces, and rarely had time to come to London. Hal was tied by her work, and could not spare the time to go to Lorraine.

There was for a little while a cessation of intercourse. Neither was the least bit less fond, but circumstances kept them apart, and they could only wait until opportunity brought them together again. Both were too busy for lengthy correspondence, and only wrote short letters occasionally, just to assure each other the friendship held firm, and absence made no real difference.

Then Hal went off to America, and while she was away Lorraine came to her cross-roads.

It is hardly necessary to review in detail what her life had been since she joined the theatrical profession. It is mostly hard work and disillusion and disappointment for all in the beginning, and only a very small percentage ever win through to the forefront.

But for Lorraine, on the top of all the rest, was a mercenary, unscrupulous, intriguing mother, who added tenfold to what must inevitably have been a heavy burden and strain—a mother who taxed her utmost powers of endurance, and brought her shame as well as endless worry; and yet to whom, let it be noted down now, to her everlasting credit, no matter in what other way she may have erred, she never turned a deaf ear nor treated with the smallest unkindness.

It would be impossible to gauge just what Lorraine had to go through in her first few years on the stage. She seemed to make no headway at all, and at the end of the third year she felt herself as far as ever from getting her chance.

That she was brilliantly clever and brilliantly attractive had not so far weighed the balance to her side. There were many others also clever and attractive. She felt she had practically everything except the one thing needed—influence.

Thus her spirits were at a very low ebb. She was still touring the provinces, and heartily sick of all the discomfort involved. Dingy lodgings, hurried train journeys, much bickering and jealousy in the company with which she was acting, and a great deal of domestic worry over that handsome, extravagant mother, who had once taken her, in company with the so-called uncle, to the select seminary of the Misses Walton.

How her mother managed to live and dress as if she were rich had puzzled Lorraine many times in those days; but when she left the shelter of those narrow, restricting walls, where windows were whitewashed so that even boys might not be seen passing by, she learnt many things all too quickly.

She learnt something about the uncles too. One of them was at great pains to try and teach her, but with hideous shapes and suggestions trying to crowd her mind, the thought of Hal's freshness still acted as a sort of protection and kept her untainted.

A little later, after she had commenced to earn a salary, she found that directly the family purse was empty, and creditors objectionably insistent, she herself had to come to the rescue.

There were some miserable days then. It was useless to upbraid her mother. She always posed as the injured one, and could not see that in robbing her child of a real home she was strewing her path with dangers as well, by placing her in an ambiguous, comfortless position, from which any relief seemed worth while.

Then at last came the welcome news that Mrs. Vivian had procured a post as lady-housekeeper to a rich stockbroker in Kensington, who had also a large interest in a West-end theatre.

Lorraine read the glowing terms in which her mother described her new home and employer with a deep sense of relief, seeing in the new venture a probable escape for herself from those relentless demands upon her own scanty purse. A month later came the paragraph, in a voluminous epistle:

"Mr. Raynor says you are to make his house your home whenever you are free. He insists upon giving you a floor all to yourself, like a little flat, where you can receive your friends undisturbed, and feel you have a little home of your own. I am quite certain also that he will try to help you in your career through his interest in the Greenway Theatre."

If Lorraine wondered at all concerning this unknown man's interest in her welfare she kept it to herself.

A home instead of the dingy lodgings she had grown to hate, and the prospect of influential help, were sufficiently alluring to drown all other reflections.

When the tour was over she went direct to Kensington, to make her home with her mother until her next engagement. She was already too much a woman of the world not to notice at once that her mother and her host's relations seemed scarcely those of employee and employer, and there was a little passage of arms between herself and Mrs. Vivian the next morning.

In reply to a long harangue, in which that lady set forth the advantages Lorraine was to gain from her mother's perspicacity in obtaining such a post, she asked rather shortly:

"And why in the world should Mr. Raynor do all this for me, simply because you are his housekeeper?"

A red spot burned in Mrs. Vivian's cheek as she replied: "He does it because he wants me to stay; and I have told him I cannot do so unless he makes it possible for me to give you a comfortable, happy home here."

Lorraine's lips curled with a scorn she did not attempt to conceal, but she only stood silently gazing across the Park.

She had already decided to make the best of her mother's deficiencies, seeing she was almost the only relative she possessed, but she had a natural loathing of hypocrisy, and wished she would leave facts alone instead of attempting to gloss them over. Ever since she left school she had been obliged to live in lodgings, because her mother would not take the trouble to try and provide anything more of a home.

It was a little too much, therefore, that she should now allude to her maternal solicitude because it happened to suit her purpose. She felt herself growing hard and callous and bitter under the strain of the early struggle to succeed, handicapped as she was; and because of one or two ugly experiences that came in the path of such a warfare. She was losing heart also, and feeling bitterly the stinging whip of circumstances. As she stood gazing across the Park, some girls about her own age rode past, returning from their morning gallop, talking and laughing gaily together.

Lorraine found herself wondering what life would be like with her beauty and talent if there were no vulgarly extravagant, unprincipled mother in the background, no insistent need to earn money, no gnawing ambition for a fame she already began to feel might prove an empty joy.

She had not seen Hal for a year, and she felt an ache for her. In the shifting, unreliable, soul-numbing atmosphere of her stage career, she still looked upon Hal as a City of Refuge; and when she had not seen her for some time she felt herself drifting towards unknown shoals and quicksands.

And, unfortunately, Hal was away in America, with the editor to whom she was secretary and typist, and not very likely to be back for three months.

No; there was nothing for it but to make the best of her mother's explanation and the comfortable home at her feet.

As for Mr. Raynor himself, though he seemed to Lorraine vulgarly proud of his self-made position, vulgarly ostentatious of his wealth, and vulgarly familiar with both herself and her mother, she could not actually lay any offence to his charge. And in any case, he undoubtedly could help her, if he chose, to procure at last the coveted part in a London theatre. With this end in view, she laid herself out to please him and to make the most of her opportunity.

And in this way she came to those cross-roads which had to decide her future.

Before she had been a week in the house, Frank Raynor deserted his housekeeper altogether, and fell in love with the housekeeper's daughter. Within a fortnight he had laid all his possessions at Lorraine's feet, promising her not only wealth and devotion, but the brilliant career she so coveted.

The man was generous, but he was no saint. Give him herself, and she would have the world at her feet if he could bring it there. Give any less, and he would have no more to say to her whatsoever.

It was the cross-roads.

Lorrain struggled manfully for a month. She hated the idea of marrying a man better suited in every way to her mother. She dreaded and hated the thought of what had perhaps been between them; yet she was afraid to ask any question that might corroborate her worst fears.

All that was best in her of delicate and refined sensitiveness surged upward, and she longed to run away to some remote island far removed from the harsh realities of life.

Yet, how could she? Without money, without influence, without rich friends, what did the world at large hold for her?

How much easier to go with the tide—seize her opportunity—and dare Fate to do her worst.

At the last there was a bitter scene between mother and daughter.

"If you refuse Frank Raynor now, you ruin the two of us," was Mrs. Vivian's angry indictment. "What can we expect from him any more? How are you ever going to get another such chance to make a hit?"

"And what if it ruins my life to marry him?" Lorraine asked.

"Such nonsense! The man can give you everything. What in the world more do you want? He is good enough looking; he could pass as a gentleman, and he is rich."

A sudden nauseous spasm at all the ugliness of life shook Lorraine. She turned on her mother swiftly, scarcely knowing what she said, and asked:

"You are anxious enough to sell me to him. What is he to you anyway? What has he ever been to you?"

Mrs. Vivian blanched before the suddenness of the attack, but she held her ground.

"You absurd child, what in the world could he be to me? It is easy enough to see he has no eyes for any one but you."

"And before I came?"

Lorraine took a step forward, and for a moment the two women faced each other squarely. The eyes of each were a little hard, the expressions a little flinty; but behind the older woman's was a scornful, unscrupulous indifference to any moral aspect; behind the younger's a hunted, rather pitiful hopelessness. The ugly things of life had caught the one in their talons and held her there for good and all, more or less a willing slave, the soul of the younger was still alive, still conscious, still capable of distinguishing the good and desiring it.

The mother turned away at last with a little harsh laugh.

"Before you came he was nothing to me. He never has been anything."

Without waiting for Lorraine to speak, she turned again, and added:

"If you weren't a fool, you would perceive he is treating you better than ninety-nine men in a hundred. He has suggested marriage. The others might not have done."

"Oh! I'm not a fool in that way," came the bitter reply, "but I've wondered once or twice what your attitude would have been, supposing—er—he had been one of the ninety-nine!"

Mrs. Vivian was saved replying by the unexpected appearance of Frank Raynor himself. Entering the room with a quick step, he suddenly stopped short and looked from one to the other. Something in their expressions told him what had transpired. He turned sharply on the mother.

"You've been speaking to Lorraine about me. I told you I wouldn't have it. I know your bullying ways, and I said she was to be left to decide for herself."

Lorraine saw an angry retort on her mother's lips, and hurriedly left the room. She put on her hat and slipped away into the Park. What was she to do?... where, oh where was Hal!

Within three months the short cut was taken. Lorraine was engaged to play a leading part at the Greenway Theatre, and she was the wife of Frank Raynor.

CHAPTER IV

When Hal came back from America and heard about Lorraine's marriage, it was a great shock to her. At first she could hardly bring herself to believe it at all. Nothing thoroughly convinced her until she stood in the pretty Kensington house and beheld Mrs. Vivian's pronounced air of triumph, and Lorraine's somewhat forced attempts at joyousness.

It was one of the few occasions in her life when Lorraine was nervous. She did not want Hal to know the sordid facts; and she did not believe she would be able to hide them from her.

When Hal, from a mass of somewhat jerky, contradictory information, had gleaned that the new leading part at the London theatre had been gained through the middle-aged bridegroom's influence, her comment was sufficiently direct.

"Oh, that's why you did it, is it? Well, I only hope you don't hate the sight of him already."

"How absurd you are, Hal!... Of course I don't hate the sight of him. He's a dear. He gives me everything in the world I want, if he possibly can."

"How dull. It's much more fun getting a few things for oneself. And when the only thing in all the world you want is your freedom, do you imagine he'll give you that?"

Lorraine got up suddenly, thrusting her hands out before her, as if to ward off some vague fear.

"Hal, you are brutal today. What is the use of talking like that now?... Why did you go to America?... Perhaps if you hadn't gone—"

"Give me a cigarette," said Hal, with a little catch in her voice, "I want soothing. At the present moment you're a greater strain than Dudley talking down at me from a pyramid of worn-out prejudices. I don't know why my two Best-Belovèds should both be cast in a mould to weigh so heavily on my shoulders."

Sitting on the table as usual, she puffed vigorously at her cigarette, blowing clouds of smoke, through which Lorraine could not see that her eyes were dim with tears. For Hal's unerring instinct told her that, at a critical moment, Lorraine had taken a wrong path.

Lorraine, however, was not looking in Hal's direction. She had moved to the window, and stood with her back to the room, gazing across the Park, hiding likewise misty, tell-tale eyes.

Suddenly, as Hal continued silent, she turned to her with a swift movement of half-expressed protest.

"Hal! you shan't condemn me, you shan't even judge me. Probably you can't understand, because your life is so different—always has been so different; but at least you can try to be the same. What difference has it made between you and me anyhow?... What difference need it make? I have got my chance now, and I am going to be a brilliant success, instead of a struggling beginner. What does the rest matter between you and me?"

"It doesn't matter between you and me. But it matters to you. I feel I'd give my right hand if you hadn't done it."

"How could I help doing it? Oh, I can't explain; it's no use. We all have to fight our own battles in the long run—friends or no friends. Only the friends worth having stick to one, even when it has been a nasty, unpleasant sort of battle."

That hard look, with the hopelessness behind it, was coming back into Lorraine's eyes. She was too loyal to tell even Hal what her mother had been like the last few months before the critical moment came, and at the critical moment itself. She could not explain just how many difficulties her marriage had seemed a way out from.

There had been other men who had not proposed marriage. There had been insistent creditors—her mother's as well as her own. There had been that deep hunger for something approaching a real home, and for a sense of security, in a life necessarily full of insecurities.

Obdurate, difficult theatre managers, powerful, jealous fellow-actresses, ill health, bad luck! Behind the glamour and the glitter of the stage, what a world of carking care, of littleness, meanness, jealousy, and intrigue she had found herself called upon to do battle with.

And now, if only her husband proved amenable, proved livable with, how different everything would be? But in any case Hal must be there. Somehow nothing of all this showed in her face as she fronted the smoker, still blowing clouds of smoke before her eyes.

"What has become of Rod?" Hal asked suddenly.

Lorraine winced a little, but held her ground steadily.

"Rod had to go. What could Rod and I have done with £500 a year?"

"My own"—from the blunt-speaking one—"it surely seems as if you might have thought of that before you allowed Rod to run all over the country after you, and get 'gated', and very nearly 'sent down', and spend a year or two's income ahead in trying to give you pleasure."

Lorraine flung herself down on the sofa with a callous air, and beat her foot on the ground impatiently. The parting with Rod was another thing she did not propose to describe to Hal. It had hurt too badly, for one thing.

"When you moralise, Hal, you are detestable. Besides, it's so cheap. Any one can sit on a table and hurl sarcasm about. I daresay in my place you would have married Rod, from a sense of duty or something, and ruined all the rest of his life. Or perhaps, after gently breaking the news, you'd have let him come dangling round to be 'mothered'. Well, I don't say I haven't been a bit of a brute to him; but anyhow I tried to do the square thing in the end. I cut the whole affair dead off. I told him I would not see him nor write to him again. I've since sent two letters back unopened, and though you mightn't think it, I was just eating my heart out for a sight of him. But what's the good! He's got to follow in the footsteps of whole centuries of highly respectable, complacent, fat old bankers. His father and mother would have a fit if he didn't develop into the traditional fat old banker himself, and beget another of the same ilk to follow on.

"I daresay with me he would have developed a little more soul, and a little less stomach—but what of it?" with a graceful shrug. "For the good of his country it is written that he shall acquire weight and stolidity, instead of an ideal soul, and for the benefit of posterity I sentenced him to speedy rotundity, and dull respectability, and the begetting of future bankers. He will presently marry some one named Alice or Annie, and invite me to the first christening in a spirit of Christian forgiveness."

Hal smiled more soberly than was her wont.

"And what of you?"

"What of me?... Oh, I don't come into that sort of scheme. I never ought to have been there at all. Still, I'm glad I showed him he'd got something in himself beside the stale accumulations of many banker ancestors; if it's only for the sake of the next little banker, who may want to lay claim to an individual soul."

"But it hurt, Lorraine?... don't tell me it didn't hurt after... after—"

"Oh yes, it hurt," with a low, bitter laugh; "but what of that either? It's generally the woman who gets hurt; but I suppose I knew I was riding for a fall."

"I don't suppose you are any more hurt than he is. You know he worshipped you."

"Yes; only presently it will be easy for him to get back into the old, orthodox groove with 'Alice', and persuade himself that I was only a youthful infatuation, whereas I— Oh, what does it matter, Hal! Come out of that 'great-aunt' mood, and let's be jolly while we can. I'll ring for coffee and liqueurs, and then we'll make lots of ripping plans to see everything in England worth seeing—until I can find time to go abroad."

Hal sprang off her table.

"Oh, very well," she rejoined, "Let's get rowdy and sing the song 'Love may go hang.' When I've got it over with Dudley, we'll just go straight on, keeping a good look out for the next fence. You'd better tell me something about this paternal husband of yours, just to prepare me for our meeting. He doesn't put his knife in his mouth, and that sort of thing, does he?"

"No; not quite so bad. His worst offence at present, I think, is to call me 'wifey'."

"Wifey!" in accents of horror. "Lorraine, how awful!"

"Yes; but I'm breaking him of it by degrees: that and his fondness for a soft felt hat."

They sat on chatting together with apparent gayness, but Hal's heart was no lighter after she had duly been presented to the paternal husband, as she called him, and she journeyed solemnly home on a bus, feeling rather as if she had been to a funeral. She tried at first to hide her feelings from Dudley—no difficult matter at all, since he usually contributed little but a slightly absent "yes" and "no" to the conversation, and if the conversation languished he took small notice.

However, he had to be told, and Hal rarely troubled to do much beating about the bush, so, in order to rouse him speedily and thoroughly, just as he was settling down to his newspaper she hurled the news at his head without any preliminary preparation.

"What do you think Lorraine has done now? Been and gone and married a man old enough to be her father!"

"Married!... Lorraine Vivian married!"

Dudley's newspaper went down suddenly on to his knee.

Hal had squatted on the hearthrug, tailor fashion, before the fire, and she gave a little swaying movement backward and forward, to signify the affirmative. He looked at her a moment as if to make sure she was not joking, and then said, with sarcastic lips:

"A man old enough to be her father?... then it isn't even Rod Burrell!"

"No; it isn't even Rod Burrell."

"Some one with more money and influence, I suppose? Well, I don't know that Burrell needs any one's condolences."

"He does, badly."

"He won't for long. The Burrells are a sensible lot, and no sensible man frets over a heartless woman."

"Lorraine is not a heartless woman. She has too much heart."

"She is certainly very generous with it."

"I don't know which is the more detestable, a sarcastic man or a sensible one." Hal shut her lips tightly, and stared at the fire.

"I imagine you hardly expect any sort of man to admire Miss Vivian's action."

"It doesn't matter in the least what 'any sort of man' thinks. I am only concerned with the possibility that she will weary of matrimony quickly and be miserable. I told you, because I wanted you to hear it from me instead of from a newspaper."

Dudley suddenly grew more serious, as he realised how it must in a measure affect Hal also.

"Who is he?"

"He is a stockbroker, named Frank Raynor, aged fifty."

"And of course she married him for his money?"

"I suppose so. Also he partly owns the Greenway Theatre."

"Pshaw . . . it's a mere bargain."

Hal was silent. She had rested her chin on her hands, and was now gazing steadily at the embers.

"Of course if he is not a gentleman, you will have to leave off seeing so much of her."

"Not at all. She would need me all the more."

"That is quite possible," drily; "but you owe something to yourself and me."

"I couldn't owe failing a friend to any one. But he is a gentleman almost—a self-made one, and he doesn't let you forget it."

"Then you've seen him?"

"Yes, today." Her lips suddenly twitched with irresistible humour. "He called me 'Hal' and Lorraine 'wifey.' We bore it bravely."

"What business had he to call you by your Christian name?"

"None. I suppose he just felt like it. He also alluded to my new hat as a bonnet. Also he used to be an office-boy or something. He seemed inordinately proud of it."

"I loathe a self-made man who is always cramming it down one's throat. I don't see how you can have much in common with either of them any more."

Hal got up, as if she did not want to pursue the subject.

"It won't make the smallest difference to Lorraine and me," she said.

Dudley knit his forehead in vexation and perplexity, remarking:

"Of course you mean to be obstinate about it."

"No," with a little laugh; "only firm." She came round to his chair and leant over the back it.

"Dear old long-face, don't look so worried. None of the dreadful things have happened yet that you expected to come of my friendship with Lorraine. The nearest approach to them was the celebrated young author I interviewed, who asked me to go to Paris with him for a fortnight, and he was a clergyman's son who hadn't even heard of Lorraine. Next, I think, was the old gentleman who offered to take me to the White City. I don't seem much the worse for either encounter, do I? and it's silly to meet trouble halfway."

She bent her head and kissed him on the forehead.

"Dudley," she finished mischievously, "what are you going to give Lorraine for a wedding-present?"

"I might buy her the book, 'How to be Happy though Married,'" he said dilly, "or write her a new one and call it 'Words of Warning for Wifey.'"

"We'll give her something together," Hal exclaimed triumphantly, knowing that, as usual, she had won the day.

Then she went off to bed, feigning a light-heartedness she was far from feeling, and dreading, with vague misgivings, what the future might bring forth.

CHAPTER V

It was a little over two years later that the crash came. There was first a commonplace, sordid tale of bickering and quarrelling, with passionate jealousy on the part of the middle-aged husband, and callous, maddening indifference on the part of the now successful and brilliant actress.

To do Lorraine justice, she was not actively at fault. Her sense of fair play made her try sincerely to make the best of what had all along been an inevitable fiasco. She did not sin in deed against the man to whom she had sold herself, but in thought it was hardly possible for her to give him anything but tolerance, or to feel much beyond the callous indifference she purposely cultivated, to make their life together endurable. The things that at first only irritated her grew almost unbearable afterwards.

Lorraine's father had been a gentleman by birth, breeding, and nature. If she inherited from her mother an ambitious, calculating spirit, she also inherited from her father refinement, and tone, and a certain fineness character, that showed itself chiefly in unorthodox ways, for the simple reason that her life and conditions were entirely removed from a conventional atmosphere.

As a man she might merely have lived a double life, conforming to the conventions when advisable, and following her own ambitions and bent in secret, without ever apparently stepping over the line.

As a woman she could but cultivate callous indifference to a great deal, and satisfy her soul by "playing fair" according to her lights, in the path before her, but nothing could save her from a mental nausea of the things in her husband which belonged to his plebeian origin and nature, and which crossed with a shrivelling, searing touch her own inherent refinement and high-born spirit.

The objectionable friends he brought to the house she found it easier to bear than the things he said about them behind their backs; neither, again, was his addiction to drink so trying as his mental coarseness. A man who had drank too much could be avoided, but the lowness of Frank Raynor's mind seemed to follow and drag her down.

Yet for two years she held bravely on, cultivating a hard spirit, and throwing herself heart and soul into the first delicious joy of success. This last surprised even her friends and admirers. A moderate hit was quite expected, but not a triumph which placed her almost in the first rank, and was due not merely to her acting, but to a bigness of spirit and comprehension she had never before had an opporturnty to reveal.

It was, indeed, the justification of Hal's devotion. Hal, by her very nature, could not love a small-minded woman. What she so unceasingly loved and admired in Lorraine was a hidden something she alone had had the perspicacity to perceive, and could so instinctively rely upon. It was the something which, given once a fair opening, carried her quickly through the company of the lesser successes, and placed her on that high plane which demands soul as well as skill.

Then came the dreadful climax. In a drunken, mad moment her husband hurled at her that he had been her mother's lover, and proposed to return to his old allegiance—had, in fact, already done so.

Lorraine immediately packed up her own special belongings and left his roof for ever.

Expostulations, promises, threats, passionate assurances that he had not been responsible for what he said failed alike to move her. She knew that whether responsible or not he had spoken the truth, and that everything else either he or her mother could say was false.

Finding her obdurate, he swore to ruin them both; but she told him she would sing for bread in the streets before she would go back to him; and he knew she meant it.

Fearing his influence against her and his sworn revenge, she went to Italy for a year, and hid in quiet villages until his passion should somewhat have died, finding herself in the dreadful position, not only of being betrayed by her mother, but quite unable to obtain any sort of freedom without revealing the black stain upon her only near relation.

She could not seek a divorce under the terrible circumstances, and she was far too proud and spirited to touch a farthing of her husband's money. It was like a dreadful chapter in her life, of which she could only turn down the page; never, never, obliterate nor escape from.

In the black days and weeks of despair which followed, she often felt she must have lost her reason without Hal, and even to her she could not tell the actual truth. Hal asked once, and then no more. Afterwards it was like a secret, unnamed horror between them, from which the curtain must not be raised.

For the rest there was the usual but intenser scene of remonstrance between Dudley and Hal with the usual resentful and obdurate termination. This time Dudley even got seriously angry, unable to see anything but a foolish, unprincipled woman reaping a just reward of her own sowing; and for nearly a week his displeasure was such that he addressed no single word to Hal if he could help it.

Hal, for once, was too wretched about everything to resent his attitude, and merely waited for the sun to shine again and the black, enveloping clouds to roll away.

She saw Lorraine everyday, in the apartments whence she had fled, and helped her to make the necessary arrangements to cancel the short remainder of an engagement and get away. She even had one interview with the irate husband, but no one ever knew what took place, except that Raynor sought no repetition, and seemed afterwards to have a respectful awe of Hal's name which spoke volumes.

Accustomed to intimidating women with a curse and an oath, he had found himself unexpectedly dealing with two who could scorch him with a scorn and contempt far more withering than a vulgar tirade of blasphemous language.

Finally the break was made complete. Lorraine got safely away to Italy, her mother retired to an English village, and Raynor departed to America for good.

For him it was merely a case of fresh pastures for fresh money-making and fresh intrigues.

For Mrs. Vivian only a passing exile from the gaieties and extravagance she loved.

For Lorraine it meant a hideous memory, a hideous, overwhelming catastrophe, and a hideous tie from which she could not hope to free herself.

She went away in a state of nervous prostration that was an illness, feeling the horror of it all in her very bones, and clinging with a silent hopelessness to Hal in a way that was more heart-rending than any hysterical outburst.

Yet that Hal was there was good indeed. Hal, who, though only twenty-one, could look out on an ugly world with those clear eyes of hers, and while seeing the ugliness undisguised, see always as it were beside it the ultimate good, the ultimate hope, the silver lining behind the blackest cloud. Hal, who could criticise unerringly, with direct, outspoken humour,and yet scorn to judge; who had learnt, by some strange instinct, the precious art of holding out a friendly hand and generous friendship, even to those condemned of the orthodox, sufferers probably through their own wild and foolish actions, without in any way becoming besmirched herself, or losing her own inherent freshness and purity.

It was not in the least surprising that a man as wedded to his books and profession as Dudley should fail to realise what was, in a measure, phenomenal. By the simple rule of A B C, he argued that ill necessarily contaminates, if the one to come in contact is of young and impressionable years. There might of course be exceptions, but hardly among those as frivolous and obstinate as Hal.

He worried himself almost ill about it all, until Lorraine was safely out of England, adding seriously to poor Hal's troubled mind, seeing she must stand by the one while longing to soothe and please the other, and fretting silently over his anxious expression. But once back in their old groove, he quickly recovered his spirits, and even tried to make up to Hal a little for what she had lost. Unfortunately, however, he hit upon an unhappy expedient.

He tried to persuade her to make a friend of a certain Doris Hayward, instead of Lorraine.

Doris's brother had been Dudley's great friend in the days when both were articled to the same profession, but a terrible accident had later lain him on an invalid couch for the rest of his life.

When clerk of the works of one of London's great buildings, a heavy crane had slipped and swung sideways, flinging him into the street below. He was picked up and carried into the nearest hospital, apparently dead, but he had presently come back, almost from the grave, to drag out a weary life as an incurable on an invalid sofa.

Soon afterwards his father died, leaving Basil and his two sisters the poor pittance of £50 a year between them.

Ethel, the elder, was already a Civil Service clerk at the General Post Office, earning £110 a year, and on these two sums they had to subsist as best they could.

Basil earned occasional guineas for copying work, when he was well enough to stand the strain, and Doris remained at home with him in the little Holloway flat, as nurse and housekeeper.

Dudley, with his usual lack of comprehension where women were concerned, evolved what seemed to him an admirable plan, in which Hal and Doris became great friends, thereby brightening poor Doris's dull existence, and weaning Hal from her allegiance to the unstatisfactory Lorraine.

His plans, however, quickly met with the discouragement and downfall inevitable from the beginning. At first he tried strategy, and Hal, in a good-tempered, careless way, merely listened, while easily avoiding any encounter.

Then Dudley went a step too far.

"I have to be out three evenings this week, so I asked Doris Hayward to come and keep you company, as I thought you might be dull."

"You asked Doris to come and keep *me* company!" repeated Hal, quite taken aback.

"Yes; why not? She is such a nice girl, and just your age. I can't think why you are not greater friends."

"It's pretty apparent," with a little curl of her lips.

"We haven't anything in common: that's all."

"But why haven't you? You can't possibly know if you never meet. She seems such a far more sensible friend for you than Lorraine Vivian," with a shade of irritation.

"Probably that is exactly why I don't want her friendship," with a light laugh.

"But you might try to be reasonable just once in a way. Try to be friendly tomorrow evening."

Hal, with her quick, light gracefulness, crossed to him, and playfully gave him a little shake.

"Dudley, you dear old idiot. I don't know about being reasonable, but I can certainly be honest; and it's honest I'm going to be now. I think it is almost a slur on Lorraine to mention a little, silly, dolly-faced, conceited creature like Doris in the same breath; and as for being friendly to her tomorrow evening, that's impossible, because I shall not be here. I'm going to the Denisons, and I don't intend to postpone it. You will have to write and tell her I am engaged."

Dudley's mouth quickly assumed the rigidity which denoted he was greatly displeased, and his voice was frigid as he replied:

"You are very injust to Doris. You scarcely know her, and yet you condemn her offhand: the fault you are always finding in me. As for any comparison between her and Miss Vivian, it is very certain she would not sell herself to a man, and then run away from him because things did not turn out as she wanted them."

Hal turned away, with a slight shrug and a humorous expression as of helplessness.

"We won't argue, *mon frère*, because, since you always read books instead of people, you are not very well up in the subject. To put it both candidly and vulgarly, I haven't any use for Doris Hayward at all. Ethel I admire tremendously, though I don't think she likes me; and Basil is a saint straight out of heaven, suffering martyrdom for no conceivable reason, but Doris is like a useless ornamental china shepherdess, which ought to be put on a high shelf where it can't get itself nor any one else into trouble. I'm really dreadfully afraid if I had to spend a whole evening alone with her, I should drop her and break her to relieve my feelings."

"Well, you needn't worry"—moving coldly away. "I have far too much respect for Doris to allow her to come here just to be criticised by you. I will explain that you are unexpectedly engaged," and he opened a paper in a manner to close the conversation.

Hal made a little grimace at him behind it, and retired discreetly to prepare for her daily sojourn in the City.

It happened, however, when, a year later, Lorraine came back to take up her theatrical career again in England, there was some vague change in her that made Dudley less severe in his criticisms. Trouble had not hardened her, nor softened her, but it had made her a little less sure of herself, and a little more willing to please.

Hitherto she had taken rather a pleasure in shocking Dudley, under the impression that it would do him good and open his mind a little. Now she had a greater respect for his sterling side, and could smile kindly at his little foibles and fads. The result was that Dudley admitted, a trifle grudgingly, she had changed for the better, and rather looked forward to the occasional evenings she spent with Hal at their Bloomsbury apartments.

He also had to admit that success had in no wise spoilt her, that it probably never would. The year of absence, it was soon seen, had not injured her reputation in the least. She came back to the stage renewed and invigorated, and with still more of that depth of feeling and atmosphere of soul which had so enriched her personations before.

She became, very speedily, without any question, one of the leading actressess of the day; and the veil of mystery that hung over the sudden termination of her short married life, if anything, enhanced her charm to a mystery-loving public. And all the time, as Dudley could not but see, she never changed to Hal.

From adulation and adoration, from triumphs that might easily turn any head she always came quickly back to the little Bloomsbury sitting-room when she could, to have one of their old gay gossips and merry laughs. She seemed in some way to find a rest there that she could not get elsewhere, in the company of people who expected her to live up to a recognised standard of individuality.

And the change in Lorraine was a change for the better in Hal too, who began now to tone down a little, and at the same time to strengthen and deepen in character.

They were, in fact, a pair it was good to see and good to know. In the first few years after the break-up of her home Lorraine was at her handsomest. Her dark, thick hair had a gloss on it that in some lights showed like a bronze glow, and she wore it in thick coils round her small head, free from any exaggerated fashion, and yet with a distinction all its own. Her dark eyes once more showed the roguish lights of her schooldays, and her alluring red mouth twitched mischievously when she was in a gay mood.

A little below the medium height, she was so perfectly built as to escape any appearance of shortness, and carried herself so well, she sometimes appeared almost tall.

Considering what her life had been, she looked strangely young for her years, seeming to combine most alluringly the knowledge and sympathy of a woman of thirty-five with the freshness and capacity for enjoyment of twenty-five. The irrevocable tie so far had not clashed with any new affection; her husband remained in America and made no sign; and her art was all-sufficing.

Hal was built on quite different lines. Tall, and slender, and well knit, she moved with the surging grace of the athlete, and looked out upon the world with a joyfulness and humorous kindliness that won her friends everywhere. She was not beautiful in any sense that could be compared with Lorraine, but she had pretty brown hair, and fine eyes, and a clear, warm skin that made up for other defects, and helped to produce a very attractive whole.

Lorraine had taught her how to dress—an art of far deeper significance than many women trouble to realise; and wherever Hal went, if she did not create a sensation, at least she carried a distinction and pleasingness that were rarely overlooked. Her daily sojourn in the City, among the bread-winners, had made her large-hearted and generously tolerant, without hurting in any degree her own innate womanliness and charm.

She showed in her every gesture and action how it was possible to be of those who must scramble for buses, and press for trams, and live daily in the midst of panting, struggling, working, grasping humans, without losing tone, or gentleness, or a radiant, fearless spritit.

At the office of the newspaper where she filled the post of secretary and typist, she was a sort of cheerful institution to smooth worried faces and call up a smile amidst the irritability and frowns.

Blunderers went to her with their troubles, and felt fairly secure if she would break the news of the blunder or mistake to the irritable and awe-inspiring chief. He, in his turn, would be irritable before her, but never with her; and it was a recognised fact among the staff that she was almost the only one who could make him laugh.

Thus a few intervening years passed happily enough, briging Lorraine to her thirty-first birthday and Hal to her twenty-fifth, without any further upheavals to strike a discordant note across the daily round, except such inevitable trials as Lorraine continued to meet through her mother, and Hal through her devotion to a non-comprehending brother. Only, while they had each other and their work, such difficulties were not hard to cope with; and life sang a gayer, happier song to them than she usually sings to the mere pleasure-seekers.

For work in a wide interesting sphere is a priceless boon, and the men who would condemn women solely to pleasure-seeking and the four walls of their home are showing the very acme of selfishness, in that they are endeavouring to keep solely and entirely for themselves one of the best things life has to give.

CHAPTER VI

It will be remembered, perhaps, that an occasion has already occured when Hal had cause to congratulate herself upon the possession of a cousin, named Dick, who acted as an antidote to a brother who sometimes resembled a great-aunt.

Dick, or to give him his full name, Richard Alastair Bruce, was indeed her best friend and boon companion next to Lorraine. He was her earliest playmate, and likewise her latest. For many months together they had been companions in the wildest of wild escapades as children, at Dick's country home; and now that they were both responsible members of the community, in the world's greatest city, they were equally attached.

If Hal was down on her luck, she telephoned Dick to come instantly to the rescue, and if it was humanly possible he came. If Dick wanted a sympathetic or gay companion, either to go out with him or to listen to his latest inspirations, he telephoned to Hal, and little short of an urgent, important engagement would delay her.

At the time he becomes of any importance in this narrative he was established in a flat in the Cromwell Road, as one of a trio sometimes known as the Three Graces. The other two were Harold St. Quintin and Alymer Hermon.

The appellation was first given to them when they were freshmen at New College, Oxford; partly because they were inseparable, partly because they were a particularly good-looking trio, and partly because they all three came up from Winchester with great cricket reputations. Within two years they were all playing for the 'Varsity' and one of them was made captain.

Three years from the term of their leaving, after each had gone his own way for a season, they gravitated together again, and finally became established in the Cromwell Road flat, once more on the old affectionate terms.

Dick Bruce was following a literary career, of a somewhat ambiguous nature. He wrote weird articles for weird papers, under weird pseudonyms, verses, under a woman's name, for women's papers, usually of the *Home*

Dressmaker type; occasional lines to advertise some patent medicine or soap; one or two Salvation Army hymns of a particularly rousing nature: and sometimes a weighty, brilliant article for a first-class paper, duly signed in his own name.

Besides all this he visited a publisher's office most days, where he was supposed to be meditating the acquirement of a partnership. Hal was very apt at terse, concise definitions, and she was quite up to her best form when she described him as "the maddest of a mad clan run amok."

Harold St. Quintin, or Quin, as every one called him, was idealist, etherealist, and dreamer. His original intention had been to enter the Church, but having gone down into East London to give six months to slum work, he had remained two years without showing any inclination to give it up. Sometimes he lived at the flat, and sometimes he was lost for a week at a time somewhere east of St. Paul's, where one might as well have looked for him as for the proverbial needle in a haystack.

Alymer Hermon, after a sojourn on the continent to study languages, was now established with a barrister, waiting, it must be confessed, without much concern, for his first brief.

Of the three he was the most striking. Dick Bruce was only ordinarily good-looking, with a very white skin, a fine forehead, and an arresting pair of eyes—eyes that were like an index to a brain that held volumes of original observations and whimsicalities, and revealed only just as much or little as the author chose.

Harold St. Quintin was small and rather delicate, with never-failing cheerfulness on his lips, and eyes that seemed always to have behind them the recollection of the pitiful scenes among which he voluntarily moved.

Alymer Hermon was Adonis returned to earth. He stood six foot five and a half inches in his socks, and was as perfectly proportioned as a man may be; with a head and face any sculptor might have been proud to copy line by line for a statue of masculine beauty.

When he was captain of the Oxford Eleven, people spoke of his beauty more than his cricket, although the latter was quite sufficiently striking in itself. There were others who had sweepstakes on his height, before the score he would make, or the men he would bowl.

The 'Varsity' was proud of him, as they had never been proud of a captain before, because he upheld every tradition of manliness and manhood at its best. And they only liked him the better that so far his attitude to his own comeliness was rather that of boredom than anything else. Certainly it weighed as nothing in the balance against the joy of scoring a century and achieving a good average with his bowling.

He was equally bored with the young girls who gazed at him in adoration, and the women who petted him, and it was a considerable source of worry to him that he might appear effeminate, because of his blue eyes and golden hair, and fresh, clear complexion, when in reality he was as manly as the plainest of hard-sinewed warriors, though the indulgence of a slightly aesthetic manner and way of speech, learnt at the University, increased rather than counteracted the suggestion of effeminacy.

But, taking all things into consideration, he was singularly unspoilt and unassuming; and sometimes blended with an old-fashioned, paternal air a boyishness and power of enjoyment that could not fail to charm.

The first time that Lorraine met the trio was when Hal took her to spend the evening at the flat one Sunday, by arrangement with her cousin. She herself knew all three well, having been to the flat many times, but it had taken some little persuasion to get Lorraine to go with her.

"Of course they are just boys," said grandiloquent twenty-five, "but they are quite amusing, and they will be proud of it all their lives if they can say they once had Lorraine Vivian at the flat as a guest."

"What do you call boys?" asked Lorraine, looking amused; "I thought you said they had all left college,"

"So they have, but that's nothing. Dick is only twenty-five, and the others are about twenty-four."

"A much more irritating age than mere boyhood as a rule."

"Decidedly; but they really are a little exceptional. Dick, of course, is quite mad—that's what makes him interesting. Alymer Hermon is a giant with a great cricket reputation, and Harold St. Quintin is a sort of modern Francis Assisi with a sense of humour."

"The giant sounds the dullest. I hope he doesn't want to talk cricket all the time, because I don't know anything about it, except that if a man stands before the wicket he is out, and if he stands behind it he is not in."

"Oh no; he doesn't talk cricket. He mostly talks drivel with Dick, and St. Quintin laughs."

"Dick sounds quite the best, in spite of his madness. A cricketer who talks drivel, and a future clergyman working in the East End, don't suggest anything that appeals to me in the least."

Nevertheless, when Lorraine, looking very lovely, entered the small sitting-room of her three hosts, her second glance, in spite of herself, strayed back to the young giant on the hearth-rug. He was looking at Hal sideways, with a quizzical air; and she heard him say:

"It may be new, but it's not the very latest fashion, because it doesn't stick out far enough at the back, and it doesn't cover up enough of your face."

"Oh well!" said Hal jauntily, "if I had as much time as you to study the fashions, I daresay I should know as much about them. But I have to *work* for my living," with satirical emphasis.

"What a nuisance for you," with a delightful smile. "I only pretend to work for mine."

"We all know that. You sit on a stool, and look nice, and wait for a brief to come along and beg to be taken up."

"It's a chair. I'm not one of the clerks. And I shouldn't get a brief any quicker if I went and shouted on the housetops that I wanted one."

"Besides, you don't want one. You know you wouldn't know what to do with it if you got it. Well, how's East London?..." and Hall crossed to the slum-worker, with a show of interest she evidently did not feel for the embryo barrister. Lorraine smiled at him, however, and he moved leisurely forward to take the vacant seat beside her on the sofa.

"Is Hal trying to sharpen her wit at your expense?" she asked him, in a friendly, natural way.

"Yes; but it's a very blunt weapon at the best. People who always think they are the only ones to work are very tiring; don't you think so?"

"Decidedly; and I don't suppose she does half s much as you and I in reality."

"Oh well, I could hardly belie myself so far as to assert that. You see, it takes a long time to make people understand what a good barrister you would be if you got the chance to prove it."

Hal could not resist a timely shot.

"Personally, I shoud advise you to try and prove it without the chance. The chance might undo the proving, you see."

"What a rotten, mixed-up, meaningless remark!" he retorted. "Is it because you find I am so dull, you still have to talk to me?"

"Quin is never dull, he is only depressing. Dick, do hurry up and begin supper. I always feel horribly hungry here, because I know Quin has just come away from some starving family or other, and I have to try and eat to forget."

Lorraine leant across to the dreamy-eyed first-class circketer, voluntarily giving his life to the slums.

"Why do you do it?" she asked with sudden interest. "It seems, somehow, unnatural in a—" she hesitated, then finished a little lamely, "a man like you."

"Oh no, not at all," he hastened to assure her. "It's the most fascinating work in the world. It's full of novelty and surprises for one thing."

She shuddered a little.

"But the misery and want and starvation. The … the… utter hopelessness of it all."

"But it isn't hopeless at all. Nothing is hopeless. And then, knowing the misery is there, and doing nothing, is far worse than seeing it and doing what one can."

"Oh no, because one can forget so often."

"Some can. I can't. Therefore I can only choose to go and wrestle with it."

"Of course it is heroic of you, but still!—"

Harold St. Quintin gave a gay laugh.

"It is not a bit more heroic than your work on the stage to give people pleasure. I get as much satisfaction in return as you do; and that is the main point. Slum humanity is seething with interest, and it is by no means all sad, nor all discouraging. There is probably more humour and heroism there per square mile than anywhere else."

"And no doubt more animal life also," put in Dick Bruce. "It's the superfluous things that put me off, not the want of anything."

"It's feeling such an ass puts me off," added Hermon; "they're all so busy and alert about one thing or another down there, they make me feel a mere cumberer of the earth. A woman manages a husband, and a family, and some sort of a home, and does the breadwinning as well. The children try to earn pennies in their playtime; and the men work at trying to get work."

"Whereas you?..." suggested Hal with a twinkle, "work at trying not to get work."

"Come to supper, and don't be so personal, Hal," said her cousin. "I wrote a poem on you last week, and called it 'Why Men Die Young.' It is in a rag called *The Woman's Own Newspaper*. It is also in *The Youth's Journal*, with the pronouns altered, and a different title; but I forget what."

"What a waste of time—writing such drivel," Hal flung at him. "Why don't you compose a masterpiece, and scale Olympus?"

"Too commonplace. Lots of men have done that. Very few are positive geniuses at writing drivel. I claim to be in the front rank."

They sat down to a lively repast, and Lorraine found herself, instead of an awe-inspiring, distinguished guest, treated with a frank camaraderie that was both amusing and refreshing. They all made a butt of Hal, who was quite equal to the three of them; and when the giant paraphrased one of her (Lorraine's) most tragic utterances on the stage into a serio-comic dissertation on a fruit salad they were eating, lacking in wine, she laughed as gaily as any, and felt she had known them for years.

Then Hal insisted upon playing a game she had that moment invented, which consisted of each one confessing his or her greatest failing, and the gaiety grew.

She led off by informing them that she found she always jumped eagerly at any excuse to avoid her morning bath. Dick Bruce followed it up with a confession that he found he was never satisfied with fewer than four "best girls", because he liked to compare notes between them, and write silly verses on his observations; while Harold St. Quintin owned to an objectionable fancy for bull's-eye peppermints and blowing eggs.

Alymer Hermon confessed that he loved giving advice to people years older than himself, concerning things he knew nothing whatever about.

Lorraine tried to cry off, but, hard pressed, she admitted that she liked the excitement of spending money she had not got, and then having to pawn something to satisfy her creditors. "Spending money you will not miss," she finished, "is very dull beside spending money you do not possess."

Alymer Hermon then suggested they should tell each other of besetting faults, and at once informed Hal her colossal opinion of herself and all she did was only equalled by its entire lack of foundation.

Hal hurled back at him that every inch in height after six feet absorbed vitality from the brain, and that, though his dense stupidity was most trying, the reason for it claimed their compassion.

"You pride yourself beyond all reason on your stature," she said, "and are too dense to perceive it is your undoing."

Lorraine leant towards him and said:

"Inches give magnanimity: big men are always big-hearted; you can afford to forgive her, and retaliate that too much brain-power sinks individuality into mere machinery. I should say Hal's besetting fault was rapping every one on the knuckles, as if they were the keys of a typewriting machine."

"And yours, my dear Lorraine, is smiling into every one's eyes, as if the world held no others for you. Were I a man, and you smiled at me so, I would strangle you before you had time to repeat the glance on some one else."

"And Dick's besetting sin," murmured St. Quintin plaintively, "is a persistent fancy for other people's ties and other people's boots. I have cause to bless the benign and other people's boots. I have cause to bless the benign providence who fashioned my shoulders sufficiently smaller than his to prevent his wearing my coats."

"And yours, Quin," broke in Hermon, "is a fond and loathsome affection for pipes so seasoned that the Board of Trade ought to prohibit their use."

"After all," Hal rapped out at him, "that's not so bad as love of a looking-glass."

"And love of a looking-glass is no worse than love of throwing stones from glass houses," he retorted.

"Of course it isn't, Hal," broke in her cousin, "and probably if you had anything nice to look at in your glass—"

Hal stood up.

"The meeting is adjourned," she announced solemnly, "and the honourable member who was just spoken has the president's leave to absent himself on the occasion of the next gathering."

"Excellent," cried Quin, while Hermon in great glee rapped the table with his knife handle and exclaimed, "Capital, Dick!... That drew her... I think you might say it took the middle stump."

"Oh, thank goodness he's got on to cricket," breathed Hal. "He does know a little about that, and may possibly talk sense for ten minutes. Come along, Lorraine, and don't address Baby at present, for fear you distract him from his game and start him off struggling to be clever again. As it is Sunday night, perhaps Dick would like to read us his latest effusions in the way of boisterous hymns!"

She led the way back to the bachelor sitting-room, and for some little time Dick amused them greatly with his experiences over editors and magazines, and then the two went off together to Lorraine's flat.

At this time she was living at the bottom of Lower Sloane Street, with windows looking over the river, and it was generally supposed that her mother lived with her.

As a matter of fact, Mrs. Vivian only occupied the ground floor flat in company with a friend. Lorraine give her an income on condition she should live there, and so, in a sense, act as a sort of chaperone to silence the tongues ever ready to find food for scandal in the fact of brilliance and beauty living alone; but mother and daughter had never again been on terms of cordiality.

So Hal was often Lorraine's companion for several nights, coming and going as she fancied, always sure of a welcome. To her the flat was a constant delight, and in the evening she loved to sit on the verandah and watch the gliding river—not to sentimentalise and dream, but because she loved London with all her heart and soul and strength, and to her the river was as the city's pulsing heart.

The moist freshness of the air coming across from Battersea Park was only the more refreshing after Bloomsbury, and the vicinity of several well-known names in the world of art and letters appealed powerfully to her imagination. Lorraine usually sat just inside the long French window, taking care of her voice, and listening contentedly to Hal's chatter.

They sat thus for a little while after their return from Cromwell Road, and it was noticeable that Lorraine was even more silent than usual. Hal told her something about each of their three hosts in turn, while showing an unmistakable preference for the slum-worker and her cousin. At last Lorraine interrupted her.

"Why do you say so little about Mr. Hermon?... you merely told me he was a cricketer, which doesn't, as a matter of fact, describe him at all."

Hal shrugged her shoulders.

"I suppose he doesn't interest me except in that way."

"But it is a mere side issue. If he weren't a cricketer he would be just as remarkable."

"But he isn't remarkable. He's only exceptionally big."

"He's one of the most remarkable men I've ever seen, anyway."

"Oh, nonsense, Lorraine. Besides, he is hardly a man yet. He's only twenty-four."

"I can't help that," with a little laugh. "I've seen a great many men in my life, but I've never seen any one before like Alymer Hermon."

"Why in the world not? What do you mean?"

"Well, to begin with, he's the most perfect specimen of manhood I've ever beheld. He's abnormally big without the slightest suggestion of being either too big or awkward. He's simply magnificent. Most men of that size are just leggy and gawky: he is neither. Again, other men built as he, are usually rather brainless and weak, or probably made so much of by women that they become wrapped up in themselves, and are always expecting admiration. Alymer Hermon has the freshness of a delightful boy, with the fine face and courtly manners of a charming man. If you can't see this, it's because you don't know men as well as I do."

Hal stepped over the window sill into the room.

"Pooh!" she said impatiently. "What in the world has happened to you? He's just a stuffed blue-and-gold Apollo."

Lorraine got up also.

"He's more than that. Some day you will see; unless... unless...."

"Well, unless what?"

"Oh, nothing, only a man like that can't expect to escape being spoilt. A certain type of woman will inevitably mark him down for her prey, and ruin all his freshness."

"Then you had better take him under your wing," Hal laughed. "It would be a pity for such a paragon to be lost to society. Personally, stuffed blue-and-gold Apollos don't interest me in the least. Come along to bed. I'm dead tired," and she dragged Lorraine away.

But instead of sleeping, the actress lay silently watching a star that shone in at her window, and thinking a little sadly about the man nature had chosen to endow so bountifully. In a few weeks she would be thirty-two and he was twenty-four.

Supposing it had been twenty-two instead of thirty-two, and out of his splendour he had given his heart to her dark beauty, what a tale it might have been—what a fairy-tale of sweet, impossible things, with a golden-haired prince and a dark-eyed princess.

She awoke from her day-dream with a touch of impatience, apostrophising herself for her folly. After all, what had a beautiful, successful woman at her prime to do with a youth of twenty-four, who played foolish games at a supper-table, and was only just beginning to know his world? Of course he would bore her intolerably at a second interview, and, closing her eyes resolutely, she drove his image from her mind.

CHAPTER VII

The second interview, however, by a mere coincidence, took place at Lorraine's flat. She was walking leisurely down Sloane Street one afternoon, after visiting her milliner's, when she ran into the young giant going in the opposite direction.

"How so?..." she asked gaily, as is face lit up with a pleased smile, and he stopped in front of her. "Whither away at this hour? Are you chasing a brief?"

"Much too brief," he told her. "I had to carry some important papers to a certain well-known Cabinet Minister; and he did not even vouchsafe me a glance of his countenance. I was given an acknowledgment of them by the footman, as if I had been a messenger boy."

"Too bad. I think you deserve that another celebrity should give you a cup of tea, to redeem your opinion of the immortals. My flat is quite near, and I am now returning. Will you come?"

"Oh, won't I?" he said boyishly, and turned back.

It was the fashionable hour in Sloane Street, when many well-dressed, well-known people are often seen walking, and when the road is full of private motors and carriages. Lorraine found herself moving still more slowly. She was accustomed to being gazed at herself, had in fact grown a little blasé of it, but the frank admiration bestowed on her giant amused and pleased her.

Covertly she watched, as she chatted up to him, for the tell-tale consciousness and perhaps heightened colour. But when he was looking back into her face he looked straight before him, over the heads of the admiring eyes, and paid no smallest heed to them. Neither was he in the least self-conscious with her. She wondered if he even realised that the tête-à-tête he accepted so simply would have been a joy of heaven to many. Anyhow, far from resenting his seeming want of due appreciation, she found it made him more interesting.

She spoke of Hal, and he immediately exclaimed: "Hal is a ripper, isn't she? I can't help teasing her, you know; it's the best fun in the world."

"Do you usually tease your feminine friends?" she asked. "I've no doubt you have a great many."

"Oh, no, I haven't. Men pals are far jollier."

"Still, I expect your inches bring you many fair admirers."

He shrugged his shoulders slightly, and looked a trifle bored, and she divined that he disliked flattery and probably the subject of his appearance. She adroitly turned the conversation back to Hal, and spoke of her until they reached the block of flats.

"Is this where you live? What a ripping situation!" he exclaimed. "I would sooner be near the river than near Knightsbridge, even if it is not so classy."

He followed her into the lift, and then into her charming home, full of enthusiasm, and still without exhibiting a shade of self-consciousness.

Lorraine found her interest growing momentarily, as he took up his stand on her hearth and gazed frankly around, with undisguised pleasure.

"What a jolly nice room. It's one of the prettiest I've seen. You have the same color-scheme as the Duchess of Medstone in her boudoir, but I like your furniture better."

Lorraine glanced up a little surprised.

"Do you know the Duchess of Medstone?"

"Well, yes" —a trifle bashfully. "You see, those sort of people ask me to their houses because of my cricket. Private cricket weeks are rather fashionable, and I get invitations as the late Oxford captain."

"And do you go to people you don't know?"

"Yes, rather, if I can raise the funds. The nuisance is the tipping. There's always such a rotten lot of servants; and I'm too much afraid of them to give anything but gold."

The tea came in, and she saw him glance round for the chair best suited to his bulk.

"My chairs were not designed for giants," she told him laughingly; "you will have to come and sit on the settee."

He came at once, stretching his long legs out before him, with lazy ease, and then drawing his knees up sharply, as if in sudden remembrance that he was a guest and they were comparative strangers. Lorraine liked him, both for the moment's forgetfulness and the sudden remembrance, and as she glanced again at his beautiful head and splendid shoulders, she was conscious of a sudden thrill of appreciative admiration.

Hal was right in naming him Apollo. The Sun God might have been fashioned just so, when first he ravished the eyes of Venus.

"And so the duchess took you into her boudoir?" she asked, with an unaccountable twinge of jealousy. "I do not know her. I'm afraid my friends are not so aristocratic as yours. But I believe she is considered very handsome."

"Hard," he said, with an old-fashioned air. "Handsome enough, but very hard. I did not like her nearly so much as Lady Moir, her sister."

"Still no doubt she was very nice to you?"

Lorraine rather hated herself for the question. The ways of aristocratic ladies, whose idle hours often supply a field of labour for the Evil One, were perfectly well known to her; and she wondered a little sharply how far he was still unspoilt. The majority of big, strong, full-blooded young men in his place would assuredly have sipped the cup of pleasure pretty deeply by now, even at his years, but with that fine, strong face, and the clear, frank eyes was he of these? She believed not, and was glad.

He did not treat her question as if it implied any special favours, and merely replied jocularly:

"Well, I suppose, since her blood is very blue and mine merely tinged, she was rather gracious, but of course the really 'blue' people generally are."

"Tell me who you happen to be?" Lorraine leant back against her cushions, with her slow, easy grace, asking the question with a lightness that robbed it of all pointedness or snobbery.

He seemed amused, for he smiled as he answered frankly:

"I happen to be Alymer Hadstock Hermon, one fo *the* Hermons all right, but not the drawing-room end, so to speak; at the same time tinged with her family shadiness—'blue' of course I mean—though no doubt it applies in other ways as well. Does that satisfy your curiosity, or do you want to know more?"

She loved looking at him, particularly with that humorous little smile on his lips, so she said:

"Not half. I want to know all the rest."

"Very well. It's quite an open book. I was born twenty-four years ago. I am an only child, and, as usual, the apple of my mother's eye and the terror of my father's pocket. He, my father, is not much else just now except a recluse. He was recently a member of parliament, a Liberal member, and, God knows, that's little enough. I believe he even climbed in by a Chinese pigtail.

"My grandfather was a Judge in the Divorce Court, which doesn't somehow sound quite respectable, and my great-grandfather was a writer of law books, for which, personally, I think he ought to have been hanged. I can't go any farther back; at any rate I don't want to, because I'm certain it's all so correct and dull there isn't even a family skeleton."

"Is it the women or the men of the family that are beautiful?"

"Oh, both," with humorous eagerness. "Skeletons and ghosts we sought, and clamoured for, but ugliness, never."

"Well, it's a pity you were not a woman. Looks are wasted in a man. Give a man a ready tongue and a taking manner, and he can usually get what he wants, if he's as ugly as a frog. With you, on the other hand, things will come too easily. You will miss all the fun of the chase. On my soul I'm sorry for you."

"The briefs don't come anyway, nor the 'oof': that's all I can see to be sorry for."

"You don't want them badly enough, that's all. If you want the one, you'll make love to an influential woman who can get them, and if you want the other, you'll marry an heiress."

"I say, you're giving me rather a rotten character, aren't you?"

He faced her suddenly, and a new expression dawned in his eyes, as if he were only just awakening to the fact that she was beautiful.

"Do you really think I'm such a rotter as all that?"

She glanced away, lowering her eyelids, so that her long lashes swept the warm olive cheeks, and with a little callous shrug answered:

"Why should you be a rotter for doing what all the rest of the world does? Four-fifths of mankind would give anything for your chances."

"But you just said you were sorry for me?"

"So I am. So I should be for the four-fifths of mankind, if they got all they wanted just for the asking."

He smiled with a sudden, charming whimsicality.

"I don't feel much in need of sympathy, you know. It's a ripping old world, as long as you can indulge a few mild fancies, and be left alone."

"Mild fancies!"

She turned on him suddenly.

"What have you to do with mild fancies? Why, you can have the world at your feet with a little exertion. Haven't you any ambition? Don't you even want to plead in the greatest law court in the world as one of the first barristers in Europe?"

"Not particularly. Why should I? It would be no end of a fag. I'd far rather be left alone."

"You... you... sluggard," breaking into a laugh. "If I were Fate, I'd just take you by the shoulders and shake you till you woke up. Then I'd go on shaking to keep you awake. You shouldn't be wasted on mere nonentity if I held the threads."

But his blue eyes only smiled whimsically back at her.

"I'm jolly glad you haven't a say in the matter. Why, I should have to give up cricket, and take to working! You're as bad as Quin with his slumming, and Dick with his rotten verses."

"You don't know yet that I haven't a say in the matter," she remarked daringly. "Have a cigarette. I'm awfully sorry I didn't remember sooner."

"Indeed, you ought to be," was the gay rejoinder. "I've been just dying for the moment when you would remember."

An electric bell rang out as they were lighting their cigarettes, and a moment later Hal danced into the room with shining eyes and glowing cheeks. A few paces from the door she stopped suddenly.

"Hullo, Baby," she said, addressing Hermon, "where have you sprung from?"

"I found it wandering alone in Sloane Street," Lorraine remarked, "and now we've been teaing together."

Alymer did not look any too pleased at Hal's frank appellation, but former remonstrance had only been met with derision, and he knew he had no choice but to submit with a good grace.

"I might ask the same question, Lady-Clerk," he replied.

"Don't call me a lady-clerk—I hate the term. I'm a typist, secretary, bachelor-girl, city-worker, anything you like, not a lady-clerk—bah!..."

"Then don't call me Baby."

Hal's face broke into the most attractive of smiles.

"I can't help it. Everything about you, your size, your face, your ways just clamour to be called 'Baby'. Of course if you'd rather be Apollo—"

"Good Lord, no: is that the only alternative?"

"I'm afraid so; you needn't go if you don't want to," as he prepared to depart. "We are not going to talk grown-up secrets."

"If I were Mr. Hermon, I'd give you one good shaking, Hal," put Lorraine. "I'm sure you deserve it."

"Not a bit. Nothing could do him more good than regular interviews with me, to undo all the harm he has received in between from silly, idiotic women, who make him think he is something out of the ordinary. Isn't that so, Baby? Aren't you labouring under the delusion that you're a remarkable fine specimen of humanity? And all the time, Heaven knows, you've about as much honest purpose and brains as a big over-grown school-boy."

"I hope you are not intending to imply he is more richly endowed with dishonest purpose?" said Lorraine.

"Oh, I wouldn't mind that," Hal declared, "so long as it was energy and purpose of some kind."

"Even to giving you that good shaking," he asked, coming forward a step menacingly.

"Not in here," in alarm; "you and I scrapping in Lorraine's drawing-room would cost a hundred pounds or so in valuables. I'll cry 'pax'," as he still advanced. "Of course you are rather a fine boy really, I was only pulling your leg."

Hermon subsided with a laugh, and Hal proceeded to explain that she had come on business, having been asked by the editor of one of their small magazines to write up an interview with the actress for him.

"I shall say I found you having a cosy tête-à-tête with a young barrister of many inches and little brains," she laughed. "Come, Lorraine, spout away. What is your favourite *hors d'œuvre*? Did you feel like a boiled owl at your first appearance? And which horse do you back for next year's Derby?"

She started scribbling, to the amusement of the other two, carrying on a desultory conversation meanwhile.

"This isn't anything to do with my department, but I like Mr. Hadley, and he was keen about it, and offered me three guineas, so I said I'do do it... Are your eyes yellow or green? For the life of me, I don't know. Which would you rather I called them? ... I've got to go to Marlboro' House tomorrow to get up a short and vivid account of a garden party, because Miss Alton, who generally does it, is down with 'flu'. Were you a prodigal as a kid? no; I mean a prodigy... Fancy me at Marlboro' House! Awful thought, isn't it? How they dare?

"What is your favourite pastime? Shall I put down shooting? I know you don't know one end of a gun from the other, but it doesn't matter; and it reads rather well—something unique about it in an actress."

"Why not put angling, and give some of my dear enemies a chance to ask what for?"

"Or jam-making," suggested Alymer, "and redeem the stage in the eyes of the British matron."

"Oh, don't talk... how can I write? Shall I bring myself in, and dig up the dear old chestnut of David and Jonathan?... or shall I describe Dudley's disapproval melting into undisguised worship," she rippled with laughter as she scribbled on. "Oh dear, think if Dudley were to find it, and read it, because he hasn't even discovered yet that he has ceased to disapprove.

"Who's your favourite poet? I might say Dick Bruce; he would write a book of poems at once. And Quin might be your hero in real life. Do you know where you were born? Up in the Himalayas sounds nice and airy, and it might as well have been there as anywhere."

"If you want anymore you must get it while I eat my dinner," said Lorraine, rising. "I have to try and be at the theatre at seven just now. You may as well both dine with me, and you can come to my dressing-room afterwards if you like, Hal."

"No, thank you"; and Hal pulled a wry face. "I've seen quite enough of the wings, and the green-room, and all the rest of it. You might take Baby, just to show him the real thing, and put him off it once for all."

She turned to Hermon.

"Have you ever been behind the scenes? I used to go sometimes, just for the fun of it, while it was a novelty; but it quite cured me of any possible taste of the stage. Most of the performers were so nervous they could hardly speak, their teeth just chattered with cold and fright mingled, and the gloom of it was like a vault. And then all the gaping, staring faces in rows, looking out of the darkness. You can't think how idiotic people look seen like that. It always suggested to me that both stage and stalls were like children playing at being lunatics."

"That's only your dreadfully prosaic, unromantic mind, Hal. You just like to write newspaper articles, and type letters, and smother your imagination under dry-and-dust facts."

"Smother my imagination," echoed Hal, with a laugh. "Why, it would take the imaginations of fifty ordinary people to concoct some of the paragraphs we fix up during the week. My imagination is a positive goldmine at the office, at least it would be if they dare print all that I suggest."

"You should run a paper yourself," suggested Hermon; "a few libel actions would made it pay like anything."

"Ah, you haven't seen Dudley," with a little grimace. "Dudley would have a fit and die before the first action had had time to reach its interesting stage. I'd take you home to see him now, but he happens to have gone up to Holloway to dinner."

"I'm dining out myself, so I must fly." He turned to Lorraine, with a gay smile. "I say, may I come and dine with you some other time?"

"Come to the Carlton on Sunday, will you?"

Lorraine hardly knew why she made the sudden decision; she only knew perfectly well she would have to break another engagement to keep it, and that she was foolishly glad when he accepted.

"It's all right; you needn't ask me," volunteered Hal, as her friend glanced at her. "I'm going motoring with Dick, and I shall insist upon staying out until ten or eleven. I always try and fill my Sundays full of fresh air. "Where are you going tonight, Baby?" she added, with a charmingly impudent smile.

"The Albert Hall, with Lady Selon"; and a twinkle shone in his eyes.

"Goodness gracious! What in the world are you going to the Albert Hall for? and who is Lady Selon?"

"She is Soccer Selon's sister-in-law, and she asked me to take her to a concert. Is there anything else you would like to know?"

"Her age?" archly.

"Somewhere about thirty-five, I should imagine."

"Oh! your grandmother, or thereabouts. Well, skip along. Tell Dick to call for me early on Sunday."

When he had said good-bye to Lorraine and departed, Hal held up her hand, hanging in a limp fashion.

"I wish you'd teach him to shake hands, Lorry. It feels like shaking a blind cord and tassel. Are you going to mother him? What an odd idea for you to bother with a boy! You surely don't mean to tell me he interests you?"

"I like to look at him. He's such a splendid young animal. I feel—oh, I don't know what I feel."

"Lots of London policemen are splendid young animals, but you don't want tête-à-tête teas with them if they are."

"You absurd child! Is there any reason why I shouldn't have tea with Mr. Hermon, if it amuses me?"

"None specially; but if it's just a splendid young animal to look at, you want, I daresay it would be safer to import a polar bear from the Zoo."

Lorraine felt a spot of colour burn in her cheeks, but she only laughed the subject aside, and alluded to it no more before they parted at the theatre door.

Only at a late supper-party that night she was quieter than was her wont; and, contrary to her habit, one of the first to leave. A well-known rising politician, who had been paying her much attention of late, prepared, as usual, to escort her home. She wished he would have stayed behind, but had no sufficient reason for refusing his company. He taxed her with silence as they spun westwards, and she pleaded a headache, wondering a little why all he said, and looked, and did, somehow seemed banal and irritating tonight.

He was so sure of himself, so fashionably blasé, so carelessly clever, so daringly frank, with all the finished air of the modern smart man, basking callously in the assured fact of his own brilliance and superiority. She knew that most women would envy her the attentions of such a one, and that his interest was undoubtedly a great compliment, as such compliments go; but tonight she found herself remembering all the other women who had reigned before her, all those who would presently succeed her, and she was conscious of an impatient disgust of all the shallowness and insincerety of the fashionable, successful man.

"May I come in?" he asked, when they reached the flat, looking rather as if he were conferring a favour than soliciting one.

"No; it is too late. Good-night."

"Too late!..." he laughed a little, and Lorraine felt her temper rising. "It is not exceptionally late, a little earlier than usual in fact. Why mayn't I come in?"

"Because I don't want you," she said coldly, and she saw him bite his lip in swift vexation.

"I shall certainly not press you," he retorted, and turned away.

At the window of her drawing-room Lorraine lingered a few moments, gazin with a half-longing expression at the gleam of the lights on the dark flowing river. What was it that gave her that strange sense of heartache tonight? Why had her usual companions bored and irritated her? Why did Alymer Hermon's fine, boyish, refreshing face come so often to her mind?

She was certainly not in love with him. The mere idea was ridiculous, but it was equally certain that something about him had given rise to this vague unrest and longing. Was it perhaps that he called to her mind the youth she had never known, the young splendid, whole-hearted years, when it was so easy to believe and hope and enjoy that which life had never given her time for?

True, the world was at her feet now, just as much as it would ever be at his, but with what a difference? For her, with the work and stain of the knowledge of much evil, and little good. For him, at present, with all the glorious freshness of the morning.

She glanced back into the dim room, and among the shadows she saw him standing there again, towering up upon her hearthrug, before her hearth, with that youthful, frank assurance that was so attractive. Of a truth he was unspoilt yet, unspoilt and splendid as the dawn of the morning—but for how long?

What would they make of him presently, the women of the world, who must needs worship such a man, and strew their charms before him. How was he to keep his freshness, when temptation hemmed him in on every side?

She felt a sudden yearning as of hungry mother-love towards him. If he had been her son, her very own son, how she would have fought the whole world to help him keep his armour bright, and his colours flying high.

And instead?...

The wave of hungry mother-love was followed by one as of swift and angry protest. Who had ever cared whether she kept her armour bright and her colours flying high? Had not life itself mocked at her early aspirations, and trampled jeeringly on her untutored, unformed high desires? What chance had she ever had, long as she might, to keep the morning freshness?

Well, what of it? She had sought and striven for fame, and fame had come; she was a poor creature if she could not look life in the face now, and laugh above her wounds.

And in the meantime perhaps she could help him fight some of those other women still; the women who would drag him down for their own satisfaction, and care nothing for the hurt to him.

Anyhow, she would try to be a good pal to him, and not a temptress. For once she would fight for some one else's hand instead of her own, and gain what satisfaction she could in feeling herself a true friend.

CHAPTER VIII

About the time that the three in the Chelsea flat were leave-taking, a stream of women-clerks in the long passages of the General Post Office proclaimed that pressure of work had again meant "overtime" to these energetic City-workers.

In consequence, there was a lack of elasticity in the many passing feet, and the suggestion of a tired silence in the cloak-room; for though the girls hastened to get away from the dreary monotony of the huge building, they were, many of them, too tired to depart as joyfully as was their wont.

Yet most of them, behind the tiredness, looked out upon the world with clear, capable eyes, and strong, self-reliant faces, that spoke well for the spirit of their set. Up there in the big office-rooms, year in year out, these refined, well-educated women kept ledgers and accounts and did the general office work of the Civil Service with a precision and neatness and correctness equal to the work of any men, and invariably to the astonishment of any interested visitor who was permitted to inquire into the system.

Yet the majority of their salaries ranged from £90 a year to £210, and they were obliged to pas an examination of no mean stamp to attain a post. Small wonder that many of them, having to help support others as well as keep themselves, had the delicate, listless, anaemic appearance of underfed women badly in need of fresh air, good food, and wholesome exercise.

The policy of Great Britain towards her women workers is surely one of the greatest contradictions of our enlightened age. Even putting aside the vexed question of suffragism, how little has she ever done to try and cope with the needs of working womanhood?

In some Government departments, as, for instance, the Army Clothing Department, it is a known fact that the women are actually sweated; and that in the higher branches, employing gentlewomen, they pay them the lowest possible wage, not because the work is ill-done, but because, owing to present conditions, plenty of gentlewomen are found to accept the offer.

Many of these gentlewomen lose their health in their struggle to obtain good food, decent lodging, and a neat appearance on Government salaries, knowing full well that the moment they fall out of the ranks numbers will be waiting to fill their places.

And in the meantime enlightened authors and politicians write articles, and make speeches, holding forth upon the charm and beauty of the Home Woman, and drawing unflattering comparisons between her and the worker.

Comfortable elderly gentlemen, who have had successful careers and can now afford to dine unwisely every night, and keep their daughters in well-dressed indolence, self-satisfied, self-aggrandising, self-advertising young politicians, who, having obtained an attentive public, delight to cant about the rights of the citizen and the good of the Empire, clever, intuitive, charming novelists, who apparently possess an unaccountable vein of dense non-comprehension on some points—all harp upon this theme of the Home Woman, and the Home Sphere, and the infinite superiority, in their own lordly eyes, of the gentle, domesticated scion of the family hearth.

As if one-fourth of the women wage-earners, gentle or otherwise, in England today had any choice in the matter whatever. The rapidity with which a vacant place in the ranks is filled and the numbers waiting for it is surely sufficient proof of that; to say nothing of the pitiful conditions under which many, gentle and otherwise, cling to their posts long after a merciful fate should have given them the opportunity to save the remnants of their shattered health amidst country breezes.

It is useless to cry out to the woman that work and competition with men is unbecoming to her. She *must* work, and she *must* compete, and seeing this, it is surely time the British Government accepted the fact magnanimously, and took more definite steps to assure her welfare.

If it can only be done through woman's suffrage, then woman's suffrage must surely come, because, whether British legislators care for the good of women or not, nature does care, and as the race moves forward the working woman will have to be protected.

It has been seen over and over again that no band of politicians, nor powerful men, nor tape-bound State can long defy any advancing good for the needs of the whole.

Whether women work or not, they are the mothers of the future; and because this fact is greater than the sum of all other facts brought forward by the narrowness and short-sightedness of men, we may safely believe that, since they *must* work, nature will see to it that they work under the most favourable conditions, no matter what rich men have to go the poorer for it.

Pity is that the hour is so delayed; that narrowness, and selfishness, and self-aggrandisement still flourish, to the eternal cost of those of England's mothers who bring weaklings into the world, through the hard conditions of their enforced labour.

The *true patriot* of today will agitate not only for the highest possible efficiency in the Navy and Army; but, with no less resolve and sincerity, for the best possible conditions obtainable for all women-workers, that the Empire may not later sink suddenly to decay, in spite of her defences, through the impoverished, feeble, sickly off-spring who are all the men she has left.

The *true patriot* will accept the ever-strengthening fact, however unpalatable, that the development and emancipation of womanhood has brought women to the front as workers, *to stay*; and he will perceive that therefore it is incumbent upon the men to endeavour to find that happy mean, where they can work together to the advantage of both, and to the stability and greatness of a beloved country.

Only now the women-workers toil bravely on, heartening each other with jests under conditions in which it is extremely likely men would merely cavil and sulk and fill the air with their complainings; dressing themselves daintily through personal effort in spite of meagre purses; throwing themselves with a splendid joyousness into their few precious days of freedom; banding themselves together often and often to wring occasional hours of gaiety from the months of toil; keeping brave eyes to the front and brave hearts to the task, while they wait steadfastly for the day when their worth shall be appreciated and their claims recognised.

Hastening to the office in the morning, or hastening home (probably to cook their own dinner) at night, they read those clever, carefully worded articles and speeches by the men of power and weight, harping upon the charm and beauty and superiority of the Home Woman; and they laugh across to each other with a frank, rather pitying, rather irritated laughter, at the extraordinary dull-wittedness of some brilliant brains.

They wonder gaily how these enlightened, clever gentlemen would like it if they all became sweet Home women in the workhouses, cultivating elegant gardens, and floating round in flowing gowns at their expense.

The men call them "new women" with derision, or mannish, or unsexed; but those who have been among them, and known them as friends, know that they hold in their ranks some of the most generous-hearted, unselfish, big-souled women to exist in England today; and that it is just because of that they are able to plod cheerfully on, and laugh that indulgent, pitying little laugh, when an outraged man swells with virtuous indignation, and waxes eloquent upon their want of womanly attributes.

Of such as the best of these was Ethel Hayward. Among the crowd now hurrying more or less tiredly into the open air, she might not have been noticed. So many had white faces, dark-circled eyes, shabby-genteel clothing, and just a commonplace fairness, that in the throng it was difficult to discover distinguishing attributes.

One had to see her apart, and note the quick, urgent step, the independent, lofty poise of her head, and the steadfastness of the tired eyes, and firm, strong mouth, to feel that life had given her a heavy burden, which only a noble soul could have supported with heroism.

As she left the portals of the General Post Office she hesitated a few seconds as to her direction. "Should she go straight back to the little flat in Holloway, or should she go west, and get the drawing-paper Basil was wanting?"

Doris could easily get the drawing-paper the next day, if she chose; and at the flat Dudley Pritchard would have arrived for the evening. She surmised hastily that it was extremely probable Doris had made some other engagement for herself that she would be unwilling to delay, and that Dudley would in no wise regret her own tardy return.

The last thought caused her eyes to grow a little strained, as she walked quickly westwards—strained with the determination to face the fact unflinchingly, and try to overcome the deep, insistent ache it caused.

But the love of a lifetime is not dismissed at will, and looking a little pitifully backward, though she was but twenty-eight, Ethel felt she could not remember the time when she did not love Dudley Pritchard, though it had perhaps only crystallised into the great feature of her life at the time when, in silent, heroic endeavour, he had given of all he had to win his friend back to life and health.

It was Dudley's careful savings that he had paid for the great specialist and the big operation; Dudley's courage and devotion that had nerved the stricken man to take up the awful burden of perpetual invalidism; Dudley's never-failing encouragement and friendship that helped him still to bear the dreary months of utter weariness, in the little home kept together by his sister's salary.

High up in the dreary-looking block of flats in Holloway, attended through the day by the erratic ministrations of Doris, and at night by the yearning tenderness of Ethel, Basil Hayward dragged out a weary martyrdom, that prayed only for release. In vain Ethel murmured over him, that to work for him was a glory compared to what it would be to live without him; in the silent, tedious hours of her absence, his soul broke itself in hopeless, passionate protest against the decree that compelled him to accept his daily bread at the hands of the sister he would gladly have striven for day and night.

It as a martyrdom across which one can but draw a curtain, and stand "eyes frontt". Look this way, look that, what answer is there, what reason, what explanation, of the hidden martyrdoms of the work-a-day world, which the blank wall of heaven seems to regard with utter unconcern?

Mankind today is less disposed than ever of yore to calmly fold the hands and say, "It is the will of God." They can no longer do so honestly without either blaming or criticising the Divine Will that not merely permits, but is said to send, such martyrdoms.

Better surely to accept bravely the enigma of the universe, and strive to lessen the suffering in our own little sphere, believing that same Divine Will is striving with us to mitigate the ills humanity has brought upon itself through blind disobedience and careless indifference to the laws of nature.

Uncomplaining resignation may help by its example, but the resignation which sits with folded hands and makes no effort to amend, is only a form of feebleness. The strong soul accepts life silently as a field of battle, asking for energy, resource, courage, and that fine spirit which obeys the unseen general in unquestioning faith.

It was only in such a spirit, through those years of pain and mystery, that Ethel was able to witness her passionately loved brother's martyrdom, and give all the years of her youth to earn that pour salary from a wealthy Empire, to keep some sort of a home for the three of them in the little, dingy Holloway flat.

For even if Doris had been capable of sustained endeavour, the bedridden man could not have been left alone for long, and no choice was left them but to eke out Ethel's pitiful £110 salary between them.

Often perhaps a passionate resentment burned in her heart concerning the heavy handicaps under which a woman achieves work equal to a man's; but she had no time to lend herself to any open protest, and toiled on, silently fighting her individual daily battle the better encouraged by those brave women taking all the opprobrium of the warfare upon their own shoulders, for the sake of working womanhood as a whole.

Only, of late a fresh burden had been added in the fear that Dudley was growing to care for her sister Doris.

It was not that she grudged Doris the happiness, nor the prospect of a home in which she and Dudley might together take care of Basil; but she saw ahead the tragedy of the awakening, when Dudley learnt of the shallow, selfish little heart behind Doris's charming exterior.

That he, of all people, should be drawn to such an one was only the contradiction seen on all sides in life. Because he had that old-fashioned distrust of the independent, self-reliant woman, he must needs go to the opposite extreme, and let himself be drawn to one capable of little else in the world but ornamentation. Doris, she knew, was fitted only to be a rich man's plaything. Dudley, she felt instinctively, would start off by expecting of her things she had never had to give, and in his dismay and disappointment might wreck both their lives.

Yet she felt powerless to take any step that might save them from each other, knowing full well that Doris, bored with her life at the flat, had decided that even life with Dudley would be better. And even as Ethel hastened westwards, instead of towards home, Doris with infinite pains put the finishing touches to her pretty hair, and took a last survey of her dainty person before the well-known step should sound on the stone staircase outside their unpretentious little door.

She had been very irritable with the invalid, because he was trying to get a plan copied quickly, and wanted a special arrangement of light, just when she was ready to go and dress after preparing the dinner; but when at last Dudley knocked on the door, Doris opened it to him with a face of such charming innocence and smiles that irritability would never have been imagined in the répertoire of her characteristics. A little helpless, a little childish, she might be, but what clever man does not love a clinging woman?

"It was so nice of you to come," she said. "It is such a dreary place to turn out to after your long day at the office."

"But I love coming," he answered simply. "You know I do."

He looked at her with unconscious admiration, and Doris noted for the hundredth time that although he was not particularly tall, nor particularly good-looking, nor particularly anything, yet his thin, clean-shaven face had a clever, distinguished air, and he had unmistakably the cut and breeding of a gentleman. She knew that even if he were only moderately well off, and could not afford the dash she loved, he was at least good to be seen with, and a man who might one day make his mark. So, though she deprecated most of the qualities which were in reality his best points, she decided in her calculating little head she would seriously contemplate becoming Mrs. Dudley Pritchard.

His greeting with the invalid was, for Dudley, a little boisterous—the result of a hint from Ethel. He would probably never have had time to see for himself that such a man as Basil Hayward would hate a pitying air or invalid manner, but he was sympathetic enough to respond quickly to a suggestion that the latest cricket or football news, gaily imparted, was far more pleasing to the invalid than a sympathetic inquiry after his health.

For Basil Hayward, sufferer and martyr, was prouder of his near relationship to a celebrated international cricketer than he would ever had been of his own sublime courage had it been lauded to the skies. Life had left him little enough, but "give me the power still to glory in every manly and athletic achievement of my countrymen," was his unspoken request.

So they discussed the latest sporting news of the world, and then had a great argument on a plan of Dudley's for a competition for a grand-stand and pavilion on a celebrated aviation ground, while they waited for Ethel.

The small flat had only one sitting-room, and while they talked Doris flitted gracefully about, putting the finishing touches to the table. Afterwards she sat on a low chair under the lamp, so that the light fell full on her pretty hair, while she bowed her head with unwonted industry over a piece of sewing.

Occasionally she glanced up at the two men, meeting Dudley's eyes with a pretty confiding look that only added to her charm.

"Ethel is so late. I wonder if we had better wait," she said at last. "She told me on no account to do so."

Basil glanced at the clock a little anxiously.

"It is too bad," he murmured; "they have no right to expect so much overtime work. She is sure to come soon."

"Yes; but I think she would like us to begin"; and Doris rose slowly. "It will save time when she does come in."

It was plain Basil disapproved, but she pretended not to see it, and in a short time she and Dudley were seated tête-à-tête, while the invalid remained on his couch. They were gay from spontaneity of pleasure, and Hal would have been surprised at the cheeriness of her grave brother, had she seen how he responded to Doris's playful mood.

Then Ethel's key sounded in the door, and it was as though a slight shadow fell upon them. Doris wished she had been later still; Dudley seemed to grow grave again, from habit, and Basil watched the door like a big devoted dog, with eyes of hungry love.

As she entered her first glance was for him, and her nod and smile ere she turned to greet the visitor hid all her own weariness, and was reflected in a light of glad welcome on the sick man's face.

"I'm so glad you didn't wait," she said; "I stayed to get the drawing-paper."

"But why did you, dear?" he asked, with quick remonstrance. "Doris could easily have gone tomorrow."

"Of course I could"; and Doris skilfully threw a hurt tone in her voice, which Dudley was quick to detect.

"I wanted to walk," was all Ethel said, as she moved away to take off her hat and coat.

But in spite of her efforts the gaiety did not return, and Doris grew a little pensive and sad.

Dudley, with his surface reasoning, saw in her attitude something that suggested the other two were in the habit of being entirely wrapped up in each other, to the exclusion of the young sister.

Ethel might be a remarkably clever and capable woman; he knew perfectly well that she was just as able with her fingers as her brain, and did nearly all the upholstering and dressmaking of the household in her evening free time; but wasn't she just a little superior and self-satisfied also—just a little unkindly indifferent to the monotony and dullness of her young sister's existence?

Dudley found his sympathy go out more and more to those childlike eyes, and the pretty, clinging ways; and a sort of half-fledged resentment grew up against the elder sister. He could not choose but admire her, if it were only for her devotion to her brother, but he felt a vague something, in his thoughts of her, that he could not express, and remained grave.

Ethel, watching them both covertly while she moved about helping Doris to clear away the dinner things, guessed at much that was passing in his mind, and unconsciously grew a little strained in her manner to him. That he should pity Doris and blame her seemed at last irony, but it could not be helped; and not even to win his love could she attempt to change her natural manner, and appear what might better please him.

She even said "good-night" a little coldly, and remained beside Basil while Doris went out into the tiny hall with him to get his hat and coat.

Doris seemed to Dudley a lonely little figure out there in the dim light, with just the suggestion of a droop about her lips and wistfulness in her eyes. He believed that she found herself left out in the cold with those other two, but was too proud to complain. He felt a tenderness springing up in his heart and spreading to his eyes as he leaned towards her with a protecting air.

She was small and fragile. It made him feel big and protective; and he liked it. Hal was so tall and straight and slim and boyish—not in the least the sort of person one could really feel protective to; and he liked clinging women... His head bent down quite near to hers as he said in a low tone: "I suppose they are like lovers, those two, and you feel a little out of it, eh?"

"Yes"—confidingly and gratefully—"and it makes me very unhappy, because I love to slave for Basil just as much as Ethel does. But he does not want me..." with a little sad air.

"Oh, I think you are mistaken. It could never be that. It is only that they have always been so devoted, and I expect it is too lonely for you here. You do not get enough change. Would you care to go to the White City with me on Thursday evening?"

"Oh, I should love it!" and there was a quick gleam in her eyes.

"Very well, I will arrange it." His hand closed over hers lingeringly. "Good-bye. Don't be despondent. I will let you know where to meet me. We might have dinner at a restaurant first; shall we?"

Again she expressed her delight, and Dudley went off with a glow of pleasure that was a surprise to him.

But behind the closed door Doris smiled a little smile in the darkness, that had none of the artless innocence of the smiles reserved for him.

"Ethel would just give her head to go with him," was her first thought; and then, "I hope he won't go to a cheap restaurant."

In the sitting-room Ethel was putting the last touches to the invalid's comfort for the night, moving about busily. Doris leaned against the table, and made no attempt to help her.

"Dudley wants me to go to the White City with him on Thursday evening. I said I would."

"Thursday is the night I have to go and see Dr. Renshaw"; and Ethel glanced round with a shadow of vexation on her face.

"I know it is, but you will not be very late." She paused, then added, "I do not get so many treats that I can afford to miss one."

"Dudley could probably have gone any other night. Did you ask him?"

Ethel spoke a little quickly, and Doris looked ready with a sharp retort, when Basil interposed.

"Thursday will be all right, chum. Doris won't leave before six and you will get in by half-past seven. I shall have nearly two whole hours in which to do any silly thing I like, without getting scolded"; and his smile was very winsome.

"I don't like you to have to wait so long for your dinner. You always get faint. Perhaps Dr. Renshaw would see me another evening... I—"

"Oh, nonsense, chum"—in the same cheery voice—"I'll have a tin of sardines, and eat one every ten minutes until you come."

Ethel let the matter drop, seeing it would please him best, and Doris retired to their room with a slightly sulky air.

"There always seems to be something to damp it if I am to have a treat," was her complaint.

"I don't think you will feel damped after you start," Ethel replied quietly, and they went to bed in silence.

CHAPTER IX

When Dudley got back he found Hal waiting up for him, with an expression of shining eagerness on her face.

"Oh, Dudley, such fun!" she began, "Lorraine has got the royal box for me for Thursday evening. We must have a little dinner-party. Who shall we take? It holds four comfortably, and two men could stand at the back."

"Thursday evening!" looking a little taken aback. "I am engaged."

"Engaged! Well, you must put it off. Why didn't you tell me? I thought you said you had any night free except Friday."

"I only made the engagement this evening."

"Are you going to see Basil again? He won't mind being put off."

"No. It isn't Basil."

"What then?"

Dudley turned away, threw his gloves carelessly down on a sidetable, and picked up some letters.

"I asked Doris to go to the White City with me."

"You—you asked Doris to go to the White City?..." she repeated incredulously. "What in the world for?"

"To see it, of course. What else should I ask her for?"

"Oh, Heaven only knows! Why ask her at all? I should certainly upset her into the canal from sheer irritation if she came with me."

"Such nonsense." He knit his forehead into a decided frown. "You are so unfair to Doris. You used to complain that I was unfair to Lorraine. I was never as unfair as you are now. You don't really know Doris at all; and she has never done anything to hurt you."

"It doesn't follow that she wouldn't if she had the chance. You're so awfully dense about women, Dudley. Why didn't you invite Ethel instead? She is worth a hundred Dorises. Then we could have taken her to the theatre."

His voice and manner grew very cold.

"I don't agree with you, but it is not a subject I care to discuss. Is there any reason why Doris should not be invited to the theatre?"

"None whatever, except that I don't propose to ask her."

They faced each other a moment almost angrily, except that whereas Dudley was distinctly vexed, Hal was a little scornful, and half-laughing.

"Then I cannot come either, and"—he paused a moment, to add with decision—"I object to your going unchaperoned."

"Do you mean that you wish me to give up the box?"

"You know what I mean."

Hal was thoughtful a moment, and then remarked with sudden glee:

"I know what I'll do. I'll take the Three Graces, and persuade Quin's aunt to come as chaperone. Then we'll all have supper with Lorraine afterwards. You shall have a nice, quiet, interesting evening with Doris, and I'll get two stalls for you for another night."

She moved about, gathering up her things.

"You don't know Quin's aunt, Lady Bounce, do you? She's the dearest old soul, and she loves a theatre. Night-night, old boy; don't keep Doris too long near the canal, in case you are taken with my inclination"; and she went gaily off, humming a popular air.

Dudley read through his letters without grasping any of their contents. For the first time Hal's attitude to Doris seriously worried him, and he felt vaguely there was trouble ahead.

But when Thursday came, and they were together, she again had the same pleasing effect upon his senses, and he let himself be persuaded that if Hal grew to know her better, she could not choose but grow fond of her.

In the meantime a group in the royal box at the Greenway Theatre was causing no small interest to a crowded house.

There was Hal, with her smart, well-groomed air, gleaming white neck and arms, and her white, even teeth that looked so attractive even in the distance when she smiled.

Dick Bruce, spruce and scholarly, hugely pleased with himself, because he had an article in *The National Review*, on the strength of the colonies in war time; and some lines entitled "Baby's Boredom" in *Fireside Chat*, concerning which he had already announced his intention of standing the champagne for their supper with the cheque.

Of the other two occupants it would be difficult to say which attracted the most attention. Alymer Hermon, with his immense stature and splendid head, or Quin's aunt, Lady Bounce, who presented so striking a resemblance to another well-known little old lady sometimes seen at the theatre, that friends of the last-mentioned were utterly puzzled.

Surely only one little lady in London wore that early Victorian dress, with the ringlets and "grande dame" air, and sat with such genuine delight and enjoyment through a play? And yet why did she not look out for her numerous friends, down there in the stalls, and recognise them?

And who in the world was she with? If that were indeed Lady Phyllis Fenton—and it seemed incredible it should not be—who was the splendid young giant, and who the white-faced girl with the brilliant smile?

And all the time, absorbed in the play and her companions, the little old lady smiled and talked, calmly indifferent to the many eyes below waiting for the expected bow of recognition.

Quin, apparently, had not been willing to desert his slummers for a gay West-end theatre; so Hal was only escorted by two Graces instead of three, but the light in her eyes, for any one near enough to see, suggested she was enjoying herself to the utmost in spite of it.

Then came the final sensation, of the little old lady in her strange costume and ringlets, passing through the vestibule, on the arm of the young giant, followed by the sleek-looking, well-groomed pair of cousins, who chatted to each other with an air of the utmost unconcern towards the curious glances now levelled at them upon all sides.

"It *must* be Lady Phyllis Fenton," said some. "It *can't* be," said others. "Then who the devil is it?" asked the men.

And still the little group passed on, smiling and unconcerned, though a red spot burned in the giant's smooth cheeks, and he carefully avoided any possibility of meeting Hal's gleaming eyes.

A roomy electric brougham was awaiting them, and then the watchers said it glided away: "Surely that is Lady Phyllis's car and liveries?"

But what they would have made of the scene inside the car it is difficult to say, for the dear little old lady suddenly collapsed backwards on her seat, with a howl of laughter, and shot into the air a pair of trousered legs.

"Oh my conscience!" gasped Quin, amid choking laughter. "It will be the sensation of the season; and when Aunt Phyllis gets to hear about it she'll first have a fit with wrath and then laugh until she's ill."

"I'd no idea you were such an actor, Quin," Hal exclaimed admiringly when she could speak; "you ought be holding crowded houses enthralled, instead of slumming."

"Heaven preserve me. Theatres are mostly mummies looking at mummies. Down east I get in touch with flesh and blood—the real thing; and I prefer it. But I wouldn't have missed tonight for something. Oh, lord!... just think of the people who know Aunt Phyllis that I must have cut; and all the fuss there will be when aunt is admonished for supping at the Savoy with an actress! We aren't half through the fun yet."

With which they all went off into fresh peals of laughter, at various reminiscences, and were bordering upon a condition of imbecility when Lorraine at last joined them with the latest news.

"It's positively immense," she said. "The manager told me Lady Phyllis Fenton had come with Miss Pritchard, and tomorrow every paper will announce it, and the mystery will grow. I 'phoned for a private room at the Savoy, to keep the puzzle up. She must only be seen passing through on Mr. Hermon's arm. How splendid they must look. I almost wish I wasn't in the secret."

"Oh, they do!" Hal cried. "Alymer ought to have had knee breeches and silk stockings, and they would look just perfect. I have to talk fast to Dick, or I should give it all away in my face."

"You'll have to settle with your aunt," Lorraine laughed to Quin. "I hope she won't cut you off with a shilling."

"She will be furiously angry and terrifically interested," he said. "I expect I shall have to take you all to dinner to show her what the party looked like. Of course, Bonne, her maid, will give it away, because I borrowed the garments from her, and said they were for a play I was getting up in the East End."

"You'll have a bad half-hour with Dudley," Dick remarked to Hal, with enjoyment. "He is sure to hear of it somewhere."

"Quite sure," resignedly; "but if it were a bad two hours it would still have been worth it. It reminds me of the old days at school, Lorraine, when we used to get into scrapes on purpose, if the fun made it worth while."

There was no gayer supper party in the Savoy that night, and the champagne paid for with the proceeds of "Baby's Boredom" proved none the less vivifying for the insipidity of its source. Dick insisted upon reciting his doggerel, and Quin was not only much toasted as "Lady Bounce", but carried kicking round the room by the giant, because in a moment of forgetfulness he used a swear-word, which they all insisted was a reflecton upon the conversation of his illustrious aunt.

Lorraine, in most amusing form herself, laughed until she was tired out, and wondered why she was not bored. She asked the question of Alymer Hermon, who was privileged to see her home, while Dick returned with Hal, and Quin beat a hasty retreat to get rid of his disguise.

"After all, you are only boys," she said, with a little smile, "and I'm... well, I'm Lorraine Vivian."

The giant gazed thoughtfully out of the brougham window a moment, and from her corner Lorraine looked long, and a little sadly, at the finely modelled head and profile.

"Perhaps," he said at length, "a great many people you meet make a special effort to please you, and try to make an impression on you. We being all so young, and just nobodies, realise the uselessness of wasting our efforts, and are merely natural."

She smiled in the shadow, and glanced away from him with the sadness deepening.

"I feel tonight I should like to be one of you—so young and just nobody. It would be a pleasant change."

"I don't think you would like it at all."

He looked at her with a slightly puzzled air.

"Only the other day you were speaking to me of achievement and ambition. You seemed to care so much. You must be glad."

"Oh yes, yes," wearily; "but it isn't enough by itself. There is something I have missed, and tonight I feel that it might outweigh all the rest— something to do with being young, and careless, and fresh, and just nobody."

Still looking at her with slightly puzzled, very kindly eyes, he answered simply, "I'm so sorry."

She seemed to shrink away suddenly into her corner. The very simplicity of his sympathy, and the quiet, natural friendliness in his face, stirred some strange chord in her heart with a swift, unaccountable ache. He looked so big and strong and splendid there in the shadow, with his freshness and his charm; and she felt very brain-fagged and world-weary; and without in the least knowing why, or what led up to the desire, she wanted to feel his arms about her, and his freshness soothing her spirit.

And instead he was not even attempting to make love to her, not even flirting with her. Would any other man she knew have ridden beside her thus after the gentleness she had shown? Was that perhaps the very secret of his attraction? Or was it a physical allurement—the irresistible charm of bigness and strength, independent of anything else, drawing with its time-old sway?

She had no time to probe further, as the brougham stopped at her door. He handed her out with the deference so often met with in big men, remarking with an old-fashioned air that suited him to perfection:

"I'm afraid we have all tired you very much. It was good of you to come with us. I can't tell you how much we appreciate it."

"Oh, indeed no; you refreshed me. Good-night. Stevens will run you home. Don't forget Sunday", and she moved away.

"It must be his bigness," was her last thought as her head touched the pillow. "When I am used to it, no doubt the novelty will pass, and I shall find him merely boyish, and be rather bored."

"I wonder if it is her dainty smallness," Dudley was musing, away in his Bloomsbury lodging, feeling still, with a pleasant thrill, the touch of Doris's small hand on his arm, and seeing again the upward, confiding expression in her wide blue eyes. "Odd that Hal should be so far astray in her judgment, when she is usually so clever; but if she knew her better she would change her mind."

As for Hal herself, she hastily tumbled into bed, still chuckling in huge enjoyment over her evening.

"Those boys are just dears," was her thought, "and I wouldn't have missed Lady Bounce for the world. What a good thing Dudley was taken with paternal affection for that little fool Doris, and I had to have a chaperone. Heigh-ho! what a scene there will be if he hears about it; but what's the odds so long as you're happy? And oh dear! what will Lady Phyllis Fenton say when she finds out"; and once more the even teeth flashed an irresistible smile into the darkness.

CHAPTER X

It was force of habit chiefly that caused Lorraine, as a rule, to sleep long and late on Sunday mornings; and it was greatly to her advantage that for so many months, and even years, no mental anxiety had robbed her of a splendid capacity to rest. She seemed to have a faculty for limiting her worrying hours to the daylight, and being able to lay them aside, like her correspondence, at night.

Yet on the following Sunday morning she found herself early awake, with a brain only too ready to begin probing restlessly, and having little of the calm friendliness she intended it should have towards her guest of the evening.

To add to her unrest, her mother paid her an early visit, of a sort that had been growing too frequent of late. It was not enough that Lorraine paid her rent, and gave her a handsome allowance; when there chanced to be no one else to pay her debts, these came upon Lorraine's shoulders also.

T-day it was a long, rambling tale of a hard-hearted dressmaker who, having had a new frock back for alteration, had taken upon herself to return the skirt, without the bodice, with an intimation that she was retaining the delayed portion until her long account was settled. Hence Mrs. Vivian found herself with what she called a most important engagement, without the equally important new frock to go in.

Lorraine lay under the bedclothes, with only her head showing, and watched her a little coldly, as she moved restlessly about the room airing her woes. She had promised Madame Luce, over and over again, to settle in a week or two; and who would have believed the odious woman would serve her such a trick?

Never again, if she had to go naked, would she order a garment from her of any description whatever. And the friends she had sent to her as customers! Why, half the woman's trade was owing to her introduction.

"Perhaps the friends don't pay their bills," Lorraine suggested in a tired voice.

Mrs. Vivian drew herself up a little haughtily.

"I do not think there is any occasion to cast reflections on my friends, even if you do not choose to be sociable to them," which remark was intended as a dignified hit at Lorraine's invincible determination to maintain friendly relations with her mother, without having anything whatever to do with her mother's friends.

As many previous hits, it fell quite harmlessly; it was doubtful if Lorraine even heard it, half hidden there in the bedclothes with her tired eyes.

"I suppose it isn't any use reminding you that your personal expenditure exceeds mine?" she hinted, "and that you have already far overstepped the allowance we stipulated?"

"You do not have time to go about as much as I do, and it makes a great difference not having hosts of friends."

"You don't seem to get much pleasure out of them," Lorraine could not resist saying, knowing as she did how much of her salary went into the pockets of these so-called friends, in order to buy their adherence.

"Do I get much pleasure out of anything?" irritably. "My only child is one of the first actresses in London, and what is it to me? Do I have the pleasure of going about with her? or living with her? or taking any part in her success?"

"I suppose it isn't such a small thing to live by her. If I were not successful, we could certainly not live here. It might have been Islington and omnibuses," and she smiled.

"As if that were all. Probably, as real companions we might have been even happier in Islington."

Lorraine stiffened. "Companions!... Ah, I, with whom else ever dancing attendance, and changing in identity every few months?"

But she made no comment, for the days of her hot-headed, deep-hearted judging were over; and from behind inscrutable eyes she looked upon the things that one sees without seeming to see them, and accepted facts that hurt her very soul, with a callous, cynical air that defied the keenest shafts of probing.

It was her armour in an envious, merciless world, that would have rejoiced before her eyes if it could have driven in a barbed arrow even through her mother.

More than once a jealous enemy had tried and failed, routed utterly by Lorraine's cynical, cool treatment of a fact that she knew no persuasion nor arguing could have helped her to refute. She did not even weep about it now in secret.

It was as though she had shed all the tears she had to shed during that year of utter revulsion spent in the Italian Riviera, companied by the passionless solitudes of snowtopped mountains. Something of a great patience and a great gentleness had come to her then, helping her to hide the loathing she could not crush, and place the fact of motherhood first of all.

As her mother, she had taken Mrs. Vivian back into her heart, and given her generously of what worldly possessions she had. And she had done it with a wondrous quiet and absence of all ostentation either outwardly or inwardly. It had never occured to Lorraine that, whether it was a duty or not, after what had passed it was certainly a fine act upon her part.

She had not questioned about it at all. To her mother's apologetic gush she had merely turned calm eyes and a strong face.

"It isn't worth while to remember the past at all," she had said; "we will just begin again on rather different lines. I'll always let you have as much money as I can spare."

Mrs. Vivian had been a little taken aback by the new Lorraine who returned from Italy; and not a little afraid before the calm, inscrutable eyes; so that she had secretly rejoiced at the arrangement which gave her a separate establishment of her own; but none the less, in bursts of righteous indignation supposed to emanate from her outraged feelings as a mother, she usually chose to make it her pet grievance.

And still Lorraine only smiled the tired smile, and glanced carelessly aside with the inscrutable eyes until the tirade was over, the coveted cheque made out, and her own little sanctum once again in peaceful possession.

Only just occasionally, if the interview had been specially trying, she might have been seen afterwards to glance whimsically across to the picture, recently enlarged from an old photograph, of a fine-looking man in full hunting-rig standing beside a favourite hunter.

"Poor old dad," she murmured once; "I don't wonder you couldn't keep up the old place. I don't know how you got along at all without my salary."

Once when she was feeling the drag of it all a little keenly she told the man in the picture: "Mother is splendidly handsome, and I daresay I owe her a good deal; but thank God you were there with your fine old name and family to give me the things that matter most. It sometimes seems as if we had got each other still, dad, and, for the rest, some are frail in one way and some another, and fretting doesn't help any one." The fine eyes had grown more whimsically wistful looking into the face of the huntsman as she finished: "Anyhow, the last favourite is second cousin to a duke, and she pointed out to me, he might have been only a butcher."

How much Hal knew of her mother's life Lorraine had never been able to gauge, but she had reason to think she knew something and was sporting enough to pretend otherwise. If so, she blessed her for it, feeling that by that generous non-acknowledgment she rendered a service both to her and her dead father.

Yet it seemed strange that any one so young and fresh as Hal should be able to act thus, instead of suffering a violent repulsion. Was it the depth of her splendid friendship; or was it a naturally adaptable, common-sense nature; or was it non-comprehension?

As time passed and she grew to know Hal yet better, she felt instinctively it was the first of these, coupled with that true sportsman-spirit which was one of her strongest attributes.

Lorraine was not the only one who felt that whether Hal had any religion or not, or any faith, through good and ill, by easy paths and difficult, one might be absolutely sure that she would "play the game." It made her feel herself richer with her one friend than with her mother's admitted hosts, and though she seemed to hesitate and reason on that Sunday morning, both knew the cheque would finally be written, and the coveted garment rescued in time for the important lunch.

Only, afterwards, a shadow seemed to linger today that heretofore would have vanished with the departing figure. The sunshine crept through the drawn curtains, lying like a shaft of hope across the gloom, but it brought no answering gleam into the beautiful eyes, with their tired, far-off gaze.

It was all very well for Hal to be a main feature in her life, blessing it with her friendship, while she turned kindly, unseeing eyes away from the corners where the murky shadows lay: Hal, who knew about the mad, discreditable marriage and its violent termination, and probably also of her mother's insatiable thirst for admiration and excitement at any cost.

There was something about Hal in herself that was as a shining armour, against which unkind barbs fell harmlessly, and enabled her to go on her serene and joyful way in blissful non-attention.

But could it be the same with this treasured only son, who was doubtless destined for a high place in the world by doting parents, and other proud bearers of the same old name? Of course he might sup and trifle with certain denizens of the theatrical world galore; it would only be part of his education, and a thing to wink at, but she already doubted whether such a slight companionship would have any attraction.

In spite of his youthfulness, there was something in him that would naturally and quickly respond to the fine shades in herself, and grow into a friendship that had no part with the casual, gay acquaintanceships of the theatre and the world.

In a sense he was like Hal, and she knew that just as she attracted Hal's devotion in spite of all disparity of years and circumstances, so, if she chose, she could make this young giant more or less her slave.

But was it worht it?

What did she, on her high pedestal, want with his young admiration? What did she want with a companion so undeveloped that she herself must awaken his strongest forces?

Through the gloom, unheeding the shaft of sunlight, she saw him again, towering up there on her hearth, with his young splendour, so extraordinarily unspoilt as yet; and she knew that, reasonable or unreasonable, she was attracted far beyond her wont.

And then she thought of his easy-going temperament, his lack of ambition, his half-sleepy attitude towards life.

What if the wheels ran so smoothly for him that the latent forces were never aroused, and little achieved of all that might be?

If love came at his asking, and a sufficiency of success to satisfy an easy-going nature, what would there ever be to stir depths which she truly believed were worth stiring? Was it so small a thing to help a fine soul forward to its best attainment?... was such an aim not worth some going aside for both?

She felt there were things she could teach him, which without her he might entirely miss; and if without her he were the better according to a conventional standard, he might yet be far the poorer in the big, deep things of life.

Well, no doubt circumstances would end by suiting themselves, with or without her agency. In the meantime why worry, in a world that it would seem worked out its own ends, sublimely indifferent to the individual?

They were going to dine together tonight anyhow; their first tête-à-tête dinner and evening: time enough to probe and worry when she was more sure a mutual attraction existed; wiser at present to seek a counter attraction for her own sake, that she might not uselessly build a castle without foundations.

Prompt as ever, she reached out for the receiver beside her bed and rang up the Albany to know if Lord Denton were awake yet.

"I'm not awake," came back a sleepy answer. "I am asleep, and dreaming of Lorraine Vivian. If my man wakes me now, I shall curse him solidly for half an hour."

"Well, will you dream you are going to take her for a spin into the country shortly? I happen to know she is fainting for the longing to breathe country air."

"In my dream I am already waiting at her door, with the Yellow Peril spluttering its heart out with delight, and eagerness to be off. I have even dreamt she managed to put a motor bonnet on in half-an-hour—is it conceivable—or should it be half a day?"

"No, your dream is right. Be outside the door in half an hour, and you will see."

An hour later they were spinning out into Surrey at an alarming pace, both silently revelling in the freshness and motion and the fact that they were too old friends to need to trouble about conversation. When they dived into the lanes he slowed down, remarking:

"I suppose we mustn't risk scrunching any one up."

Lorraine only smiled, remaining silent a little longer, and then she suddenly asked him:

"When you feel yourself inclined to fall in love foolishly what do you do?"

"Well… as a rule…" he began slowly and humorously, "I either cut and run, or I hurry to see so much of her that I am bound to get bored."

"The first plan sounds the safest, but would often be the most difficult of execution. Supposing the second miscarries and you don't get bored?"

"Well, then I think—usually—there is an awful moment when I have to tell her I can't afford both a motor and a wife; and to be motorless would kill me."

A sudden little twitching at the corners made Lorraine's mouth dangerously fascinating.

"Evidently you have never fallen in love with me," she said, "for you have not been driven to either way of escape."

He looked into her face with an answering humour, and a twinkle in his eyes as alluring as her smilling lips.

"Because when I fell in love with you I did it sensibly, and not foolishly," was his answer; "instinct told me I couldn't have you for my wife however much I wished it, so I said myself: 'Flip, old boy, she'll make a thundering good pal, you close with it,' and I did."

She made no comment, and he went on more seriously:

"You see, even if you became marriageable and I cut out the motor, you wouldn't be attracted to an ordinary sort of cove like me. I suit you down to the ground as a pal, but it wouldn't go any farther."

"I wonder why you think that?"

"I don't exactly *think* it—thinking is too much bother—but it's just there, like a commonplace fact. You are all temperament, and high-strung nerves, and soul, and enthusiasm, and that sort of thing, which makes you a great actress. I'm just a two-legged, superior sort of animal, who hasn't much brain, but knows what he likes, and usually does it without wasting time on pros and cons. Consequently, I'm just as likely to end in prison as anywhere else, and take it without much concern as all in the day's work. You are more likely to end in a nunnery, as the most devout of all the nuns."

"What an odd idea! Why a nunnery?"

"Oh, because it's an extreme of one sort or another, and you are made for extremes. You'll perhaps be very wicked first" —he smiled delightfully— "after which, of course, you'd have to be very good. It's the way you're made. I'm cut out on quite a different plan. I can't be 'very' anything, unless it's very drunk after the Oxford and Cambridge at Lord's."

"Do you think I could be very wicked?" She asked the question with a thoughtfulness that amused him greatly, and he answered at once:

"I haven't a doubt of it. You are probably plotting the particular form of wickedness at this very moment."

She laughed, and he went on in the same serio-comic mood:

"I quite envy you. It must be very thrilling to think to oneself, 'I've dared to be desperately wicked.' You cease to be a nonentity at once and become a force. You get right to hand-grips with the big elemental things. Of course that is interesting, but it usually means a confounded lot of bother."

"You are as bad as Hal Pritchard. She announced the other day she would rather have a dishonest purpose than no purpose at all."

"It's the same idea, only Miss Pritchard lives up to her creed by being full of energy and purpose; whereas I can't be anything but a mediocre waster. I've neither the pluck to be wicked, not the energy to be good, nor enough purpose to regret it. I believe I'm best described as an aristocratic 'stiff', a 'stiff' being a person who spends his life trying to avoid having to do things.

"I fill a niche all the same," he finished, "because I make such an excellent foil for the other chaps, who like to pride themselves on their superiority and hard work. It's nice for them to be able to say contemptuously, 'Look at Denton,' and it's nice for me to be able to feel I'm of some use, without the bother of making an effort."

"You are certainly quite incorrigible as an idler, if that can be called a purpose, and, Flip, don't change; I love you for it; you are one of the most restful things I have ever known."

He glanced into her face with a keenness that somewhat belied his professed incapacity to be in earnest, and remarked with seeming lightness:

"Feeling a bit down on your luck, eh? Are you thinking of falling in love foolishly?"

"I'm thinking of trying to guard against doing so."

"You ought not to find it difficult. Crowd him out with other admirers."

"It seems as if he were going to do the crowding out."

"Why, is he so big?" jocularly.

"There's six foot five-and-a-half of him."

"Whew! And thin as a lathe, I suppose; a sort of animated telegraph pole."

"No; broad in proportion, cut to measure absolutely."

"Then he is a fine fellow," with conviction.

Lorraine felt a swift glow of pride, and then inwardly admonished herself for being silly. What, after all, was size? As Hal had trenchantly remarked, plenty of London policemen were just as big and fine. Half in self-defence she added:

"He has brains as well, and he is as handsome as Apollo."

"Then run," was the laconic response; "don't stop to buy a ticket; pay the other end."

She smiled, but grew suddenly serious. Leaning forward with eyes straining hard to the horizon, she said: "Flip, I've had a hard life, in spite of the success. Shall I run?... or... shall I stay, and snatch joy, while there is still time?"

He looked at her with a growing interest.

"If I were you I should run," he said; "but, all the same, I think you'll stay."

"No; I don't think I shall. There are other reasons. He is a good deal younger than I—and—well, I've a fair amount on my soul already."

The tired shadow was coming back to her eyes, but she laughed suddenly with an attempt at gaiety.

"You ought to have heard Hal Pritchard on the subject. She remarked there were plenty of London policemen just as big, and suggested if I wanted a fine young animal to play with, I should be safer with a polar bear from the Zoo."

"Well done, Hal. We ought to have brought her. Where is she today?"

"Careering across England in a haphazard fashion with her cousin Dick Bruce. Do you mind turning towards home now? I'm dining out, and have some letters to write."

"Who's the happy man tonight?... I thought of course I was to have the whole day."

"With a view to getting wholesomely bored! No, Flip, I don't propose to let you find that way out just yet."

"I should have found it for myself long ago if it were possible. As it is, I have grown resigned, and accept what crumbs fall to my portion." He paused a moment and then asked, "Is it Goliath tonight?"

"It is."

"Rash woman; and just when I have advised you to run."

"But it is not in the least serious yet. I only asked you in view of it becoming so."

"Which means you will try and start to run, *after* you are firmly in the trap."

"Not at all. I won't go near the trap. I'll tell him I'm old enough to be his mother, and talk down to him from years of detestable common sense and sagacity."

"Which sounds as if it would be even duller than dining with me."

"Oh no. It holds novelty anyway. You are never dull, but likewise you are no longer novel."

They made for the high roads again, and spun along mostly in silence until the car once more came to a standstill at Lorraine's door.

"Come in," she said, "I've lots of time."

"No," with a little smile. "I've had my crumbs for the day. I'm going to have a good solid crust now to keep the balance. Do you know Lottie Bird?… Fourteen stone, if she's an ounce, and a tongue like a sixty-horse-power motor. There are times when she's so damned practical and overpowering she does me good. This is one of them. Good-bye. Don't kill the giant with a glance; and don't be silly enough to get hurt yourself."

"All right. I'll go in full armour," and she nodded gaily enough as he moved off down the street.

CHAPTER XI

What Lorraine exactly meant by full armour she did not quite know, but it might very well have been taken to mean the shining armour of her own best loveliness. Certainly after no small consideration she chose what she believed to be her most becoming gown, and she was unusually critical about the dressing of her hair.

All the same, at 7.45 she was ready, and her cavalier had not yet arrived. She waited five minutes until he came, and then it was necessary to wait another five minutes that he might not know she had been more up to time than he. Then she entered the drawing-room in a little bit of a hurry, and cut short his simple, direct apologies by regretting her own tardiness, and saying she had been out motoring until late.

But she had time to note quickly that he also had dressed himself with special care, plastering down resolutely the unruly determination of his fair hair to curl. That was good. Any suggestion of a curl must have produced an effect of effeminacy, whereas that neat, plastered wave showed the shapeliness of his head, and gave him a touch of manly decision. Her electric brougham was at the door, but she kept it waiting a few minutes, that they might be later than the majority of diners, and pass up a well-filled room.

In the end their arrival was equal to her best expectations. She led the way slowly, with a queenly grace that was one of her best attributes; but as she nodded casually to an acquaintance here and there, she had plenty of time to observe the curious eyes from all around, looking with undisguised admiration, not so much at her faultless appearance, which was more or less known, but at her striking cavalier.

She had engaged a small table at one of the top corners and arranged the seats sideways, so that both could look over the room if they wanted to, and at the same time be easily seen by others. She did this because it amused her to see people gazing at him, and to watch his quiet self-possession. She almost wondered if he even realised how much attention he attracted, but perceived that he could hardly help doing so, though he took it all with so simple and unabashed an air.

She watched also to see if, as most of the strikingly handsome men she had known, he courted tell-tale glances from other eyes, and sipped honey from any flower within reach, as well as from his own particular flower. And when she found that his absolute and undivided attention was given to her, and that all the power of entertaining he could muster was called into her service, she felt a glow of gratitude to him that he had not disappointed her, but proved himself the simple, high-bred gentleman she longed to find him.

It made her show herself to him at her very best. Not showily witty, nor callously gay, nor fashionably original, but just her own self of light humour and dainty speech and kindly sympathy, the true, best self that held Hal's unswerving devotion through good account and ill.

Unconsciously she left the time-worn paths of beauty and success, and became young, and fresh, and whole-hearted as he; tackling abstruse problems with a childlike, vigorous air; holding him spell-bound with her own charm of conversation one moment, and leading him on to talk with ease and frankness the next.

The other diners got up and retired to the lounge, and still they sat on; no hint of boredom, no note of disparity, no need of other companionship. As they were preparing to rise, she told him lightly that he talked amazingly well for his tender years.

"Only twenty-four," he answered; "it does seem a kiddish age, doesn't it!"

"Dreadfully kiddish. It makes me feel old enough to be your grandmother."

He glanced up, half-questioning, half-deprecating.

"That would be the oddest thing of all, unless I really appear to be about twenty years before my time."

For a reason she could not have fathomed, she looked into his eyes with a sudden seriousness and said:

"I was thirty-two last week."

She saw a quick look of surprise he did not attempt to hide, followed by a very charming smile, as he asserted:

"It is impossible. You could not sit there and look like that if you were thirty-two."

"The impossible is so often the true. I'm glad you don't think I seem old. It is nice to believe one can keep young at heart, in spite of the years. Shall we go to the lounge?"

Again they moved through the admiring crowd, but this time Lorraine felt less idle interest and more inward wonder; and without any misgiving she steered to a quiet alcove, where they could talk without again being the cynosure of many eyes.

Here, in a pleasant, friendly way, she led him once again to talk of the future, and was glad to find, in answering sincerity with sincerity, he was ready to admit that he was a little sorry about his own lack of ambition and want of application. He did not pretend now that it was of no moment. He told her he would like to achieve, only somehow he always found his attention wander to other things, and his desire grow slack after a week of rigid application.

She recognised that the motive-power was missing, and that unless something deeper than mere desire of achievement stirred him, he would probably never attain. He needed a goal that should make everything else in the world pale before it, and something that seemed almost as life and death to hang on his success. But how get it for him? If he loved, and was bidden wait until he had prospered, the end was all too sure and the love too easy.

It was something different that was needed; something that would bring him up with dead abruptness against a blank wall, and leave him with a taste of life that was dust and ashes unless he found a way through. Either that or some sweet, wild, unattainable desire, that might drive him to work and ambition by way of escape.

And there again, where should he encounter such a desire? One had only to look into his calm, fine face to feel that the unattainable in the form of love, barred by marriage vows as lightly made as broken, would never stir the depths of his heart, nor appeal to his real self in any way whatever.

He would not love such a woman, however for a time she might fascinate him; and afterwards there would only be the nausea and the memory that was like an unpleasant taste. Such a woman might teach him many things it is no harm for a man to know; but she would never call to the best in him, nor help him to realise himself.

"Have you seen your friend the duchess lately?" she asked, with a disarming smile, not wishing to appear merely curious.

"Yes; I saw her on Friday, at a ball. She was in great form."

"You danced with her?"

"Yes. She's not a good dancer."

"Then you only had one, I suppose?"

"No, three." He smiled a little. "We sat out two."

"You ought to have felt highly honoured."

"Oh, I don't know. She is very amusing. A very funny thing happened last week. Out of sheer devilry, she and a friend and two men went to the Covent Garden Fancy Dress Ball, disguised of course, and just for an hour or two. To their horror, after the procession, the friend was handed a large glass-and-silver salad bowl, as a prize for being the best 'twostep' dancer in the room. Of course she had to go off with the beastly thing; but she was so proud of winning it, she couldn't resist giving their escapade away, and it got round everywhere."

"I wonder if our escapade with Lady Bounce is out yet? I haven't seen Hal since Thursday."

"Oh yes, it is," eagerly; "the duchess had heard about it. She was pumping me to know who was in the joke. We are longing to see Quin and hear the latest, but he is down east."

"What an oddity he is!" thoughtfully. "I liked him so much: but it is difficult to reconcile him with slumming."

"He's one of the best. Every one loves him. And he does his slumming in quite a way of his own. I've been with him sometimes, and he just goes among the rough characters down there as if he hated being a swell and wanted to be one of them. He positively asks them for sympathy, and of course it takes their fancy and he is friends with them all."

"I think you are a remarkable trio altogether. Hal's cousin Dick is just as original in his way as St. Quintin. And you, of course, are somehow different to the majority. I wonder how you will each end? St. Quintin will perhaps become a bishop. Dick Bruce will write an astounding, weird novel, and bound into fame. And you? ..."

He flushed a little. "I shall be left far behind by both of them, futilely wishing to catch up."

"I hope not. Your chance is just as good as theirs, if you choose to make it so,"

"I fail to see that I have any chance at all."

"Most chances rest chiefly with ourselves. It's a great thing to be ready for them if they come. I hope you'll be that."

"I hope so too, but it would be easier if one were more sure they were coming," and he laughed with a lightness that jarred a little.

She rose to go, as it was getting late, feeling slightly disappointed in some vague way; and when they parted she noticed that his handshake was slightly limp, as of one who would not grasp life tightly enough to compel it to surrender its good things to him.

But in her own sanctum she rallied herself, and hardened her heart, asking what had it to do with her after all, and how could his success or non-success in any way concern her.

Doubtless in the end he would share the fate of the great majority and attain only mediocrity; having missed that one great blinding shaft of pain or joy that might have stabbed him into tense, pulsing life, and spurred him up the heights of fame and glory.

She let her evening-cloak slide to a chair, turning to glance at a calling card on the table, with a renewal of the old, callous, cynical air. The practical force of Flip Denton's conversation was making itself felt. Of course it was an absurdity for her to imagine herself in love with a youth of twenty-four— almost the dullest of all ages—be he never so good to look at. She might very well keep a motherly eye on him, and show him a side of life he might perhaps not see otherwise, but it must end there.

No doubt a certain novelty had made the evening unusually pleasant: after two or three more they would certainly pall, and then she would go back to her old chums; the men of the world who had paid their footing and won their experience, and come through, careless enough devils at best in their own phraseology, but non the worse for a fall or two, and a win or two, and a self-taught hardihood for most things life was likely any more to send.

She smiled a little as she remembered how calmly he had thanked her and said good-night. Of a surety he took his fruits quietly and unconcernedly enough. She wondered if he were secretly in love with some pink-and-white débutante, who flushed and smiled when he spoke, and gazed up at him with fond, adoring eyes. It was likely enough.

No doubt he would tell her all about it soon, as a very young man tells a favourite sister, or a jolly, not too elderly aunt. She rather hoped he would. It would be an anti-climax humorous enough to cure her all in a moment of seeming anything to him other than that jolly, not too elderly aunt. Then she would invite Flip to dinner, and they would be gay together—she could imagine the tone in which he would call her "aunty"—and her folly would fall from her like an outgrown chrysalis, leaving her sane, and cynical, and wordly, and whole again.

The train of thought pleased her, and soothed in some way an indefinable rasping sense of the general futility of all feeling and all striving. Surely she, with her young-old heart, her world-worn memories, and her youth that never was, should know that worldly-wise dictum full well.

Of course she kew it.

The things that mattered were beauty and brilliance and success; and these she had in good measure, brimming over. Her mood made her cross suddenly to the many-sided mirror, and switch on a blaze of light that would brook no feigning.

In its searching gleams she looked at herself with clear, fearless eyes. Yes; it was all there still, untouched and unimpaired by those thirty-two years: the colouring, the skin, the rounded, supple figure—all the things for which men loved her and the world gave her fame.

She gave herself a little mocking salute, and then turned away to hurry into her pretty, cosy bed.

But what the blaze of light had not seen the mothering darkness hid tenderly. Two bright tear-drops, filling tired eyes that had tried so often to fool themselves into blind and callous content.

CHAPTER XII

"Dick Bruce will write an astounding, weird novel, and bound into fame," Lorraine had remarked to her companion, and away somewhere down in Kent, an hour or so earlier, Dick had remarked to Hal as they spun along:

"I've got the maddest idea for a novel you ever heard of. I'm going to make the hit of next season."

"I hope it's not about babies," said Hal, thinking of his doggerel.

"Yes, it is—babies and vegetables."

"Oh, nonsense. You can't make a novel out of babies and vegetables."

"You see if I can't. The vegetables are all to be endowed with life, and of course the scene of my tale will be the vegetable kingdom."

"And where do the babies come in?"

"The babies will represent mankind."

"I never heard such rot. Why should mankind be represented by babies? Much better let them be represented by green peas or gooseberries."

"Not at all. Mankind can only properly be represented by babies; mankind being in its infancy."

"But it isn't. It's much older than vegetables."

"It is not. Man was made last, and instead of developing into a reasonable, rational object, like a potato or a cabbage, he has strayed away into all manner of wild side-issues, and is still nothing but a very much perplexed infant."

"And do you propose to try and help him to emulate the reasonable, rational condition of the potato and cabbage?"

"I propose to show him his inferiority to these delectable creations."

"Then if he has any sense he will just duck you in the Serpentine and make you apologise. Personally I consider myself anything but a baby, and far superior to any of the cabbage tribe."

"Ah!..." he cried gleefully. "You are actually proving my theory. I can't explain now, but just wait till that book is written."

"Are you taking rooms at Colney Hatch while you do it?"

"I have thought about it. You show more understanding in that remark than in any of the others."

"It doesn't require much effort of understanding to think that out. Is the onion or the mangel-wurzel to be your hero?"

"You are unsympathetic. I shall not tell you any more."

"Not at all. I am most interested really. I should make the cabbage your hero, and the onion your heroïne, then she can weep on his breast." They swerved violently, and with a little gasp she added, "All the same, I've no desire to weep on the highway underneath a motor-car. What *are* you doing?"

"I don't know. The steering-wheel seems a bit odd."

They stopped to examine the wheel, and almost immediately, out of the gathering darkness behind shot another car, hooting violently to them to get out of the way. Unable to stop the oncoming car in time, Dick tried to move aside, failed, and in less than a minute the newcomer, in spite of brakes swiftly adjusted, crashed into them, smashing their lamp, and badly damaging the back near-side wheel of the car.

"Well, I'm blowed!" said Dick, "that's the only moment in the whole day you shouldn't have been on that particular square yard of the entire globe. Any other moment, I could either have moved aside or stopped you in time."

The occupant of the other car, who was driving alone, sprang out and came briskly forward.

"What the devil!..." he began, then noticed the lady, and stopped short.

"It was certainly the devil," said Dick, ruefully examining his battered wheel, and "I always thought he was credited with the deceny to look after his own. How have you fared?"

"Well, he seems to have looked after me all right," in a cheery voice; "there's nothing that will prevent my going on to town. But if you will pardon my curiosity, why take root in the middle of the road and ask for trouble?"

Hal's smile suddenly flashed out in the lamp-light irresistibly.

"It's a new theory about vegetables being wiser than mankind, but of course we took root too soon."

A pair of grey eyes looked quizzically at her in the darkness, discerning only the gleam of a white face in a close-fitting bonnet, and the flash of white, even teeth.

"The blasted steering wheel wouldn't act," said Dick. "We had just that second slowed down to examine it. You might have come along here to all eternity and not have been as inopportune."

"You take it very well." The big-coated apparition, in motor-cap with the ear-flaps down, and motor-goggles, and the suggestion of a rotundity about the centre, was not at all engaging to look at, but he had a charming voice.

"I'm taking it so ill that I daren't express myself out loud," said Hal. "What in the world are we to do? Is there a train anywhere near?"

"I'm afraid not, but there is a decent enough inn close by."

"An inn isn't much use to me." She paused, then added solemnly: "I've got a strait-laced brother."

Hal's voice was rather deep and rich for a woman, and it had a dangerous allurement in the darkness. The stranger took off his goggles and tried again to see her face, while Dick took a minute stock of his damage.

"Well," he suggested, a little daringly, "if he is able to chaperone you at the inn himself?—"

"He isn't," said Hal; "he's somewhere east of Piccadilly, studying Phœnician Architecture, and the herringbone pattern on antique masonry."

"Oh, damn!" intercepted Dick, "the old man has let me down badly this time; this car won't move before daybreak. It means a red light burning all night, and we must go to the inn."

"But, Dick," Hal exclaimed in quick alarm. "How can I let Dudley know? He'll have a fit at the idea of my being out all night like that."

"He ought to be too thankful you are safe and sound to mind anything else."

"But he won't; because he is always grumbling at my not getting back before dark. There must surely be a train from somewhere?"

Her voice had grown seriously alarmed as she began to realise what sort of a fix she was in. The stranger came forward to lend his aid to the inspection, and after a cursory glance added his verdict to Dick's.

"You won't move her before morning; and there are no trains anywhere near here on Sunday night. I am going to London myself; you must let me give you both a lift."

Dick stood up with an air of finality.

"I can't leave her. She isn't exactly all my own, you see. I must stay at the inn, but if you wouldn't mind taking Miss Pritchard—" he looked at Hal a little anxiously.

"I shall be delighted," came the brisk response from the stranger.

Hal for once was nonplussed, but her habitual humour reasserted itself.

"I don't know which Dudley will think the most dreadful," she remarked comically, "for me to stay at the inn unchaperoned, or motor back with a stranger. I seem to be fairly between the devil and the deep sea."

The men laughed, but Dick made the decision.

"You had better go back," he said. "He will at least have you safe under lock and key by midnight that way and not lie awake worrying all night himself."

"Then let me run you to the inn first," said the stranger, and after fixing his red lights, Dick went off with them in search of help to make the car safer for the night.

A little later the stranger's motor turned Londonwards with two occupants only, one in front and one behind. After a few miles he stopped.

"Won't you come and sit in front? It seems so unsociable to travel like this."

"Most unsociable," said Hal, "but it would please Brother Dudley."

"Never mind Brother Dudley now." The voice was very attractive. "Mind me, instead. I'm very dull here, and I hate driving in the dark. My chauffeur is down with the 'flu', and I couldn't beg, borrow, nor steal any one else's."

"Are you a doctor?" she asked, taking her seat beside him.

"Why do you think I should be a doctor?" tucking a warm rug cosily round her, in a leisurely fashion.

"Only because I thought perhaps you were obliged to go, in spite of your chauffeur being ill."

"I was obliged to go, but I'm not a doctor."

They started forward again, but the pace was noticeably slower.

"I hope you don't mind going slowly, it is so difficult to steer in te dark?"

Hal was perfectly aware he had not found it so difficult before, but she only said lightly:

"Anything to keep safe from another mishap. I might have to walk home next time."

"Or stay at an inn with me!..." with an amused laugh. "What would Brother Dudley do then?"

"Have brain fever first, I expect, then creeping paralysis, then sleeping sickness."

He chuckled with enjoyment, and presently remarked: "I don't think you treat Dudley respectfully enough if he is an affectionate elder brother."

"Oh, yes I do. I sort of leaven the lump. Without me he'd be just a clever prig; he couldn't help it. With me he is only better than most men; and his lofty ideas don't get top-heavy, because I keep him in touch with commonplace humanity."

"Why is he better than most men? What is the matter with the rest of us?"

"The rest of you don't bother to have lofty ideas at all, much less struggle to live up to them."

"You are a little sweeping. Do you like men to have lofty ideas, and be priggish?"

"They don't necessarily go together. It's only Dudley who thinks all the rest of the world ought to be good too."

"And don't you agree with him?"

"I look at things from a different standpoint. I admire him tremendously, and feel his superiority; but it is more natural to me to take things as I find them and make the best of them as they are."

"You are evidently a very sensible young lady. You can find a warm spot in your heart even for a sinner, for instance!"

"I rather like them," and she gave a low laugh.

"Of course you do, if you're a true woman."

"Oh, I'm a true woman right enough. I like a man to have a spice of the devil in him; and I like playing with fire; and I love getting into mischief."

"Capital!... you and I must be friends. I'm beginning to think it was a lucky mishap for me at all events."

"I haven't finished my qualifications yet. You may change your mind. I like all those sort of things, but at the same time I like the big things as well. Also I'm told I'm most annoyingly practical, and most irritatingly capable of taking care of myself, and never getting burnt, so to speak."

"Who told you that?"

"I think it was some one at the office."

"What office?"

She mentioned the name of one of the leading London papers.

"Oh, you're a working young lady, are you?" He asked the question with a new note in his voice, though it would have been difficult to tell just how the information struck him.

Hal gave another laugh.

"A working young lady! How awful! I shall not be friends with you if you call me anything so dreadful as that."

"What do you call it?"

"Well, I think I like 'Breadwinner' best, as that is what I do it for—but I don't mind working woman."

The stranger looked hard into the darkness a few moments, then he asked suddenly, sitll with the new note in his voice:

"And I suppose you want the vote?"

Mentally he was wondering whether, if she knew who he was, she would attack him physically or insist upon writing in chalk all over his car.

"I don't want it for myself, because I shouldn't know what to do with it, and I haven't much time to find out. But I want fair play for women-workers generally, and if that is the only way to get it, I hope it will come quickly."

"What do you mean by fair play?"

"Just whatever is fair play. I don't think women ought to be making iron chains at Cradley Heath for a penny a yard, for instance, and that sort of thing. I think it is a slur on the men who govern the country that it is possible. If you were one of them, and drove about in this beautiful car, not caring twopence whether starving women were sweated or not, I should—" she hesitated.

"Well, what should you—"

Detecting the mysterious note in his voice, she added with mischievous, half-serious intent:

"I should want to scratch you, and bite you, and push you into the first available ditch, for a poor coward, who was afraid to take care of the interests of woman, in case she got too well able in the end to take care of herself—so there."

He could not help laughing, and when he subsided she added:

"I suppose you are one."

"Why do you suppose it?"

"Never mind. Are you?"

"You promise you won't scratch me and bite me?"

"I'll give you a sporting chance to run away."

"I'm not very likely to run away from you, I think."

They had reached the well-lit roads now, and he turned and looked keenly into her face, partly to see if by chance he might recognise her, and partly to get a cleaner idea of her appearance.

"You look too nice to be a suffragette," he said.

"Such rot! Do I look too nice to care whether working women and outcast women are fairly treated or not?"

"That's only the bluff of the movement. What they really want is power and notoriety."

Hal tossed her head.

"You're a positive worm," she told him frankly.

Again his engaging laugh rang out.

"That's a nice thing to say to a man who has brought you all the way from Millington to London, and helped you out of a tight corner."

The white teeth gleamed suddenly.

"I'll qualify it if you like, and call you a cross between a worm and a brick."

"Not good enough. I won't pass the worm at all. If you don't retract it wholly I shall put you down at the first tram, and let you get back to Bloomsbury on your own."

"I'll retract, if you'll tell me who you are."

"I'll tell you afterwards."

She shook her head.

"Perhaps you are going to Downing Street even now, to plan a crushing blow to the Cause."

"I am going to Downing Street, but it has nothing to do with the Cause, as you call it."

It was her turn to glance round, but she only saw that he was clean-shaven, and somewhat lined. His grey, quizzical eyes met hers full of humour.

"I wonder who we both are?" he said.

"I can easily tell you who I am, as I'm so comfortably of no account. My name is Harriet Pritchard, and my friends call me Hal. I live with Brother Dudley, who is an architect; and if the world isn't any the better for me, I hope it is sometimes a little gayer, that's all."

"And are you engaged to the young man whose steering gear went wrong?"

"No; I am not engaged to any one at all."

"Very nearly perhaps?"

"No; not even within sight of it. Being engaged, and always having to go out with the same pal, would bore me to tears."

"I see." There was a note of satisfaction in his voice. In the brighter lights he had observed that the warm ulster clung to a very shapely figure, and covered a pair of fine shoulders, and even if she was not pretty, for he could not be quite sure on the point, she was certainly very attractive, and had a delightfully engaging smile.

"I wonder if there is room for another in the ranks."

Something a little condescending in the way he made the suggestion nettled Hal.

"Aren't you a rather old?" she asked.

Again his ready laugh rang out.

"I'll give frankness for frankness. I am forty-eight."

"Goodness!... and I am twenty-five."

"Is that all? Then allow me to say you are a remarkably clever young woman."

"A good many breadwinners are; they have to be. Some of them are too clever even for Cabinet Ministers," and she chuckled joyfully.

In the darkness, she did not see the quick gleam in his eyes, as he retorted:

"I don't think many Cabinet Ministers have the luck to meet a breadwinner who is as attractive as she is clever."

"And if they did," sarcastically, "I suppose they would drop the notoriety yarn and find time to consider whether the working woman is treated fairly or not. The weakness in her defence at present seems solely that not enough pretty women make up her defenders. Bah! You all ought to have kittens to play with, and nanny goats and woolly lambs."

"I don't know why you include me. What have I done?"

"Well, if you're going to Downing Street?"

"Why shouldn't I be going to a dinner-party?"

She turned and glanced up with a daredevil light in her eyes that delighted him.

"I not only think you a member of Parliament, but, judging by your fatuous air of superiority, I should imagine you are positively a full-blown Cabinet Minister."

He busied himself with his steering wheel, while little chuckles of enjoyment came out of his muffler.

"And supposing I were?" he said at last.

"Goodness!... I hope you're not?..." in quick alarm.

"Why do you hope so?"

"Oh, I don't know, except that I've never known a Cabinet Minister in my life, and I never expected, if I met one, to treat him like... like—"

"An old and fatuous lump of superiority!" with a gay laugh. "Well, little woman, you needn't be in the least sorry. I don't know that I've ever enjoyed a motor ride more. When will you come again?"

"*Are* you a Cabinet Minister?..." she asked helplessly.

"Well, I hope you won't disapprove, for I have to plead guilty to being Sir Edwin Crathie."

"Sir Edwin Crathie?" in abashed tones.

"They called me Squib at school." He said it in a whimsical, humorous voice, looking down at her with very friendly eyes.

But Hal had grown silent.

"I'm afraid by your manner you do disapprove?"

"It is certainly embarrassing. I would rather you had been... well, just any one."

"You'll get used to it," still with the twinkle in his eyes. "In the meantime you haven't answered my question. When will you come for another ride?"

She did not reply, and he leaned a little closer.

"You will come again?"

"I'm afraid Brother Dudley wouldn't like it"; and then they both laughed.

"Will you come in?" as they drew up before her door.

"I'm afraid I haven't time; and besides, I'm a little afraid of Brother Dudley. I only feel equal to the Prime Minister this evening."

She held out her hand.

"Well, thank you ever so much. You saved me from a dreadfully tight corner."

"The thanks should be all mine; you saved me from unmitigated boredom. I cursed my chauffeur for going down with 'flu' today, but now I feel ready to raise his salary for it."

He had pulled of his thick motoring-glove, and was holding her hand in a firm, lingering clasp, which she quickly cut short, tucking both her hands into her ulster pockets, and standing up very straight and slim in the lamplight.

"I'll have to go though the confessional now," she told him, "and sit on the stool of repentance for supper."

"No; don't repent; come again." He moved nearer.

"I'm naturally a very busy man, and I can't make engagements offhand, but I can easily get at you on the telephone. Will you come some afternoon, about half-past four?"

"I think you are very rash. How do you know I shall not bring the colours, and wave them wildly down the street, shouting 'Votes for Women'?"

"I'll risk it. Will you come?"

She moved away, latch-key in hand.

"I don't know. I won't promise, anyway. Good-bye, and my best thanks."

There was a rush of light through an open door, a last bright smile, and he found himself alone in the street.

CHAPTER XIII

When Hal entered the sitting-room and met Dudley's eyes she felt, as she afterwards described it to Lorraine, that she was in for it. Yet it was not so very late, barely half-past nine. On the table her supper was still waiting for her.

"We've had a slight accident," she said, taking the bully by the horns; "something went wrong with the steering gear, and it delayed us. Have you had supper?" noticing the table was still laid for two.

"I always have supper at eight on Sundays, because Mrs. White has to clear it away herself, as you know. Isn't Dick coming in?"

"No. He's—" Hall stopped short, considering the advantages of prevarication.

"I wanted to see him," testily. "He said he would give me a particular address tonight. Why is he in such a hurry?"

"It wasn't Dick who brought me."

She took off her motor-bonnet and threw it on the sofa, running her hands through her bright hair, and rubbing her cheeks, which were a little cold.

"Not Dick?..." Dudley looked up from his book peremptorily. "Who did bring you?"

Hal took her seat at the table.

"Well, you see, we had a slight accident. We had just stopped to examine the steering gear, when another car came round a curve and crashed into us. Dick's car was damaged, and..." she reached across for the salad, and helped herself with as unconcerned an air as she could muster... "Oh!... onions!... how scrumptious!... Mrs. White always remembers my plebeian tastes, but not my patrician ones."

"Well!" he suggested coldly. "Dick's car was damaged, and—"

"Dick had to stay and nurse it."

"Then did you come home by train?"

"There was no train. There was nothing else."

"Nothing else than what?"

"Nothing but the car that run into us, or going to an inn for the night with Dick. I was afraid you wouldn't like that," with a mischievous gleam.

"My likes and dislikes are not, apparently, of the smallest moment to you, or you would not have been motoring late on Sunday at all."

"Dick can't go other days."

"Who was in this other car?"

"A man."

Again he glanced up quickly.

"Any one else?"

"No. His chauffeur is down with 'flu'."

"Was it some one you knew, then?"

"No. He told me on the way in."

"Am I to gather that you returned to London alone, in a motor-car, with a perfect stranger?"

"I'm afraid you are."

"Why didn't Dick come with you? Surely if he takes you out for the day he might at least see you safely home. I never heard of such proceedings in my life. The man might have been a positive blackguard. Had you any idea who he was?"

"No, none; but what's the use of making a fuss! It's all right now, and I'm safely at home; which is surely better than being in some weird village all night, and you wondering what on earth had become of me."

"That is not the question. It's the whole circumstance from beginning to end. I consider Dick's behaviour most reprehensible."

"He couldn't leave his car alone there in the middle of a Kentish high road. He had to stay somewhere near."

"I think he should have considered you of more importance than the car. To let you return alone, at that hour, with a perfect stranger, is the most unheard of proceeding. I shall certainly tell Dick what I think of him."

"It wasn't Dick's fault," loyally. "I just took the matter into my own hands and came. Dick had nothing to do with it. In fact, I insisted upon his remaining behind."

"Oh, of course you would. You only seem to be happy when you are flying in the face of some convention or other. But Dick is older than you, and he knows my views on these matters. He owed it to me to see you safely home."

"But since I am safely home!..." obstinately.

"You very well might not have been. What the stranger himself must think of you I don't know. Have you any idea who he was?"

"Yes. Sir Edwin Crathie?"

"Sir Edwin Crathie! Do you mean the Cabinet Minister?"

"So he said."

"And did you tell him who you were?"

Again there was a gleam under the lowered lashes.

"I did; but I can't say he either recognised our historie name or seemed much impressed. I really don't believe he had ever heard of me."

Dudley refused to smile. Instead the frown deepened on his face.

"That is probably just as well. Your actions of late cannot be said to be entirely to your credit. What is this tale about Thursday night? I met St. Quintin's father with Uncle Bruce this morning in the Park. You told me Quin's aunt was going to chaperone you. Did she or did she not?"

"I told you Lady Bounce was going to chaperone me. Lady Bounce *did* chaperone me."

"Is Lady Bounce Quin's aunt?"

"That depends." Hal pushed away her chair, wishing vaguely that fathers and uncles would mind their own business. Either incident alone she could have coped with, but it was a distinct imposition to expect her to manage both at once, and on Sunday night into the bargain.

"I can only presume you lent yourself to such a vulgar proceeding as Quin dressing up as a woman and acting chaperone. Is that the truth?"

"Not entirely. You see, he wasn't an ordinary woman. He went as his aunt, Lady Phyllis Fenton. His personification was a masterpiece."

Dudley began to pace the room. His thin lips were compressed into a straight line, and his whole air distincly worried.

"What you seem quite unable to perceive is the way in which these incidents reflect upon your good taste and upon my guardianship."

Hal grew suddenly nettled.

"It is nonsense to talk of guardianship now. I am twenty-five, and I earn my own living. I am perfectly well able to take care of myself."

"No; that is just what you are not. You are so rash and inconsequent."

"Well, anyhow I get a good deal out of my life, while you—"

He remembered his own Thursday evening and intercepted:

"It is possible to get a great deal out of life without outraging every convention. Do you imagine either Ethel or Doris Hayward would do the wild things you do?"

"Ethel Hayward is a brick. She couldn't be straitlaced anyhow, nor narrow-minded. Doris would do anything under the sun that suited her own ends."

She got up, and turned away without perceiving his frown, beginning to gather up her paraphernalia. He stopped short in his walk.

"If it really was Sir Edwin Crathie who brought you home, I must write and thank him, I think."

"I shouldn't bother; probably it wasn't him at all; only some third-rate actor."

Dudley tried to see her face, not sure if she was serious or not, but she kept her head averted as she added:

"Quite possibly it was Lord Bounce."

"You are always treating a serious subject with levity," he complained. "What am I to think? Do you or do you not believe your escort was Sir Edwin Crathie?"

"Well, as he was awfully afraid I might be a militant suffragette, I think he really was a Cabinet Minister."

"I hope you entirely undeceived him on that score," drily.

"Not at all. I told him I was tingling to scratch him and bite him," and the ghost of a smile crossed her lips.

Dudley relapsed into silent displeasure, and for a few moments neither spoke. Then Hal, with her garments on her arm, came round to him with a frank, affectionate air.

"Dudley, don't make mountains out of molehills over nothing. I know I am a little wild. I can't help it—we seem to have got mixed up somehow.

You've got all the decorum and nice, refined feelings of a charming woman, and I've got the enterprise and 'don't-care' spirit of a man. It isn't any use fighting against facts. You must take me as I am, and make the best of it. I can't change now; and I don't know that I would if I could."

"I don't suppose you would. You positively glory in the very traits that I deplore"; but his voice sounded mollified.

"Oh well, old man, you wouldn't like me to be helpless, and foolish, and woolly-lambified, would you? It wouldn't be half so interesting. Just fancy if you had a sister like Doris Hayward, can you imagine anything tamer?"

He stiffened again, but she did not notice it.

"As for Thursday night, you never ought to have heard about it, and you never would have done if Uncle Bruce had not been such an old telltale. Just wait till I get him alone; that's all. Anyhow, he didn't think it a heinous crime did he? I expect he gave a great laugh that startled every one within hearing."

As that was exactly what had happened, Dudley made no comment.

"And Sir Edwin Crathie would only have thought me a fool if I had been afraid to come back with him. These things will happen occasionally. They are not worth worrying about. You are too anxious over trifles, Dudley." She moved away towards the door. "Well, good-night, don't forget to return thanks that anyhow I am not in a hospital, generally smashed up."

She left him, and retired to bed, feeling a little depressed. Of course he had not forgiven her, nor would he see things from her point of view. She almost wished he did not mind; but all her life she had had an affection that was almost adoration for her one brother, and it always depressed her to displease him, however indifferent she might seem.

She awoke next morning with the sense of depression still lingering, and set off for the City in far from her usual spirits. The office seemed dingy and dull, and the routine wearisome. It felt like ages and ages since she had driven home through the darkness in Sir Edwin's beautiful car. She wondered if it was real at all; only what else should make all the old friends at the office appear so uninteresting and commonplace.

She speculated a little forlornly as to whether she would ever be likely to see him again, and decided it was most unlikely, and that probably he had already forgotten the whole incident.

And just when she had reached that point in her meditations, the telephone boy came to tell her some one was asking for her. She asked him dispiritedly who it was, and he replied that the gentleman had declined to give a name.

Hal shut herself into the case, took down the receiver, and, still dispiritedly, asked: "Hullo! Are you there?"

"Is that Miss Pritchard?" asked a voice that made her pulses hasten.

"Yes? Who is that?"

"The mere worm," came back the cheery answer.

"What's the matter? You sound somewhat funereal. Was Brother Dudley very angry?"

"Terrible. I am still recovering. He seemed to have grave doubts as to whether you really were the eminent person you professed to be!"

"Oh, he did, did he? And what did you say?"

"That it was quite possible you were only a third-rate actor all the time."

"Thanks. I shall not grow vain on your compliments. Have you any grave doubts yourself?"

"I don't mind either way."

"Thanks again. Well, I am speaking to you from my own private sanctum at the House of Commons; and if you want to make sure, you can take my number, and ring up the Exchange and inquire."

"I'll take your word for it."

"Good girl. You don't sound quite so obstreperous as you were last night. What's the matter?"

"I'm only Mondayfied. The office is always boring on a Monday."

"I'm sorry I can't suggest a spin this afternoon, but I'm too much engaged until Wednesday. Will you come on Wednesday? Well?" as Hal, appeared to be meditating.

"Where do you propose going?" she asked.

"Anywhere you like. I'd better not fetch you from the office though. I'll pick you up just casually in St. Jame's Park. Will you be there at five, near the Archway?"

"All right, if I can get away. How shall I let you know if I change my mind?"

"Don't do anything so childish. The run will do you good after a stuffy office. I'll be there to the minute. Good-bye," and he rang off without waiting for a reply.

Hal went back to her work, with a pleasurable sensation that instead of grey stuffiness there was joyful sunshine. She had never imagined for a moment he would actually carry out his suggestion of a meeting; and here they were with an actual appointment.

It was so odd, too, that they had not properly seen each other yet; only having met in the light of street lamps; and she fell to wondering eagerly what he was like in broad daylight. A voice whispered, "Perhaps you won't like him at all, and will wish you had not gone"; but her love of adventure easily silenced it, and she looked forward to her outing without any misgivings.

Once she thought she would go an tell Lorraine about it first, but later decided it would be more enjoyable to do so afterwards, and kept her own counsel; which perhaps was not entirely wise, seeing how much more cause Lorraine had to know the world than she had.

CHAPTER XIV

Sir Edwin Crathie had come to the front very rapidly under the auspices of the Liberal Government. Without having any special worth, he was sufficiently brilliant and unscrupulous to brush obstacles aside without compunction, and assert himself in a manner that impressed his hearers with the notion that he was very clever, very thorough, and very reliable.

Those who knew him superficially believed him extra-ordinarily clever. Those who knew him intimately sometimes shrugged their shoulders. He was possessed undoubtedly of a certain flashy sort of cleverness, but some of his greatest skill existed in imposing it upon others as strength and insight.

As may be imagined, such a man was not much troubled with principles. If a step was likely to help him forward with his ambitions, he took it without considering the moral aspect. If no help was likely to follow, he only took it if it happened to please his fancy. To say that he had climbed by women was to put it mildly.

Many of his steps he had taken on women's hearts, trampling them mercilessly in the process. And since he was admittedly unscrupulous, it was not surprising, for he was possessed not only of an attractive appearance, but of great personal magnetism when he chose to exert it.

He was a bachelor because so far he had considered the single state best forwarded his aims, but a growing and imperative need for money was now causing him to look round among the richest heiresses for some one to pay his debts in consideration of being made Lady Crathie.

In the meantime Hal's independent spirit and freshness suggested an entertaining interlude; and as she attracted him more strongly than any woman had done of late, he decided to follow up their chance friendship just for the amusement of it.

In consequence, he felt quite boyishly eager for the hours to pass on Wednesday, and when at last it was time to start, dismissed his chauffeur with a curt sentence, and started off alone. The chauffeur, it may be mentioned, merely glanced after him, and with a shrug of his shoulders wondered "what the master was up to now."

When Sir Edwin reached the meeting-place he was not particularly surprised to find no signs of Hal. He believed she would come; but evidently she liked being perverse, and would purposely keep him waiting. He ran the car slowly back again, scanning each pedestrian ahead with a certain anxious eagerness, wondering how he would like her in broad daylight.

On returning to the Archway, and still finding no one waiting, he alighted with a pretence of examining some part of the car, and looked back over the paths leading down from Piccadilly.

And something in his mental regions felt rather foolishly glad when he recognised her afar off.

He had never seen her walk, but his instinct told him Hal would move with just the graceful, swinging stride of the tall, slim figure coming towards him, and carry her head and shoulders with just such a dauntless, grenadier attitude.

He found himself standing quite still, with his hands deep in his overcoat pockets, watching her. Her costume, too, pleased his fastidious taste. Of course a first-class tailor had cut a coat and skirt with a fit and hang like that; and the small hat, if it had nothing Parisian about it, anyhow suited the wearer and dress to perfection.

He noted with quiet pleasure that she showed no signs of embarrassment when she met his watching gaze, merely crossing the road with the same jaunty, upright walk, and a gleam of fun in her eyes.

"Hullo!" was her greeting. "Hope I haven't kept you waiting. I've had a busy afternoon helping my chief to give you and The Right Honourable Hayes Matheson a good slanging."

"Oh, you have, have you?"

The grey eyes were growing more and more approving, as he noted each detail most likely to appeal to a man who had made a study of women for many years. The shapely little ears with the glossy hair curling round them, the full, rounded throat, the determined little chin, the frank, fearless eyes.

He still hardly knew whether she was pretty or not, but he discerned wery quickly that she was amply blessed with that rare gift of personality and humour that is so much more durable than a pretty face.

Hal, for her part, was no less interested in him, but she found little else than that she had already seen: humorous, quizzical grey eyes, a face a good deal lined, and a mouth and chin suggesting a nature fond of enjoyment and self-indulgence, which it had never seen any cause to deny itself. She saw that he was very grey about the temples, and a trifle inclined to stoutness, but tall enough and broad enough to carry it off.

A fine figure of a man, though one, she felt instinctively, belonging to a very different world to hers. Because she felt his careful scrutiny, and because she wanted to assert her indifference to it, she remarked suddenly, after a moment:

"Well, how do you like me by daylight?"

"How do you like me?" he retorted, and laughed.

She shook her head, and her eyes grew mischievous.

"Old," she said; "quite old and grey."

"Old be damned! Forty-eight is the prime of life."

She was taking her seat, and gave a low chuckle of enjoyment at having drawn him.

"Ah, you may laugh now," he said, "but I'll soon show you forty-eight is far more attractive than twenty-eight. Where shall we go?"

"I don't mind in the least, but I should prefer to steer for tea and buns."

"Tea and buns!... how like a woman!... How can you expect to get the vote on tea and buns?"

They were spinning along the Broughton Road now, heading for Putney and Richmond, and Hal felt her spirits rising momentarily with the joy of the motion and comfort and fresh air.

"We don't expect to get in on tea and buns; we expect to get it on whisky and beer. That is to say, we expect the course of events to prove that tea and buns conduce to a frame of mind better able to cope with the questions of the day than the whisky and beer drained in such quantities by men."

"And when you've got it you'll all vote for the man who happens to be good-looking, and who can pay you the prettiest compliments."

"A few will vote that way, no doubt, but not the majority. Women are not so fond of pretty men as they were"; and her lips curled significantly.

"Pretty men!..." he echoed, with enjoyment.

"Little woman, you have a neat way of putting things."

He was silent a few minutes, then added:

"I suppose, down at that office they are all in love with you?"

"I don't know. I haven't asked them," with twinkling eyes. "I'm a bit in love with the chief myself."

"Oh, your are, are you? And what aged man might he be?"

"Oh, he's quite old," she laughed; "somewhere about forty-eight."

"And is he in love with you?"

"It just depends. Sometimes he's rather fond of me on a Saturday; but on Mondays he loathes me."

"I see. And are you as changeable?"

"No, I love him always; but on Mondays it's mostly from habit. On Saturdays it's from choice."

He looked down at her, and it was on the tip of his tongue to state some commonplace about being jealous. Then suddenly he looked back to his steering wheel, and the commonplace sentence died unspoken. Quite unaccountably he felt less inclined to flirt and more inclined to be really friendly, and for some distance they skimmed along in silence.

They had tea at the Star and Garter, both chatting volubly on the most interesting topics of the day. Hal's newspaper work had made her cognisant of many subjects very few girls of her age would even have heard of, and her original criticisms delighted him. It was a gay little tea-table, and the time slipped by with extraordinary rapidity. Hal noticed it first.

"Do you know it is half-past six?" she said, "and I'm dining out tonight. We must fly."

"Is it really past six?..." in astonishment. "How the time has flown! You know, you are such an entertaining little woman, you make me forget everything but yourself." He looked at her hard, and the force of habit caused him to add: "I doubt if any other woman I know today could have given me so much pleasure."

"Well, you needn't thank me," with her low, fresh laugh, "because I came entirely to give myself pleasure."

"Then I hope you have succeeded. I see it is quite hopeless to expect any sort of a complimentary speech from you."

"Quite; though I don't mind admitting I have been very enjoyably entertained as well."

"That is something, anyhow. And now I suppose you are going straight off home to dress, and dine with some one else, and forget about me?"

"I don't suppose I shall forget you. It happens to be a journalist dinner, and probably we shall tear you to pieces between us before we have finished."

"Well, I'd rather you did that than forget me."

She felt him looking hard into her face, with something a little sinister in his expression, and she got up and turned away.

"Why do you turn away when I am interested? Don't you think you might be a little pleased that I don't want you to forget me?"

He asked the question with a humorous twinkle, though she felt that he meant it seriously as well. This last, however, she was clever enough to ignore, and merely threw him a mischievous glance over her shoulder as she answered:

"Well, I have to consider Brother Dudley's attitude, you see; and I've a notion he would be best pleased for both the incident and motorist of Sunday evening to be forgotten."

He got up slowly, looking amused.

"I suppose he would be horrified at this outing?"

"I strongly suspect he would."

"What if he hears you were out motoring at Richmond with me?"

"Oh, well, I shall tell him you are old enough to be my father, and not to be absurd."

"Why do you harp on my age so?... If I am old enough to be your father, it doesn't follow that I'm too old to be your lover?"

He was standing close to her now, looking down into her face, and Hal felt a little conscious tremor run through her blood. She faced him squarely, however, and answered in a gay, careless voice:

"Of course it doesn't, only, as I don't happen to want a lover, it's a contingency not worth considering."

"Perhaps the post is already filled?" he suggested, refusing likewise to be daunted.

"Quite filled. It's a case for a placard stating 'House Full', and you," she finished, "would naturally be at the tail end of the queue which has to go away."

He laughed with relish, and gave it up.

"I can see you will take some taming," he said, as he handed her into the car. "My weighty and important position evidently does not impress you in the least."

"Of course not, as you're a Liberal. They have so few really good men, they have to take anything they can get. Back up the Budget and the Chancellor, and exhibit a colossal amount of impudence, and there you are!"

"Well, there isn't much to boast of in the way of men on the Conservative side, is there? Chiefly a collection of cousins, and second-cousins, and cousins by marriage, shoved in by a few interfering old aunts. You don't need me to tell an enlightened young woman like you that even impudence might serve the country better than cousin-ship."

"I wonder sometimes if any of you honestly put the country first at any time; or whether it is just a popular name for a very big 'me'?"

"You are such a little sceptic. Do you always credit people with self-interested motives?"

"I don't know that I do; but if you are a city-worker it is a fairly safe basis to work upon, until you can find proof that you are wrong."

He looked down at her with amusement.

"What a wise little head it is! Do you know, I don't think I ever met any one quite like you before,"

"What you have missed!" was the gay rejoinder, and they both laughed.

"I suppose I mustn't take you home?" as they neared Piccadilly. "Brother Dudley might see us?"

"No, thanks. If you will drop me at Hyde Park Corner I will take a homely bus, and return to my Bloomsbury level."

"Until my next free afternoon, I hope. Will you come again soon?"

"Perhaps."

"What do you do on Sundays?"

"I generally go out with Dick Bruce."

"Does Dick Bruce consider himself entitled to every Sunday?"

"Well, I consider myself entitled to Dick!..." laughing.

"You're evidently very fond of Dick."

"Very," with enthusiasm. "I have been for twenty-five years. We were like the two babies in *Punch* which said, 'Help yourself and pass the bottle.'"

"Dick's a lucky devil. Does he take Saturday afternoons as well?"

"No; he plays cricket or hockey then."

"Then may I have a Saturday afternoon?"

"It would be jolly;" and a swift gleam in her eyes told him she meant it.

"Very well. I shall consider that a promise. The first Saturday I can arrange, we'll run down to some little place on the coast, and get some sea air. And if you feel inclined to write me a letter between now and then, send it to York Chambers, Jermyn Street."

He pulled up, and instantly she exclaimed in haste:

"Oh, there's my bus. Good-bye, thanks awfully; I must fly"; and before he could get in another word, he saw her clambering on to a motor-omnibus, with the utmost unconcern for his sudden, astonished solitariness.

"Gad!... what a woman she'll be one day," was his comment. "If she'd a hundred thousand pounds I wouldn't mind marrying her myself; she'd never let a chap get bored. I'll warrant," He moved slowly down Piccadilly. "Most of them do," he cogitated; "it doesn't seem as if there were one woman in a thousand who didn't soon become a bore. Heigh-ho, but debts are more boring still sometimes, and I want a fifty-thousand cheque badly."

CHAPTER XV

When Hal went to tell Lorraine of her adventure she found her a victim of the prevailing malady, kept indoors two days with influenza. She was not in bed, but lying on a sofa, by a small fire, looking very frail and ill. Hal did not say much, as Lorraine disliked fussing, but her heart smote her to think she had been absent two days while her friend was a prisoner.

"Why didn't you tell Jean to 'phone me?" she asked. "I would have got here somehow."

Instead of answering, Lorraine nestled down into her cushions, and said:

"It's dreadful nice to see you, chummy."

Hal drew up a footstool, and sat down with her head against the sofa.

"What does the court physician say, Lorry? Of course he is generally fathering and brothering and mothering you as well as doctoring?"

"Yes; he is taking care of me in a sort of all-round, comprehensive fashion. I don't know what I should do without him."

"Do!..." with a little laugh. "Why, just have another court physician instead." Hal's eyes strayed round the room. "What lovely flowers, Lorraine! Don't they almost make you feel a corpse?"

"They would if they were white, I dare say."

On a little table by the sofa was a bowl of violets, looking very sweet and homely among the beautiful exotics filling all the other vases. Hal buried her nose in them.

"How delicious! Who ventured to send your royal highness anything so homely as violets?"

Lorraine's eyes rested on them with a look of tenderness. "Some one not very well off," she said, "who had the perspicacity to know I should value them from him more than the choicest blooms."

"It sounds as if it might have been Dick. Was it?"

"No."

Lorraine replied in a careless tone, suggesting there was no special interest attached to the giver, but, for some unknown reason, Hal chose to be inquisitive.

"The Three Graces are your only 'hard-up' friends, and Quin is down east, so he would not know you were ill. Surely Baby didn't think it at all out by himself, and actually go into a shop and buy them?"

"You shouldn't call Mr. Hermon Baby, Hal; it isn't quite fair."

"Oh, yes it is, as long as he is so objectless and purposeless. Besides, his face is so cherubic I can't help it."

"I call his face very manly."

"Well, so it is—in a way: but it's cherubic also; and then he's so dreadfully placid. If he'd only wake up, and boil over about something."

She was silent a few moments, and then said suddenly;

"Do you know Sir Edwin Crathie, Lorraine?"

"No; why? I now of him."

"What do you know of him?"

"Oh, nothing much. I believe he is a great lady's man."

"I've met him," said Hal; and she proceeded to tell of the motor mishap and subsequent meeting.

Lorraine was interested and amused, but for some strange reason Hal did not tell the tale with her usual gusto, and nothing in her voice or manner suggested it was more than the most casual of meetings. Lorraine, a little preoccupied with her own feelings, for a wonder did not discern that Hal treated the incident with a lightness not quite natural, considering how exceedingly unlooked-for it was, and before the recital was quite finished Jean looked in to inquire if Lorraine would see Mr. Hermon. Lorraine replied in the affirmative, and a moment later Alymer Hermon entered the room.

"I'm so sorry you are not well," he said, in his frank, pleasant way. "I only heard of it last night."

"And then you sent me violets. It was nice of you. I appreciate them so much."

"I guessed Dick," put in Hal, who had not risen from her stool. "I did not think you would have the energy to think of them."

"I have been feeling rather exhausted since," he told her lightly.

"Take the arm chair," said Lorraine smilingly, "and have a good rest."

"Do," echoed Hal. "I'm sure you are tired out with your day's work."

"Don't be so superior," he retorted. "Just because you can type a certain number of words per minute, you give yourself such airs."

"Well, that's a better reason than the fact of being a few inches longer than most people."

"Now you two," put in Lorraine, "don't start quarrelling in such a hurry. Try and be nice and polite to each other for a few minutes."

"Baby doesn't like me when I'm polite," said Hal.

"I've never had a chance to judge."

"Liar. What about the first time we met?"

"I thought you were rather nice in those days. Your offensive attitude is only of comparatively recent date."

"Oh, don't sit there like a stodgy old book-worm, reeling off nicely rounded sentences."

"I hope it might impress you with the incongruity of addressing me as an infant."

Hal looked up from her lowly seat with a mischievous, engaging expression.

"You know you really are rather clever in a useless sort of fashion," she informed him.

"Thank you," making a bow.

"Can't you tell him how to be clever in a useful sort of fashion, with all your practical experience?" suggested Lorraine.

"Oh, I *could*; but what's the use? he doesn't want to know. It would mean hard work."

"Give him the benefit of a suggestion, anyhow."

"Well, other briefless barristers peg away at journalism, and political agency work, and coaching, and studying. Baby just sits down and looks nice, as if he thought the briefs would come fluttering round him like all the silly, pink-cheeked, wide-eyed girls. You ought to have seen our little maid the night he dined with us. When she first saw him she seemed to mutter 'O my' in a breathless fashion, and when she handed him his plate, she spilt all the gravy on to his knee, gazing into his face."

Hermon looked a little annoyed. "Very few people can talk absolute rot in a clever way," he aimed at her.

Hal laughed.

"Why, that drew you, Baby! You look quite ruffled. I was only pulling your leg: the pink-cheeked girls don't really flutter round, they run away in terror at your scowl. You know he can scowl, Lorraine. At least it isn't exactly a scowl; it's more a cast-iron solemnity of such degree that it has a Medusa-like effect and freezes the poor little peach-blossom girls into putty images."

"I'm sure Mr. Hermon never gives his personal appearance a thought," Lorraine replied, "except when you insist upon harping on it."

"I can't help it. I feel he's hemmed in with such a sticky, treacly, simpering amount of youthful adoration generally, that I simply have to rag him for his good!"

"It's very kind of you to be so interested in my welfare"—a twinkle gleamed suddenly in his blue eyes—"I certainly like your way of adoring the best."

"Ah"—with an answering twinkle—"I didn't think you had guessed my secret. How embarrassing of you! You have positively driven me away." She rose to her feet. "I must go, Lorry. I can't sit out any more. He has discovered that I adore him."

"You both seem rather imbecile tonight," Lorraine commented; "but surely it needn't drive you away, Hal."

"I must go all the same. We have visitors coming. I shall run in again tomorrow. Be sure and 'phone me if there is anything I can do for you." She kissed Lorraine, and turned to Hermon. "Good-bye. Don't display all your best allurements to Lorraine this evening, because she isn't strong enough for it. Remember my unhappy plight, and let one victim satisfy you for the present."

"What about your victims?" he asked. "Dick is kicking the toes of his boots thin because he saw you yesterday with Sir Edwin Crathie."

Hal coloured up, much to her own disgust, and greatly to Hermon's enjoyment, who immediately followed up his advantage with:

"I suppose we shall all have to cry small now, because of the right honourable gentleman."

"It will be a puzzler for you to cry small," was her rather feeble retort, as she passed out.

Hermon came back and reseated himself in the big arm chair.

"May I stay?" he asked, and Lorraine answered:

"Yes, do," in the frank spirit she had told herself must be her attitude towards him.

So he sat on with an air of content, seeming to fill some place in the pretty room by right of an old comradeship, or some blood-tie, or a mutual understanding—an intangible, indefinable attitude that had sprung into being between them of itself.

Lorraine did not talk much, because she was tired, but she let the goodly sight of him, and the quiet rest of him, lull and soothe her senses for the passing moment without any disturbing questioning. Hermon likewise did not question. He liked being there, and she seemed willing for him to stay, and it seemed enough.

Once or twice lately he was conscious that he had been rather foolish with different admiring friends of the fair sex; and though he was no prig, and knew most men took kisses and caressess when offered, and would have thought it a needless throwing away of good things to refuse, he yet felt a little irritated with himself and the givers without quite knowing why.

And there was another trying incident over a girl he had met at various country-houses the previous summer, and greatly enjoyed a flirtation with. Unfortunately, she appeared not to have understood it in the light of a flirtation; and now she was writing him miserable, reproachful love-letters which had at any rate succeeded in making him wish he had been more circumspect. It soothed his ruffled feelings to be with Lorraine; and it flattered his vanity to feel that she liked him there.

They had been sitting quietly some little time when the front-door bell announced another caller, and Jean came to inquire if her mistress would see Lord Denton. Lorraine half unconsciously glanced at Hermon, and seeing an expression of disappointment on his face, said quietly. "Ask him to come tomorrow, Jean. I am very tired tonight."

Jean went away, and presently returned with a loverly bouquet of malmaisons, and three or four new books. "His lordship will call about twelve," she said: "and he hopes, if you feel able to go out, you will let him take you in his motor." Then she went out, leaving them alone again.

In the pause that followed, Lorraine lay silently watching him for some minutes, wondering what was passing in his mind. Although it was only September still, the evenings were drawing in quickly, and there was little light in the room except the flickering glow of cheerful flames on the hearth. They caught the glint of his hair and shone on his face, throwing the delicate, aristocratic features with cameo-like dinstinctness on the black shadow beyond.

Lorraine looked again, with the eyes of a connoisseur, and she knew that in very truth no merely handsome face and form were here, but a nature and character corresponding to the outward beauty of line and lineament. She wondered once more as she lay there what it must be to have borne such a son; and a surging, aching, tearing pain filled her heart for the longing to have known from experience. She felt she could have been a saint among women for very joy, and an ideal companion, as well as a mother to such as he.

And instead?—

Well, there were murky corners in the background for her as well as her mother, but never from actual seeking. When necessity had not driven her, loneliness had, and the gnawing ache of a fine, fearless soul to grasp some satisfaction from the sorry scheme of things. And always the satisfaction had passed so quickly... so quickly, driving the starved soul back on itself again, with a little extra weight added to its burden of bitter knowledge.

Was there then no counterpart for her—no twin soul—no strong, true comrade, to say "You and I" when sorrow and disillusion came, and so rob pain of its deepest sting?

Then, as if he felt her scrutiny, he turned his face to her slowly, and looked into her eyes.

"You know you are looking rather bad," he said a little awkwardly and shyly. "I'm awfully sorry. I hope you are taking care of yourself."

"I don't suppose I should worry much if left to myself," she told him, with a touch of lightness; "but a very stern physician, and a most resolute maid, insist upon giving me every possible attention."

"It doesn't tire you... my being here?..."

"No; I like it."

"I wonder why?"

"Do you always want to know the why of things?"

"I'm afraid I don't as a rule bother much, but this is a little amazing, isn't it?"

"I don't see why you should think so."

He studied the fire again.

"Only that you are at the top of the ladder, and I am at the bottom."

"I was once there too."

"And did it seem as if it would be impossible ever to reach the top?"

"Yes, often. I don't think anything but resolute, iron determination ever takes any one up. Influence helps a good many up the lower rungs, and saves them a lot of the drudgery, but it cannot do much else, and unless one is full of grit and purpose at heart, one sticks there."

"Still, it must be a great help to be pulled through the drudgery."

"It may mean a good deal of loss also."

"How?"

"I don't suppose success that is won through favour means half so much to the winner as success that is wrenched from Fate by one's own resolute hands. The only thing is, one wonders so often afterwards if it has been worth while."

"Do you wonder that?"

"Ah!... don't I?"

He said nothing, and she went on:

"All the same, I imagine I had to succeed or die. I was built that way. Nothing less than success would have satisfied me. I often crave for quiet, restful happiness now, but if it had been offered then I should have passed it by and struggled blindly for fame. Still, it is hard to think how easily one can take a false step, and suffer for it till the end."

"Did you do that?"

He turned his eyes to her again, and she saw as sympathy in them that was deeper than any feeling he had shown her yet.

"Yes. I was in a very tight corner, and I took a short cut out. I married for money and influence. The step brought me all I anticipated, but it brought other things as well, that I had chosen not to remember: nausea, ennui, self-disgust, loneliness, emptiness. I think I should never have won through without Hal."

"And is your husband living?"

"Yes. In America. We have not troubled each other for a long time. I suppose I am fortunate in being left alone." She was silent a few minutes, and then she told him kindly: "Hal says they always chaff you about marrying an heiress, for the sake of being rich without any need to work; but take my advice, and don't force the hand of Fate before she has had time to give you good things in her own time."

He turned to her with a very engaging smile as he answered:

"They chaff me about a good many things, but most of them are a little wide of the mark. I haven't any leaning at present towards a paid post as husband."

"I'm glad; but I didn't for a moment suppose you had seriously. I wonder what you have a leaning towards?" she added.

"I should like to succeed." He sat forward suddenly and leaned his chin on his hands, resting his elbows on his knees, and stared hard at the flames. "I care a great deal more about succeeding really than any one believes; but I'm afraid I'm not cut out for it."

"I should like to help you," she said simply.

"You are very good," he answered, still looking hard into the fire.

Lorraine got up and moved slowly about the room, touching a flower here, and a flower there, and rearranging them with deft fingers. She turned on an electric light with a soft shade, and glanced at the books Flip Denton had brought her.

Hermon sat back in his chair and watched her. He thought he had never seen her lovelier than she looked in the homely simplicity of a graceful tea-gown, and her thick black hair coiled in a large loose knot low on her neck. It gave her an absurdly youthful air, that somehow seemed far removed from the brilliant star as he knew her on the stage.

Then she came towards him, and stood beside him, resting one foot on the fender and one hand on the mantelpiece; and he saw, with swift seeing, the shapeliness of the long, thin fingers and the graceful, rounded arm.

"You are thoughtful, *mon ami*," she said, with a soft lightness. "Tell me what you are thinking of."

"I don't know. I don't think I am thinking at all. I feel rather as if I were sunning myself in your smiles, like a cat."

"You like being here, like this?"

"I love it."

"Then come often. Why not?"

"I shall bore you."

"I think not. It is pleasant to me also to have some one keeping me company in such a natural, homely way. You see, I am very much alone. I have no women friends except Hal, who is nearly always engaged; and there are not many men one can invite to come and sit by one's fireside. You seem to come so naturally and simply. It is clever of you. Very few men could. It is difficult to believe you are only twenty-four."

"I fancy years often do not go for very much. I have travelled about alone a great deal. Anyhow, you are just as young for thirty-two as I am old for twenty-four."

"Hal has helped to keep me young. She restores me like some patent elixir. I suppose I love her more than any one in the world."

"I'm not surprised," he answered. "A good many people love Hal. Dick and Quin just dote on her."

She looked at him keenly a moment.

"I am spared wasting my affection," he added, "by her obvious contempt for me."

"She doesn't mean any of it. She only wants to rouse you."

"Still, she succeeds in making me feel rather a worm."

Lorraine made no comment, but she could not resist a little inward smile at the thought of any one making such a man feel a worm. She realised there might be no harm in the leavening influence.

The clock struck seven, and he gave a start, rising quickly to his feet beside her. Lorraine was a little under medium height if anything, and as they stood together he seemed to tower above her like some splendid prehistoric human, while she appeared as some exquisite miniature, or frail and perfect piece of Dresden china.

And again it seemed as if his physical beauty acted upon her with some irresistible magnetism, flowing round her and over her and through her, till she was enveloped and obsessed by him.

His age was nothing, years are mere detail; she felt only that he was a splendid creature, and everything in her gloried in it. She rested her hand lightly on his arm.

"How big you are. You almost overpower me."

He smiled down at her, but it was just a quiet, friendly smile, and she could not tell if her touch stirred him.

"I'm afraid I am rather a monster. It is sometimes a nuisance."

"Ah, don't say that. I am quite sure the first Adam was as big as you, and Eve was frightened and ran away, but she wouldn't for the world have had him an inch smaller. And every true Eve since has gloried in the man who towered above her, and was a little terrifying in his strength. Don't let them spoil you," she added with a note of wistfulness, "all the Eves who must needs follow with or without your bidding."

"I imagine Hal will counteract much of that; and the feeling, when I am with you, that I am just a great, brainless, useless animal."

"No; you are not that; and you are quite extraordinarily unspoilt as yet. Come and see me again soon, when you've nothing better to do."

"How soon?"

He was looking hard into her face now, almost as if he were only just fully realising her beauty, and she flushed a little as she met his ardent eyes and answered:

"As soon as you like."

"Friday is my first free evening."

"The come and dine here quietly. I shall not act this week at all. I shall run down to the sea from Saturday to Monday."

She had intended to go on Friday afternoon, but with his nearness all Flip Denton's sage advice vanished from her mind, and instead of running away as he urged, she went a step nearer to the temptation.

When he had gone she sat down in the arm chair he had used, and stared hard at the fire. Jean came in to urge her to go to bed, but she only said:

"No; I like this room and the fire. Bring me the fish, or whatever it is, here. I will go to bed about half-past eight if you like, but not before."

So she sat on, and in her heart she saw still the fine face, with its unspoiled freshness, and felt his presence still filling the room.

It would seem Fate had brought her and Hal together into the arena of new happenings and new feelings, for among the crowded houses of Bloomsbury, in a little high-up bedroom near the sky, Hal sat on the edge of her bed leisurely brushing her long, bright hair, and pondering a telephone message that had asked her to go for a motor ride the following Saturday.

"It means putting Amy off," was her final cogitation, "but I think I'll go. It will be such fun, and I'm rather sick of work."

So, in spite of strong wills and common-sense warning, we still, as ever, let our footsteps follow the alluring paths, and go boldly forth to meet a joy, ever careless of the following sorrow that may accompany it, until the hour of shunning is past.

CHAPTER XVI

The following Friday afternoon Lorraine went out with Flip Denton in his motor, and among his first questions was:

"Well, how is the foolish falling in love progressing?"

"It is stationary. I've got another friend I want to keep, Flip; another friend like you."

"Ah, I can't pass that. You were never even remotely in sight of falling in love with me. And you know what Kipling says: 'Love's like line-work; you can't stand still, you must go backward or forward.' You don't propose to take my advice and run away from it?"

"Not before I am sure there is danger, anyhow."

They were silent some moments, then she asked him:

"Do men ever run away, Flip?... My experience has been that the average man always has a good try to get what he wants, without much consideration for outside things, or for youth, or for harm."

"That's because beautiful women necessarily come up against the worst in men. It is their fate: one of the balancing conditions perhaps to make things more even with the less-favoured women."

"I suppose great beauty generally undoes a woman. Is it the same with men too? It seems a pity when Nature produces anything beautiful she should not guard it better—beautiful flowers, beautiful birds, beautiful creatures all ravished the quickest; while the little, comfortable daisies, and sparrows, and homely people go serenely on unharmed."

He did not reply, and they sped along in the understanding silence they were both so fond of.

Denton was thinking, as a man may, of various pretty faces that had been the undoing of their owners, and wondering a little dimly and confusedly about the paradoxical contrariness of Nature, who gives a man his strongest desires nearly always towards forbidden ends. Why create a beautiful thing, and then create a longing for it, and then probably descend in wrath upon both heads which did but follow the bent she herself had given them?

Lorraine was wondering a little bitterly why a man may taste forbidden fruit again and again and go unpunished; and why a woman, so often set amid sterner temptations, was yet left so strangely unprotected: the one so quickly able to put an incident aside, and seek fresh fields for conquest; the other so terribly liable to be branded for life in that same incident.

It made a bitterness surge up in her soul for her own unprotected girlhood and struggling youth; and for all they had brought her to learn of the tree of knowledge. No doubt she had been callous enough about it at the time; eager only to dare, and triumph, and achieve; but how should it have been otherwise, since no kindly guiding hand had told her she was wasting her powers and her substance to achieve an end that would never satisfy her soul?

Did she even know she had a soul that would presently crave a satisfaction found only among the higher and better things, and turn away with infinite scorn from the petty triumphs of an hour or a day?

Well, she had fought her fight with the rest, and triumphed greatly in the world's eyes; and now she must abide by the path she had chosen, and glean the best satisfaction she could out of it.

And yet—

Later in the afternoon, when she sat drinking a lonely cup of tea by a lonely fireside, the questioning, probing mood returned again; the significant "and yet" still left the last conclusion without any finality. Looking backward, a sense of resentment seemed to creep over her; a combative desire to get even with Fate about many things while there was time and opportunity.

She remembered particularly the first man who had tried to lead her astray. He had been considerably more than twice her age, a hardened sinner without any compunction, with a devilish cunning at breaking down defences without any seeming over-persuasion, and at whitewashing his actions into passionate devotion to youngn inexperienced years. She remembered how she had struggled to resist him. It was good to remember now that she had not been his victim.

And yet, what of it, while such men could triumph again and again and go seemingly unpunished, and young, eager, ambitious souls were often so pitifully stranded at the beginning of a career?

Men of his age and his character usually did triumph. How often had she seen it since! The first wrong step not a generous-hearted, hot-headed youth; but a hardened sinner who had wearied of other hardened sinners and turned his evil designs to youth and freshness, hoping perchance to be rejuvenated thereby.

And Nature stood by with folded hands, and saw her fairest creations soiled and ravished before they had reached maturity, without apparently the smallest compunction.

Her first wrong step had been her marriage, and though it had given her a good deal in the beginning, in the end how it had robbed her!... ah! how it had robbed her of those things that could never be won back.

And now, by an unlooked-for turn of events, she found herself among the world-wearied ones, asking for the divine freshness of youth. If she chose to make him love her she believed she could.

And yet?—

She stood beside the window and leaned her head against the framework, gazing at the river. It was gliding smoothly along now, beautified and glorified by the reflected light of a setting sun. How light transfigured!

The murky, muddy, sullen Thames, so often going with its countless burdens, as one enslaved unwillingly to the needs of commerce, now flashing, shining, silver waters hastening joyfully out to sea. She felt that often and often her life had been as the shadowed, murky waters, enslaved unwillingly by bonds that circumstances had created.

She thought how his life, the life of this man who was beginning to fill her soul, was still like the joyous, shining, waters reflecting sunlight. Was it possible she wanted to bring the shadows and dim its silver radiance for her own gratifications?

And even so, was it in any case likely to go undimmed much longer? The shadows were certain enough to come, if not through her, perhaps through some one with less soul, and less fineness of aim, who would do him far greater harm. Her love for him was not, at least, entirely selfish.

She knew that she cared very much for his future. She cared very much that life should give him a chance to fulfill the best of his promise.

And if the chance came by shadows, well, across the river of a man's life they flitted lightly enough as a rule, chasing each other away, and leaving the waters still flowing joyfully. It was only for a woman, apparently, the shadows left a stain that even the sunlight could not chase away.

It would seem woman was made a helpmeet for man in many ways beside that of keeping his home and bearing his children. How often did he owe his best development and best achievements to her, absorbing light from her in some mysterious ordering, and soaring away afterwards while she was left among the shadows.

Yet, by some equally mysterious compensation, a woman was often so fashioned that if she could feel the upward flight was won through her, she might rest statisfied even though him she loved had soared away. It was the mother-love blending strangely with the wife-love; the protecting, inspiring, unselfish, mothering instinct, lying in the soul of every true-hearted woman.

Standing gazing at the flashing river, Lorraine, in the midst of her probing, knew that it was his ultimate success and good she wanted, as well as his freshness to sweeten her own life.

And yet?—

What if she brought a shadow where there would otherwise have been no shadow, dimmed a brightness that, without her, had gone undimmed? She knew he was not weak naturally. He did not need any strengthening; only impetus, ambition, aim, and some safeguarding by the way.

She smiled a little drearily at the recollection that it was from her, herself, that probably his own people would think he needed safeguarding. She could foresee that they would likely enough hurl themselves between him and her, oblivious that by doing so they might very possibly be the cause of driving him to far worse. But that, of course, no one could help; as how should they know the fine shades between the women who lived outside the conventions?

But then again, they need not know that the great friendship existed— why should they? After all, few would credit the celebrated, beautiful actress with anything beyond a passing fancy for the youthful, briefless barrister.

And yet?—

Across every fresh pathway she turned her thoughts along, was still that arresting, intangible, "and yet".

The pity of it! At least he was strong, and true, and unspoilt now. Why not give life a chance to leave him so?

Why not give Fate a chance to endow him quickly with the rich, blessed love that kept a man walking straight and strong along his steadfast way?

But again the thought came back of what he would lose, what he must inevitably lose, if he missed the storm and stress and struggle that are as the mill and furnace through which the gold is refined, and hardened, and separated from the dross.

She went back to the fireside feeling that her probing had brought her nowhither, and that she was only very tired and very depressed.

Then she went slowly away to dress, and chose, somewhat to Jean's surprise, one of the simplest evening frocks she possessed. Jean, knowing the tall, beautiful new friend was coming to dinner, had laid out an elaborate dinner-dress, and arranged the jewel cases for selection.

"Put them away at once," was all her mistress said, with one sweeping glance round. "I shall wear that little blue Liberty gown and a single row of pearls."

When Alymer came he found her already seated by the fire, engaged with some knitting.

"How nice and homely," he said. "I never associated you with anything so commonplace as sewing."

"I'm afraid I can't sew very well," with a little smile. "I can knit this, and that is about all."

"Are you better?" and he scanned her face critically, in an old-fashioned way that gave her secret joy.

"Yes, sir, thank you," with a low laugh.

He laughed too, and took up his stand on the hearthrug, with his hands behind his back, in a natural, quite-at-home way, that seemed to come easily to him.

"How jolly it is to see a fire. My mater always seems afraid of beginning too soon. I think she has a sort of feeling that if winter sees fires started he will hurry."

"I never leave them off. My fire is one of my staunchest companions. An empty grate always depresses me, because if it is sunny and hot I want to be out-of-doors, and if it is not, I want my fire. Let us go to dinner, then we can get back and purr over it to our hearts' content."

Because it pleased her to make him an honoured guest, Lorraine had been at considerable pains in ordering her dinner, and she was gratified to observe that it was not wasted on him.

Certainly, among other things at Oxford he had learnt to know a good dinner and good wine, and enjoy them as a connoisseur. It amused her also to observe that the old-fashioned air with which he had inquired a little masterfully after her health, grew upon him as the evening progressed.

She thought he must be a little bit of a tyrant to his mother, and any one he was specially fond of. Not dictatorially so, but with a humorous, half-satirical insistence that was very engaging.

When the sat over the fire together, later, she found herself telling him many things about her early struggles, and first successes, not in the least in a "talking down" attitude, but as to a very sympathetic companion of her own age.

It was evident he was truly interested, and this made him a charming listener. And he told her yet further of his own hopes, and disappointments, and discouragements. Several times since he took his degree, one friend or another had held out hopeful expectations of being able to put him on to this case of that, which might bring a brief. And always the hope had failed, and the promise ended in smoke.

She gave him sympathy in her turn, and said she would not raise his expectations unkindly, but she believed she could really help him to get a start. She would speak to Lord Denton about it. He was always ready to do a little thing like that for her.

"He is one of those dear people," she told him, "who seem to try to make up for their own incorrigible laziness by going out of their way to put some one else in the way of a start."

She saw the colour deepen in his face, and a subdued light shine in his eyes, as he thanked her rather haltingly. The little show of diffidence was very charming. How far removed, how amazingly far removed he was from the average good-looking youth of twenty-four, who was usually so anxious to impress every one with his attributes and his powers.

And he was not even average. Every time she saw him she wondered afresh at his extraordinary wealth of attraction. One could have forgiven him a few airs and mannerisms; but no forgiveness was asked: in every single phrase she found him always the modest, unassuming, high-bred gentleman.

So they sat on and talked, and for the time being the warfare of the afternoon passed from her mind. Probing seemed suddenly out of place. Why probe?... Their friendship had slipped of itself into an old companionship. What need for more? She knew instinctively he would come often to fill her lonely hours, and tell her all about his work and his doings.

And sometimes they would go out together on little jaunts. If they did, who need know, or who, at any rate, need gossip? She felt a gladness grow in her mind at the thought of the happy friendship they might have; guarded perhaps from harm by the disparity in their years, and at the same time of inestimable benefit to him, and pleasure to her. She felt almost motherly as she laid her fingers lightly on his arm, with a little laughing jest, as they stood together before parting.

"I have enjoyed my evening of invalidism so much. Come and see me again soon, won't you?"

"I should love to. You are very good to me."

"Oh, no; I'm not. Don't let us talk of goodness in that way. I like your company; and it is good to have what one likes. I shall expect you again soon, Alymer—I may call you Alymer, mayn't I?... Mr. Hermon is so overpowering."

"I wish you would. I would have asked you, only I was afraid you might think it cheek."

"Very well then, *Alymer*," with emphasis, "when I have spoken to Lord Denton I will telephone you; and I hope he will be able to start you off on a road that will very nearly end in a verdict of 'Suffocated with briefs.'"

"Or 'briefly suffocated'," he laughed, and beat a hasty retreat, for fear of a reprisal.

When he had gone, Lorraine sat again in the firelight, and it seemed as if the stress and unrest had fallen from her, and only the memory of a pleasant companionship remained. They were going to be the best of pals— why not—and why seek to probe any further?

Apparently he was not susceptible, and cared more for his profession than any one supposed, and so, since she liked to have him there to glory in his comeliness, they could form a mutual benefit society, and no one need be hurt at all. It was all quite simple, and she went to bed feeling rested and refreshed, and looking forward hopefully for the pleasant meetings to come?

Flip Denton was running down to Brighton for the weekend also, to take her out on the Sunday in his car; and he noticed at once that a shadow which had hovered over her eyes of late had vanished.

"You are looking topping," he told her. "What about the love affair, is it all satisfactorily off? It has been worrying you a little of late."

"It is not exactly off," she replied, "but it is more satisfactorily placed. We are going to be real good pals. He is going to keep me company in some of my lonely hours, and I am going to try and help him to get briefs. I am relying on you for the first one, Flip."

"The dickens you are. My dear girl, why should I put myself out to acquire a brief for a rival?"

"Oh, just because you are you. You know you will love it, Flip! You will get him a brief, and then you will pat yourself on the back and say: 'I know I'm a lazy dog myself, but I'm a devil of a good chap at getting other fellows work.'"

"So I am" —enjoying her thrust— "and it's a splendid line, and gives far more satisfaction in the end. If I tried to work I should only make a mess of it, and drive some one nearly crazy, whereas, in putting another chap on to a job I give such a lot of folks pleasure, I feel I am getting square with the Almighty."

"Then you'll try, Flip?"

"It is humanly possible, he shall have a brief of his very own within the next month."

"You are a dear. Sometimes I think you are the most adorable person I know."

"You don't think it long enough at a time, Lorry. You are too prone to go off suddenly after false gods measuring six-foot-five-and-a-half inches and with the faces of Apollo Belvederes."

"Probably it is a merciful precaution on the part of our guardian angels, Flip; and, anyhow, you know you like a little variation yourself in the way of bulk, and sound, practical, indecorous chorus girldom."

"I do," was his unabashed affirmative. "Nice, comfortable, elevating palliness with you; and a right down rollicking bust-up occasionally with the ladies of the unpretending school of wild oats."

"I want my giant for the present to be satisfied with his palliness with me and his work. Do you think he will?"

"As I haven't seen him I can't say. If I get the chance, however, I'll tell him that 'wild oats' are the very devil, and I'd give all I've got to have stuck to work and had naught to do with 'em."

"You know you wouldn't, Flip," with a little laugh.

"I know I couldn't, you mean; but I never admit it to juniors."

"Well, you shall come to the flat to meet him. If he gets a brief, we'll have a little dinner party, and I'll ask Hal and her cousin and St. Quintin."

"Right you are. I haven't seen Miss Pritchard for ages. Shall we turn now, and go back by Rottingdean?"

"Let us go whichever way has the best view of the sea. I feel I want to look at wide, breezy spaces for a while, and not talk at all."

"You shall," he promised, and they sped along in silence.

CHAPTER XVII

When Hall sat on the side of her bed, brushing her hair and meditating on her irritation, she had not misjudged when she anticipated great enjoyment from an afternoon run with her new friend.

It would have been difficult indeed to say who enjoyed it the most. Hal was in great form, and Sir Edwin Crathie half unconsciously took his tone from her, dropping his usual attitude towards women he liked, and adopting instead one as gay and careless and inconsequent as hers.

It was not in the nature of the man to desist from flirting with her, but his pretty speeches were coupled with a humour and chaff that robbed them of any pointedness, and merely resulted in an amusing amount of parry and thrust, over which they both laughed whole-heartedly.

"You are an absolute witch," he told her as they sat enjoying a big tea at an hotel on the south coast; "ever since we started you have made me behave more or less like a school-boy, and a tea like this is the climax."

"It's a good thing I am the only witness," she laughed. "The poorness of your jokes alone would have horrified your colleagues, but to see you eating such a tea must have meant a request for your resignation—it is so incompatible with the dignity of a Cabinet Minister."

"I had almost forgotten I was a Cabinet Minister. Gad! but it's nice to get right away from the cares of office occasionally like this. When will you come again?"

"Oh, I don't think I must come any more," roguishly. "I'm sure Brother Dudley will not consent."

"What has Brother Dudley go to do with it?... Did he consent this time?"

"Not exactly. I anticipated his willingness."

"You little fibber. You mean you anticipated his firm refusal, and took French leave, so that you need not disobey him."

"It is true that Dudley and I differ occasionally, but I do not disobey him... if I can help it."

"Well, if you took French leave this time, you can easily do it again."

"But this time it was a novelty. I was curious to find out how I should enjoy an afternoon with you?"

"Rubbish. You knew perfectly well you would enjoy it immensely. So did I. Two people who like each other always know those kind of things at once."

Hal leaned back in her chair, and her expressive mouth twitched in a way that made him long to kiss it hard.

"There are occasions when I don't like you at all," she said.

"Fibber again. When don't you like me?"

"Chiefly when you are quite positive certain sure that I do."

"Well, that is never; so you are a fibber."

"I thought you seemed particularly confident nine seconds ago."

"I was only teasing you. I could hardly have been serious after you have called me a worm, and an old man. So now—when will you come again?"

"In about a month. Let's go out as Guys on the fifth of November."

"A month be blowed! I want to know which day next week?"

"I am full up next week."

"Full up of what?"

"Lorraine Vivian, Dick Bruce, Quin, the Beloved Chief, and the Baby."

"What a list! Is Lorraine Vivian the actress? Who are Quin and the Baby?"

"She is... and they are!..."

"Who does the Baby belong to?"

"It would be difficult to say. About a dozen probably claim him."

"And doesn't he know his own mother?"

"Oh, I wasn't thinking of mothers."

"Who were you thinking of?"

"The ladies who have lost their hearts to him."

"I see. Are you one of them?"

"I am not. You see, his beauty has never struck me all of a heap, because I've got so used to it."

"Is he a beautiful baby, or a youth, or a man?"

"A bit of all three. He stands 6 ft. 5 ½ in., and is superbly handsome. I call him sometimes, for variation, the stuffed blue-and-gold Apollo."

"Well, that's better than 'a positive worm'," laughing, "but I don't mind him. Who is Quin?"

"Quin is a philanthropist, sentimentalist, and hero. He spends his life working in the East End."

"I don't mind him either, and Dick Bruce I've seen. The actress doesn't count, and your precious chief you see every day. Now, then, when will you come again?"

He got up from his seat and came round to her side of the table. He had a vague intention of imprisoning her hand, and perhaps her waist, but some indescribable quality held him off. It was difficult to suppose she did not half guess what was in his mind, and yet, without showing the smallest consciousness or shyness, she faced him with a look so boyishly frank and open it utterly disarmed him.

"I am not a bit more persuasive on my right side than my left, and I have promised next Saturday to the Three Graces — who are Dick and Quin and Baby. We are going to the Crystal Palace to see a football match."

"Then what about Sunday?"

"Oh, I can't come on Sunday."

"Why not?"

"I hardly know, except that it usually belongs to Dudley or Dick."

"Next Sunday needn't."

"Well, that's what I don't know."

"Yes you do." He moved a little nearer. "You've got to keep next Sunday for me. It's my turn. We'll have a splendid day. We'll take Peter, and we'll start early and fly down to the New Forest. It's glorious in the autumn. We'll have a picnic-lunch, and tea at an hotel on the way back. So that's settled." He got up, and lifted her ulster from the back of a chair. "Now come along, and we'll slip home before it gets late enough to cause trouble."

Hal let it pass for the time, and got into her ulster. She was clever enough to see the advantage of retaining a way of escape if she changed her mind, or accepting the invitation if she wanted to later on.

She knew perfectly well a girl did not always go out for a whole day with a man like Sir Edwin with impunity; but she had also something of contempt for a girl who missed a great treat for want of pluck. She preferred to leave the question open, and if she badly wanted to go at the end of the week she would not, at any rate, stay away because she was afraid.

As it happened, circumstances played into Sir Edwin Crathie's hands. About Wednesday, with a diffidence that made Hal secretly amused and secretly curious, Dudley asked her if she would mind if he was away for the whole day on Sunday. As she was generally away herself as long as the summer lasted, she wondered why he should ask her in that manner. It was just as they had finished breakfast, and he busied himself with his pipe-rack as he made the announcement.

"Of course I don't mind," she said. "Are you going into the country?"

"Ye-es." He seemed about to add something further, but changed his mind. Hal, with a little inward chuckle, divined by his manner he must be going somewhere with a lady, and she was pleased, as she liked a man to have woman friends, believing they made him more broad-minded and tolerant and generous-hearted if well-chosen.

She asked no further question, however, and Dudley commenced to whistle softly as he drew on his boots. Evidently his mind was somewhat relieved after the sentence was said.

So now it remained to discover Dick's attitude. She could, of course, quite easily put him off; but she was not quite prepared to do this of her own initiative, as he had so generously placed all his Sundays at her disposal. On Friday, however, he was speaking to her through the telephone.

"I say, Hal, you're coming to the Footer match tomorrow, aren't you?"

"Yes, of course I am. Why?..."

"Well, it's just this way. I was going to motor the pater to Aunt Judith's, and I forgot all about it. He wants me to take him on Sunday instead. What shall I do?... Would you care to come too?"

Hal had not the smallest wish to go to Aunt Judith's, who belonged to the old school, and disapproved in a most outspoken manner of lady-clerks of every sort and description. It was a constant grievance to her, when she set eyes on Hal, that she did not gratefully accept £20 as secretary to a well-known, interesting editor.

In consequence, Hal encountered her as little as possible, accepted gratefully her interesting, easy billet, and consigned the imaginary young children to a Hades peopled with nursery governesses.

"Awfully sweet and good and kind of you, Dicky dear," she called back to him mockingly, "but I think I'll practise a little self-denial this time, and stay away."

"Odd you should say that," he laughed, "because I consider I'm practising a little self-denial in going. What shall you do with yourself? Will Dudley be at home?"

"No; he's going somewhere for the day, that has a nervous, apologetic sort of air about it. I didn't press for particulars, but I'm dying to know. I can't believe he would really take a gay young person out, and yet, judging by his manner, it might be a real flyer from Daly's."

"Good old Dudley!... Then I suppose you will go to Lorraine?"

"Yes, I daresay I shall. Good-bye, see you Saturday."

Hal returned to her work in a meditative mood. She was beginning to wonder why she had not had any message from Sir Edwin all the week. Had he changed his mind, or had he possibly forgotten? If he rang her up presently what was she going to say?

The notion that he had perhaps forgotten was not pleasing; and yet, with all he must have to think about during the week, it was equally not surprising. As a matter of fact, it had been a most trying week for all Ministers.

The party was emphatically growing into disfavour, and all brains had to be utilised to find the most efficacious remedy. Sir Edwin had been very useful in his suggestions, for he had had considerable practice in getting what he wanted by artfulness if no straighter mode offered.

His suggestions to His Majesty's Cabinet were masterpieces of political trickery, and their adoption was a foregone conclusion in spite of the Ministers who raised objections. The party had to win back favour somehow, and at any rate his were the best plans that offered.

But all through the stirring meetings of the week he never once forgot Hal. His silence was merely an adaptation of the policy he was urging upon his colleagues. "If I leave her alone till Friday she will get piqued," was his thought, "and then she will come."

Accordingly, soon after the luncheon hour he rang her up.

"Hullo," he called. "At last I have got a moment to speak to you."

"What has happened to all the other moments?" she asked.

"We've had a very anxious, worrying week in the House. I've scarcely had time to get my meals. You surely didn't suppose I had forgotten you— did you?"

"I didn't suppose either way. It didn't matter."

The man at the other end of the wire smiled openly in his empty room. "Prevaricator," was his thought "but, by Gad, she's game."

"Well, anyhow I hadn't, and I wasn't likely to. I only hope you haven't made another engagement for Sunday? I'm badly in need of a long day in the country. Are you still free?"

"It depends—"

"Oh, nonsense; you can't desert me at the last moment. If I can't get that day off to run down to the New Forest, I shall have to go to a tiresome political luncheon party. Now, be patriotic, and serve your country by attending to the needs of one of her harassed Ministers."

"I am always patriotic."

"Then that settles it. I suppose I'd better not call for you. I'll pick you up at South Kensington Station at 9.30. Peter will make an excellent chaperone, so you needn't worry—good-bye"; and he rang off, leaving Hal to hang up the receiver, not quite sure whether she had been trapped or not.

At his end he moved across to a window with the smile still lingering on his face.

"Nothing like making up a woman's mind for her," he mused; "they're all alike when they are on the edge of the stream, hesitating about the plunge. Give 'em a little shove, and once they're in they swim out boldly enough. The trouble is, when they want to keep the whole river for themselves and will not brook any other swimmers.

"I expect I'm going to have a devil of a time with Gladys, and she'll take a lot of squaring. Women are the deuce when you're short of funds. But I can't help being susceptible, and Hal has caught my fancy altogether. Dear little girl, I expect she'll want a big shove yet before she'll take the real plunge. But it's interesting, by Jove! it's interesting; and when she looks a veiled defiance at me with those candid, mischievous eyes of hers, I know I've got to win somehow."

Hal went back to her work, feeling a little as if she had been swept off her feet; and she was not entirely without misgivings. The possible impropriety of going out alone with a man for the whole day did not trouble her, but the nature of the man, she was shrewd enough to perceive, was a doubtful point.

Of course she was perfectly aware that Aunt Judith, for instance, and Dudley, and probably her mother, had she been alive, would have been scandalised at such a proceeding; but then she had pluckily fended for herself so long, she did not consider she was any longer called upon to mould her actions according to their views. She belonged to the large army of women who have to spend so much of their time on office chairs that their comparatively few hours of pleasure have no room for the ordinary conventions that hem round the leisured, home-walled maiden.

If a treat offered, and it was reasonably within bounds, they took it and were thankful and gave no thought to the possibly uplifted hands of horror among possibly restricted relatives. She was one of those who enjoy the freedom of the American girl, without being of those who, unfortunately, often fall short of her level-headed characteristics; largely perhaps through those very uplifted hands which suggest harm, where harm otherwise might never have been thought of.

It was not, now, any suggestions born of uplifted hands that gave Hal that faint misgiving. It was that growing doubt concerning the nature of the man, and a consciousness that she was unduly pleased the treat was actually to take place—a growing consciousness that in spite of the doubt she cared more about seeing Sir Edwin Crathie than most men, with a like recognition that this might seriously endanger her own peace of mind.

It was all very well to go out together on a basis of good-fellowship and mutual enjoyment, so long as neither cared anything beyond; but what if this unmistakable attraction he exercised over her deepened and widened? What if the commonplace, middle-class Hal Pritchard, secretary and typist, fell in love with Sir Edwin Crathie, the Cabinet Minister, and nephew of Lord St. Ives?

But she thrust the thought away, and apostrophised herself for a silly goose, who deserved to get hurt if she had not more sense. Was he not twice her age, and brilliantly clever (so his own party said), and so obviously out of her range altogether that it would be sheer stupidity to allow herself to feel anything beyond the frank fellow-ship they now enjoyed? She insisted vigorously to herself that it would, and went off to have dinner with Lorraine, who was once more delighting her London audience nightly.

It was a curious thing which occured to both afterwards, that there had been some indefinable change, observable in each to each, dating from that particular evening.

Lorraine was more contentedly gay than she had been for some time—a quiet, natural light-heartedness, born of some attainment that was giving her joy. Hal was not clever enough to actually perceive this, but she did perceive that a certain restless, anxious indecision of manner and plans had passed away. For the time being Lorraine was happy in a sense she had not been over her success. That Alymer Hermon had anything to do with it never entered Hal's head. She had treated the whole matter of Lorraine's attraction to him with the lightness that seemed its only claim, and scarcely remembered it at all.

And yet, all the time, it was the young giant who was bringing the soothing and restfulness into the actress's storm-tossed life. He was beginning to be with her constantly—to come to her with all his doings, and his imagings, and his hopes. And, as she had suspected, natural or unnatural, he was the companion of all others who gave her the most pleasure at the time.

World-wearied and brain-wearied with her own unsatisfying successes, she found a new interest in entering into his projects, and scheming and dreaming for his future instead of her own.

She was quite open to herself about the probability that she would have felt nothing of the kind had he been merely a giant, or had he been plain. It was the rare, and indeed remarkable combination of such physical attributes, with brains, and nobility and an utter absence of all assumption.

She forgot about his youth and a certain natural crudity; and what he lacked in experience and development she easily balanced with the extraordinary physical attraction that had never ceased to sway her.

For the rest, the future might go. Her friendship would not hurt him, and his had become necessary to her. If they dreamed over a volcano, what of it? Most dreams for such lives as hers usually were in close proximity to sudden destruction. Waves from nowhere came up and overwhelmed them. Rocks from unseen heights fell on them and crushed them. If she was wise she would take what the present offered, and leave the future alone.

For Hal, on the other hand, had developed something of the restlessness that had fallen from Lorraine. The new element dawning in her life was not a restful one; neither did it lend itself to her usual spontaneous chaff and gay badinage.

She told Lorraine about her afternoon drive, without giving half the particulars she would have done ordinarily; and when Lorraine asked her about Sunday, she only said she was perhaps going for another run with Sir Edwin. Lorraine did not press the point, because she was having a day with Alymer, and was chiefly glad that Hal was happily provided with a companion to take Dick's place.

Then she went off to her theatre, and Hal went home, wishing the next day were Sunday.

CHAPTER XVIII

Dudley hardly knew, himself, why he spoke diffidently about his plans for Sunday, and why he did not tell Hal outright that he was taking Doris Hayward to a picnic at Marlow, given by mutual friends of his and theirs— friends of the old vigorous days, when he and Basil Hayward had gone everywhere together, and Hal had still been a boisterous schoolgirl. Perhaps he felt she might seem to have been rather unkindly left out.

As a matter of fact, an invitation to include his sister had been given; but, for reasons he hardly stopped to face, he chose not to mention it. That was after he had learnt from a visit to the little Holloway flat that nothing would persuade Ethel to leave her brother, who had been ailing more than usual of late, and Doris would accompany him alone.

It had been with a curious mixture of feelings he had heard this. Things were very pitiful up at the little flat, and though his inmost sympathy had gone out generously enough to both girls, with a perversity born of narrow insight he had reserved the deepest of it for Doris.

It seemed to him that she was so young to face such circumstances, and at such an early age to become saddened by the vicissitudes of life. In the depths of her wide blue eyes he saw unshed tears, and the little droop of her pretty mouth went straight to his heart. He wanted to gather her up in his arms, and kiss her and pet her till she was again all sunshine and smiles.

He was not unaware that Ethel probably suffered more, but her way of showing it, or perhaps hiding it, appealed to him less. Instead of that mute distress of unshed tears, her quiet eyes wore an inscrutable veil. It was as if the anguish behind the veil were something too terrible and too sacred to be looked upon by a workaday world; but Dudley only knew that a wall of reserve was between him and her trouble.

And her firm, strong mouth had no engaging droop at the corners. It was only if anything a little firmer, almost to sternness.

Dudley believed that Basil was dying at last, after his weary martyrdom, and he believed that Ethel knew it; and in some vague way it hurt him that she gave no sign, and refused to be drawn into any speech concerning his increased weakness.

Doris, on the other hand, spoke of it in a faltering, tearful voice, adding a little pitifully that it made it harder for her that Ethel was so distant and unsympathetic.

In a sense the circumstances nonplussed Dudley altogether. Some inner voice told him that such a depth of wondrous, unselfish devotion as Ethel showed to her invalid brother could not live in the same heart with hardness and want of sympathy; and yet there was the evidence of the swimming, melting eyes and drooping lips of the younger sister left out in the cold.

Perhaps it was unfortunate that on that very evening of Dudley's visit Ethel had come home rather earlier than her wont, to find Doris not yet returned from her daily outing, and, in consequence, the fire out and the sick man shivering with cold. He had looked so dreadfully ill that she had hastened first to get some brandy to revive him, only to find Doris had forgotten her promise to get the empty bottle replaced that morning.

In desperation she had hastened to the other little flat on the same floor, hoping its inmate might chance to have a little to lend.

The tenant was a lonely, harsh-featured spinster, who eked out a precarious living by teaching music. Ethel knew her slightly, as a gaunt woman who usually toiled up the stairs with a sort of scornful weariness of herself and everything else.

She knew that because she was not fashionable, nor striking, nor well-dressed, she taught mostly in rather second-rate schools, and often had to take long journeys to her pupils, coming home tired and worn at night to an empty, comfortless little dwelling, to light her own fire and cook her own evening meal.

She knew, too, that she was a gentlewoman, the daughter of a poor clergyman, left penniless, to fight a hard world alone. Had her own home been happier, she would gladly have asked her to join them sometimes; but the weight of Basil's illness, and her own usual condition of weariness, had left the invitation always unspoken.

"A little brandy," the music-teacher echoed, with a quick note of concern; "yes, I believe I have a drop. Is it your brother? Let me come and see if I can help?"

"Thank you," Ethel had replied, trying not to allow her voice to show how much she would have preferred not to accept the proffered help. "I think I can manage quite well."

But the gaunt spinster followed her across the little landing obstinately. She had seen Doris out half an hour before, and knew that she had not yet returned.

"Ah, you have no fire," she said, in her somewhat grating voice; "if you will let me I will light it," and without more ado she had procured coals and wood for herself, and was down on her knees before the empty grate.

Ethel turned away with a sick, helpless feeling over Doris' selfishness, and after administering a few drops of brandy, chafed the sick man's hands and feet. When Basil felt better he glanced up curiously at the strange, dried-up-looking female who had just succeeded in persuading a cheerful blaze to brighten the room. She looked back into his face frankly.

"You needn't mind me," she informed him; "I'm only the music-teacher from the opposite flat."

"You seem to be rather a kind sort of music-teacher," he said, with his winsome smile, "even if you do only come from the opposite flat."

The hard face relaxed a very little, and she shrugged her shoulders.

"Oh, well, it isn't easy to be kind," she answered, "when you don't stand for much else in the universe but a letter of the alphabet." She turned back to her grate and commenced sweeping up the ashes.

Basil roused himself a little further and looked interested.

"What letter do you stand for?"

"Just G." She gave a low, harsh laugh. "G is the letter that distinguishes my flat from the others, and it is all I stand for to God or man."

"I see." His white, pain wrung face looked extraordinarily kind. "Well, G, I'm very deeply grateful to you for coming across to light my fire; and I'm glad there happened to be a G in the universe this afternoon."

She turned her head away sharply, that neither of them might see the sudden, swift mist that dimmed her eyes, but she only answered:

"All the same, if there had been no G, and no you, the universe would have had an atom less pain in it, and no one have been any the worse."

"That's where you're wrong," he told her, "because Ethel couldn't have done without me, and if you put your head in at my door occasionally, and just remark to F that G is across the passage, F will be glad the universe didn't decide to leave G out of the alphabet."

The woman looked at him a moment with a curious expression in her eyes. Then she said:

"Well, if *you* can take the insult of a maimed, or joyless, or cursed life like that, it oughtn't to be so very hard for me to be glad I happened to be able to come over and light your fire."

"Nor so very hard to come again."

"Ah!..." she hesitated, then said to him, looking half-defiantly towards Ethel: "Time after time, when I thought you were alone, I've wanted to just look in and see if you were all right. But I didn't like to. People don't take to me as a rule, and I'm... I'm... well, I'm not an ingratiating sort of person, and I guessed, probably, you'd all rather do without any help I had to give."

"It was kind of you to think of us at all," Ethel said, not quite sure whether Basil would like her to come in or not.

"You guessed wrong," was his answer. "*I* think it would be very nice of you to look in occasionally. It certainly seems rather absurd for you to be all alone there, and I all alone here, when we both want a little company. I'm sure the alphabet was not meant to be so unsociable."

"It just depends."

She got up from her kneeling posture on the hearth, and stood, a grotesque apparition enough, looking at him with her greenish, nondescript eyes. Her hay-coloured hair was tightly drawn back from a high, bulging forehead, her eyebrows were so light they scarcely showed at all, while her nose, which started in a nice straight line, had failed her at the last moment by suddenly taking an upward turn in an utterly incongruous fashion. She had high cheek-bones, a parchment skin, and a mouth that was not much more than a slit; the grotesque effect of the whole being heightened by a long, thin neck, which she made no effort to cover with a neat high collar, but accentuated by a half-and-half untidily loose one.

She wore a cheap, ready-made blouse, with absurd little bows tacked on down the front, which Ethel longed to abolish with one sweep, and her skirt, which had shrunk considerably in front, sagged in a dejected fashion behind.

Yet to Basil's kindly eyes, there was something behind it all that was attractive. For one thing, she was so eminently sincere. One felt she had no delusions whatever, concerning her appearance or her oddities; and though she looked out upon life with that scornful, resentful air, she had yet a keener sense of humour and a clearer brain than most women. Under different circumstances she might have been a success.

As it was, she appeared to have got into a wrong groove altogether, and, unable to extricate herself, to have merely become an oddity. Basil, from his couch, looked up at her with friendly eyes, and she finished:

"One may want a little company, without wanting just any company."

"You think you will find me even duller than nothing?" and his eyes twinkled.

"You know I didn't mean that. You are clever, and well-read, and probably fastidious. I'm... well, you see what I am! and no good for anything except trying to restrain horrible children from thumping till they break the notes."

"I thought you said you were a music-teacher?"

"That's what they call it," with a dry grimace; "but when I dare to be honest, I have too much respect for music."

"Well, you won't have to weary your soul restraining me from thumping anything, so it will be a change to come and talk to me. We'll turn the tables, and I'll try and restrain you from thumping the universe too hard."

"It would be much more to the point if we thumped together: I, because I'm not wanted, and it's an insult to foist me on to mankind whether I like it or not; and you, because... well, because you are a strong man cursed with helplessness."

"Very well, if you come in that particular mood, we'll just play football with the bally old universe, so to speak. The main point to me is, that we take a rise out of the powers that be, by being a source of entertainment occasionally to each other. As our alphabetical significance in the general scheme is next door to each other, we may as well get what we can out of the circumstance."

She turned aside, looking half humorous and half satirical.

"It sounds well enough as you say it, but I expect the powers are sneering diabolically at us both. However, if you'll let me try to be some sort of company, I'll come across again soon—"

A latch-key was heard in the door, and a moment later Doris entered. When she saw the two women she looked taken aback, and stammered something about not knowing the time.

"When I got in Basil's fire was out, and he was perished with cold," Ethel said coldly; "and as I had to go to Miss... Miss -"

"Call it G," put in the music-teacher, with a comical twist of her mouth.

"—for brandy, she came over and lit the fire for me."

"I couldn't help not knowing the time," Doris murmured in a low, grumbling voice, and went away to take her hat off.

The music-teacher glanced from one to the other, as if about to say something, but changed her mind and moved towards the door. On the threshold she looked back, and said in her short, dry way:

"If F wants anything of G, G will be ready to come instantly."

"Thank you," Basil and Ethel replied together, the former adding, "And don't forget to put your head in at the door occasionally, by way of a reminder."

Ethel said no more to Doris, because she felt it useless, but her silence as they prepared the evening meal together signified her disapproval. She was deeply worried about Basil's failing strength, and longed to speak of it to someone who could understand; but felt such selfish forgetfulness as Doris showed shut her out from any sympathetic discussion.

Then Dudley came, and while Doris looked woebegone and sad, Ethel's face was a little stern with stress and anxiety. Basil tried valiantly to be cheerful enough for all three, but the effort cost him almost more strength than he could muster.

After Dudley had gone, carrying with him the image of Doris's plaintive prettiness and pathetic solitariness, and thinking gladly of the pleasure it would be to take her to Marlow on Sunday, Ethel slipped on her knees beside Basil's couch, overcome for a moment by the burden of his suffering, and the difficulties of their lives.

Often after Dudley had been, and some little act or glance or word had seemed to emphasise the barrier between them, her yearning over Basil had broken down her courage. When she had lost them both, what would become of her then? was the question that utterley undid her, finding no reply beyond a sense of empty darkness.

She told herself she would go right away to another land—to some far colony—where she could begin life afresh, with her haunting memories kept in the background. She would not stay to see the awakening come to Dudley, if Doris were his wife, nor struggle through the long months at the General Post Office, when the end of each day's labour brought no welcoming smile from Basil.

She would not settle down alone in a dingy little flat as their opposite neighbour, to become a mere letter of the alphabet to God and man, surrounded by countless other cyphers of as little meaning and account. She would go away to some new, young land, with her vigour and her courage, and carve out a path with some semblance of reality and value.

Only, could she ever get away from the awful emptiness that would come to her with the loss of Basil, and the utter lack of any incentive to carry on the unequal struggle?

Basil laid his hand on her bowed head, and for a little while seemed unable to speak. Then he steadied his voice, and rallied her with his brave, whimsical thoughts.

"Wouldn't the dear old pater have enjoyed G? She's just the kind of oddity he doted on. Fancy her teaching music of all things. It must be only scales and exercises. I think she's splendid to see the incongruity herself, and refuse to call it music when she dare be honest. What a grotesque figurehead she looks, chum, doesn't she? I thoroughly enjoyed talking to her."

But Ethel could not answer to his cheeriness just yet.

"Basil, why are so many humans just mere letters of the alphabet in the general scheme?"

She had slid into a sitting posture now, and leaned her head against his arm.

"It doesn't matter so much about the men; they can go out into the world and make friends by the way, and become something more if they wish; but what of the single women, who have to work for their living, and have nothing much to look forward to but a sort of terror as to what will become of them when they can work no more? If you could see some of them at the office, with that drawn, dried-up, joyless look, scraping and saving and starving for dread of the years ahead: it's so unfair, so grossly, hideously, cruelly unfair."

"It perhaps won't be when you see all round it, chum. It is so obvious we only see one side of things here. When we see the other side it will all look so different."

"Perhaps, but in the meantime they are here, now, in our very midst, all *these unwanted* women. If you saw as much of them as I do, I think you would feel even the letter had better not have been supplied. A blank would have meant so much less suffering. A penniless woman without attractiveness, and with neither husband, child, nor father wanting her, is such an anomaly. She just drags on, hating her loneliness, dreading and fearing the future or illness, merely existing because she is called upon to do so for no apparent reason."

"But she can always make friends, chum. If she is kind and cheerful and hopeful she will soon win love of some sort."

"Yes... yes... but, Basil, to be all that, when one is weighed down with the inequality of chance and a horror of the future calls for a heroine; and Life didn't bother to make many of them heroines. She doesn't seem to have paid much attention to them at all. Orphans and widows and sick people she remembers; but the lonely, ageing, hardened, unwanted spinster! It sometimes seems to me it is just sentimentality to be persuaded everything is all right.

"I don't believe it is all right. There's too much useless, silent aching, and useless, passionate resentment over circumstances that it seems should either never have been, or should be remedied if any Guiding Hand has power. I have determination and I'm strong, Basil; the future doesn't frighten me badly yet, but when you are gone, I feel as if the loneliness might half kill me, and as if then I ought to have the right to become a blank if I wish, since I was never consulted about becoming a letter in the great alphabet."

He did not seek to stay her, knowing with his deep insight that to get such thoughts spoken was better than to brood inwardly; and because of his unshakable faith in her courage, he was not alarmed by them.

Yet he could not offer any comfort. Had not the enigma of useless pain racked and torn his soul piteously through the long years of his illness, leaving him indeed with a wonderful courage, but not with a theory that would fit the needs of suffering mankind? He could bear his own ills, because he had trained and taught himself to take them as a soldier takes the miseries of a hard campaign; but the general sum of suffering was another matter; and he shrank from saying either that suffering was sent by God to do good, or that it was necessary to the human race.

All he knew was simply that ills bravely borne seemed aided by some mysterious power outside their bearers; whereas the craven and the grumbler seemed but to add to their own burden. For the rest, though he would not say it for the pain it gave her, the knowledge of his growing weakness was already a solace to him, and he watched with hidden eagerness for the day that should set him free. At least a corpse was no drain upon the slender purse of a beloved sister; and the gnawing ache of his helplessness and uselessness would be stilled for ever.

If only Dudley had cared for her? From his vantage-ground of the looker-on, with his unnaturally sharpened sensitiveness, he knew perfectly how matters stood and how hopeless the desire seemed.

Dear old Dudley, his life-long friend, would probably marry Doris and learn his mistake too late; and Ethel, with her fine nature, would go to some one else.

Well, one could not change either one's own little circle of fate, or the universe, just to suit oneself; one could only hope for the best, while there was still room for hope, and cultivate that soldier-spirit, undaunted even in a losing fight.

In the meantime there was the lonely, unwanted spinster opposite, with her immediate claim of nearness and loneness; and, as if to direct her thoughts into another channel, he said:

"You know, chum, I believe G was quite serious about wanting to come in here sometimes. Why not find out which afternoons she comes home early, and let her come and get tea and have it with me here. Then Doris need not worry about getting back in time."

"But if you are feeling weak it will tire you so, Basil, to have a stranger. You will feel obliged to talk to her."

"No, I don't think I shall; and it would be nice to feel she was rather glad not to be a blank after all. Let her come one afternoon and try. Perhaps one way of grappling with the problem of human suffering—the best way—is to try and alleviate the atom of pain that is nearest each one of us."

She assented to please him, and then kissed his forehead with a lingering, adoring tenderness, marvelling that such a sufferer could so think for others. Then she went quietly to bed, feeling, as the gaunt spinster had tried to put it, "If *you* can bear your ills so, surely I might manage to bear mine more courageously."

CHAPTER XIX

The next evening Ethel crossed the little landing to the lonely flat, and gave the invitation from F to G.

A good deal to her amusement, she found the gaunt spinster knitting babies' socks, with a basket containing several completed pairs beside her. She picked a pair up, and said with a kind little smile:

"I hardly expected to find you doing this."

"Of course not," in a short way, that sounded uncivil without being so. "It's an occupation about as much suited to me as teaching music."

"I wonder why you do it?"

"I do it for bread, naturally. They bring in a few shillings. It is just a fluke that I can make them at all. I know as much about a needle ordinarily as a flying-machine; but I learnt to knit once under protest. I sprained my ankle and was laid up for some weeks, and I told the doctor I should go stark, staring mad if he kept me shut up in a house doing nothing. He said knitting was a very good preventive to madness, and he'd send his wife along. She was a great missionary worker, and she pounced on me like a hawk, and started me off knitting socks for little gutta-percha babies somewhere in the Antipodes, almost before I knew where I was. Such insanity!... as if white babies wanted to be bothered with socks, much less black ones! I told the doctor it was adding insult to injury to allow it to appear I hadn't more common sense than to occupy my time with garments for the heathen. As if there weren't too many garments in the world already, half the community over-dressed, and ready to sell its soul for more. 'Leave them clean and healthy and naked, that's my advice, doctor,' I told him; 'and if you weren't afraid of your wife you'd agree.'"

Ethel leaned against the table, enjoying the rugged face and comically twisted mouth.

"But I thought you were a clergyman's daughter?" she said.

"So I am; but I don't see why I shouldn't be credited with a little common sense even then. I know they haven't much as a rule; what with their sewing-classes, and praying-classes, and mothers' meetings smothering up their minds till they can't see beyond their noses. I never had much to do with that part of it. They didn't like me well enough in the village to want to pray with me nor sew with me; which was just as well, for if I'd prayed, I should have implored the Almighthy to open their minds a little, and widen their views, and give them each a good thick slab of devilry to counteract their general soppiness and short-sighted stupidity. Ugh!… to hear some of those soppy folks praying to be delivered from the Evil One, and to have strength given them to cast the devil from their hearts! Just as if the devil had time to bother with that sanctimonious, chicken-hearted crew. He wasn't very likely to do them the compliment of acknowledging their existence."

"Did no one do any parish work then?"

"Oh, yes, the doctor's wife did most of it. And when a new doctor came they daren't for the life of them have a word to say to him, for fear of the next prayer-meeting, when she would preside. You see, she'd pray for the lost sheep in the fold for about half an hour, and how he went to the wolf for healing, which was the new doctor—instead of the saviour, which was her husband, the old one, and drew lurid pictures of the fiery poisons and deadly draughts the wolf gave the poor sheep to kill him instead of cure him."

"And what became of the new doctor?"

"Oh, of course he had to go—which was a pity, as he was the first person with a sense of humour who ever entered that village as a resident. One could positively talk sense to him, without being regarded as a lunatic. As a rule, you had to feign imbecility there if you didn't want to be considered mad. I had just made up my mind to learn to knit men's ties, instead of babies' socks, when he departed"—and she looked at Ethel with a grimness, and at the same time a lurking humour, that made it quite impossible for Ethel to keep her face.

"And did you change your mind then?" seeing the gaunt spinster was not in the least annoyed at her for laughing.

"Yes; I stuck to the babies' socks. I thought on the whole it was less incongruous for a woman with a face like mine to work for a baby than a man. And that's the nearest I ever got to a love affair. Just to wonder if I'd knit a man a tie, and change my mind, and knit socks for a little black heathen whelp instead."

"O dear!" said Ethel, with a little smothered gasp, "you don't mind if I laugh, do you? You really are very amusing."

"Amusing!..." with a little humorous snort. "Well, I don't mind amusing you; but I do think it's about the most monstrous thing in the way of a practical joke I know, for Nature to create a creature like me, with a natural inclination to want a mate. Just as if any man could bear to get up every morning of his life and see me there."

"Nonsense," Ethel exclaimed. "Basil thinks you are very attractive."

"Does he?" drily. Then, with a sudden, swift humour, "Perhaps it's a pity I didn't learn to knit ties after all!"

"Tell him about why you didn't instead—and about the village and the doctor's wife. He'll be so interested. You will be a positive godsend to him. May I tell him to expect you to tea tomorrow?"

"Yes. Tell him, to add to the humour of the situation, I'll bring across a baby's sock to knit. We're both so likely to have a mutual interest in babies."

Ethel kept Basil entertained most of the evening with the account of her interview, rather to the annoyance of Doris, who, for some vague reason, was not at all pleased about the new acquaintance.

Perhaps it was because, on one or two occasions when she had remained out later than she should, she had met the music-teacher and encountered a fierce and disapproving glare. Doris was quite willing to be relieved of her charge occasionally, but she did not at all appreciate the idea of a strong-minded individual, who would certainly not hesitate not only to condemn her selfishness, but to look her scorn of it.

On the evening of Dudley's visit, when she first found the gaunt spinster at the flat, she had gone to bed feeling out of sorts with herself and all the world.

She hated having been caught in her selfish forgetfulness; she hated the idea of the opposite tenant coming in to help Ethel; she hated being Doris Hayward and living in a stuffy Holloway flat. It caused her to turn her thoughts more seriously to a way of escape, and, as a natural sequence, to how much Dudley's attentions might mean.

And further, if they were meant in earnest, how she would feel about marrying him. She made no pretence to herself of loving him; personally, she thought love mostly sentimental nonsense; but she liked being with him, and she liked going about with him.

On the other hand, he was not rich, and she hated poverty. If she waited a little longer, a richer man might turn up?... or, again, he might not, and Dudley might change his mind. Certainly it was very awkward to know which was the wisest course, but in the meantime it would be just as well to keep Dudley attracted.

To this end she gave her hair an extra curl on Saturday evening, and arose betimes on Sunday morning for further preparations. Ethel took a bow off her hat, ironed, and remade it, and finally put the finishing touches to her appearance.

"You look very nice," she said. "I hope you'll have a splendid day. Run and show yourself to Basil."

Basil told her she would certainly be the belle of the luncheon party, and finally she departed feeling very pleased with herself.

Dudley was waiting for her at Paddington, and his eyes showed plainly that he echoed Basil's opinion, though he did not actually express it in words.

"How did you leave Basil?" he asked. "I wish I felt happier about him."

"He is much brighter altogether. I really think Ethel might have come, as the tenant of the opposite flat would have been only too pleased to go and sit with him. She never seems to have any pleasure, does she? But it is really her own fault. I would have stayed at home today if she would have let me."

"I think I'm rather glad she wouldn't; though I am sorry she could not have had the treat as well. We are going to have a lovely day, in spite of its being so late in the year."

As it was only a small birthday luncheon, and the others of the party had either gone overnight or lived near, they were easily able to get a compartment to themselves, and Dudley was conscious of a pleasurable quickening of his pulses at the prospect of the long tête-à-tête.

And indeed it was not surprising, for Doris looked adorably pretty and winsome, and many a wiser man might have shared his pleased anticipation. Moreover, Doris was not in the least stupid or vapid, however selfish and shallow her nature; and if she chose she could be a very pleasant companion.

And today she did so choose, hovering still in indecision over the subject that had filled her thoughts often of late.

Finally, it chanced that during much of the day they were thrown together, and all the time she thought how nice it was to be of so much consequence to any one; while he enjoyed again the sense of her clinging, engaging dependence.

And when they were once more alone in a compartment, steaming back to town, it was not in the least surprising that, almost before he knew it, Dudley was pouring into her ears a tale of love.

True, it was a very calm and collected tale, but it was none the less genuine for that; and from the bottom of his heart he believed that she, above all women, was the one he desired as his wife. Transports of any description were foreign to his nature. He imagined they always would be.

Joyous excitement and enthusiasm he left to Hal, except such enthusiasm as he kept for old ruins and ancient architecture. Still, it warmed all his blood and quickened all his pulses to have his way at last, and hold Doris in his arms, and try to kiss away the unshed tears and the little droop from her lips.

He took her home from the station, but did not go in because of the lateness of the hour, and the probability that Basil was just getting off to sleep; only kissing her again with a certain old-fashioned, deferential air and promising to come in the course of a day or two to see Ethel and Basil.

Doris let herself in with somewhat mixed feelings.

She had had a delightful day and thoroughly enjoyed it, but, now that the die was cast, and the difficult point settled, she found herself beginning to be more critical of Dudley.

She wished he were not quite so old-fashioned, nor so good. She was a little afraid she would find his sterling qualities distinctly boring, and his high standard a difficult and tiresome one to bother with.

And then, of course, there was Hal. Hal never had liked her and probably never would. Not that it mattered very much. In fact, it was rather pleasant than otherwise to think of Hal's discomfiture and dismay, Doris wondered if she would expect to live with them, and made up her mind then and there, very decisively, that she would never agree to anything of the kind.

She had suffered quite enough from Ethel's superiority, without encountering a second edition in Hal. As she thought of it, and of how she would checkmate Hal's possible plans to make her home with them, she smiled to herself a little cruelly in the darkness.

CHAPTER XX

It was Hal also who filled Dudley's thoughts as he made his way homeward. In her attitude to his engagement he was afraid she was going to personate what is known as a "tough nut to crack." He wondered if she would be waiting up for him, and what in the world she would say when he told her.

As it happened, she was waiting, sitting over the remains of a little fire she had lighted for company. The reason she felt the need of company, and the reason she was waiting, was the fact of a perturbed frame of mind she was endeavouring to soothe, until he came in to give the final touch.

She was perturbed because of the change in Sir Edwin Crathie, and the closing scene of a somewhat eventful day. Until tea-time he had been as gay and lighthearted and inconsequent as ever.

Their lunch in the New Forest had been an immense success, and both had enjoyed it thoroughly. On their way home they further enjoyed a big tea at an hotel.

Moreover, the drive had been delightful. The glory of the autumn tints; the delicious stillness of the autumn weather, and the sunny coolness of the atmosphere had all contributed to make the day perfect. After her long hours of office work and monotony, Hal was only the better tuned to enjoy it, and as she leant back in blissful ease in the luxurious motor, she thought what a goose she would have been to let prudish thoughts influence her to forgo it.

Then, once more, after tea, he had deliberately moved his chair nearer to hers, and struck a personal note that she found it difficult to combat.

"Do you know," he told her blandly, "you're the dearest little woman I've met for a long time? I don't know when I've enjoyed a whole day with any one so much as this."

"It's just the novelty," she said, adopting a note of unconcern to head him off; "most of your friends flatter and try to please you. It amuses me more to contradict you; that's all."

"Oh, that's all, is it! Well, I dare say if I found a special joy in being contradicted, I could easily humour the fancy without going for a whole day into the country."

"Ver likely—only, since you wanted your day in the country, you kill two birds with one stone, don't you see?"

"And supposing I badly wanted something else from you besides contradiction!... a little affection, for instance!"

"Oh, I'm giving you a lot of that thrown in," gaily, but she pushed her chair a little farther away; "if I didn't rather like you I shouldn't bother to contradict you."

"Rather like me!... that's very cold—I, a great deal more than *rather* like you."

"That, of course, is different," with a jaunty air, that made them both laugh.

"Still, I don't think we can stop at 'rather liking', now—do you?"

"I don't see why we shouldn't; we are getting on very nicely."

He got up suddenly, and walked away to the window. In his heart of hearts he was a little nonplussed. Of course they couldn't stop where they were, he argued; but how, with a girl of Hal's practical level-headedness get any farther?

Then he remembered he was a firm believer in swift and sudden measures, and usually found they fitted all contingencies. So he swung round, crossed the room, put his hand on her shoulders, and boldly kissed her.

"There," he said—"that is how I 'rather like' you."

Hal was quite taken aback—almost too taken aback to speak; but a red spot burned in each cheek, and a sudden flash seemed to gleam angrily in her eyes. Her quick brain, however, took in the position instantly. If she grew indignant and melodramatic, he would merely laugh at her.

Of course he knew she must be perfectly aware that men often kissed a girl who stood to them in her position, without thinking much of it. To make a fuss would be rather absurd. On the other hand, of course, he had to be disillusioned concerning what he apparently supposed would be her feelings on the subject.

"I call that bad taste," she said coolly. "You might have given me a sporting chance to let you know beforehand I should object." He looked about to repeat the action, but she edged away from him. "Of course I know lots of girls don't mind, but that's nothing to do with you and me. I do."

"Why do you mind?" He felt rather small before the directness of her eyes, and tried to bluster himself on to his former level. "It's very silly of you, especially nowadays. There's no harm in a kiss, is there?"

"None that I know of, but I think we were getting on very nicely without it. We won't risk spoiling things. Come along, I'm longing to be off"; and she moved towards the door.

"Are you angry with me?" he asked.

"Yes; very; but if you'll promise not to do it again I'll try to forget. If you transgress further, we shall just have to leave off being friends—that's all."

He took his seat in the motor beside her in silence, and Peter whizzed them away at a good speed.

Hal, enjoying the motion, kept her face averted, and drank in the lovely, fresh country air.

Presently a hand stole firmly over hers.

"You're not to be angry with me any more, little woman. I'm afraid I was rather a cad, but you've got such a fascinating mouth. I'm sorry."

She looked frankly into his eyes.

"Well, don't do it again, then."

He tried to look no less frankly back, but it was as if some forbidden thought flashed across his mind.

"I'll try not," he said, a trifle lamely, and looked away.

He still kept possession of her hand, however, until she resolutely drew it from him.

"Will Brother Dudley be in?" he asked, when they drew up in Bloomsbury.

"No; he won't get back much before nine."

He took her latch-key from her, and opened the door, entering himself, instead of taking her proffered hand.

"Which way?" he asked, and she opened the door into their sitting-room.

"I'll show you Brother Dudley's photograph now you're here," she said in a frank voice—"and the very latest of Lorraine Vivian. I wish I had one of Apollo; but I've never asked for one, because I always make a point of pretending not to admire him."

"It's only pretence, then?" he asked, glancing at the others as if his thoughts were elsewhere.

"It can only be. One is bound to admire him at heart. Nature seldom made a fairer gentleman, and it would be mere perversity to deny it, except, as I do, for his good."

Then suddenly she saw he was scarcely listening to her, and looking at the photographs without seeing them, and instinctively she moved away, feeling a little at loss. The next moment he had caught her shoulders, and kissed her again.

"I said I'd try, and so I have, but it's no use. Little woman, don't be prudish; kiss me back again."

But she pushed him away, and in the firelight he saw she was very white and determined.

"I asked you not to. It is much worse taste still now."

"No, it isn't—don't be silly. Why shouldn't I kiss you? I... I... have got awfully fond of you, and I know you like me somewhere down in your heart."

"I shall cease to do so from this moment."

"I dare you to. Hal, if you like me, why not take the sweets that offer? I'll be bound you've never been kissed in your life as I will kiss you. Don't be prudish. Let me teach you."

She seemed to hesitate a second, in indecision as to what was her best course to withstand him, and, seizing the opportunity, he suddenly caught her in his arms and kissed her on the lips with swift, eager kisses. Then, not giving her time to speak her resentment, he snatched up his hat and moved to the door.

"Don't be angry," he said. "I did try, honour bright, but it's no use; good-bye. I must see you again soon"; and he went out, closing the door behind him.

For some minutes Hal stood quite still, feeling a little dazed. She saw him cross the pavement, give some directions to Peter, and then drive away without a backward glance. She stood still a little longer, then slowly took off her hat, threw it on the sofa, ran her fingers through her hair and sat down.

After a little, the emptiness of the room seemed to oppress her, for though it was not cold, she jumped up and put a match to the fire. Then the landlady came in with her supper.

"'Ad a nice day, miss?" she asked pleasantly.

"Very nice. How's Johnnie? Did you get to see him?" alluding to a small son boarded out at Highgate for his health.

"Yes; I went up to tea with 'im. 'E looks years better already."

"I'm very glad."

Hal sat down to her supper with a preoccupied air, and instead of having a little chat, she relapsed into silence, and the landlady departed. She felt vaguely that something had upset entirely the even tenor of her mind, and she wanted to think. Any other Sunday evening she would have told the landlady something about her motor-ride, for she and Dudley had now been in the same rooms for seven years, and it is quite a fallacy to condemn all London landladies as grasping, bad-tempered tyrants.

Hal was quite fond of Mrs. Carr, and had found her unwearingly thoughtful and attentive. But tonight she wanted to think, and was glad to be alone again, almost immediately returning to her arm chair over the fire.

She was conscious, in a vague, uncertain way, that though Sir Edwin had kissed her because he cared for her, he could not have acted so had he cared in an upright, honest-hearted manner. She attracted him, and he wanted all the pleasure he could get out of the attraction, but there, no doubt, it ended.

For the rest, he was Sir Edwin Crathie, Cabinet Minister, and member of a proud, patrician family. She was Hal Pritchard, secretary, typist, and occasional journalist at the office of a leading London paper.

She grew restless, and commenced roaming round the room. Her knowledge of life, as it is lived near its teeming, throbbing, working centre, warned her that the new turn of their friendship held danger. If she was wise, she would shun the danger, and go back to her old life before he had come into it. She would firmly and resolutely refuse to see him again.

To do so without regret was impossible. Now that the friendship seemed about to cease, she realised it had meant more than she knew. She held her face in her hands, and her cheeks tingled at the memory of the last eager kiss.

She was woman enough to know it was good to be kissed like that by a man who, even if his morals and principles left much to be desired, was still very much a man, and had won a distinction that made most women proud of far less attention than he had shown her.

Still?—

In a different sense she was struggling in a net of circumstances something like Lorraine's. Lorraine wanted to do the right thing, or, at any rate, the sporting thing.

So did Hal.

In a world full of temptations, and backsliding, and much suffering thereby, the sporting thing for the strong woman is to stand to her guns. If Hal dallied with Sir Edwin now, she felt she would be deserting her post. At the judgment-bar of her own heart, which, after all, matters far more than the judgment-bar of public opinion, she would be allowing herself to compromise for the sake of the fleeting, dangerous pleasure.

She stopped short by the window, and stared out into the gloomy, lamplit street. And it crossed her mind to remember the bitter price so many women had paid for that dalliance and compromise, so many now probably gazing out with dull eyes into gloomy streets, hopeless, reckless, and joyless.

Yes; dalliance and compromise were mistakes. The real pluck was the sporting spirit that stood to its guns, even if it cost a big and wearisome effort. She would not dally. She would answer to her own Best, and try to go on her steadfast way.

After all, she had Dudley and Lorraine. It was good to have a brother all to oneself, who was incontestably a dear, in spite of a little priggishness and narrowness. He would be home soon, and then they would have a last chat over the fire together; and that would help to renew her in her determination to cut the dangerous friendship adrift.

She leaned back in the chair a little wearily, and waited for the welcome sound of his key in the latch. She wished he would come quickly, because she did not quite like the way her mind kept reverting to those eager kisses. The memory had the danger of making most other thoughts seem thin and dull; and she wondered how she was going to replace a friendship that had been so full of interest and enjoyment.

If she had dared, she would like to have persuaded herself that he cared for her in the real way; and her cheeks glowed, and her heart thumped a little at the thought of all the real way meant. But her practical side told her only too decidedly that this was not the case.

Perhaps he was not the sort of man who could care in the real way at all. He was too selfish, and grasping, and ambitious by nature. That he was interesting and a delightful companion as well did not help matters. Men were very often all these things together, but the selfish, ambitious, unscrupulous side usually outweighed all the rest in big questions that affected their whole lives.

Then she remembered that many of the girls she knew—quite nice, jolly girls—would have taken the fun that offered, and not bothered about anything beyond the present. Still, that did not affect her own particular case.

One had to try and live up to one's own ideals, not other people's, and in her inmost heart she knew that she thought but poorly of the girls who run foolish risks for the sake of a little extra pleasure and gratification, just as she thought poorly of the man who amused himself, trifling with a girl's affections, to pass a little time.

Then came the welcome sound of Dudley's key, and she sat up and turned an eager face to the door to greet him.

He came in quietly, and returned the greeting with his usual calm, undemonstrative appreciation; only, he did not look at her, nor ask her any questions about her day.

The supper was still waiting for him, and he took a few mouthfuls, in a preoccupied manner, with his face turned away. Hal asked him about the day's outing, wondering not a little at his manner. He seemed anxious, and somewhat ill at ease, and she observed that he did not eat anything to speak of.

At last he got up and came to her side near the fire.

"Aren't you going to sit down?" she asked. "I thought a little fire looked so cosy."

He did not seem to hear her, for instead of replying he coughed nervously, cleared his throat, and said:

"I've something to tell you, Hal—a piece of news."

She waited, watching him with a puzzled, curious air. Then, without any further preamble, he finished abruptly:

"I'm—I'm—engaged to be married."

Hal gave a gasp, and became suddenly taut with amazement and incredulity. "You're—engaged—to—be—married!"

"Yes; you're not very surprised, are you?"

A sudden, awful fear seemed to envelop and clutch at her.

"Who to?" she asked, a little hoarsely?

"To Doris Hayward."

For some reason he seemed unable to look at her. Vaguely he knew he had dealt her a blow, and that it was of a nature he could not soften.

Hal stared hard at the fire, then suddenly started to her feet.

"You can't mean it," she exclaimed, forgetting to be circumspect. "You couldn't possibly think seriously of marrying Doris Hayward?"

Instantly he stiffened.

"I don't know why you speak of it in that way. Certainly I am serious. It is hardly a question I should joke about."

There was a tense silence, then Hal turned to the sofa and picked up her hat as if she were a little dazed. She seemed suddenly to have nothing to say, and she knew herself to be no good at prevarication. To congratulate him seemed an impossibility just yet.

"Of course I know you have never cared for Doris," he said; "but probably you did not know her well enough. I hope you will soon see you have misjudged her."

"I hope so," she said lamely. "Good-night—I—I—hadn't thought about your getting married. I must get used to the idea. I—" she paused in sudden, swift distress. "Good-night; of course I hope you'll be happy, and all that," and she went hurriedly out, and up to her own room.

CHAPTER XXI

When Hal reached her room she sat down on the bed in the dark, and stared at the dim square of the window. She was feeling stunned, and as if her brain would not work properly. It grasped the significance of old, familiar objects as usual, but seemed quite unable to grip and understand the something strange and new which had suddenly come into being. She remembered she had waited for Dudley to come with soothing for a perturbed frame of mind, and instead, he had brought her—*this*.

What could it mean? Surely, surely, not that Doris Hayward was to rob her of her brother.

A wave of swift and sudden loneliness seemed to envelop her. The blackness of the night closed in upon her, and desolation swept across her soul.

"If only it had been Ethel," was the vague, uncertain thought: "any one in the world almost but Doris."

And again,

"Why had Dudley been so incredibly blind to Doris's real nature? Why had he of all men been caught by a pretty face? Was it possible he thought his life would need no other help and comfort but that of a charming exterior in his wife?"

How childlike he seemed again to his young sister's practical, worldly knowledge. Of course he knew almost nothing of women, buried in his musty old architectural lore, and giving most of his brain to the contemplation of ancient ruins and edifices.

He had looked up from his books, and Doris had smiled at him, that diabolically winsome, innocent smile of hers; and something in his heart, not quite smothered and likewise not healthily developed, had warmed into sudden, surprised pleasure, and straightway he thought himself in love. Hal was sure of one thing, that if Doris had not decided it would suit her plans to be Dudley's wife, the idea would not have occured to him.

After all, what did he want with a wife for years to come, going along so contentedly and placidly with his books and his thirst for knowledge, and the peacefulness of their sojourn with Mrs. Carr? No servant troubles, no housekeeping worries, no taxes, no gas and electric-light bills; everything done for them, and for company each other.

Oh, of course, it was all Doris's doing. She wanted to get away from the dingy flat and the poverty, and she had hit upon Dudley as a way out.

Hal got up suddenly with a bursting feeling. Of course she did not even love him, would not even try to change her nature to become more in touch with his, would not trouble in the least what obstacles stood between any real and deep understanding. Perhaps she was not even capable of love, but in any case her affections could not have been given to any one as quiet, and studious, and old-fashioned as Dudley.

She went to the window and threw it open that she might lean out and breathe the open air. Her head burned and ached, and her eyes smarted with a smouldering fire in her brain. She felt more and more how entirely it must have been Doris's doing. Doris had smiled at him, and confided in him, and managed first to convey a pathetic picture of her own loneliness, and then to suggest how happy her life might be with him.

And of course Dudley was all chivalry at heart, and trusting, and tender-hearted; that was one reason why he had always deplored her, Hal's, boyish independence and determination to fend for herself. He did not understand the vigorous, enterprising, working woman.

Immersed in his books and his studies, he had allowed himself to be influenced largely by caricatures, and by the noisy stir of the platform woman. But he understood the Doris type, or thought he did, and placed their engaging dependence before such spirited resolution as her own and Ethel's.

And how to help him? How, now, to thwart the carrying out of Doris' cleverly carried scheme.

Her first thought was Ethel and Basil. She would go to them, and appeal to them to help her.

And then she remembered that "blood is thicker than water." How could they thwart their own sister; and in any case what would Dudley ever see in it but a persecution that would intensify his affection? One hint that Doris was victimised, and she knew Dudley well enough to realise he would only marry her the more quickly, whether he had learned the truth or not.

Opposition of any sort would probably do far more harm than good at present. There was nothing for it but to meet the blow with the best face possible, and hope time might yet bring release.

Then her thoughts went back to Sir Edwin, and quite suddenly and unaccountably she longed to tell him about it. He would be interested for her sake, and he would cheer her up, and make her hopeful in spite of herself.

And yet—

No; to see him again, feeling as she felt now, would only mean to see him in a mood of weakness, that might make her less able to withstand him.

She must rely only on Lorraine and Dick, and try to stand by her previous determination. She would see Lorraine directly she left the office the next day, and in the meantime she would try and hide from Dudley the extent of her dismay.

But in spite of her resolve, when she rested her head on the pillow, the hot tears squeezed through her closed eyelids, and in dumb misery she told herself Dudley was lost to her for ever.

She awoke the next morning with a dull, aching sense of misery that had robbed the sunshine of its warmth, and the day of its brightness; but as she dressed she strengthened herself in a resolve to try and hide her chagrin, and make some amends to Dudley for her reception of the news.

"I suppose you felt pretty disgusted with me last night," she said at the breakfast-table. "I'm sorry, but you took me so violently by surprise."

He had taken his seat, looking grave and displeased, but his face relaxed as he replied:

"I'm afraid I was rather sudden. It seemed the easiest"—he hesitated, then added—"I hope you'll try to get on with Doris."

"Of course." Hal turned away on some slight pretext. "I'd hate giving you up to any one—you know I would—we've—we've—been very happy together here, and—" but her voice broke suddenly.

Dudley looked unhappy, but he steadied his voice and said cheerfully:

"Well, it needn't be very different. If you and Doris will get fond of each other, it will be the same, only better. Of course you will live with us."

"Oh no"; and she tried to smile lightly—"I couldn't—possibly live without Mrs. Carr now. I should never be properly dressed, for one thing, and I should always be forgetting important engagements." She changed the subject quickly, seeing he was about to remonstrate. "Have you seen Ethel and Basil since—since—"

"No; I'm going to see Basil this afternoon, after taking Doris to Wimbledon to see Langfier fly, and I shall stay to dinner. Will you come up this evening?"

"No; I'm going out. Perhaps tomorrow—" she hesitated, as if swallowing a lump in her throat. "You might give my love to Doris, and say I'll come soon." She saw Dudley glance at her inquiringly, and recklessly dashed into another subject, talking at random until she left.

In the afternoon she hurried straight off to Lorraine's flat, arriving a few minutes after Lorraine had come in from a walk in the Park. She was standing by the window, drawing off some long gloves, and even Hal was struck by a sort of newness about her—a bloom and a quiet radiance that was like a renewal of youth.

She was beautifully dressed as ever, but with a far simpler note than usual—something which suggested she wished to look charming, without attracting attention; something which suppressed the actress in favour of the woman.

It was as if, surrounded with success and attention night after night, and for several years, she had wearied of the rôle, and put it aside voluntarily whenever opportunity offered. She had been wont to be very fashionable and striking in her dress and general appearance, but now Hal noticed vaguely a simpler note all through.

Her face and expression seemed to have changed also. A certain hardness and callousness had gone. Her smile was more genuine, and her eyes kinder. In some mysterious way, it was as though Lorraine had won from the past some gleaming of the woman she might have been under happier circumstances, and without certain harsh experiences.

And it was all owing to her feeling for Alymer Hermon and his youthful pride in her.

They met continually now. Her flat was open to him whenever he liked. He came to her when he had anything interesting to relate—when he was depressed and when he was hopeful. With the inconsequent acceptance of youth, he took from her what an older man would have regarded a little shyly, and perhaps feared to take.

She was his pal, his excellent friend, who gave him such sympathy and interest and encouragement as she could find nowhere else. Because he was young, he drank deep and asked no questions.

He did not imagine for a moment that she was in love with him. True, other women were; but then they told him so, and alarmed him with their attentions. Lorraine was more inclined to laugh at him and make fun of him, in a jolly, pally sort of way, which made him feel perfectly at home with her, and successfully banish any questions.

She was more like a man friend, only better, because a man would have wanted an equal share of interest, whereas Lorraine seemed content to be interested in him. She never encouraged him to talk about her triumphs and her other friends. She rather implied they were so public and apparent already she did not want to hear any more of them.

But she was always ready to talk of his hopes and aspirations, and help him to build foundations to his aircastles. And already, under her tuition and help, he had made immense strides. His work and his objects had become real to him, ambition had taken root and begun to push out little upward shoots. He saw himself one of the leading lights at the Bar, and instead of lazily scoffing, he liked the picture. He wanted to get there, and if Lorraine was ready to help him, why should she not? Why bother to ask questions?

Of course she must be fond of him, or she would not do it; but then he was fond of her too—very fond—and why not? The mere suggestion of danger did not occur to him. She was so many years his senior, and so celebrated, it never crossed his mind to suppose she could have any feeling for him beyond the jolly palliness that seemed to have sprung up naturally between them.

So he came and went between the Temple and her flat and his own quarters, and life began to assume a bigness of possibility that drowned all else, and kept him eager and hard working and safe from the hurtful influences and actions that attend idle hours.

And Lorraine, for the present, walked in her fool's paradise and was content. She watched him slowly and surely fill out both physically and mentally into the promise of his splendid manhood.

She saw his youthful beauty solidifying into the beauty of a man, and carefully watered and tended those budding shoots of ambition that were to help him attain his best promise.

For the time being the thwarted mother-love that is in every woman satisfied her with the evidence of his progress, and she lulled any other into quiescence, hugging to herself the knowledge that it was she alone to whom he would owe greatness, if he won it, and that even his own doting mother had not done, and never could do, the half that she was doing to start him on a steadfast way that should lead to fame and usefulness.

She made it her excuse for ignoring the questions which her wider knowledge could not entirely banish. To what other results the friendship might lead she turned a deaf ear. The other results must take care of themselves, was her thought; it was enough for her that she could help to make him great.

She smiled a little at the thought of the women she had won him from. He talked to her now freely and openly, though always with that unassuming modesty which was so attractive. She knew what he had already had to combat. What a life of self-pleasing and gay-living lay open to him if he chose to take it. She knew that, if he chose it, though he might still win a certain amount of fame, it would never be the well-grounded, staunch, reliable success that she could spur him to.

And so she drew a curtain over the dangers her course might hold, and, in a light and airy way, threw over him the glow and the warm attractiveness of her many fascinations and allurements, that she might keep him free from any foolish engagement or low entanglement, to concentrate all his mind and his heart upon his work and her.

How long such an aim was likely to satisfy her, or how natural or unnatural her course, she left with all the other questions, to be faced, if necessary, later on, or to pass with the swift joy into oblivion.

At least it was not the first time a woman, scarcely young, and having her full measure of success, had turned unaccountably to a man very much her junior, for something she apparently sought in vain from men of her own age. It might be strange, but it was not unique; and for the rest, were not the ways of the little god Love like the ways of many events—"stranger than fiction"?

His magnificent physique, his extraordinarily beautiful head, and his no less extraordinary, unassuming modesty, attracted and held her with links that grew stronger and stronger, and her happiest hours now were those in which he made himself delightfully at home in her flat, and added to his charm by talking to her with the old-fashioned, grandfatherly air she had enjoyed from the first.

And so Hal found a younger and softer Lorraine than she had known for a long time, waiting to hear the burden of her tale of woe.

They talked it over in every aspect, Hal sitting in her favourite attitude on a stool at Lorraine's feet; but very little light could be won through the clouds. All the consolation Lorraine could suggest was a possibility that to be engaged and married to a man like Dudley might change Doris altogether for the better; but Hal, beyond feeling brighter for having spoken out her dismay, felt there was little indeed hope of that.

"Have you seen Sir Edwin Crathie again?" Lorraine asked presently, and she was surprised to see a spot of colour instantly flame into Hal's cheeks.

"I've had a long motor ride with him," she said, speaking as if it were a mere detail.

"*Have you?*" was Lorraine's very expressive rejoinder.

"Why do you say it like that?" Hal laughed with seeming lightness. "He just took me for a treat. He's rather sorry for me, being boxed up in an office, as he calls it."

"I see. Well, don't forget he has the reputation for being rather a dangerous man, old girl."

Hal laughed again.

"I'll tell him so, and go armed with a revolver next time." She noticed an inquiring look in Lorraine's eyes, and added: "Don't look so serious, Lorry; he is old enough to be my father. He likes a little amusement, the same as you and Baby Hermon."

She turned away as she spoke, and did not see the swift deepening of the look of inquiry, nor a certain strange expression that flitted across Lorraine's face; and almost immediately the door opened, and Alymer Hermon walked in unannounced.

"Hullo, Hal!" he exclaimed—"it's quite a long time since I ran into you here."

"Hullo, Baby!" she retorted. "Why, I declare, you are beginning to look quite a man."

"If you don't mind I'll pick you up and carry you all the way down the stairs to the street; then you'll see if I'm a man or not."

"Tut; any big creature could do that! Got any briefs yet?"

"I have."

Lorraine looked up instantly with an eager, questioning glance—while Hal asked gaily:

"What is it?... I suppose the original holder is sick, or dead, or something, and you are a stop-gap."

"You are wrong, Miss Sharp-tongue. I hold the brief entirely on my own. It hasn't even anything to do with any one in Waltham's Chambers."

And still Lorraine, with shining eyes, watched his face.

"I suppose," said Hal, "the other side have got a very small man, and they wanted a big one to frighten him?"

"Wrong again. The other side has Pym, and he is quite six feet in height."

"Then perhaps he looks clever, and they believe in contrasts."

"I shall carry you down to the street yet," threateningly; "you are running grave risks."

"So is the poor man trusting his defence to you."

"It happens to be a lady."

Hal clapped in her hands.

"Of course," she cried; "now we are getting at it. The lady chose you because she thought your wig and gown becoming. How many interviews shall you be having with her?"

"I couldn't say, but we had one this afternoon."

"And was she very charming? Did she call you Baby?"

He shrugged his shoulders and turned to Lorraine.

"I only waste my substance trying to cope with any one as obtuse as Hal. Is she going to stay to dinner?"

"I'm afraid so," smilingly.

He took up his stand on the rug, with his back to the fire and looked down at Hal on her footstool.

"It's a pity about the obtuseness," he commented, "because she is really rather nice to look at. She has improved so much lately."

"Oh no, I haven't," tilting her nose in the air. "I am exactly the same; but you have acquired better taste. Is *he* going to stay to dinner, Lorraine?" "I'm afraid so. You will have to call a truce, because I want to hear all about the brief; and I shall hear nothing if you persist in wrangling."

"It isn't my fault," he said. "I always try to be friends."

"Well, as far as that goes, I always *try* to like you," Hal retorted with a laugh.

"You would find it much easier if you did not hurl insults at me. Begin another plan altogether."

"Come along to dinner," put in Lorraine, rising, "and let us hear about this brief."

She led the way to the dining-room, and they had a merry little meal, arranging all about the congratulatory dinner Lorraine proposed to give for Alymer to celebrate the important occasion of his first brief.

Afterwards Hal drove to the theatre with her, and stayed a short time in her room while, as Lorraine phrased it, she put on her war-paint.

Then she went rather sadly home alone, feeling lost and unhappy about Dudley. It crossed her mind once that Lorraine and Alymer Hermon seemed be on very much more familiar terms than previously, but she paid little heed to the thought, merely supposing that it amused Lorraine to help him in his profession.

She sat over the fire and tried to read, but presently the book went down into her lap, and her eyes sought the cheery flicker of the flames. Only there was no answering glow in her usually bright face, rather a sad uneasiness and perplexity, as if circumstances she hardly knew how to cope with were closing in upon her.

She felt she had come to a difficult path in life she would have to face alone; for in her friendship with Sir Edwin Crathie neither Dudley nor Lorraine could help her.

And, gazing into the fire with serious, thoughtful eyes, it was neither Dudley and Doris, nor Lorraine and Alymer who finally held her thoughts, but sir Edwin Crathie himself.

CHAPTER XXII

The first time Sir Edwin rang up the newspaper office after the memorable Sunday it happened that Hal had gone into the country to report an opening ceremony, graced by Royalty, so she was saved the necessity of framing a reply.

One of the usual reporters being ill, the news editor had asked her if she would like to take his place, and she had eagerly accepted the chance. It meant a day in the country, travelling by special train, and the writing of the report did not worry her at all, as she had already served her apprenticeship to journalism, and knew how to seize on the most interesting points and condense them into a small space.

She had a genius for making friends also, and after an excellent champagne lunch, and a cup of tea captured for her by a pleasant-faced man whom she afterwards discovered to be the Earl of Roxley, she motored back to the railway station with a well-known aeronaut, who promised to take her for a "fly" some day. They travelled up to town in the same compartment, and as Hal had to have her article ready for press when she reached the office, it was necessary to write it in the train.

The "flying man" wished to turn his hand to journalism too, and attempted to help her, without much success, though with a good deal of entertainment for himself. He was specially amused at her determination to lay considerable stress on the fact that one of the horses in the royal carriage fell down between the station and the park.

"What's the good of putting that in?" he argued; "it is of no importance."

"Why, it's almost the most important thing of all," she declared. "You evidently don't know much about journalism. The Public will not be half as interested in the King's speech as in the information that one of the horses fell down, and that the King then put his hands on the Queen's, and told her not to be frightened."

"But he didn't; and the horse only slipped."

"But you're too dense!" she cried, "and, anyhow, you can't be certain that he didn't. It's what he ought to have done, and the British Public will be awfully pleased to know that he did. They'll be frightfully interested in the horse falling down, too. I suppose you would leave it out, and give dates of the building of the edifice, and the different styles of architecture, and the names of illustrious people connected with it. As if any one wanted to know that! The horse will make far better reading, though I daresay I ought to work in a few costs of things. The B.P. loves to know what a thing costs."

"Well, why not value the horse, as you think so much of it? or say that it snapped a trace in half which cost two guineas, and was bought in Bond Street?"

They both laughed, and then Hal said seriously:

"I think I'll make it kick over the centre pole, only then perhaps some of the other reporters will catch it for not having seen the kick also. I once wrote an account of a garden party, and left out that the horses of the Prime Minister's carriage shied and swerved, and one wheel caught against the gate-post. As a matter of fact, it did not do much more than graze it, but some journalist wrote a thrilling account of how the carriage nearly turned over; and I've never forgotten the chief's face when he asked me why I hadn't mentioned the accident to the Prime Minister's carriage. I said there wasn't an accident, and he snapped: 'Well you'd better have turned them all in a heap in the road than left it out altogether!'

"I've never made the same mistake since," she finished, "and now, if the chief sees my paragraphs, he has to ring some one up occasionally, and make sure I haven't gone out of bounds altogether."

"Well, if you're quite determined to lie... I mean romance... why not do it thoroughly? Let the King leap out of the carriage, with the Queen in his arms, and the royal coachman fall backwards off the box—and—and—both the horses burst out laughing?"

"I'd get the sack for that," Hal spluttered, busily plying her pencil, "and then I'd break my heart, because I'm in love with the chief."

"Oh"—with a low laugh, "and is it quite hopeless?"

"Quite. The most hopeless *grande passion* that ever was. He's been married twice already, and the second is still very much alive. Did the Queen wear a black hat, or a dark purple one?"

"Dark purple, of course, like her dress. Why, I could write the thing better than you."

"I'm sure you could, if you might have half the newspaper. I don't know where you'd be in thirty-six lines!"

"By Jove! Have you got to squeeze it all into thirty-six lines?"

"Less, if possible. There's been a row in Berlin, and we have to allow for thrilling developments, which may crowd out lots of other paragraphs."

"And supposing you want it a few lines longer?"

"Then the compiler will add a bit on about the weather, or throw in another dress description, or something. I'm putting you in now," scribbling on; "but I don't know your name?"

"And I'm not going to tell it to you for your precious paragraph, so you'll have to cross that bit out again."

"Not at all," airily: "a well-known aeronaut, who has recently beaten the distance-record, and is looking remarkably well in spite of his advanced years, was among the distinguished guests!"

He had to cry "pax" then.

"I give you up," he said; "you're too much for me! But I'll take you for a fly the first opportunity I get. Will you come?"

"Will I come!..." in eager tones. "Oh, won't I?"

And he promised to arrange it.

When they reached Euston, Hal had to dash for the first taxi, and tear to the office with her report, and it was not until she was leaving that the call boy told her a gentleman had asked for her on the telephone in the afternoon.

"Did he give any name?" she asked.

"Yes, Mr. Crathie."

Hal suppressed a smile. "I suppose you told him I was out."

"Yes, miss. He wanted to know when you would be back, and I asked Mr. Watson, and he told me to say 'Not before evening.'"

Hal climbed to the top of a bus, and journeyed homewards with a thoughtful air. Of course he would ring her up again the next day, and then what was she to say?

In the meantime, looming big in her immediate horizon was the visit to be paid to Holloway that evening. She was going up without Dudley, having expressed a wish to do so, with which he had willingly complied. She felt it would be easier not to appear forced without him, and would be fairer on Doris also. Yet she dreaded the visit very much, and longed that it was over.

Ethel opened the door to her, as she happened to be in the little kitchen close beside it, and Hal thought she looked very ill as she grasped her hand with warm friendliness, saying:

"How nice of you to come and see Doris so soon."

"What are you doing in the kitchen?" said Hal. "I want to come and help."

"I'm only making a salad, and shall not be long. You must go to the parlour"; and she laughed at the quaint, old-fashioned word.

"No, I'm coming to help," and Hal walked past her, through the open door. "How's Basil? Dudley spoke as if he was not quite so well just now."

"I'm afraid he isn't," with sudden, hardly veiled anxiety; "but it may only be the foggy weather."

To any one else Ethel would probably have asserted that he was well as usual, and changed the subject; but she liked Hal specially, and showed it by being quite honest with her. She also knew perfectly well that Dudley's engagement must have been a great shock to his only sister, not solely because she had nothing whatever in common with Doris, but because she herself must love him; and her heart felt very tender and friendly over her.

Although Hal had come to see Doris, she did not refrain from following her inclination, and seating herself on the kitchen table to chat to Ethel while she made the salad. Doris would keep, was her rapid mental conclusion, and they two might not get another chance of a few words alone.

Chatting thus, it was interesting to note the similarity that existed between these wielders of the pen, each daily immersed in a City office.

Each had the same clear, frank eyes, the same independent poise of head, the same air of capable energy and self-dependence. Each, too, had the same rather colourless skin, from lack of fresh air, though whereas Ethel looked tired and worn, Hal seemed strong and fresh and wore no air of delicacy.

Then Doris came, with her pink-and-white daintiness, and spoke to them both with a little triumphant air of condescension; for was not she engaged to be married, whereas clever, working women usually became "old maids"?

Hal tried not to seem too offhand, but it was quite impossible for her to gush, and she could not pretend a sudden affection just because of the engagement. So she just said something about Dudley being very happy, and hoped they would have good luck, and then went to the sitting-room to talk to Basil, entertaining him immensely with her account of the day's ceremony, and her haphazard friendship with the "flying man", who was going to take her in his aeroplane.

"Who was he?" Basil asked. "Has he won any prizes?"

"I don't know. He did not tell me. I did not discover his name either, but he was some relation of the 'Lord-of-the-Manor' person who received the King."

"You don't know his name?" asked Doris in a shocked voice. "Weren't you introduced?"

"Never a bit of it," laughed Hal. "I was left behind when the last fly had gone to the station, and he heard me asking anxiously how soon one would get back again, and immediately offered me a seat in the motor he was going in. Another man was with him, a much be-medalled officer, who was somewhat heavy in hand to talk to, and at the station we gave him the slip."

"How can he take you for a fly if you don't know who he is?"

"Well, I dare say he won't; quite likely he didn't mean it; but if he did, he can easily find me at the office. He knew my name, and what paper I was there for. They both knew, which probably accounts for the gentleman with the medals being somewhat ponderous—soldiers are usually snobbish—and he may not have liked having to ride to the station with a newspaper woman."

"But if the other man was the Lord of the Manor's brother?"

"Oh, that wouldn't make any difference. He might very well be less self-important than anything in a bit of scarlet and medals if he had been the Lord of the Manor himself. Why, the Earl of Roxley got tea for me, and was most attentive."

Doris's eyes opened wider. She had always secretly entertained rather a superior attitude towards Hal and her sister, and was glad she was not an office clerk. The big, breezy, working world, where the individual is taken on his or her merits apart from birth, or standing, or occupation, was quite unknown to her; and that Hal's original, attractive personality might open doors for ever shut to her mediocre, pretty young-ladyhood, would never enter her mind.

"I don't think I should care to talk to any one without being introduced," she remarked a little affectedly, to which Hal shrugged her shoulders and commented:

"It's just as well you haven't to knock about in the world, then. Any one with an ounce of common sense and perspicacity knows when it is safe, and when it is sheer folly."

Basil watched her with an amused air.

"I'm sure you do," he said.

"Yes." She smiled infectiously. "I've only once been spoken to unpleasantly in London, after knocking about for seven years, and then I offered the man a sixpence. I said: 'I'm sorry I haven't any more, and I can't spare that, but if you are hungry!...' He looked as if he would like to slay me, and vanished."

Doris still looked slightly disapproving, and when at last Hal rose to go, she half-unconsciously asked Ethel with her eyes to accompany her to get her hat, instead of her prospective sister-in-law. And when they were alone, Ethel looked into Hal's expressive face, and guessing something of what she carefully hid, said sympathetically:

"You and Dudley have always been so much to each other; I am afraid you must feel it a little having to share him already with another."

Suddenly and inexplicably Hal's eyes filled with tears, and she turned away quite unable to answer.

Ethel pretended not to notice, but her heart bled for her, knowing how much worse it was than just the fact of the engagement.

"I'm so wrapped up in Basil," she went on, "that if it had happened to me I should have felt quite heartbroken, however much I told myself I wanted his happiness."

Hal dabbed her eyes a little viciously.

"Of course I want him to be happy," she managed to say; "but it is nice of you to understand."

"There's one thing," Ethel continued, "you will become a sort of relation, and you've no idea how pleased Basil and I will be about that."

"Will you?" Hal smiled through her tears, "I rather wonder at it."

"Of course we shall. Basil and I think you are one of the finest characters we have ever known. You've no idea how proud we are when you come to see us," which proved Ethel's understanding heart, for a little generous praise is a kind healer to a sore spirit.

Hal looked into her eyes, with a pleased light in her own.

"You are too generous, but it's nice to be thought well of by any one like you and Basil. I shall remember it when I am silly enough to be downhearted, and it will cheer me up."

She had to hurry away then to catch a train, and as she went her mind was full of the thought:

"Why, oh why, had Dudley, in his blindness, wooed the younger sister?"

"Well?" he said, as she entered their sitting-room, where he was reading over the fire. "How did you get on?"

"Oh, splendidly"—trying to throw a little enthusiasm into her voice. "Doris looked amazingly pretty."

She show a soft light in his eyes, and because it rather maddened her, she hastened to add: "But I see a great change in Basil."

"Yes?... I wondered if you would. I was afraid he did not seem so well."

"Dudley"—with sudden seriousness—"when Basil dies, it will just about break Ethel up. She idolises him."

"I know; but she can hardly wish him to live on if he continues to grow worse."

"I suppose not; but it's rather awful to think of what it will mean to her to lose him. And she's so sympathetic and tender-hearted." Hal stood a moment looking gravely at the fire—"you know, I think she's the most splendid person I've ever known."

"Splendid!..." a trifle testily. "Why? Splendid seems an odd word to use."

"It's the one that suits Ethel Hayward best of all. Anything else would be too commonplace. When I think what her life is—the endless struggle to make both ends meet—work morning, noon, and night—and on the top of it all the brother she adores a helpless, suffering invalid, it quite overawes me. If she were bitter and complaining it would be different, but she is nearly always cheerful and hopeful and ready to think of some one else's troubles. And yet she isn't goody-goody—nor what one describes as 'worthy'; she's just human through and through."

"She sometimes seems to me a little severe," he said.

"Severe!... Oh, Dudley, she is the kindest soul alive."

"Perhaps she was tired; but it seemed to me, considering Doris's youth, she expected rather a lot of her."

"Ah!..."

Hal turned away, and picked up an evening paper. The exclamation might have meant anything, yet Dudley half knew it meant that in some way Hal believed Doris had wilfully misrepresented her sister, and, naturally resenting the inference, he returned to his book and said no more.

Hal lingered a little longer, passed one or two remarks on the evening news, told him of her day in the country, and then went to bed.

Yet, in spite of her soreness towards Doris, something in her evening with Ethel had unaccountably cheered and refreshed her—the kindly praise, the warm-hearted affection, the sight of the strong, womanly face, unembittered by its heavy sorrow.

Hal stood at her window, and glanced out over the City, and felt renewed in her determination to withstand Sir Edwin Crathie's advances. She knew that he was treating her with a lack of respect he would not have dared to show a woman in his own circle.

He was treating her as a City typist; and however much she wished to prolong it, she knew she owed it to herself to cut it adrift.

And the next day, when the anticipated telephone call came, her resolution was firm and unshaken.

"Tell the gentleman I am engaged," she told the call boy.

He came back again a moment later to know what time she would be disengaged, and she gave the message: "It is quite impossible to say. I have some most important work on hand."

The small boy grinned in a way that made Hal long to box his ears, but she returned to her work, and pretended not to see.

At the other end of the wire the speaker sat back in his chair and muttered an oath; then for some moments he stared gloomily at his desk.

"Damn it! I like her pluck," ran his thoughts; "but I don't mean to be put off like that. I've got to see her again somehow, if it's only to prove I'm not the cad she thinks me."

CHAPTER XXIII

The following afternoon when Hal left the office about half-past four she saw a motor she recognised a little way down the street, and was almost immediately accosted by Sir Edwin himself.

"I knew you left at this time," he said frankly, "so I came to meet you."

Hal looked a little taken aback.

"I wonder why you did that," was all she found to say.

"Well, it was the only way, since you won't come to the telephone, and I am afraid to call on you in Bloomsbury. I want to talk to you. Come along and have some tea."

Hal hesitated, looking doubtfully at the motor, but he urged her on.

"Come; surely you're not afraid to have a cup of tea with me. We'll go to the Carlton—or the Ritz if you prefer it—and take a conspicuous table."

"In my office garments!" with a low laugh. "I don't want to be taken for your housekeeper."

"My housekeeper is a deuce of a swell," laughing in his turn. "She certainly wouldn't be seen in a last year's frock; but you're one of the lucky people who manage to look smart, even in office clothes, as you call them—so come along."

Hal got into the motor.

"Which is it to be? Ritz or Carlton?"

"Oh, Carlton—and not the centre table."

"How do you manage it?" he said, as they glided off, looking at her with critical, admiring eyes.

"Manage what? I wish you wouldn't look at me like a doctor studying my health. I shall put my tongue out in a minute."

"Don't do that. A colleague or an opponent would be sure to be looking, and I don't know which would be worse. Manage to look smart in anything, of course I mean."

"Oh, it's Lorraine Vivian and her maid; they loathe to see me dowdy."

"With a little help from the Almighty, who gave you a haughty little nose and a short upper lip," he told her laughingly. "You're been very angry with me, I'm afraid, and no doubt I deserved it, but I'm going to make you be friends again and forgive me."

"You won't find it easy."

"I dare say not; but I'm going to try all the same. Shall I begin with a humble apology?"

"You couldn't be humble. I shouldn't believe in it."

"I believe I could with you—which means a great deal. Tell me, were you fully determined not to speak to me on the telephone, and not to see me again?"

"Most certainly I was."

"What nonsense! And did you really suppose I should submit without making an effort to see you, and persuade you to be friends again?"

Hal tilted her nose up a little, and glanced away as she replied a trifle scathingly:

"I supposed, having found I was not the sort of girl you imagined, and not one you could take liberties with, that possibly our friendship would cease to interest you."

He coloured slightly.

"You hit hard, but I suppose I have deserved it. I shall now have to prove to you that I've turned over a new leaf, and deserve it no longer."

They stopped before the Carlton as he spoke, and he led the way into the lounge, and to a side table.

"I'm sure you'll trust me this far," he said; "people stare so when one is in the middle of the room."

Hal sat down and drew off her gloves, feeling, in spite of herself, unmistakably happy. It was good to be there, instead of trudging home to Bloomsbury; and it was specially good to be chatting to him again.

A dear friend may be always a dear friend, and yet not just the one one wants at the moment. When things are difficult, and irritating, and disappointing, the pleasantest companion is apt to be one with so much individual regard for us at the time that we can hold forth upon our troubles without any fear of boring our listener.

When Hal had poured her tale of woe into Lorraine's ear, she had known that Lorraine was genuinely interested and sorry—and yet, also, that something else occupied her mind at the same time. Sitting now, opposite to Sir Edwin Crathie, it was perfectly apparent for the time being that his mind was entirely at her service.

This was further shown by the fact that he realised something was worrying her before she told him.

"What's the matter?" he asked abruptly; "you look as if something very boring had happened."

"It has."

Hal kept her eyes lowered a moment, with a thoughtful air, and the corners of the fascinating mouth drooped a little.

"What has happened?... Tell me what is bothering you."

He spoke peremptorily, yet with an evident concern for her that made the peremptory tone dangerously alluring. Hal remained silent, though she felt her pulses quicken, and he added:

"Come, we are going to be friends again; aren't we? I've told you I'm very sorry; I can't do more. You will really have to forgive me now."

She looked into his face, and something in his eyes told her he was quite genuine for the time. Of course it might be rash, and unwise, and various other things, but it had been a difficult, trying week, and his sympathy was passing good now. Sir Edwin met her gaze for a moment, and then lowered his.

He thought it was chiefly when her eyes laughed that he wanted to kiss her, but when they had that serious, rather appealing expression, he began to feel they were more disturbing still. Mastering his unmanageable senses with an effort, he looked up again, and said:

"Well, what is it? Of course you must tell me."

"Brother Dudley is going to be married," said Hal with her usual directness.

"When?" And Sir Edwin gave a low exclamation of surprise. "Isn't it rather sudden?"

"Very," in dry tones.

"And I suppose you don't want to love your prospective sister-in-law all in a hurry."

"I don't want to love her at all."

"Then I don't suppose you will," with a little laugh. "Presumably you know her."

"I have known her a long time. If I had been asked, she is the last girl I could have believed Dudley would care for. I don't believe he does care for her in the real sense. She is very pretty, and she wanted to marry him, and she just played on his feelings."

"What do you call 'in the real sense'?" he asked pointedly.

A pink spot burned in Hal's cheeks; she felt the question a little beside the mark, and did not want to answer it.

"She has rather a dull home, and is very poor, and I think she thought on the whole life would be improved if she were Dudley's wife."

"And that is not the real sense?" insistently.

"It certainly is not love."

"Well, you haven't yet told me what is?"

"I don't know much about it, and"—hastily—"I don't want to. When it's real it hurts, and when it isn't real it's just feebleness."

"Still, you must know some day."

He liked to see the spot of colour spreading in her cheeks, and the frank eyes growing a little defiant as he pressed her against her will.

"It doesn't follow that I must. Perhaps I shall just be feeble, and marry for a home and luxuries."

"Never," with conviction. "You'll—Hal, you'll get it badly when once you're caught."

"I never said you might call me 'Hal'."

"Didn't you? Well, I apologise. May I?"

She could not help laughing.

"You evidently mean to; and I suppose you usually have your own way."

"Very often. That's sensible of you. Of course you are sometimes annoying sensible and practical. I don't know that I ever liked any one quite so level-headed before. It never appealed to me. Yet, somehow, I think you could lose your head. You've got it in you to do so. I wouldn't give tuppence for a woman who hadn't."

Hal was silent, and, as usual, he pressed his point.

"Do you think you could lose your head?"

"I don't think I shall," was the evasive answer.

"I wonder," he said.

She felt him looking hard into her face, and moved restlessly beneath a scrutiny that quickened her pulses and warmed her blood in a way that was altogether new. Then suddenly she looked up.

"Don't you think we are rather talking drivel? Let's get back to the original subject. I don't want to lose my head — it's rather a nice one — sound and reliable and all that."

He sat back in his chair with a laugh.

"You're very clever," he told her admiringly. "I always seem to be out-flanked in the end. Very well then, Brother Dudley has got engaged foolishly, and Hal has been quietly fretting, instead of being a sensible little woman, and telling her friend all about it straight away. What are you going to do now?"

"I can't do anything. He won't get married for a few months anyway."

"And when he does?"

"Then I shall stay where I am, and make the best of it, I suppose... but... but" — her voice broke a little — "I'm a positive fool about Dudley. I can't bear to lose him."

"Poor little woman. Well, I'll be good to you if you'll let me. I dare say I can brighten things up a little. Every cloud has a silver lining, you know."

"I don't know where Dudley's will be," with a wintry smile. "It wouldn't be so hard if I thought there was any chance of his being happy. But there isn't. He doesn't in the least know her real character."

They sat on until seven o'clock, and then Hal rose to go, feeling happier than she had done ever since they last met.

"Well, am I forgiven?" he asked, as she buttoned her gloves.

"You are, for the present," with an arch glance; "but I reserve the right to retract at a moment's notice."

"And in the meantime you will prove it by coming out to lunch on Sunday? We might go to the Zoo afterwards, and make friends with some of the animals."

At the first suggestion of lunch Hal had been ready to shy away, but the idea of the Zoo on Sunday afternoon was too much for her, and she said with unmistakable longing:

"I should simply love the Zoo." Then, after a pause: "Couldn't I meet you there about three?"

"But why wait until three? It is not very friendly of you to refuse to lunch with me."

"I usually go to Lorraine" —somewhat lamely.

"Why not bring Miss Vivian with you?"

"Oh, could I?" eagerly; "that would be splendid—if she is disengaged."

A curious little half smile crossed his eyes at her eagerness; but he only said:

"Certainly, and if she cares to bring a friend, to make the party an even number, I shall be only too pleased. Shall we say the Piccadilly, for a change, at 1.30?"

Hal thanked him, and as she sped homewards in a taxi he had procured for her, she viewed the prospect with real delight.

Dudley, of course, would be spending his Sunday with Doris, and she and Lorraine, supposing the latter were disengaged, might have found the afternoon a little long alone. The evening was the occasion of the dinner-party to commemorate Alymer Hermon's first brief, so it was very likely Lorraine would be free at midday.

She thought it was nice of Sir Edwin to invite her friend as well, and as she reviewed the afternoon meeting, her heart was foolishly glad over his apology, and insistent determination to be friends. It was evident, she believed, that if she adhered to her resolute resistance of familiarity, she would be able to keep him at a discreet distance, and they might enjoy a really delightful friendship.

Her eyes were smiling and glad at the little upper window that night. She had hated cutting off their friendship. The days had been dull and dragging without even a telephone chat with him; and though she still told herself it was chiefly because of the shock of Dudley's engagement, she knew it was a little for his sake also.

And she thought further, if they might now include Lorraine in some of their meetings, it would be an added safeguard, and very entertaining as well. She meant to telephone to her the first thing in the morning to fix up their Sunday engagement.

Inquiries on the telephone, however, the next morning, elicited the information that Lorraine had already arranged to go out to lunch; and thus Hal found herself unexpectedly thrown on her own resources. A little note from Ethel asking her to accompany Dudley if she had nothing better to do, placed her in a further awkward position.

She did not want to go to Holloway, to swell the number of mouths to be fed out of Ethel's slender housekeeping purse, and add one more to be cooked for, etc., on Ethel's one free day. Finally, because it was the simplest, as well as the pleasantest thing to do, she telephoned Sir Edwin, and told him Lorraine could not accompany her on Sunday, but she would be there herself, and afterwards go to the Zoo.

And at the other end of the wire Sir Edwin smiled, an enigmatical smile that was unmistakably pleased, as he put back the receiver, and glanced towards the cosy fire in his grate.

"I wonder," he said to himself meditatively, "if one could make her care, whether she could care enough to lose her head."

CHAPTER XXIV

It was rather a curious circumstance, that on the occasion of Lorraine's dinner-party, Alymer Hermon was the first to notice an indefinable change in Hal. To the others she was only gayer than usual, more sparkling, better-looking.

From the Zoological Gardens Sir Edwin had taken her home in a taxi, and after being a delightful companion all the afternoon, had said good-bye in just the friendly, pally spirit that Hal wished, without exhibiting any alarming symptoms whatever to disturb her peace of mind. He had indeed been at his very best; far nicer than ever before; and together they had thoroughly enjoyed their intercourse, through iron bars, with the animals they both loved.

Moreover, his knowledge on most subjects did not exclude zoology, and he was able to tell her numberless little details of the ways and habits of beasts that Hal rejoiced to hear, because she loved all four-footed things.

And then there had been the pleasant consciousness of a new winter costume, that was not only very up to date, but remarkably becoming; and Hal was true woman enough to enjoy the knowledge that she looked her best. Neither was it in any degree a mediocre "best"; and even Sir Edwin was a little surprised to find himself with a companion who attracted nearly as many admiring glances as various lady friends who were recognised beauties.

Her slim, graceful figure was singularly perfect, and, as he observed with fresh pleasure each time they met, she walked with a natural elegance and grace that were a delight to the eye. And happiness gave a faint pink flush to her cheeks and a light to her eyes, that somehow seemed to radiate gaiety; and her intense power of enjoyment communicated itself to others in a way that was wholly delightful.

So they spent a gay afternoon, which cemented the former acquaintanceship into a firmer bond of friendship, and because of it he vowed within himself he would play fair with her, and make no more advances he was not prepared to follow up in an honourable spirit.

For Hal, it was enough that the past mistake seemed genuinely regretted and wiped out, and that all his manner to her now held deference and respect. And she was intensely glad—almost alarmingly glad, if she had stopped to consider; only that would have cast a shadow on the sunshine; and she preferred to take the sunshine while it offered, and leave the future to take care of itself.

And in the meantime there was Lorraine's dinner-party, instead of a lonely evening, and once more she dressed herself with care and skill; and later stood up straight and slim in Lorraine's pretty drawing-room, radiating happiness, and surprising even old friends with her good looks.

Alymer Hermon remarked it first. He was standing beside her on the hearth, and he looked down from his great height with laughing, quizzical eyes and said:

"You're looking astonishingly pretty tonight. Have you been consulting a beauty specialist?"

Dick Bruce and Quin laughed delightedly.

"Why, of course!" cried Dick, digging his hands deep into his pockets, and giving himself a little gleeful shake, "I've been puzzling my head to grasp what it was. I'd forgotten all about the beauty specialists. It must have cost an awful lot, Hal."

"It did," she told them; "but you've no idea how clever they are. They can renovate the most hopeless faces. I'm sure you'd all find it worth while running to the expense."

"Now, come Hal," objected Quin laughingly. "We can't have the ornament of our flat insulted like that. The rising barrister needs no beauty specialist, you must admit."

Hal looked up at the giant with twitching lips.

"I was going to suggest a brain specialist for him. It won't be much use getting lots of briefs because he looks nice in his wig and gown if he hasn't the brains to win his cases."

Hermon caught her by the shoulders to shake her, and at that moment Lord Denton quietly entered the room.

Lorraine had met him in the hall, while hastening across for something she had forgotten, and told him to go in, so that he entered unannounced, and saw the group before they knew of his presence.

Especially he seemed to see the two on the hearthrug. Hal, with her shining eyes, rising coulour, and laughing lips, and Hermon with a sort of answering glow in his face, boyishly gripping her shoulders as if to shake her. He stood and looked at them a moment without speaking, then Hal espied him, and thinking he had that instant entered, exclaimed:

"Help!... Help!... Lord Denton, I am caught in the clutches of Leviathan."

He came forward smillingly.

"Leviathan does not look as if he meant to eat you; and even if he did, I don't believe my courage would run to closing with six-foot-five-and-a-half."

"Awful, isn't it?" she said, releasing herself and giving him her hand. "He is like those lanky pieces of corn which are all stalk and no head. Have you seen him before?"

"Once," offering his hand to Hermon. "Delighted to see you again. I hear you've made a hit already. My cousin tells me his friend is charmed with your way of grappling with her case."

"Did you take her by the shoulders?" asked Hal wickedly, rubbing her own.

"No," Lord Denton told her. "He was very grave indeed. You must give him his due, Miss Pritchard. You've seen him grave yourself, haven't you now?"

"Yes; and he looked like a boiled owl. On the whole, I prefer him imbecile."

Alymer turned on her threateningly, but she slipped behind the other two, saying:

"Have you met these also, Lord Denton. Mr. St. Quintin, of Shoreditch, and my cousin, Dick Bruce, poet, novelist, and mother's help."

Denton shook hands with them genially, and then Lorraine came back, and they all followed her to the dining-room.

The repast was a very gay one. Every one was in the best of spirits, and, which is more important still, all were in attune, and there was no dissentient note. Hal was perhaps the gayest, and Lord Denton found himself watching her almost if he were seeing her for the first time. She seemed to him to have developed amazingly in the few months since he last met her, but he supposed girls of her age often developed quickly.

Yet even then it seemed a little strange that the merry, rather crude young typist, as he had regarded her before, should so easily appear a sparkling, distinguished guest. He could not help a little mental comparision with Lorraine, not in any way to the latter's detriment, but with a vague thought at the back of his mind concerning her and Hermon.

Lorraine would always be beautiful: her whole face and form were modelled on lines that would stand the ravages of many years; and for him she would ever be one of the dearest of women; but could she match Hal's young, vigorous, independence, that was very likely to prove more attractive than a generously given devotion?

Men, like women, are drawn to an indifference that piques them; and he, man of the world that he was, foresaw a strong irresistible attraction about Hal's spirited independence.

But, on the other hand, Lorraine was intensely sympathetic and understanding, as well as beautiful; and it seemed strange indeed if any man she chose to enslave could resist her.

He watched Hermon bend his fair head down to her dark one, with an affectionate, protective air, that was very becoming to him; and observed that with Hal it was all sparring, and told himself Lorraine had nothing to fear.

They toasted Hermon on his brief, and on the laurel wreath Dick announced he already perceived sprouting on his manly brow. Hal said it was only a daisy chain, or the halo of a cherubim; and the laurels were rightly sprouting on Dick's brow as a novelist.

Hermon returned thanks in a witty, clever little speech, during which Lorraine seemed scarcely able to take her eyes from his face, and Lord Denton recognised more fully the extraordinary attraction such a man must wield, whether by intention or quite unconsciously.

He pictured him towering a head and shoulders above nearly every one around at the law courts, with his clear-cut, fine face, looking yet more striking in the severe setting of a wig and gown; and he knew that Lorraine had made no mistake when she said he only wanted impetus and a chance to make a name for himself. If he could rap out a dainty little speech like this at a moment's notice, wearing just that air of unpretentious, boyish humour, his path ought undoubtedly to be a path of roses, petted by women, admired and appreciated by men.

"In conclusion," he was saying, "may I suggest a toast to Miss Pritchard? I am sure you will all join me in offering her our warmest congratulations upon her sudden and unlooked-for promotion, from a somewhat nondescript young person to a brilliant and beautiful society belle."

"Speech! speech!" cried Dick and Quin to her gleefully, noisely rattling their glasses, and Hal got to her feet.

"Ladies and gentlemen and Baby Alymer Hermon," she began. "You must allow me to acknowledge your kind toast by congratulating you all, in return, upon the sudden and swift development of you powers of vision and perspicacity: equalled only, I may say, by your extraordinary dullness in not having observed long ago those traits for which you are pleased, at this late hour, to offer me your congratulations. Before I sit down I should like to suggest we all drink the healths of the celebrated actress who is our hostess, of a bishop in the making—" signifying Quin; "a great novelist in the brewing, and a gentleman justly celebrated for the eloquence and ease with which he does nothing at all"—and she bowed to Lord Denton.

"Capital!" he exclaimed. "I am evidently dining in very distinguished company tonight"; a little later, turning to Dick, he added: "How soon, may I ask, will this great novel be procurable by the general public?"

Before Dick could reply, Hal intercepted gaily:

"Well, I think the carrots and turnips have fallen out as to which takes precedence at a dinner-party: isn't that so, Dick? And until the difficult question is settled, progress halts."

"Something of the kind," agreed Dick promptly; "and there is also discord among the vegetable marrows and pumpkins on a similar question; but when the Baby Brigade has settled the views of the Trade Unions, and reversed the Osborne Judgment, we shall be able to proceed smoothly."

"It sounds a very extraordinary type of novel," said Lorraine.

"It is. I wanted, if possible, to write something even more imbecile than has ever yet been written. I have not the patience for great length; nor the wit for brilliant satire; nor the imagination for the popular, spicy, impossible, ill-flavoured romance; so I have chosen the other line, adopted by the great majority, and aim at purposeless, pointless imbecility."

"And is Hal the model for your heroine?" asked Hermon.

When Hal's indignation and epithets had subsided, Quin remarked that he supposed the book fairly bristled with mothers, and with paragraphs of good advice to them.

"Well, yes," Dick admitted. "There are certainly a good many mothers—far more mothers than wives, in fact."

"Oh, naughty!" put in Lord Denton.

"Not at all. It has to do with a theory. It is to bring out the common sense of vegetables compared to humans. Humans condemn millions of women, specially born for motherhood, to purposeless, joyless spinsterhood, all on account of a prejudice. No green, brainless, commonplace vegetable would be guilty of such unutterable folly as that."

"Don't be too sweeping," quoth Quin. "In the East End women are still mothers from choice; and given decent, healthy conditions, they would proudly raise an army to protect their country from her threatening foes. It is not their fault that 50 per cent of their offspring are sickly, anaemic little weeds."

"It sounds as if your book has a serious side in spite of its imbecility?" suggested Lorraine.

"Imbecility and madness are usually full of seriousness," Dick told her—"far more so than commonplace rationalism."

"And do you want to revolutionise society?"

"Oh dear no; what an alarming idea!"

"Then what do you want?"—they asked him.

"I want to see all the superfluous unemployed spinsters busy, happy mothers, patriotically contributing to raise a splendid fighting-force, for one thing, which will certainly be regarded as an utterly imbecile idea by a magnificently rational world."

"And have you any theory about it?" asked Lord Denton.

"Nothing but the worn-out, commonplace, absurdly natural theories of the vegetable and animal kingdoms. My only chance is that, being so ancient, and so absurdly natural, the modern world may mistake them for something entirely new, and seize upon them with the fasionable avidity for novelties."

"Or they may lock you up," suggested Quin.

"In any case I'm afraid you'll be too late," Hal commented, with a half grave, half sarcastic air; "for before your theories can make any headway, England is likely to have given all her life-blood to systems, and restrictions, and cut-and-dried conventions, utterly regardless of her need for a strong protecting force to maintain her existence at all. Taken in the aggregate, she never has bothered much about the primary necessity for the best possible conditions for the mothers of the future."

"What a learned sentence, Hal," put in Lorraine, looking amused. "Quite worthy of a militant suffragette."

"The announced suffragettes are not the only ones who care for England's future," she said. "I suppose I care a good deal because I'm in the newspaper world, and I know something of what she has to contend against in the way of petty party spirit and the self-aggrandising of some of her so-called leaders, who haven't an ounce of true patriotism, and only want to shout something outrageous in a very loud voice, just to attract public attention."

"I think Bruce is right up to a certain point," remarked Lord Denton. "We can hardly contemplate the reinstitution of polygamy, but it certainly ought to be the business of the State to see that every child born into the country is given the best possible conditions in which to become a good citizen and, if necessary, a good soldier."

"Isn't there a Poor Law for that express purpose?" asked Lorraine.

"Don't speak of it," commented Quin sadly. "Our Poor Law, like so many excellent institutions, is mostly run on a wrong basis. Huge sums of money are expended in procuring homes for homeless children, and the last thing that seems to be considered is the suitability of the home. Applications are accepted in a perfunctory, business-like way by guardians and others— and perhaps an inspector takes a casual glance round; but the moral aspect of the whole matter, as to character and habits, is mostly left to chance. We, who are on the spot, often have to rescue children from the homes the State has provided for them."

"It is more supervision, then, that you want?" asked Lord Denton.

"It is a different sort of supervision altogether. It ought to be woman's work, not man's—women who are paid and encouraged and helped."

"But that might be defying some of the precious conventions," put in Hal with a touch of scorn—"making women too important, don't you know; and encouraging them to be something more than household ornaments. We can't have that, even for the sake of the future. It would be too alarming. No; England will continue in her cast-iron rut of prejudice, until most of her soul-power is dried up, and only the husk of a great nation is left, to follow in the way of other husks."

"Then I will go to the new, young, strong nation, and watch her splendid rise," quoth Dick.

"Traitor!" they threw at him, but he was quite imperturbed. "Strength and vigour are better than old traditions and an enfeebled race; and somebody, somewhere on the globe, had got to listen to what I am bound to teach."

"You dear old Juggins," said Hal, "when England has passed her zenith, and gone under to the new, strong race, you will be found sitting meditating among cabbages and green peas, like Omar Khayyám in his rose garden. The rest of us will have died in the fighting-line—except Baby, and they will put him under a glass case, and preserve him as one of the few fine specimens left of a decadent race—in spite of his brainlessness."

"Are we a decadent race?" asked Lorraine thoughtfully.

"Only the House of Lords and a few leading Conservatives," said Lord Denton with flippancy. "The workingman who has the courage to refuse to work, and the Liberal members who have the grit to demand salaries for upsetting the Constitution, led by a few eminent Ministers who delight to remove their neighbour's landmark, and relieve his pocket, are the splendid fellows of the grand new opening era of prosperity and greatness."

"Still," put in Quin hopefully, "it is very fashionable to go big-game shooting nowadays, and an African lion may yet chew up a few of them."

"Poor lion!" quoth Lorraine; "but what a fine finale for the king of beasts, to chew up the despoilers of kings. Shall we go to the drawing-room?" And she rose to lead the way.

A Bridge table was arranged in an alcove for Hal and three of the men, and Lorraine and Hermon sat over the fire for preference. They were far enough away from the players to be able to speak of them unheard, and Hermon, in the course of their conversation, mentioned that he saw something different in Hal tonight to what he had noticed before.

Lorraine thought she was only very lively, but Hermon looked doubtful. He could not express what he seemed to see, but in some way her liveliness held a new note. He thought she had more tone and a new kind of assurance, and he tried to explain it to Lorraine.

"I expect she's had a jolly afternoon," was all Lorraine said, with a smile. "She has been to the Zoo with Sir Edwin Crathie."

"Has she?" significantly, and Hermon raised his eyebrows. "Are they still friends, then? I thought she only knew him slightly."

"That was at the beginning," and Lorraine glanced at him with the smile deepening in her eyes. "There always has to be a beginning—doesn't there?"

But no answering smile shone in Alymer Hermon's face, rather a slight shade of anxiety as he glanced across the room at Hal. "I should not like a sister of mine to have much to do with Sir Edwin Crathie," he said gravely.

"Perhaps not, you dear old Solemn-acre," giving his arm a gentle pat; "but a sister of yours would not have learned early to battle with the world as Hal has."

"But surely if she is less protected than a sister of mine would have been, there is the greater cause for caution."

"There is no comparision. A sister of yours would always have known protection, and always rely on it, and if it failed her she might find herself in difficulties and dangers she hardly knew how to cope with. Hal faced the difficulties and the dangers early, and learnt to be her own defence and protector. Some women have to, you see. It is necessary for them to wield weapons and armour out of their own strength, and be prepared to be buffeted by a heartless world, and not be afraid. If you had a sister, you would want to keep her in cotton-wool, and never let any rough, enlightening experience come near her. If I had a daughter, I should like her to have the enlightening experience early, and learn to be strong and self-dependent like Hal; then I shouldn't be afraid of her future."

She was silent a few moments, then added thoughtfully: "I think it would be better for society in general if the girls of the leisured classes knew more about the world, and were better able to take care of themselves; meaning, of course, with a pride like Hal's in going straight because it's the game."

Hermon's eyes again strayed to Hal's pretty head, with its glossy brown hair, and Lorraine continued after a pause:

"If I'm afraid of anything with Hal, it is that she might let herself get to care for some one who isn't worth her little finger, or some one who is out of her reach, or something generally impossible. She wouldn't care lightly; and she'd get dreadfully hurt."

"But surely she couldn't actually fall in love with a man like Edwin Crathie?" he remonstrated.

"I wasn't thinking of Sir Edwin specially. She goes about a great deal, you know, and meets many people. She has a strong vein of romance too. I always feel I shall be very glad when she is safely anchored, if only it is to the right man."

They were interrupted then by the Bridge players, who had finished their first rubber, and Lord Denton persuaded Hermon to change places with him for a time, and came to sit over the fire with Lorraine. Presently he too mentioned Hal.

"She is the best woman Bridge player I have ever met," he said. "She seems to be developing into something rather out of the ordinary. Hasn't she grown much better-looking?"

Lorraine smiled, a slow, sweet smile.

"Alymer Hermon has just been praising Hal too," she said; "I like to hear you men admire her; it shows you can appreciate sterling worth as well—well—shall we call it daring impropriety?"

"You are a little severe."

"Am I? Well, you see, I know a good many men pretty intimately; and I have gleaned from various confiding moments that it is not the working woman chiefly, relying only on her own protection, who strays into the murky byways and muddy corners of life. It is surprisingly often the direction of the idle, home-guarded, bored young lady. Flip, if it came to a choice, I believe I would my money on the worker. It's such a splendid, healthy, steadying thing to have a real purpose and a real occupation; instead of just days and weeks of idle enjoyment. And as for temptations! Well, they abound pretty fully in both cases; it isn't the amount of temptation likely to be encountered that matters, so much as the quality of the individual armour to meet it with."

"Still, when it comes to being hungry and cold and having no money?" he argued.

"It doesn't make much difference in the long run, except that one hopes The Man Above will surely find a wider forgiveness for the woman who was hungry and cold than for the woman who was just bored, but hadn't the grit to find an aim and purpose to renew and invigorate a purposeless life. All the same, I'd like to see Hal safely anchored to a real good fellow. Flip, if you could persuade her to try, she'd make you a splendid wife."

"And what in the world should I do with a splendid wife?" laughing frankly into her face—"what an appalling possession! Lorry, old girl, I've got a splendid woman pal, and that's good enough for me. If I ever want a wife you shall have the privilege of finding me one: but it won't be until

I am old and gouty, and then she had better be a hospital nurse, inured to irritability."

"You are quite hopeless," shaking her head at him, "but I don't particularly want to lose you as a friend, unless it is for Hal; so we'll say no more."

"Sensible woman! And now I must really be off. I like your friends, Lorry. They're very fresh. And of course Hermon is tremendous. You haven't overdrawn him at all. Only to be careful. Remember the burnt child. A man like that ought to be made to wear a mask and hideous garments, for the protection of susceptible females."

"He would need to speak through a grating trumpet as well."

"Yes, I suppose he would. Even I can hear the attraction in his voice. It will be splendid when he begins to feel his feet in the law courts. We'll make a celebrity of him, shall we—just for the interest of it. But it's to be only a hobby, Lorraine, no entanglements, mind"—and he laughed his low, pleasant laught.

"Very well, call it a hobby, or what you like—only keep him in mind now, Flip. I've got him into an ambitious spirit that means everything, if there is enough fuel at the beginning to keep it alight until it is a glowing pile quite capable of burning gaily alone."

"Right you are. I like him. You fan the flame, and I'll rake up the fuel. I'll speak to Hodson about him tomorrow. He's always ready to lend a hand to a promising junior."

When they had all gone, Lorraine lingered a few moments by her fireside.

"A hobby!" she breathed; "yes, why not? Man-making is almost equal to man-bearing. I have no son to spur up the Olympian heights; but what might I not do for Alymer, if... if—"

She placed her hands on the mantelshelf, and leaned her forehead down on them.

"Alymer," she whispered, a little brokenly, "I wonder if I ought to be ready to give you all, and ask nothing? Perhaps make you all the splendid man you might be, just for some one else, and get nothing myself but a heart-ache?"

CHAPTER XXV

The winter months passed more or less uneventfully and pleasantly. The case in which Hermon had held his first brief, though in only a very secondary position, was rather splendidly won. An unlooked-for development in it roused public interest, and filled the Hall with spectators. Lord Denton went out of curiosity, and was present when Hermon, as an unknown junior, made his first public appearance.

He was not the only man specially interested either; senior counsel on both sides had its grandiloquent eye on the new-comer, so to speak— interested to know how he would acquit himself. Afterwards they congratulated him very warmly, and Denton went to tell Lorraine he had made a hit.

"He looked splendid," he declared enthusiastically; "and he was delightfully calm and self-possessed. He'll soon get another brief now. You see."

He did; and the future began to look very full of promise to this favourite of fortune.

As Lorraine had predicted, his growing success filled his mind, and kept him safe from many pitfalls; while her sympathetic companionship satisfied him in other respects, and formed a substantial bulwark between him and the women who would have tried to spoil him.

He had other women friends as well, but Lorraine felt they were not dangerous, by the way he talked of them. As long as he did not get foolishly engaged, and cripple his career at the very outset, as he easily might while he had no income to rely on, she did not fear. Lord Denton advised her to marry him to an heiress as soon as possible, but Lorraine knew better than to risk an impeding millstone of gold, and insisted he must just win his way through on the allowance his father gave him.

In the meantime they were a great deal together, and though they seldom went to any public place alone, they occasionally broke their rule; and it was known, at any rate in theatrical circles, that Lorraine rarely went out with her own old set, and had grown reserved and quiet. Hal knew something of the absorbing friendship, but she still made light of it, and sparred with Hermon whenever she saw him — "for his good."

As a matter of fact, she did not go quite so much to Lorraine's as usual herself; for many of the hours she had been accustomed to spend there she now spent with Sir Edwin Crathie. All through the winter they continued to take motor rides into the country; and often they went together to a quiet, unfashionable golf club, where they were both learning to overcome the intricacies and trials of that absorbing pastime.

It was easy for Sir Edwin to silence curious tongues. He spoke of her quite frankly as his niece, and Hal more or less acquiesced, because it was simpler to arrange an afternoon's golf, for Dudley had managed to become very thoroughly absorbed in Doris, and she asked no questions.

The only two to raise any real objections were Dick and Alymer Hermon. Dick had to be talked round, and thoroughly impressed with Sir Edwin's great age (of forty-eight), and though Hal did not state the actual years, she was perfectly correct in insisting that he was old enough to be her father; though she need not perhaps have said it in quite such a tone of ridiculing an absurd idea.

Anyhow, Dick was pacified up to a certain point, and obliged to see that the new friendship did her good, keeping her cheerful and hopeful in spite of her bitter disappointment about Dudley's engagement, and generally brightening the whole of the winter routine for her.

With Hermon it was rather different. He was less cosmopolitan than Dick, and he insistently adhered to his first idea concerning what he would have felt had Hal been his sister.

Why she should have been specially interested did not occur to him. Dick, of course, actually was a sort of brother, being much more so in a sense than many real brothers, as far as personal interest and protection went.

When Has was first left an orphan she had been a great deal with him, at his own home, and they had always been special friends both then and since.

But Hermon was in no sense either a brother or a special friend. They had never done anything else but spar, however, good-naturedly; and Lorraine, in consequence, twitted him once or twice about looking grave over Hal's doings.

And Hermon had laughed, and coloured a little, saying something about a feeling at the flat that they all had a sort of right in Hal, and he didn't see what that brute, Crathie—a Liberal into the bargain—wanted to be taking her about for.

He even went so far as to say something to Hal herself about it; one day, when they were alone in Lorraine's drawing-room, waiting for her to come in, Hal had just told him frankly she had played golf with Sir Edwin the previous day; and in a sudden burst of indignation Hermon exclaimed:

"I can't think how you can be so friendly with the man. Surely you know what he is? He has about as much principle as my foot."

Hal had turned round and stared at him in blank astonishment.

"Goodness gracious!" she exclaimed, "what an outburst! What has Sir Edwin done to hurt you?"

But he stood his ground steadily.

"You know it isn't that. If you were my sister, I wouldn't let you go out with him as you do."

"Then what a comfort for me, I'm not. And really, Baby dear! I'm much more adapted to be your mother."

"Rot!"

He looked at her almost fiercely for a moment, scarcely aware of it himself, but with a sudden, swift, unaccountable resentment of the old joke. Hal, surprised again, backed away a little, eyeing him with a quizzical, roguish expression that made him want desperately to shake her.

"Grandpapa," she murmured, with a mock, apologetic air, "you really mustn't get so worked up at—at your advanced years."

His face relaxed suddenly into laughter.

"I don't know whether I want to shake you or kiss you... you... you—"

"Thanks, I'll take the shake," she interrupted promptly. "I certainly haven't deserved such severe punishment as a kiss."

He took a step towards her, but she stood quite still and laughed in his face; and he could only turn away, laughing himself.

Yet he was conscious that her attitude riled him. He was not in the least vain, but all the same it was absurd that Hal should persist in being the one woman who was not only utterly indifferent to his attractions, but seemed almost to scorn him for them. In some of the others it would not have mattered in the least—at any rate he thought so—but in Hal it was sheer nonsense.

He liked her better than any one, except perhaps Lorraine, and he always enjoyed their sparring; but of course there was a limit, and she really might be seriously friendly sometimes; and anyhow he hated Sir Edwin Crathie.

While he thought all this more or less vaguely, Hal watched him with undisguised amusement.

"Don't think so hard," she said; "it spoils the line of your profile."

"Hang my profile!" he exclaimed, almost crossly. "Can't you be serious for five minutes, you're always so—so—"

"Not at all. I'm perfectly serious. A frown doesn't suit you one little bit. Imagine a scowl on one of Raphael's cherubim."

"I don't want to imagine anything so silly, and I'm not in the least like a cherub. It would be more sensible if you want to do some wise imagining, to think of Sir Edwin Crathie, and imagine yourself in the devil's clutches."

"But I've not the smallest wish to be in Sir Edwin's clutches, so why should I try to imagine it?... and you're not at all polite, are you?"

"I'm honest anyway; and I'll warrant that's more than he can rise to."

"But really, dear Alymer," reverting again to the mocking tone, "at what period of your friendship with him have you had occasion to find him out?"

"Your sarcasm won't frighten me. A man knows more about this sort of thing than a girl. Of course he is all right in an ordinary way, but you are so often with him... Considering his political career, it is positively unpatriotic of you to be such close friends."

"Such nonsense! Do you want me to be as bigoted and narrow-minded as those Conservatives who are continually holding the party back, because they are quite incapable of realising there are two sides to a question? I don't hold the same views as Sir Edwin at all. I'm not likely to, being on the staff of the *Morning Mail*; but that isn't any reason why I should object to him as a friend."

"No; but his reputation might be."

Hal stamped her foot.

"Oh, don't stand there and talk about a man's reputation in that superior, self-satisfied fashion. What is it to you anyhow? My friendship can't possibly be any concern of yours."

She moved away with a restless, ruffled manner, and threw back at him:

"Of course I'm awfully grateful to you for being so interested in my welfare, but your concern is a little misplaced. I am quite capable of taking care of myself, and have been for at least seven years."

He looked hurt, and about to retort, but at that moment Lorraine's latch-key sounded in the door, and Hal went out into the hall to meet her.

"I'm so glad you've come," she remarked, as they re-entered together. "Baby is in one of his insufferable, superior moods, and is lecturing me on my friendship with Sir Edwin. And all because I casually mentioned I had had a game of golf with him."

Lorraine looked a little surprised, but she only remarked laughingly:

"It's a little fad of his to lecture. I rather like it; but I wonder he had the temerity to lecture you."

"Unfortunately, lecturing doesn't instill common sense," put in Hermon, "and it only requires common sense to understand Sir Edwin Crathie isn't very likely to prove a satisfactory friend."

"You mean it only requires dense, narrow-minded self-satisfaction. Really, Baby, if you are so good to look at, there is surely a limit even to your permissible airs and graces"; and Hal tossed her head.

"Now come, you two," interposed Lorraine; "I don't want quarreling over my tea. Give her some of that sticky pink-and-white cake, Alymer, and have some yourself, and you will soon both grow amiable again."

"He hasn't got his bib," Hal snapped, "and he knows his mother told him he was to have bread-and-butter first. You are not to spoil him, Lorry. Spoilt children are odious."

"So are conceited women," he retorted. "It's only that new hat that is making you so pleased with yourself."

"It's a dear hat," she commented. "You have to pin a curl on with it, else there's a gap. I'm in mortal dread I shall lose the curl, or find it hanging down my back."

No more was said on the subject of Sir Edwin, but when Hal was about to leave, and found that Hermon was staying on, she pursed up her lips with an air of sanctimonious disapproval and said:

"I don't want to hurt any one's feelings, but I'm not at all sure *Mr.* Hermont is quite a nice friend for you, Lorraine. His conversation is neither elevating nor improving, and I hardly like to go off now and leave you alone with him."

"Don't worry," Lorraine laughed. "He is improving every day under my tuition. I hope you can say as much for Sir Edwin."

"I can," she answered frankly. "He has learnt quite a lot since I took him in hand; especially about women and the vote. He has positively made the discovery that they don't all want it just for notoriety, and novelty; but I'm afraid he won't succeed in convincing the other dense old gentlemen in the Cabinet. Good-bye!"

"Be circumspect, O Youth and Beauty. And don't let him over-eat himself, Lorry," she finished, as she departed.

CHAPTER XXVI

When Hermon was finding fault with Hal's friendship for Sir Edwin Crathie, it had not apparently occured to him that his own friends and relations were likely enough to take precisely the same view of his friendship with Lorraine Vivian. He did not want to think it, any more than Hal had done, and therefore he conveniently ignored the probability, and indulged in the reflection that anyhow they were never likely to hear of it.

Yet it was through them, and their ill-chosen mode of interference, that the first trouble arose, when that quiet, peaceful winter was over, and the spring arrived with renewing and vigour, and with new happenings in other beside the natural world.

It was as though the one gladsome winter of pleasant companionship and firesides was given to them all—Dudley and Hal, Ethel and Basil, Lorraine and Hermon—before the wider issues of the future stepped in and claimed their toll of sorrow before they gave the deeper joys.

Alymer Hermon's father and mother were at this time living in a charming house at Sevenoaks, whither he went at least once a week to see them.

His father had become more or less of a recluse, enjoying a quiet old age with his books; but his mother was an energetic, bigoted lady of the old school, who had allowed much natural kindliness to become absorbed in her devotion to church precepts and church works.

When it first reached her ears that her only son, of boundless hopes and dreams, was continually with the actress Lorraine Vivian, she was horrified beyond words.

Undoubtedly the story had been much magnified and embroidered, and accepted as a scandalous liaison or entanglement without any inquiry. To make matters worse, Mrs. Hermon belonged so thoroughly to the old school that she could not even distinguish between a clever celebrated actress and a chorus girl.

The stage, to her, was a synonym which included all things theatrical in one comprehensive ban of immorality and vice, with degrees, of course, but in no case without deserving censure from the eminently respectable, well-born British matron. She could not have been more upset had the heroine of the story been the under housemaid; and indeed she placed actressess and housemaids in much the same category.

Of course the friendship must be stopped, and stopped instantly. What a mercy of mercies she had discovered it so soon, and that now it might be nipped in the bud. Just at the very outset of his career, too, which had so astonishingly developed of late, and caused her such proud delight.

That that surprising development, both in the career and the beloved son, might have anything to do with this dreadful entanglement was not to be thought of for a moment; and when Alymer's father ventured to suggest thoughtfully and a little wonderingly that the friendship had certainly not harmed the boy, she turned on him with bitterness, ending up with the dictum that men were all alike when there was a woman in the case, and could not possibly form an unbiased opinion.

After which, she went off to church to a week-day service, partly to pray for guidance in a matter in which she had already firmly decided what line to take, and partly to unburden her mind to her pet clergyman. Of course she must speak to Alymer that very evening. How fortunate that it was one of the nights he almost always came to Sevenoaks.

If only he had lived at home it would never have happened. It was all that hateful little flat where he lived with Bruce and St. Quintin. She ought never to have given way so easily. If his father had docked his allowance, in order to compel him to live at home, he would soon have got used to the daily train journey, and it would have been far better for him.

Now, of course, he was not likely to hear of it; and since he was making such good headway in his profession, it certainly did seem a pity to risk upsetting him. But no doubt a little quiet talk would convince him of the unwisdom of allowing his name to be associated with an actress just now; and once more she congratulated herself that she had heard in time.

The Rev. Hetherington listened to her story with all the sympathetic horror she could wish, and she felt buoyed up in her adamantine decision, although she still harped on the intention of praying for guidance.

The Rev. Hetherington, of morbid and woeful countenance, was one who looked across a world glorious with spring sunshine, as if he saw nothing but the earwigs, and black-beetles, and creepy, crawly things of existence, and he promised readily to pray also: and perhaps God smiled the smile He keeps for the good people who so often ask to be guided by His Will, when they have long before decided exactly what that Will shall be.

The pastor accompanied his parishioner to her door, walking slowly with her through a garden bursting into a joyous splendour of crocuses, and snowdrops, and promise of laughing daffodils in warm corners; and together they lamented the terrible temptations of wicked sirens that beset the paths of splendid young men in the world.

"Not that he isn't a good, affectionate son," she finished, "but he has always been made so much of—which is not in the least surprising, and no doubt he has grown lax. Still, he might have remembered how proud a name he bore, and, at least, have drawn the line at a frivolous, painted actress. His father says she is very clever and quite well known, but even he cannot deny she probably paints her face; and surely that is enough to show what her mind is! How Alymer could endure it, I don't know. He has been used to such perfect ladies all his life, and the mere sight of paint should disgust him."

"Of course, of course," murmured the mournful parson, who had great hopes of a big subscription for his Young Women's Bible Class, and was in two minds as to whether to regard the present moment as auspicious, and introduce the need of educating all young women in high and holy thoughts; or whether it was wiser to wait until his companion were in a less perturbed frame of mind.

And the crocuses nodded and laughed, holding up their little yellow staves gaily to the sunshine, and shouting to each other that it was spring, clamouring to make the most of their great day, before the flowers came in battalions to crowd them out of sight and mind.

And the gentle little snowdrops whispered secrets to each other, which only themselves could hear, about warmth and sunshine and the beauty of the new spring world—too old in the wisdom of nature to pay any heed to the two humans who would rather have had a world all maxims and rules, and rigid straight lines from which no gladsome young hearts ever strayed.

Finally the mournful clergyman went away without asking for his subscription, having made mental decision that there would be far more trouble to come over the painted woman, and yet more propitious occasion was likely to arise.

And Alymer's mother went into the house with set, severe lips; and pulled down all the blinds that were letting in sunlight, for fear some of the carpets got spoiled.

She did not, however, venture into the library, where her husband sat in a large bow window reading, with sunlight flooding all round him, and sunshine in his quiet eyes, and the sunshine of a great man's thoughts filling his mind.

He was too much of a philosopher to worry about his son, and, moreover he knew Alymer well, and had great faith in his good sense; but he realised a mother would take fright more quickly, and that it was as well to let her have her talk with the boy, and comfort herself with the belief that she had saved him. As long as she did not shut out his library sunlight, nor bring her pet clergyman into his sanctum, he found it easy to balance her sterling companionable qualities against certain others of a trying nature, and go serenely on his philosophical way.

Undoubtedly Alymer was a well-selected mixture of both parents. To his mother he owed his fine features and his power of resolve when he chose to exert it; and to his father his splendid stature, his quiet little humours, and the old-fashioned, courtly protectiveness that had so quickly won Lorraine's heart.

Yet it was a mixture that might have borne no practical results if left to itself, but rather a retarding.

As Lorraine had so clearly seen, the spur of ambition, and a resolute determination to succeed in other walks than that of the casual, charming, petted favourite of fortune, were indispensable to bring his traits into a harmony with each other that would achieve.

It was to this end that she had given him of her best encouragement and help; too old and too wise not to have seen that whatever her own personal feelings towards him, it was extremely probable that she had helped him towards realising his highest promise, for some one else to reap the deepest joy of it.

Well, at any rate she had had the interest and the companionship, and these had not been small things. He had come into her life just when it was wearying of triumph and adulation; when lovely frocks and jewels, and hosts of admirers—the very things she had craved for a few years earlier—had commenced to pall in the light of the little real satisfaction to be won from them. With some women perhaps they never palled. Perhaps each fresh conquest renewed them, and each fresh triumph invigorated.

In Lorraine's complex character, the love of success was blended with a love of the deeper and richer things of life. She was of those to whom, at times, wide spaces, and fresh breezes, and the big, sweeping, elemental things call loudly, above the noise of the world of fashion; and she knew what it was to be filled with an aching nausea of all she had practically sold her soul to win, and a yearning *nostalgia* for something that might satisfy the finer instincts of her nature.

And in a measure her interest in Hermon had filled the void. Whatever her feeling had been in the beginning, it had undoubtedly merged now into a definite purpose for his good, from which she meant to eliminate—if the time came when he wanted to be free of her—any claim her heart might clamour to assert.

Her dealings with him were, for the time being, on a par with the generous unselfishness she had shown towards her mother. For both of them she found the courage and resolution to thrust herself in the background and give of her best as the hour required.

If the friendship had been permitted to develop quietly along these lines, a future day might have witnessed Lorraine quite naturally outgrowing her infatuation, and happily satisfied with the result of her unwearying interest and effort; while Hermon, from his proud pinnacle of success, would still have felt her his best friend.

But at the critical moment the blundering, disturbing hand was permitted to jar the harmony of the strings and spoil the melody. To what end?... who knows?... Perhaps to some unseen, mysterious widening, and deepening, and learning necessary to the onward march of Humanity towards its goal of Perfection.

CHAPTER XXVII

Alymer knew directly he entered the house, and saw his mother, that something had upset her, but he did not associate it with Lorraine, and kissed her with his usual warm affection.

It was not until after dinner, when they were alone in the drawing-room, that the subject was broached, and then, with very little preliminary, Mrs. Hermon—bending Divine Guidance to her own will—made a merciless attack on "the painted woman."

It was no doubt the most unwise course of action conceivable; but Mrs. Hermon, with her quiet and philosophical husband, and her only son, had led a sheltered, smoothly flowing married life, after a yet more sheltered girlhood, far removed from the passionate upheavals of society, and she had neither practical worldly knowledge nor experience to aid her.

She told him the story that had reached her ears through the jealousy of a sister, whose only son was very plain, and a scapegrace, and who had been fiendishly glad to have an opportunity to cast a slur upon the doings of the successful, handsome, steady young barrister.

"Douglas says he is always with her," had been her sister's conclusion—"and that every one is talking about it, and there is a dreadful lot of scandal. I thought it was only kind to tell you, as if he goes on in the same way he will certainly ruin his career."

Then had come the parting shot.

"We all think so much of Alymer, that I would not believe such a story of him without proof. Douglas said he usualy went to her flat in Chelsea about five, when he leaves Chambers, and I went twice to see if he came; and on each occasion he strode along, and swung into the building almost as if he lived there."

Mrs. Hermon did not at first tell her son the source of her information, and he did not ask her. Neither, somewhat to her surprise, did he attempt to exculpate himself, nor to make any denial.

He stood up on the hearth with that straight, strong look he had, when all his faculties were acute, and heard her through to the end. Then she said in a hurt voice: "You don't deny it, Alymer. I have been hoping you went to the flat on business, and there was some mistake."

"I deny everything that you have implied against Miss Vivian. The story of the friendship is true."

His quiet self-possession seemed to disconcert her a little. She was prepared for indignant denial, or angry remonstrance even; but this calm self-possession was something almost new to her. True, he had always been calm and philosophical, like his father; but this was something deeper and stronger than she had yet known in him.

"The fact is, mother," he went on after a pause, "you have run away with a totally wrong idea of Miss Vivian. If she were the sort of actress you picture, you might perhaps be anxious; but all the same I think you might have given me credit for rather better taste."

"My dear, an actress is an actress—and everyone knows what that is; and the mere fact of her calling, or whatever you like to name it, is sufficient to seriously hurt your position."

He smiled a little.

"I dispute the dictum that everyone knows whant an actress is, in the sweeping sense you mean. I do not think you know, for one. I shall have to try and persuade Miss Vivian to come and see you."

"Indeed I hope you will do no such thing."

Again he smiled.

"In any case I should not succeed. She is very proud, and would resent patronage even more than you."

Mrs. Hermon gave a significant sniff of incredulity, but she only said:

"Well, Alymer dear, you will give me a promise not to see her any more—won't you?"

"I can't do that, mother."

"Why not?"

"It is out of the question. For one thing, I owe too much to Miss Vivian; and for another, I am too fond of her."

"All the more reason you should try to break off the friendship at once, before she has succeeded in any of her schemes to entangle you."

"She has no schemes to entangle me, as you put it. She has been a splendid friend. I owe my first brief to her, and a good deal else beside."

"Well, and no doubt you have already given her a good deal in return. Quite as much as she deserves. There is no necessity for you to ruin your whole career, just because she happens to like being seen out with you."

There was a silence, in which Alymer seemed to be cogitating how best to disarm his mother's fears; and also to be reminding himself of her natural ignorance on theatrical matters, and his own need to be patient therefore. At last he said quietly:

"Miss Vivian only wants to help me in my profession; and I can only tell you again she has been a splendid friend to me. Aunt Edith has told you a great deal of nonsense. She has always been glad to pick holes in me if she could. Most of it is lies, and you must take my word for it. It is useless to discuss the matter. I am sorry you have been so worried, but I don't know how to make you understand."

"I understand far better than you think; and I know you ought to end the friendship at once. I want you to do so."

"It is out of the question. But you need not worry. You must just forget. No..." as she attempted further remonstrance; "don't go on. I cannot listen to any more against Miss Vivian. I think I will go and smoke a pipe with the pater. Shall you come and sit with us?" And a certain expression in his eyes that reminded her of his father in his most decisive moods told her he meant to say no more. She rose at once.

She had failed, and she knew it, but she had not the smallest intention of giving in. She had started on the wrong tack, that was all. Of course the boy was too chivalrous to go back on a friend, particularly as he believed he was under some obligation to her. Her plan of mercilessly tearing the lady to pieces had not been a good one, but she would think of something else, and save him in spite of himself.

And comforting herself with this reflection, she allowed the subject to drop, and went with him to the library. Her next plan should be a more sure one. She would work in secret with an agent to help her, who could see the enormity of the danger, and appreciate more thoroughly than his father the urgent need to interfere. She had already a vague plan in her head that she believed an excellent one, and which she could put into execution immediately.

It was an old-fashioned, time-worn plan, but Mrs. Hermon was a woman of old-fashioned ideas, and she did not know but that she was the originator. She had not the least idea that quite the commonplace course of action in these questions was to send a secret emissary to the lady, to reason with her, or plead with her, or bribe her, according to her status, on behalf of the innocent young victim of her charms. The great thing, she imagined, was to find a suitable agent.

Now, besides the sister who was jealous, she had a bachelor brother of a certain well-known stamp. A good-looking, aristocratic, well-preserved man of independent means; and though over sixty years of age, still a gallant, with not much in his handsome head beyond a pathetic desire to continue to captivate, and a belief that he was as invincible as ever.

Very shady stories had more than once been written down to his account, but he had the wit always to rise above them and sail serenely on to do more mischief.

His sister rightly surmised that he would have considerable knowledge concerning actressess and the theatrical world, and without troubling to consult her husband, she took him into her confidence and unburdened all her trouble.

"Phew!" murmured the elderly beau, "so the young scamp has got entangled with an actress, has he? Shocking!… shocking!… But don't worry, Ailsa; we'll soon square the lady one way or another. Do you—er—happen to know if she is of the nature one can offer money to?"

"I think not. Alymer insists she is a lady in the real sense; though, if so, why did she go on the stage?"

"Love of excitement, I dare say. Is she, by any chance, a chorus girl?"

"No, not exactly; though really I fail to see any difference in degree between one actress and another. They are all on the stage; and no doubt they all paint their faces and snare good-looking young men."

"No doubt," agreed the man, who had more than once made it his business to snare an unsuspecting, trusting girl.

"And you will go to see her, and persuade her to drop him; won't you, Percy? It is no use talking to his father; he does not see the matter in a serious enough light. He believes Alymer will soon tire of her. So he may, but in the meantime she may irredeemably injure his career. Of course, if it is a question of money we will find it all right; but whatever it is, try to cut the whole matter off entirely. Make love to her yourself, Percy, if that is what she wants—you know you have always been rather good at that sort of thing"; and she smiled at her own astonishing wordly wisdom, feeling almost rakish at having framed such a sentence.

"Ah!" with a deprecatory shake of his head, that did not, however, hide a certain fitful gleam in his eyes, "I am getting too old for those kinds of pranks now, but I will do my best to—er—" For a moment he wondered whether he meant to do his best to make love to the actress himself, or try to rescue Alymer, and finally finished: "follow out your wishes and suggestions."

"I knew you would, Percy. It was a good idea of mine to ask you. Don't mince matters at all, will you? Make her thoroughly understand she has got to give him up under any circumstances, or we shall, well—er—take proceedings if it is possible. Anyhow, Alymer must be guarded against himself, and his father is too unpractical to help, so we must do it alone."

"I quite agree. Alymer is an exceptionally fine fellow, with an exceptionally promising future; and if he cannot see for himself how foolish a scandal would be just at the outset, we must, as you say, save him on our own account. I am fond of Alymer, very fond, and very proud, and I will do all in my power over the matter. What is the actress's name, did you say?"

"I don't think I mentioned it; but Edith told me in her letter. I will look for it."

She went to a writing-table, and returned with the epistle in her hand, glancing through it until she came to the required information, when, without looking up, she read, "Lorraine Vivian."

At the same time a sudden, curious, startled expression crossed the faded eyes of the white-haired gallant, and he turned quickly aside, stroking his moustache with a slightly nervous air.

"Eh? Do you mean the well-known celebrity?" he asked. "Surely not Miss Vivian of the Queen's Theatre?"

"I suppose so. I never go to the theatre, so I never hear these names. Edith certainly writes as if she were well known. Does it makes any difference?" she asked, as he was silent. "Don't you want to go? If you don't I must find some one else; that is all."

"But certainly I will go. I was only a little surprised. She must be a good deal older than Alymer."

"That only makes it worse. No doubt she is no longer pretty enough for older men, so she has to set her cap at young ones, who are flattered by her attention. I certainly thought Alymer had more sense—but there—one never knows, and these women are very clever, I believe."

"D—d—I mean—extraordinarily clever; but we can be clever too, and I dare say we can contrive to outwit her."

A little later he went away to catch a train back to town, leaving his sister reassured and hopeful; but as he went he repeated to himself in a low, incredulous voice: "Lorraine Vivian... Lorraine Vivian... How strange that I should be asked to undertake a mission that will cause us to meet again. I wonder if you will recognise me quickly? I flatter myself, even white hair has not destroyed my claims to a woman's favour."

CHAPTER XXVIII

Lorraine had not the smallest idea of what was coming upon her. She knew perfectly well herself that it would be most unwise for a rising young barrister to get talked about with an actress known to have a husband living, and it had made her a great deal more cautious than she would otherwise have bothered to be.

Moreover, Alymer, seeing nothing to gain by making known his mother's fears, preferred not to annoy her with any account of them. To say that he was wholly unaffected by it, however, would be to say too much. He was, indeed, exceedingly and bitterly annoyed with his interfering aunt, who had obviously tried to make trouble for some petty motive of jealousy. He only hoped that his mother would take her line from him and his father, and maintain a dignified front, unmoved by his aunt's tale-bearing gossip.

He was slightly affected in another way also. It was almost the first time he had seriously considered what the world might say if their great friendship was known. He knew it well enough to believe it would be in haste to put the worst construction on it, though their own immediate friends might stand by them loyally.

It caused him to consider that construction in a light he had hitherto been protected from by circumstances, for it thrust forward an aspect they had successfully kept in the background. It made him ask the question, What was he prepared to do if his aunt continued her persecution, and some sort of change had to be made in the friendly, delightful intercourse?

He wondered a good deal what Lorraine's own attitude would be. Would she, perhaps, now that she had given him his start, cut all the friendship off for his good, and return to her old friends and admirers? He shrank from the contemplation of such a solution undisguisedly, and meant to continue their pleasant relations if possible.

He certainly wished no change whatever, if it could be avoided. Lorraine meant everything to him just then, and he could not but know how much his companionship and affection had come to mean to her.

So the next day he paid his customary visit, and talked as usual of many things, but said no word of what had passed the previous night.

Lorraine's room was full of violets and snowdrops, cushions of them on every side, in lovely array. He moved about looking at them, and she watched him from a low chair by the fire, clad in some new spring gown of an exquisite mauve shade, that seemed to tone with the violet-bedecked room.

It gave her dark eyes something of a violet tint, and her hands looked as white and delicate as the snowdrops. Moving about from mass of blossoms, Alymer, glancing at her, thought she looked younger and lovelier than ever.

"You have a spring air about you," he said, "and all the room seems full of spring. There is something about it all I like better than the lilies and roses and malmaisons usually making a display."

"I sent them all to the dining-room," she told him. "Every spring is such a beautiful new thing, it has to be allowed to reign supreme for a little while in here. It gives me rather an ache to see them, all the same"—after a pause—"they make me dream of the smell of the new woodland, that delicious, damp, earthy smell of spring, and all the young, joyful bursting of buds and springing of seeds and the mating birds, and the showers that make the leaves glisten. I feel as if I should like to tramp out across the country in such a shower, and get healthily wet, and be a real bit of the spring for just one week."

"Why don't you go? You are not looking very well, and the country air would probably do you no end of good."

"I don't want to go alone, and I do not know who I could take. Hal is not able to leave, and mother would merely be bored to tears, and Flip Denton is at Monte Carlo. There is no one really but you and Hal and Flip who would fit in with my spring mood. Any one else would strike a discordant note."

"I wish I could come."

The wish escaped him almost involuntarily, as, with the sight of the spring flowers and the spring scent in his nostrils, he too felt the call of the fresh, wild, vigorous things in his blood.

Lorraine looked at him with a curious expression on her face. Why, she wondered, did he not seriously contemplate coming? Why did he so steadily pursue, as far as she was concerned, his serene and passionless path? She believed he cared more for her than for any one else; and, if so, was it possible the ache sometimes in her heart for a closer bond and resolutely strangled, had no counterpart in his hot, vigorous youth?

Then he looked suddenly into her eyes, as if to see whether she had heard his wish, and what she thought of it. And as their gaze met, she saw the blood mantle to his face, and a half-shamed expression creep into it, as if he had been discovered in a thought that should never have been permitted.

He looked away again to the flowers, and Lorraine turned her eyes to the fire, with a swift wonder in her mind. She felt that something had transpired since they last parted—something she did not know of, and that was entirely different to anything that had crossed their path before. Some new thought had been put into his mind. Something that made him give her that half-shy, half-wondering look.

She gazed hard at the fire, and her pulses began to beat a little fitfully. She knew instinctively that something had come suddenly into being between them, which neither might name, and which was the oldest thing in the world.

And then across her mind, as once before, swept with swift pitilessness a vision of what might have been; of what life might have held for her had she been among the blessed—an aching, tearing longing for a youthful hour she had irretrievably missed. She drew her hand across her eyes, ignoring his presence, shutting him out, seeing only the heavenly joy she had missed.

Supposing such a moment had come to her with such a man, when she, like him, was in the first flush of youth and beauty; of dreams and hopes, and rich believing. What a knight for a lovely maid! What a lover to dream of bashfully and fearfully; and with all her soul one thought of him.

From her vantage ground of much doing and much knowing, she looked back yearningly to the bloom and springtide of life, when all splendid things are possible, and any day may bring the splendid knight.

And instead had come... ah, what?

Well! For her it had been the wolf in sheep's clothing, who, beside all he had robbed her of, had taken all her chance of the one great awakening to blinding joy. Now she could only look upon the joy from afar, seeing a barrier of fateful years, and, like a drawn sword at the gate of her dream, the stern, unyielding decree that has echoed unchanged down the long centuries: "Thou shalt not—"

Alymer was silent too, standing with the thoughtful expression on his face that was so attractive, probing a little nervously into that wish he had expressed, and wondering a little uncertainly just what it meant.

Then Lorraine got up.

"You are grave, *mon ami*; and it is the springtime. Grave thoughts are for the autumn of life—recklessness better becomes the joyful spring."

"Are you ever reckless nowadays?" he asked, watching her graceful movements as she bent down and buried her face in a cushion of violets.

"I am when I smell violets. They may be modest and retiring little flowers, but they hold spring rapture and spring lavishness and spring desiring in their scent all the same."

"Then you are reckless now?"

What was it made him dally thus upon dangerous ground? What was it made him speak to Lorraine as he had never spoken before, on the very day after his mother's admonition? Why did his immense height and strength and the young vigour in his blood suddenly blot out the years that lay between them, and sweep into his soul, the knowledge of his masculinity and might, which of its own nature possessively dominated her femininity?

They seemed all at once to have strayed into an atmosphere, born of that warning admonition, and of their talk, of the reckless, creative spring; and because, in spite of his youth, he was very much a man, and she was a dangerously attractive woman, his pulses leapt fitfully and eagerly with the swift ache that has existed ever since God made man and woman.

Without looking up, Lorraine felt this. The very air about them seemed charged with it, and she too, under some spell of springtime, moved into closer proximity to the splendid knight. She brushed against his arm unconsciously; and looking down on the top of her dark head, he said half-shyly:

"You somehow seem such a little thing today, Lorraine, I feel as if I could pick you up, as one does a small child."

"Please don't," with a low laugh—"just think of my dignity."

"But you are not dignified today. You seem as young and light-hearted as the springtime. I feel as if I must be years older than you."

She raised her face suddenly, with yearning eyes:

"Oh, let us emulate the spring this once—let us both be young and foolish and real, and pretend there isn't any one else in the world."

For one second he looked at her with wondering incredulity, then, with a tender little laugh he suddenly bent down and folded his arms round her till she seemed to vanish altogether into his embrace, and kissed her on the lips.

"The scent of violets has intoxicated us," he said, and kissed her again.

Then he gently pushed her into her big, deep chair.

"I'm going now. I only ran in to see how you were after that bad headache. You must bring the lilies and malmaisons back tomorrow, or I shall be offending so grievously you will forbid me the flat. Good-bye!" And without another word he went away out of the room.

Lorraine sat quite still, and let the spell wrap her round for the precious moments that she could yet hold it. Of course it could not stay. In an hour at most she would be her old, brain-weary self again, with the best of her youth behind her; while he was still there on the threshold, young and strong and free. But even this one short hour was good. Life had not given her many such. She would fence it round with silence, and solitude, and the scent of violets.

Alymer went out into the streets wondering at himself vaguely, and yet with a pleasant glow of memory. He felt it bewildering that Lorraine Vivian, whose favours were so eagerly sought by men, should have allowed him to kiss her.

It seemed something apart altogether from her generous friendship and helpful influence. It made him pleased with himself, and filled his mind with a yet greater tenderness to her. He knew so much now of her early difficulties and following troubles—of the frivolous, unprincipled mother, and the long, uphill fight. She had honoured him with her confidence in spite of his youth, and now—

He quickened his steps, and his pulses leapt yet more fitfully. Spring was in the air and in his blood, and one of the recognised beauties of London had been gracious to him beyond all dreaming.

It was enough for the present hour. Why ask any inconvenient questions and spoil it all? Let the future look after itself.

Only one thought for a moment cast a little shadow upon his ardour. It crossed his mind, for no accountable reason, to wonder what Hal would think. He was a little afraid she would strongly disapprove.

But, after all, if she did, what matter? He owed nothing to Hal, and there was no reason why her views should disturb him in the least. Of course it did not... and yet... Hal's good opinion was a thing worth having; and, in short, he hoped she would not know.

It was not that she was straight-laced. She was too near the heart of humanity through her daily toil to be other than a generous judge; but she was also a creature of ideals for herself and for those who would be among her best friends; and she would have known unerringly that no great, consuming love had drowned his reason and filled his senses.

It was for that she would have judged him; and for that he would have stood before her direct gaze ashamed. One might be gay and irresponsible and merry, but there were just one or two things which must not be allowed in that category. Instinctively, he knew that in Hal's view he would have transgressed—not because he felt too much, but because he felt too little to be justified.

But why need she know? Why need any one know? He did not think his mother would follow up any further the story she had been told, and he would see his aunt about it personally. It was better to have it out with her, lest she took upon herself to interview Lorraine, and make more trouble still.

He ran up the stairs to the flat, two steps at a time; and scrambled to get changed for the dinner to which he was going, still feeling a pulsing thrill that, among all men, he was Lorraine Vivian's chosen friend.

In another flat—a bachelor one in Ryder Street—an elderly beau, likewise dressed for a dinner-party, though with the utmost care and precision, instead of a scramble. And to himself he said, as he took a long, last look at the image he loved:

"I must go tomorrow morning and settle this little matter about Alymer. No doubt Lorraine will be amazed to see how well-preserved I am. She cannot have any real feeling for such a boy, and, after all, a good-looking man of the world—"

He smiled to himself as over a thought that pleased him, and rang for his servant to go out and hail a taxi.

CHAPTER XXIX

It was not difficult for Alymer to persuade himself that a little diplomacy on his part would probably assuage his aunt's wish to upset his friendship, and incidentally allay his mother's fears; but, as it happened no one having his welfare so exceedingly at heart over this matter with the actress was in any degree as amenable or as quietly pacified as he imagined.

Another interview took place between his mother and his aunt, in which the latter advised writing to Miss Vivian direct to tell her what his father and mother thought of the friendship, and that an uncle of his would call upon her at once.

To say that the letter was an insult is to put it mildly, though at the same time it was not so much through intention as ignorance.

Lorraine read it with silent amazement, and thought the writer must be mad. It seemed quite incredible that any lady in the twentieth century should apparently be so ignorant concerning the status of a celebrated actress. It was evidently taken for granted that she was an adventuress of the worst type.

She was naturally somewhat angry and indignant, but decided it was not worth while to take any notice, and merely awaited with some curiosity the visit of the uncle who was to expostulate with her, and, practically, offer her terms.

He came at about twelve o'clock, and he did not give his name, merely asking to see Miss Vivian on a matter of business.

Lorraine dressed with special care, and looked her best when she quietly entered the drawing-room. She gave an order to her maid with the door half opened, in the most casual and imperturbed of voices, then she came slowly in, closed the door behind her, and advanced towards the figure standing on the hearth.

When she had taken two steps she stood still suddenly, and in a voice that was rasping and harsh, exclaimed:

"*You!*—" Alymer's uncle squared his shoulders, stroked his white moustache with a gallant air, and replied:

"Yes—er—Lorraine. We meet again, you see. I may say—er—I am very glad indeed that it is so," and he advanced a step with outstretched hand.

But Lorraine was rooted to the spot where she stood, and a sudden, sharp fierceness seemed to burn in her eyes.

"Have—*you*—come—about—Alymer—Hermon?" she asked in slow, cutting tones, as if each word was hammered out of a seething whirlpool of suppressed emotions.

"Alymer is my nephew, and his mother asked me to come and—er— talk to you about him. She is a good deal perturbed on his behalf—er— because—"

"I do not want to know any more than I am able to gather from the extraordinary epistle I received from her this morning. What I should like to know is, did you agree to come here on this errand, knowing who I was?"

The faded blue eyes of the carefully dressed old roué began to look uncomfortably from one object to another; anywhere, indeed, but into those scorching orbs, with their suppressed fires.

Then he took his courage in his hands, and tried again.

"My dear Lorraine, you seem to be taking rather a theatrical view of a very commonplace matter. Of course it is bad for the boy to get mixed up in a scandal, just at the beginning of his career, or, for the matter of that, talked about with a celebrated actress whose husband is known to be living somewhere. I have come to you as a man of the world, to ask you as a woman of the world to be generous in the matter, and help me to set the minds of his parents at rest at once—"

"Ah! It was as a man of the world you came to me before; but then I—I"—she gave a low, unpleasant laugh—"I wasn't a woman of the world, you see, until you had taught me, and left me."

He did not quite know what the laugh meant, but now his old eyes were roaming over the beauty that was yet hers, and memory was stirring, and something made him reckless.

"Don't speak of it like that," he pleaded drawing a little nearer. "I know I didn't perhaps treat you quite well; but if there are any amends I can make now?—If you will let us be friends again?—"

"Amends—amends. What do I want with amends from such as you?" And her eyes flashed dangerously. He retreated quickly, with a hurt, rather cowed expression.

"Well, Fate has thrown us together again and I am still a bachelor—and I have money—"

"Do please try not to insult me any further."

Lorraine had grown calmer, though the dangerous look was still in her eyes, and she moved away to the window, leaving a large space between them, and half-turned her back to him.

"I have already burnt the epistle I received from Mrs. Hermon—its insults were too utterly foolish to notice. You may go back and tell her her son has never received any harm from me, and I absolutely decline to discuss the question any further. As for yourself—you will doubtless find a taxi on the rank, just outside."

"But, my dear lady, I cannot go back leaving the matter like that."

He grew emboldened again, now that he could not see her eyes.

"I am here to plead on Alymer's behalf. If you are fond of him, you must at least listen to reason for his sake."

"Not from you. And who are his people that they dare to treat me like this? . . . First an insulting letter, and then an emissary such as you—"

"Alymer is my nephew, and his mother is my sister, and therefore I am a most suitable emissary, except for a certain incident of long ago, which has long been consigned to oblivion by both of us, I am sure. The boy is young. He is on the threshold of life and a great career. What will be the result, do you think, if you refuse to listen, and perhaps ruin his prospects for your own pleasure?"

She turned back to him a moment, and the smouldering fires leaped up.

"I was young. I was on the threshold of life. What did you care for my youth or my future? What do other men like you care? My mother was lax, and you knew it. I believe you gave her diamonds. And now you come to me and ask me to spare your nephew—*you* come—*you*!..." and the scorn in her voice lashed him like a stinging whip.

But he tried valiantly to stand his ground, though all his fine attire and air of bravado could not save his visible shrinking into a faded, dissipated, worthless-looking old rogue.

"If you won't listen to any plea from me, will you permit me to make one from his mother, and appeal to the woman in you to realise her anxiety?" Lorraine turned again to the window and looked out upon the silver, shining river. And suddenly it was as though all her soul rose up in arms. She felt with swift passion that it seemed to matter so much in the world that a young man with a promising future should not run any risk of harm from an older woman.

But if it was a young woman, and an older man, what did it matter then! Why, the very man who would have hurt her could allow himself to plead for another young thing, if that other were a man.

Doubtless he would argue, as all the rest of them, that years in men craved the freshness and revivifying of youth it was only natural, and a woman mattered so much less. But the mature woman herself, she has no right to indulge in any longing for that same freshness and revivifying.

Ten years ago this man had been just at the age, and with just the handsome, aristocratic appearance, in spite of iron-grey hair, that so often attracts a girl in the early twenties. She scorns boys at that age, and feels the compliment of being chosen by a man of the world before the many older women she cannot choose but see would gladly be in her place. That it is her youth and not herself that holds the attraction is unknown to her, and a clever man may often dupe her young affections.

Lorraine, with her romantic, imaginative temperament, had grown to believe herself in love with him, and then had followed the old, sordid story of insult and her consequent disillusionment. The memories stung her now with a bitter stinging heightened by the feeling that life cared so much more for Alymer's welfare than it had ever done for hers.

And then that appeal to her woman's feeling to sympathise with the perturbed mother.

Well, because she was his mother, surely she was blessed enough. What had she—Lorraines—to place against that great fact? She felt painfully that in spite of her success her life was pitifully, hopelessly barren, scarred this way and that, torn and rent and damaged by mistake upon mistake which could never now be rectified.

A nausea of it all made her feel in those tense moments, gazing at the serenely flowing river, that had she a child she would be borne away on the smooth silver water with her little one, out of the fret and turmoil, to some quiet nest in the cliffs at its mouth; and there for the years that were left her she would fill her days with the peaceful, homely joys that had never yet been hers.

But how could she go alone? Only in the uneventful days to find her loneness intensified a thousand times, and without escape.

No; the river would flow on to that serene haven; but never for ever would she and a little one of her own be borne on its motherly bosom to the country of little things and peacefulness.

And the thought only stung her afresh; driving the sting in deep and sharp while this man remained under her roof.

"Well," he said at last; and in the interval his voice seemed to have regained some of its polished, self-possessed satisfaction. "I see you are deep in thought. You were always tender-hearted, and I felt I should not appeal to your womans heart in vain."

Her face was turned away, so that he could not see her expression, nor read what was in her eyes, and purposely she let him go on.

"You will, I know, let me go back with the message Mrs. Hermon is waiting for so anxiously. It will be quite simple. No doubt you have countless admirers, and if you summon another, and let Alymer think he is replaced, after the first hot-headed wrath he will quickly become normal again, and apply all his faculties to his profession. I know you are too clever not to appreciate just everything involved, and too generous not to give the young man his best chance."

Then he cleared his throat, stroked his moustache, and waited, wondering a little why she did not speak. He squared his shoulders again, and glanced round to catch a reflection of himself in the overmantel, then once more stroked his moustache with a sleek air of growing satisfaction.

It had certainly been a most ticklish undertaking, and but for his diplomacy, he believed one foredoomed to failure. But of course Lorraine was a woman of the world, with a larger mixture of the other kind of womanliness, perhaps, than was usual, and he in his perspicacity had deftly appealed to both.

Then Lorraine turned round, and at the first glimpse of her face his own fell, and suddenly he seemed to be shrinking visibly; as if he would not ungladly have vanished through the floor.

She took a step or two forward, and stood in front of him with her head held high, and those same scorching fires in her eyes; and there was something almost over-awing in the taut intensity of her whole attitude, mental and physical.

"No," she said, in a cold, firm voice. "You may not go back and tell Alymer's mother that I agree to cease my friendship with him for you and for her. You may go back and tell her that because when I was young you had no thought of my future, and no consideration for my youth, I refuse absolutely to parley in the matter at all. I shall not change my course of action by one iota. I shall not take any single thought for the future. The future may take care of itself. If you can estrange Alymer from me, that is your affair. Rather than estrange him myself, I will bind him closer. That is my answer to you, and to the *lady*," with fine scorn, "who sat down yesterday and penned that unheard-of letter to a fellow-woman she knew nothing whatever against. Yet I think I could have charged that to her evident ignorance concerning theatrical matters, and forgiven her, if a monstrous irony had not sent you to plead her cause—"

"My dear Lorraine," he interposed, but she stopped him with an imperious gesture and continued:

"There is nothing for you to say, nothing that I am in the least likely to listen to. You have evidently misunderstood my character from first to last. Probably you even credited me with wantonness in those far-off days when I was fool enough to believe all you swore to me of love and devotion. However that may be, you tried to set my feet in the wrong path, and when it suited you, gave me a push that further evil might conveniently widen the breach between us. Probably you have done much the same again since, and with as little compunction. What I have to say to you now is just this, once again. Your mission today is not merely useless; it has considerably aggravated any danger there may have been. Because of every girl a middle-aged man has treated as you sought to treat me I shall hold Alymer to his friendship if I can, and use any influence I may have to increase rather than decrease his visits.

"It may be fiendish of me. I don't know. I am no angel; not even the obliging soft-hearted fool you and Alymer's mother seem to have concluded I might be. And what is more, if I had a vein of kindliness and unselfish consideration, you have done your utmost to stamp it out.

"Most of us are half good, and half bad. Today, you have given the devil in me an impetus such as it has seldom had before. That is your affair. Go back and explain the real truth if you dare. Tell Mrs. Hermon you found the low adventuress a devil, and one that you yourself had tried to help to make. Tell her"—again with that low, unpleasant laugh—"that you fear the worst for Alymer.

"That is all. Now you can go."

Once more he futilely tried to speak, but she only waved him aside, and walked with a haughty, scornful step ahead of him.

"Jean," she called to her maid, as she passed through the little hall, "Will you open the door for this gentleman?"

In her own room, she slid down into a large cushioned chair and sobbed her heart out.

CHAPTER XXX

It was there Hal found her. By the merest chance she had run up to the flat at her midday hour, to ask a question about Sir Edwin Crathie, and a rumour concerning him that she felt an imperative need to have answered. When she saw Lorraine in tears the question was instantly banished for the moment.

Had Lorraine been in her normal condition, she could hardly have failed to notice that the "Hal" who came up in haste to ask this urgent question was not the "Hal" of a few months, a few weeks ago. She would probably have observed that the vague, indefinable change Alymer had seen in her had grown more marked and more defined.

She seemed to have sprung suddenly into womanhood.

It was no light-hearted, careless, rather boisterous girl who appeared unexpectedly at the flat, to give her one or two eager hugs, tell her the latest news of her doings in gay, gossipy fashion, and eat an unconscionable amount of chocolates, usually kept for her special delectation.

The old, bright look was there on the surface, the ready, laughing speech, but there was also, with it, something that approached a dignified phase, and suggested a new reserve. She was also distinctly better-looking likewise, in some vague, incomprehensible way.

But Lorraine had not time to take any note of the change, for all her faculties were bent upon shielding herself.

Of course it was useless to hide that she had been crying, but at least Hal must not know that the crying had been soul-racking sobs.

With a look of consternation and dismay she, Hal, was across the room in a bound, kneeling beside the big chair.

"My dear old girl, what in the world is the matter?"

Lorraine contrived to smile with some appearance of reality, as she dried her eyes, and said:

"I don't quite know. It's idiotic of me, isn't it? If you hadn't come and stopped me, I should never have been able to appear tonight for swollen eyes." But Hal was not so easily put off. She grasped both Lorraine's hands in hers and said resolutely:

"Why are you crying, Lorry?"

Feeling it hopeless to avoid some sort of a reason, she replied:

"I had a letter this morning that upset me rather. It is silly of me to take any notice, and I shouldn't if I were well. I've been wretchedly nervy lately, and it makes me silly about things."

"What was the letter about?"

"Oh, only some one who is jealous, I suppose; trying to get a little satisfaction out of saying a few things that may hurt me. It is so silly of me to mind."

Hal's mind immediately flew to Mrs. Vivian, and instead of inquiring any further she just said:

"Poor old Lorry," and kissed her affectionately.

Then with a little laugh:

"I suppose you weren't going to have any lunch at all, but I'm frightfully hungry. I hope to goodness there is something in the house."

"Run and tell Jean to see cook about it, there's a dear. I must bathe my eyes and try to look presentable."

While they lunched Hal chatted of many things, but she noted that Lorraine was looking thin, and seemed to have something on her mind, while she made no attempt to eat what was placed on her plate.

When she was pulling her gloves on later she asked:

"Why don't you take a week's holiday and go into the country, Lorry?… It is no use going on until you are ill, as you did before."

"I think I must ask about it. I feel as if one week would do me a world of good. How is Sir Edwin? Have you seen him lately?"

"We played golf on Saturday."

A white look came suddenly into Hal's face, and she riveted her attention on an apparently tiresome fastener as she asked, with the greatest show of unconcern she could muster, the question that brought her there.

"Have you heard a rumour that he is going to marry Miss Bootes?" naming one of the richest heiresses of the day.

"No; I hadn't heard it."

Lorraine gave a quick glance at her face, but saw only the look of concentration on the fractious fastener.

"Well," Hal said in level tones, "I suppose she is worth about half a million, and I don't think he is rich."

"Probably he has only been seen speaking to her, or taking her to supper at a big reception. That would be quite enough to make some people link them at once, and fix the date of the wedding."

"There's a bun-fight at the Bruces' tonight," Hal ran on, "with Llaney to play the violin, and Lascelles to sing—quite an elaborate affair: so it is sure to be very boring; but I suppose Alymer will be there, looking adorably beautiful, and all the women gazing at him. It will be entertaining to chaff him, anyhow."

"Well, don't tell him you found me weeping," with a little laugh. "He might not realise it was only nerves."

"I'll tell him he's to take you away for a week's holiday," Hal replied lightly. "Goodness knows, you've done enough for him."

She went back to the office and settled down to her work with resolute determination, but any one who knew her well would have seen that some cloud seemed to have descended upon her, and that all the time she stuck to her work she was wrestling to appear normal, in the face of some enshrouding worry.

Through all the letter she was writing, and over the proofs she read to aid the chief, there seemed to be one sentence dancing in letters of glee, like a war-dance executed by little black devils on the foolscap of her mind. It was last night she had heard it, that ominous piece of news that took her violently by surprise, in spite of her practical common sense. Some one had said it quite casually in the motor bus—one man to another, as an item of news of the day.

"They say Sir Edwin Crathie is to marry Miss Bootes the heiress."

"What! The Right Honourable Sir Edwin Crathie?"

"So they say. He's very heavily in debt, I believe—over some bad speculations—and an heiress is about the only thing to float him. Besides, the party wants rich men, and it would be a good move on his part."

That was all, and then the two silk-hatted, frock-coated men had got out. Eminently well-to-do men—probably both stockbrokers, but men who looked as if they would know.

Hal had gone on home in a sudden torment of feeling. Of course he was free to marry the heiress if be wished, but why, if so, had he dared once again to drop the mask of companiable friendliness with her and grow lover-like? The change had been coming slowly of late, wrought with infinite caution and care. He had not meant to frighten her again, and find himself in disgrace, so he had taken each step very leisurely, and made sure of his ground before trusting himself upon it. The next time he kissed her, he had determined she should like it too well to resent his action.

And the safe moment, as he deemed it, had come the previous Saturday after a delightful afternoon at golf. They had motored down to the Sundridge Park Links, and stayed afterwards to dine at the club-house, then back to Bloomsbury, and into the pretty sitting-room, where Dudley was not likely to appear until late, because he had gone to a theatre with Doris.

And then for the second time he had kissed her.

But this was quite a different kiss. It was a climax to one of the best days he had ever had—a day in which, besides playing golf, they had talked of State secrets and State affairs. He had paid her the compliment of talking to her as if she were a man, and Hal, being exceptionally well informed on most questions of the day, was able to hold her own with him, and to make the conversation of genuine interest.

And his quick, observant brain greatly admired her power of argument, and her woman's directness of method, confirming the view that while a man usually indulges in a good deal of preamble, with many doubts and side-lights, a woman trusts to her instinct and arrives at the same conclusion in half the time. Of late, too, he had talked to her of interesting modern problems; and what had been frivolous in their earlier friendship had solidified into a real companionship.

And now as he stood on the hearth with his back to the fire, looking with rather critical eyes round the pretty room that Hal had contrived to rob of nearly all its lodging-house aspect, she stood quite naturally and unconcernedly beside him drawing off her gloves.

"It was a good game," she was saying, "if you had not messed up that sixth hole. It's a brute, isn't it. I was lucky to escape that marshy bit."

"You are getting too good for me. Your drives out-classed mine nearly every time."

"But I can't approach. I never, never, shall be able to hit a ball just far enough. If I loft on to the green at all it is always the far side, with a roll."

"You'll soon master that. A little more practice, and you'll be in form for matches. I think we'll have to go away somewhere and have a fortnight's golfing! Why not to some little French place? You would finish up a first-class player."

Hal laughed lightly.

"Just imagine Brother Dudley's face when I told him I was going to France for a fortnight with you!"

"You wouldn't have to tell him anything about me," watching her with a sudden keenness in his eyes. "I should have to be personated by Miss Vivian or some one."

"Oh, I dare say Lorry would come for the matter of that. We might teach her to play too."

"Well, I hardly meant she should actually be there," he went on in a meaning voice. "She'd be rather in the way, wouldn't she? I don't know that I could do with any one else but you."

He stepped closer to her, and slipped his arm round her shoulders. "A third person will always be in the way when I am with you, Hal."

She changed colour, and breathed fitfully, moving as if to disengage herself from his arm.

"No, don't go. This is very harmless, and I've been exceedingly good for a long time, now, haven't I?"

"All the greater pity to spoil your record," putting up her hand to remove his.

But he only clasped her fingers tightly, and drew her closer, till he could feel her heart palpitating a little wildly; and that gave him courage.

"It has been far harder than you have the remotest idea of. I deserve one kiss, if only by way of encouragement."

His face was close to hers now, and with a little murmuring sound of gladness he kissed her cheek.

"Little woman," he murmured, "I've grown desperately fond of you. I hardly know how to do without you. Be a sensible little girl, won't you?"

She disengaged herself resolutely then, but she was not angry, and her eyes were shining.

"You are transgressing flagrantly—as I should express it in a newspaper report. Collect your forces, and retire gracefully, O transgressor."

"I suppose I really must go now. It's been such a splendid day, hasn't it?"

He seemed to speak with a shadow of regret; and there was a shadow of regret in his eyes also as he riveted them on her face. Then he turned suddenly and picked up his cap.

"Well—the best of friends must part—and the best of days come to an end. Good-bye, little girl."

With his cap in his hand, he suddenly put both his arms round her and kissed her with the old passionate eagerness—then he loosed her and turned to the door.

"I'm in love with you, Hal—head over ears in love; but it's a devilish hard world, and Heaven only knows what's to come of it."

With which enigmatical sentence he let himself out and departed.

When he had gone Hal stood quite still where he had left her, and looked into vacancy. About her lips there was the ghost of a smile. In her ears was only the recollection of the words, "I'm head over ears in love with you."

So, it was coming at last—the great, glad day of love and fulfilment. If he had set out to trifle with her at first, at least he was serious enough now. She, too, had only trifled in the beginning, seizing a little fun and adventure in her workaday world. There had been no reason to suppose it need hurt any one. Now, she, too, was serious.

Perhaps the things detrimental to him that she had heard previously had some truth in them then, but he was changed now. Love had changed him. He was like another man. She had seen and felt it in a thousand ways that could not be translated into speech or writing. It was just that he was different, and in every particular it was to his advantage.

She was different too. She did not resent the kiss, because she knew that he honestly cared for her. And she knew, too, that she honestly cared for him. The end of the enigmatical sentence rankled a little, but she did not led herself dwell upon it.

She chose instead to remember how he had kissed her; and that he had confessed he was head over ears in love with her. Which only showed that Hal—for all her worldly wisdom and practical common sense—could be as blind and as romantic as anyone when her heart was touched, and her pulses romping feverishly at a memory that thrilled all her being.

Three days later she had heard the conversation.

Of course it was absurd—manifestly so—and yet, and yet—

After a miserable twenty-four hours of fighting against her own uneasiness, she paid the flying visit to Lorraine, to see if she could glean any light on the gossip from her, only to return to the office baffled and tormented.

It was the enigmatical sentence that pressed forward now, instead of the thrilling confession that he loved her. Was it possible he was indeed so base as to love her and tell her in the very same week that he had asked another woman to be his wife?

And if so, what had prompted him? What was in his mind? Why had he not left things as they were, and refrained both from the kiss and the confession?

And then above her tortured feelings rose the triumphant thought, goading and pleasing at the same time: "Whether it is true or not, he loves *me*—not her, the heiress, but me—Hal Pritchard—the peniless City worker."

CHAPTER XXXI

In the evening came the party at Dick Bruce's home, and it was necessary, she knew, to thrust all recollection of Sir Edwin aside, in order to give rise to no questioning and appear as usual.

So she dressed herself with special care, rubbed a pink tinge on to her white cheeks, bathed and refreshed eyes dulled by worry and shadows, and made her appearance, looking, if anything, a little more radiant than usual.

"By Jove! you look stunning, Hal," was her jovial uncle's warm greeting. "Who'd ever have thought, to see the ugly little imp of a small child you were, that you would grow up into a fashionable, striking woman? I congratulate you. When's the happy man coming along?"

"When I'm tired of enjoying of myself," she laughed, "and feel equal to coping with anything as trying as a husband. At present a brother keeps me quite sufficiently occupied," and she passed on.

Across the large, well-lit room, towering above every one around him, she saw the head and shoulders of Alymer Hermon. All about her, as she moved towards him, she heard the low-voiced query: "Who is he?"

No society beauty at her zenith could have caused greater interest. He was looking grave, too, and thoughtful, which suited him better than laughter, giving him something of a look apart, and banishing all suggestion of the conceit and self-satisfaction that would have spoilt him. Then he caught sight of Hal, and instantly all his face lit up, and a twinkle shone in his eyes as he edged towards her.

"How late you are! I thought you were never coming. Did your hair require an extra half-hour? I suppose you've been tearing it out by the roots over your faithless swain."

"I don't know what you mean, and anyhow I shouldn't be such a fool as to tear my own hair out by the roots for any one. If hair is coming out in that fashion, it shall be his roots."

"Come and sit down. I'll soon find you a chair."

"What's the good of that? We can't converse unless you sit on the floor. I work too hard to spend my evening shouting banalities at the ceiling."

"Well, let's hunt for a couch; there are plenty here on ordinary occasions. Isn't it a poser where all the furniture goes to at a 'beano' like this! There's nothing in the hall, nor in the dining-room; and there doesn't seem to be much here. Let's make for the lounge."

"But I can't take you away. I shall get my face scratched. You were made to be looked at, and half these silly people are staring their eyes out in your direction. I don't know how you put up with it so serenely. I should want to bite them all. If I were a man, and had been burdened with an appearance like yours, I should want to hit Life in the face for it."

"Don't be silly. What does it matter? It pleases them, and it doesn't hurt me. I get my own back a little anyway... when I want to"—with a low, significant laugh.

"Oh of course lots of women are in love with you,"—with a contemptuous sniff; "but if I were a man I wouldn't give tuppence for the woman who made me a present of her affections. You miss all the fun of the chase, and the victory. It must be deadly dull."

"That's what Lorraine has sometimes said; but what can I do? Shall I paint my face black?"

"Oh, I've seen you look black enough, but it's rather becoming than otherwise. Anyhow, it isn't insipid. But you've grown quite manly lately, I suppose. I hear about you occasionally positively working hard. Heavens!— what you owe to Lorraine!"

"I do," fervently.

"Then why in the world don't you look after her a bit? I turned up unexpectedly at half-past one today, and found her sobbing her eyes out."

"You found Lorraine sobbing her eyes out..." incredulously.

"I did. She told me not to tell you, as it was only nerves—but of course it wasn't. You know as well as I that Lorraine doesn't suffer from weepy nerves. It's worry again; and she is looking thoroughly ill."

"Why again?..."

He was looking grave enough now, and there was anxiety in his voice.

"Oh, because there's often something to worry her—either her mother, or her memories, or the future. I suppose you haven't bothered to go and see her lately to cheer her up? Been too busy with your briefs!"

"I was there yesterday, to inquire how she was after a bad sick headache. The room was all violets and snow-drops"; and his eyes grew soft.

"And did she sight of her robust health knock you backwards?"

Hal was irritable from the strain on her own nerves, and it pleased her to hurl sarcasms at him, feeling somehow angry at his calm, smoothly-flowing path to success.

"I thought she looked ill, and I advised her to go away for a week."

"That was kind of you. And why won't she take your safe advice?"

"She won't go alone, and she said there was no one to go with her."

"Too many briefs, eh?"

"What have my briefs to do with it?"

"Oh, nothing. She's given hours and hours to you and your future; but of course you couldn't risk sparing a week—"

"But!..." he began with raised eyebrows.

"Oh, don't 'but' in that inane fashion. If you say it isn't proper I shall scream. Lorraine is nearly old enough to be your mother, and she has far too much sense to be in love with you; and you wouldn't be so idiotic as to imagine it any use for you to be in love with her. Therefore it's only a companion she wants to keep her from moping and dwelling on sad thoughts; and you seem to be able to do that—as well as any of us; so why can't you get another man, or boy if you prefer it, to go for a run into the country with you? Flip would take her by the next train if he were there. He wouldn't care a farthing for scandalmongers. But I suppose he can do that sort of thing because he's a man. And, anyhow, I don't suppose she would go with you, even with a third person. She might think a whole week of you too much of a good thing."

His face has grown still more thoughtful, and he paid small heed to her taunts.

Lorraine sobbing, Lorraine ailing, Lorraine unhappy, filled his mind. What could have happened to upset her so? True, she had not been looking well for some weeks, and had complained of headaches and weariness; but he felt sure something quie apart had transpired to upset her so thoroughly.

Neither did he think it was Hal's version of the usual worries. He greatly feared his own people had made some move of which he was in ignorance. He contemplated with deep vexation the probability that he himself was indirectly the cause of her new trouble, and he mentally decided then and there to go to considerable lengths, if she wished it, on her behalf.

Probably if he travelled down to some seaside place and saw her comfortably settled, and later on ran down to fetch her, she would be more easily induced to go. At any rate he would call the very next day and see, if his proposition simplified matters at all.

Hal watched him a little impatiently, and at length remarked:

"You seem to be thinking rather hard. Are you meditating upon Lorraine's trouble, or my suggestion, that it is unlikely she could endure a whole week of you, unadulterated?"

"Both," with a humorous glance at her. "I'm thinking it would be interesting to find out the truth in both cases."

"Well, you won't do that. Lorraine never tells her troubles. Not even to me. And she's too tender-hearted to hurt your feelings on the other question."

"I'm not afraid of that."

His face grew a little brighter, and, as if satisfied with the result of his cogitations, he changed the subject.

"What's making you so ratty tonight? Is it the faithless swain?"

"I don't know what you mean."

"Perhaps you haven't seen the evening paper."

"I haven't. I'm sick to death of papers by six o'clock."

"Well, you oughtn't to have missed it tonight, and then you'd have had the pleasure of seeing the announcement of the faithless swain's engagement to the rich heiress."

Hal bit her lip suddenly, and felt her blood run cold, but she kept her outward composure perfectly, and merely commented:

"Oh, you mean about Sir Edwin Crathie and Miss Bootes!... that's very old news."

"Well, it was only in the paper tonight anyhow; and only given as a rumour then. I was going to ask you if it is true. They say he's in the dickens of a mess for money. But of course you know all about it."

He was enjoying himself now, feeling that he was getting a little of his own back, and it made him unconsciously merciless.

"It must have been rather a trying moment when you had to break to him that you couldn't possibly pay any of his debts, and that therefore you must part?"

"I don't know anything about his debts. They don't interest me. I can beat him at golf, playing level, and that's far more to the point."

"Then you are going to play golf with him, while Miss Bootes bears his proud name in return for paying his debts! Sure, it sounds a nice handy arrangement for him."

Then Hal got up.

"I don't want to *talk* to you, because you are talking such drivel; and I don't want to *look* at you, because your pink and white and blue and gold irritate me beyond words, so you'd better go and stand in the middle of the room for the benefit of those who delight to gaze; and I'll go in search of a refreshingly ugly person who can talk sense!"

Hermon gave a low chuckle of enjoyment, and continued to chuckle to himself until she was lost to sight and his hostess was introducing some charming débutante to him. The débutante was pink and white and blue and gold likewise, and gazed up at him adorably under long curling lashes; but he might have expressed a fellow-feeling with Hal, for he found himself merely bored, and longed to go in search, not of a refreshingly ugly person, but of the refreshingly irritable, snappy, unappreciative one who had just left him.

When at last he was free, however, he found Hal had complained of a headache and gone home early, unattended.

CHAPTER XXXII

On her way home Hal stopped the taxi and bought an evening paper. When she got it, however, she found Dudley there, so she merely held it under her cloak.

"You are back early," he said, in a surprised voice.

"Yes. It was very formal and very dull, and I was tired."

He glanced up with questioning eyes. It was something new for Hal not to stay untill the last moment at a festivity. He thought she looked a little paler than usual, and there were shadows about her eyes, but she interrupted any comment he might make by an inquiry after Doris.

"She is very well."

He stopped short rather suddenly, and seemed thoughtful. He had been urging Doris to fix the date of their wedding, and let him see about taking a house or a flat, but she had seemed to avoid the subject lately, and he was a little troubled.

"I suppose poor Basil is much the same?"

"Yes. He and Ethel were both asking what had become of you. They said you hadn't been up for a long time."

"I haven't. I'll go tomorrow. Good-night," and she kissed him, and went upstairs.

In her own room she sat on the bed, and read the evening paper.

Yes, it was there sure enough, but it was only given as a rumour. "We understand there is a rumour..." How well she knew the phrase, with its dangerous suggestiveness, and safe retreat. She wondered who had started the rumour, and how the paper had got it.

But, again, insistently she asserted it could not be true. If it had not been for last Saturday she might have believed it. But after that... no, he could not be so base. She put the thought away from her, and tried to sleep, but her eyes would look out into the blackness, and her brain ask questions.

"What if it were true?" She clenched her hands and fought the question. It could not be true; why worry? Yet he had never made the slightest suggestion of marrying her. She remembered that, but scorned it.

Why should he? There had been nothing lover-like between them until the previous Saturday; and of course had there been any one else, it would have been so easy to go on the same and make no change that particular afternoon.

Finding what comfort she could out of these thoughts, she fell at last into a troubled sleep.

The following afternoon, in fulfilment of her promise, she went up to Holloway from the office. Doris was out, and Ethel not home yet, but the door was opened to her by a gaunt stranger, who said:

"Come in. This is one of my days. I'm in charge this afternoon."

Hal looked into the angular face, which appeared to her as if it had been roughly hewn with a chisel, by some one who was a mere amateur, and she could not repress a little smile.

"I don't think I've met you before. Are you—are you—a friend of Mr. Hayward's?"

"Well, he's a friend of mine, if that will do as well. I'm generally know here as G. The letter isn't stamped on my face, but it's on the door of my flat, and that's much the same."

She stood aside for Hal to pass down the passage, adding grimly as Hal loitered, with rather an amused, engaging expression:

"I don't stand for much more than a door, with a G on it, as I often tell Mr. Hayward, but I suppose it's all right."

"A little more occasionally," suggested Hal. "A door wouldn't be much use to Mr. Hayward, anyhow."

"That's what he says. Won't you go down to his room?"

"What are you going to do?"

"Get the tea. It's one of the few things I can do passably well."

"Let me come and help. It won't take long. I'm interested in that door. You see, I'm not even G; and I don't possess a front door."

The music-teacher looked searchingly into her face, and was evidently pleased with what she saw, for she adopted a friendly note, and seemed ready to chat. Hal followed her into the little kitchen, and commenced to take off her hat.

"I'm an old friend," she volunteered, "and I often leave my hat in here. Are both Mr. Hayward's sisters out?"

"Miss Hayward will be late tonight, and her sister is uncertain. It depends somewhat upon which young man she is out with," in acid tones.

Hal glanced up in astonishment, but her companion was busy with the cups and saucers, and did not notice the look.

"All I can say is, I'm sorry for that nice gentleman who is fool enough to think of marrying her. Lord! he'd be safer with some one with a face like a door-knocker, such as mine. But there, they're all the same; and the nicest of them are generally the biggest fools."

Hal grasped the situation at once, and instead of enlightening her concerning her own identity, said casually:

"There's another young man as well, is there?"

"There is so. A pawnbroker I should take him to be, who wears the jewellery left in his care on his person for safety. As a matter of fact, I believe he is a South African millionaire. He brought her home one day, and Blakde—that's the housekeeper's husband down below—recognised him. He was out in South Africa in the war, and he saw him then."

Hal drummed on the table with her fingers to assume nonchalance.

"Does Miss Hayward know?"

"Know? Of course she doesn't. How should she know, particularly if that artful monkey did not want her to? I don't know where the poor sick man would be now but for me. She's always off somewhere—that minx— and I rush back from my music pupils, because I can't rest for the thought of him here all alone. I've given one up, who wanted a lesson at half-past four every day. That's the time he needs his tea."

"Why do you do all this for him?" Hal found herself asking, a little unaccountably. "He is nothing to you, is he—no relation, I mean?"

"Nothing to me!... Oh, isn't he though! I'd like to know what is anything, if he's nothing?"

She rattled the cups and saucers a little restlessly, and Hal, with growing interest, waited for her to go on.

"Before I knew him, I was nothing in the world but a door with a letter on it, as I've just told you. That's all I stood for, a mere letter of the alphabet who paid a monthly rent. I told him so, when I first came across, and he said, 'Well, I'm very glad they didn't leave G out of the alphabet.' That's all."

"But I'm his slave now. Nobody cared whether there was a G or not before. It isn't pleasant to feel you're a mere cypher, with no particular meaning to any one; just shot in haphazard to fill up a blank—a mere creature, useful to teach exercises and scales to odious children one only longs to slap.

"Fancy being expected to keep yourself alive in a dingy little flat, for ever alone, just to do that!" The cups rattled more restively still. "I say, the universe is the grimmest jester there ever was. Me to teach music to keep life in a body that doesn't want it! If I'd been employed laying out corpses in their grave-clothes there'd have been some sense in it. I'm not much more that a figurehead of an old hulk myself. But music!… music!… Oh Lord, and I haven't one real note of it in my whole composition."

Hal seated herself on the table. With her quick intuition she perceived at once entertainment of an original kind was before her, and she promptly laid herself out to obtain all she could.

"Why do you teach music? I don't think you do quite suggest a musician?"

"Of course I don't."

The gaunt spinster was cutting some bread-and-butter now with a savage air.

"Do I suggest anything, except perhaps a butcher or an undertaker? Yet I can only keep myself alive with music. That's the jest of the Arch Humorist. My father was a clergyman. He droned out services for fifty years in a hamlet, with a little square church like a wooden money-box. I was taught music so that I could—well—make the tin-pot organ groan, I used to call it. I had twenty-five years of that, with never a break. I got so that, to keep myself from turning into a stone gargoyle on the organ seat, I must have my little jest too.

"One way I had it was by making the organ groan dismallest at weddings and christenings, and squeak hilariously at funerals. Father never noticed, he'd already turned gargoyle, you see, and as for the village people!

well, it suited them, because they always wept at weddings, and overate themselves at funerals."

"And then?..." Hal was so thoroughly enjoying herself now, she had almost forgotten the invalid.

"Well, then the gargoyle died, or ran down, or something. I should think he got tired of sing-song the tender mercies of God to the devout people, and His judgments on the wicked. It always seemed to me the good folks got the nastiest knocks; and the wicked, well, they fairly left the green bay tree behind.

"Anyhow, I'd been devout enough, as far as sinning goes, for forty years. I wasn't even blessed with the chance to be anything else. Then a new parson came, an underdone young man with new fal-da-dal ideas. I wonder how soon *he'd* become a gargoyle? I defy him to stand out long against the cast-iron nonentity of that village. But he didn't take kindly either to me or my music. Hadn't any sense of humour at all. I don't know what I ever knew a clergyman who had. Perhaps a man couldn't very well go on being a clergyman if he possessed such a trait.

"Anyhow, this particular one did not think I put enough expression into the tunes. He said they hardly sounded like sacred tunes at all; which wasn't surprising, when you come to think that sometimes a low note and sometimes a high note on that little tin-pot organ would take it into its head to stick, and would either boom or squeak all through the thing I was playing." Hal burst out laughing, quite unable to contain herself any longer, but the spinster went on calmly: "The tune might just as well have been 'Down by the Old Bull and Bush' then, but it wasn't my fault, because when your hands and arms and feet and eyes and ears are all struggling to keep time with a village choir that varies its pace every few bars, you've got nothing left to release a stuck note with."

"I hope you didn't tell the under-done young parson about 'The Old Bull and Bush'?" said Hal, still rocking with enjoyment and bent chiefly upon leading her on.

"I'd never heard of it then, or I might have. Even that won't reach the village I'm thinking of for a hundred years; and then they'll play it until the very birds lose heart, and think they are uncannily up to date. So they are if you count it when things come round the second time. I told him if the organ seemed to be playing 'Yankee Doodle,' I supposed it was because it felt like it; as, for twenty-five years, it had more or less pleased itself at my expense.

"But he'll be a gargoyle soon, and then he won't notice, and it will boom and squaek to its heart's content. Of course I ought to have stayed on because I matched it all, and I didn't mind the booming and squeaking as long as the choir didn't get convulsed, and stop altogether—because that was liable to catch father's attention. A gargoyle is out of place in London. It's as mad for me to be here as that I'm here to teach music. After I became fossilised I ought to have stayed on till I died, and then that self-willed organ could have fairly squeaked itself out over my corpse. Come along and have some tea now. Poor Mr. Hayward will be getting faint."

"But you're too perfectly delicious for anything!" Hal cried, springing off the table. "Why haven't I known you for years? Why haven't I known you all my life? You must meet my cousin Dick Bruce. You absolutely *must*, with the least possible delay. He'll simply dote on you. Come along to Basil, and tell me heaps and heaps more"; and she caught her by the arm in the friendliest fashion, and half-pulled her along to the little sitting-room.

CHAPTER XXXIII

"What a gossip you two have been having!" Basil said, and, seeing the laughter in Hal's eyes, he added, "has G been telling you some of her amazing theories, or tearing the existing order of the universe to shreds?"

"Oh, I don't know, but she's simply immense. Have you heard about the tin-pot organ that will play its own way, and the choir that gets convulsed, and the underdone young parson? She's simply got to know Dick. He wouldn't miss it for the world."

"Yes; I've heard most of it. She plays an organ of laughter for me nowadays, that makes me bless the day she was born."

The gaunt spinster positively blushed.

"Oh, that's just your way," she snapped, bashfully trying to hide her pleasure. "If I hadn't been G, a pretty, charming young woman with real music in her might have been, and you'd have liked that much better."

"No, I shouldn't. She'd have played 'Home, Sweet Home,' with variations, and 'The Maiden's Prayer'—I know her at a glance. If you do only play scales and exercises I'm sure you manage to put a lot of character into them."

"That's only thumping; and who wants thumping?"

"I do, when it's the universe. I'm just as much askew with it as you are, only I haven't got the wit to thump it so satisfactorily. You are going it for the two of us now."

"Still, you're not a gargoyle..." with a queer twist of her face that delighted Hal.

"I shall positively take you to Dick myself," she said, "or bring him here to you. He'll talk to you about a mother's patience, and babies; and you'll talk to him about gargoyles and organs, and Heaven only knows where you'll both get to; but I wouldn't miss it for anything."

"I don't know who Dick may be, but if he talks to me about mothers and babies"—grimly—"I shall groan like that organ did at christenings. They may be useful in the general scheme, but beyond that I don't know how any one can put up with them at all; with their potsy-wotsy, and pucksie-ducksie, and general stickiness. It's quite enough for me that I have to knit stupid little socks for their silly little feet, for bread-and-butter. The most I can say for it is, that it's a more satisfactory plan than casting your bread on the waters, on the off-chance some kindly Elijah will butter it."

"Where are the socks, G?" Basil asked, looking round. "I should like Hal to enjoy the edifying spectacle of your knitting babies' socks."

"You don't mean that," interrupted Hal comically. "I can't believe it."

"It's the horrible truth," asserted the spinster, calmly going on with her tea—"most of them go to little black whelps in the Antipodes. After all, it isn't any more incongruous than the music—is it?"

"But you don't do it for the under-done young parson, surely?"

"Goodness gracious, no. What an idea! He wiped his hands of me long ago. The wildest stretch of imagination, you see, could not picture me ever looking like an angel; so he left me to my fate!" And again the humorous twisted smile delighted her small audience.

"Have you seen Splodgkins lately?" Basil asked. "You say all babies are sticky and objectionable; but you must admit that sticky imp down below is better than two-thirds of the other babies in the world shining with soap polish."

"So he is"; and the grim face relaxed still further. "He was sitting in my way on the stairs this morning, and as I could not get by, I said, 'Make room, please, Master Splodgkins; you don't own the universe.' 'Eth oi doth,' he lisped. 'Noime ain't thplodums. Damn th' ooniverth.'"

It was good to hear Basil's whole-hearted laughter.

"We ought to have had him to tea," he said regretfully. "He would have delighted Hal. He's two-and-a-half years old"—turning to her—"this remarkable person-age; and, like most gutter snipes, has developed as an ordinary child of four. He and G have debates occasionally. He wishes to be called D, because that is the letter on his front door, and 'Splodgkins' hurts his dignity but he's so funny when he is indignant we can't resist teasing him."

A little wistful smile crept into the invalid's eyes. "We have lots of fun in this dingy old barrack between us," he told Hal. "We are rarely silly enough to be dull, with so many queer, interesting folks under the same roof."

Hal felt something like a sudden lump in her throat, but she smiled brightly as she looked from one to the other, feeling somehow the better for knowing such waifs of life and circumstance, who could yet baffle Fate's pitilessness with genuine laughter.

"Dick is writing a most weird and incomprehensible book on vegetables and babies. I'm quite certain you could give him lots of ideas," she remarked to G.

"He'd better put Splodgkins in if he wants to make it sell," said she. "Only they mightn't allow it at the libraries. Splodgkins's vocabulary is fortunately sometimes indistinguishable for his lisp."

"Splodgkins couldn't be translated," put in Basil. "He sometimes comes to tea with me and G; but he is almost too exhausting. I think he knows every bad word in the English language; but one has to forgive him because he always saves half his cake for his baby sister, and hurls violent abuse at any one who dares to disparage her.

"Are you going?..." as G got up. "I'm sure Miss Pritchard doesn't want you to leave us."

"Miss Pritchard!..." In a horrified voice.

"Never mind," said Hal quickly. "It didn't matter." Then to Basil, in explanation: "G said something about Doris's fiancé, not knowing I was his sister, but I quite forget what it was. Good-bye, G," holding out a frank hand. "I think you're a delightful person, and I'm just as glad as Basil that you weren't left out of the alphabet."

A few minutes later Doris came in, looking flushed and stealthy, and the first thing Hal noticed was a loverly little diamond brooch she had not seen before.

"What a darling brooch," she exclaimed, after their greeting. "Did Dudley give you that? He might have shown it to me."

"No..." stammered Doris, turning red. "I've had it a long time. It's not real."

"Well, it's a wonderful imitation, then" said Hall a little drily—and remembered the man like a pawnbroker's shop.

Then Ethel joined them, and Hal's quick eyes saw the still increasing anxiety, just as surely as she saw the increased furtiveness in Doris's side-long glances. And because of all that she felt for Ethel, she trust her own care into the background resolutely, and made the evening as gay as she could while she was there.

Only afterwards she went home through the lamp-lit darkness, feeling as if some vague shadow had descended silently upon her little world.

What was this insistent, nameless fear at her own heart? Why was Lorraine weeping when she found her yesterday? Why was trouble steadily gathering on Ethel's face? What was this gossip about Doris?—

The gloom of a foggy night added to her depression. Why, in the tube railway, did all these people about her look so white and tired and lifeless? Did they just go on in their niches, in the same way that the grotesque music-teacher had gone on in hers for all those monotonous years; only to become like an uncared-for, unwanted letter of the alphabet pushed in to fill up a blank in a big city at last?

Were they all gargoyles-fixed, rigid, joyless, carved things, fastened in their respective niches, not for ornament, or for use specially, but just because the general machine seemed to require them?

And if so—why?... why?... why?—

It was so easy to be joyous if one was made for it. Such a little would make every one gay, if they were fashioned accordingly. What could be the good of disfiguring a beautiful world with all these vacant, expressionless, hopeless masks?

Hal did not read poetry. She was perfectly frank about being utterly bored with it. When she had anything to say, she liked to say it straight out, she explained, without twisting it about to make it rhyme with something just shoved in to fill up the line; and she preferred other people to do the same.

Yet, perhaps, at that particular moment, had she seen the lines:

"Ah Love! could thou and I with Fate conspire
To grasp this sorry Scheme of Things entire,
Would not we shatter it to bits—and then
Remould it nearer to the Heart's Desire?"

In her present mood she might have recognised also the stateliness and the beauty of a thought transcribed into verse.

Or possibly she would have obstinately asserted there was no occasion to introduce the word Love at all—and it was no one's Heart's Desire she wanted, but just a common-sense, reasonable amount of pleasure for all, and a spring-cleaning of all the gloomy, wooden faces.

In the sitting-room at Bloomsbury she threw her hat down on the sofa, and ran her fingers through her hair with an almost petulant air.

"I just feel tonight as if it was a rotten old world after all," she said.

Dudley, sitting poring over some plans with a reading-lamp, looked up in mild surprise.

"And what has made you feel all that?—not Basil, I'm sure."

"Well, there's no occasion to be so very sure. I think it's decidedly rotten where Basil is concerned."

She came and half-sat on one of the arms of his chair, and rested her hand on his coat-collar.

"I wonder what G would think of a sane man spending his evening ruling pointless-looking lines on a big sheet of paper?"

"And who may 'G' be?"

"I hardly know—except that she's the quaintest person I've ever struck yet—and I've seen some funny ones."

"Oh, I know who you mean. Yes; she is an oddity. Well, how was every one. How was Doris?"

"I hardly know. She was not there when I arrived, and she did not come in until a few minutes before Ethel."

"I wonder where she was?" thoughtfully. "I asked her to come for tea and a walk in the Park today, and she said she could not leave Basil."

Hal looked keenly into his face, and immediately he smiled and said:

"I suppose the tenant opposite was free unexpectedly, and Doris was able to get out after all. Poor little girl. I'm glad. But I wonder she didn't telephone me."

Hal turned away, feeling a little sick at heart.

Were they all then in the maelstrom of this gloomy sense of an engulfing cloud? What could be the meaning of Doris's behaviour? Did Dudley suspect anything? Certainly he had been a good deal preoccupied of late, and spoken very little of the future.

She looked out of her window across the blue of London lights, and her thoughts roved a little pitifully across the wide reaches of her own small world. From Sir Edwin, with his high post in the nation's councils, and Lorraine with her brilliant atmosphere of success and triumph, to the dingy block of flats in Holloway, where, in spite of almost tragic circumstances, to quote Basil, they had "lots of fun" among themselves.

She believed he meant it, too. It was no empty phrase. Rather something in touch with Life's great scheme of compensations, which she manipulates in her own great way, beyond the comprehension of puny humans.

Certainly neither Sir Edwin nor Lorraine could boast of "lots of fun." Rather, instead, much care and worry and brain-weary grappling with problems of modern succesful conditions.

She wondered, with a still further sinking at heart, if perhaps the time had come when she would have to grapple too. Was it very likely, after their delightful friendship, and after that confession of his the previous Saturday, Sir Edwin was prepared tamely to give her up? In her heart, she knew him better.

And yet, if the rumour was not false, what else could result? Vaguely she felt it might be one of those problems of modern society, coming across the evenly flowing river of her life, to demand solution. Not the solution of the crowd—to follow a beaten track is rarely difficult—but her own individual solution, which might mean much warfare of spirit and weary heartache. The foregoing of an alluring pleasure she deeply longed to take— not for any reward nor any gain, but solely for the sake of the mysterious power abroad in the world which is called Good; and which demands of the Present Hour that it is ready to crucify itself and its deep desires for the sake of the Future.

CHAPTER XXXIV

As the days of that new spring-time crept on, it appeared that the shadow descending upon Hal's little world had come to stay.

Things happened with surprising quickness, and each happening was of that particular order which presents itself enshrouded in gloom, and, with a pitilessness which is almost wanton, refuses to allow one gleam of the sunshine, carefully wrapped up in its gloomy folds, to send a single glad ray of hope to those wrestling in its sinister grip.

One knows the sunshine may possibly be hidden there somewhere— sunshine always is hidden in each event somewhere—but what is the use of expecting it weeks or months or years hence, when it seems that one single ray now would be of more help than a whole sun in some vague, distant future?

May it not be that in the development needed to fit the individual for the full and glad enjoyment of the sunshine to come, a ray of light would blur the film, and spoil the picture instead of producing one that is strong, clear and beautiful?

So, a dauntless belief in the sunshine to come, without a ray to promise it, may make for greater perfectness through steadfast courage than had one beam crept through to lessen the need for effort and for strong enduring.

Yet it was strange that the grim hand of destiny should strike at so many in that little world at the same time, and that its blows should be of that intimate nature which allows of no speech, even to one's dearest friend.

Lorraine knew that the rumour of Sir Edwin Crathie's engagement was an admitted fact; but she did not know how hard it hit Hal. She could only have learnt by accident, and, because of events in her own life, she was out of the line of such a discovery.

Hal knew that Lorraine, after a nervous breakdown, had gone somewhere into the country for a week or so, and that Alymer Hermon had run down later to see how she was getting on, and if he could do anything for her, but of the almost tragic circumstances that led up to his action she knew nothing, and imagined the merest generous attention.

She saw also the preoccupied, aged look growing on Dudley's face, and knew that the shadow was over him too.

Ethel saw the change creeping over Basil as no one else saw it, and knew that not even the far future could shed a single gleam for her upon the darkness coming.

Yet—for life is oversad to dwell upon rayless darkness even in books—bright, enduring, beautiful sunshine was wrapped up in those black clouds to flood the little world with joy at the appointed hour.

It was Lorraine's life that events moved first. After Hal left her, she spent a wretched, restless, brain-racking afternoon, and was only just able to struggle through her part at night.

And afterwards she became suddenly sickened with the need to struggle. She was not extravagant by nature, and had saved enough money from her enormous salaries to live very comfortably if she chose.

A nausea of the theatrical world and its incessant demands began to obsess her. She felt that from the first day she stood in a manager's office, seeking the chance to start, it had given her everything except happiness.

Money, success, position, jewels, fine clothes, admirers, friends, adventures, gaieties—all these had come, if by slow degrees, but not one single gift had contained the kernel of happiness.

Perhaps it was her own fault. Perhaps the trouble lay in the wrong start she had made and never been able to retrieve. But at least there was time to try another plan yet.

Finally, feeling the nerve strain of recent events was seriously affecting her health, she decided to arrange a week's holiday to think the matter out.

But then what of Alymer?

Nothing had changed her mood since his uncle paid his ill-chosen visit. She did not actually intend to try to influence Alymer against his people, but she did intend that he should not change to her, nor pass out of her life, if she could help it.

Because she, and she alone, had started him off on his promising career, she meant to be there to watch it for some time to come. Her influence might not any longer be actually needed. The devine fire to achieve had already lit into a steady flame in his soul, and her presence would make very little difference in future. He had tasted the sweets of success, and ambition would not let him reject all that the future might hold.

But she must be there to see. In her lonely life he meant everything now. There was no need for him to think of marriage for years yet; and in the meantime she felt her claim upon him was as strong as any mother's fears.

So she waited for his next visit, wondering much what would transpire if he had heard of his uncle's call.

As it happened, he had. In the interview he had sought with his aunt, to request her not to interfere in his affairs, the indignant lady hurled at him the story of the visit; or such garbled account of it as she had received from the participator himself.

That was quite enough for Alymer—that and Hal's account of Lorraine in tears. He felt that his benefactress, his great friend, had been abominably insulted, and he hastened in all the warmth of his ardour to her side.

Lorraine was waiting for him in her low, favourite chair, and when he first saw her he could not suppress an exclamation to see how frail she seemed suddenly to have grown.

Her skin of ivory whiteness, enhanced by the tinge of colour in her cheeks, and there were shadows round her eyes placed there by no cosmetic art.

All that was most chivalrous, most protective, most affectionate in his nature rose uppermost, and shone in his face as he said:

"Lorraine, it is too feeble just to say I am sorry. I heve been cursing the blunder with all my heart ever since I knew."

"That was dear of you," she said; "but of course I knew that you would."

"I hoped so. I told myself over and over, you must know it had all happened without my knowledge."

Lorraine had no mind to make light of the matter. She felt she would hold him better by simply leaving it alone, and letting his own feelings work on her side.

She knew of course that his uncle had probably tried to injure her case; but then, Alymer was a man of the world, and she trusted him, knowing what he must about his uncle, to judge her kindly.

But all this seemed to fade into nothingness when she saw the distress and the affection in his eyes—the anger that any one had dared to hurt her, and the eager wish to make amends. It made all her smouldering love leap up into flame, and the strength of the suddenly roused passion almost frightened her. She felt there was desperation in it, the desperation of the drowning man who catches at a straw, of the condemned man who seizes a last joy.

Quite unexpectedly a reckless, surging desire began to take possession of her soul. She had lost so much already; been hit so many times; missed so many things.

A picture came back to her, with a new allurement. The picture of herself with a little one of her own, floating down the peacefully flowing river to some quiet haven, far removed from the glare of the footlights. Should she make a bold bid to win that much from the years that were left?

She sat quiet, looking into the heart of the fire while the thoughts coursed through her brain, and her long lashes hid from the man above her the glowing dreamlights in her eyes.

Then he too pulled up a low chair and sat down, so that his head was more nearly on a level with hers, and still his eyes looked at her with that regretful, protecting expression.

"You must go away, Lorry," he said, using Hal's pet name; "you are beginning to look thoroughly ill."

"I don't feel well, but I haven't the heart to go alone. I should only get melancholia."

"Hal seemed to think I ought to offer you a little companionship." He said it with a slightly bashful air.

"Hal?..." in a sharp, questioning voice. "What has Hal been saying to you?"

"Not much. She was in great form at the Bruces' last night. She rubbed it into me finely on various subjects, and finally went off with her head in the air to find some one refreshingly ugly who could talk sense."

They both laughed, but Lorraine's eyes were thoughtful.

"And what did she say about your companionship?"

"Oh, that it was only some one to talk to and be company you wanted if you went away, and that I seemed to fill the post better than any one just now." He paused, then added: "Do I?"

She felt him looking hard into her face, and kept her eyes lowered. She did not want him to know that the thought of his companionship in the country was like the straw to the drowning man—the last joy to the condemned one.

"You always make me forget the years, and feel young," she said slowly and thoughtfully, "and I dare say that is a very good tonic in itself."

"You oughtn't to need help from any one for that"; and she knew there was genuine admiration in his voice. "You never look anything but young. I suppose it is temperament."

"Temperatment doesn't erase lines," with a little sad smile.

"Perhaps not, but it makes them, in some way, suit you; and they add to the character in a face."

"It is sweet of you to say so, Alymer, but it sounds a fairy tale. I don't so very much mind growing old, if only it were not so... empty-handed."

"But surely you have so much!"

"Not very much that counts. Anyhow, I hope some day you will have a great deal more."

"You are depressed. You must really get away somewhere at once."

He was grandfatherly now, the mood she always loved and laughed at, and her pulses quickened to it. He placed one of his large, strong-looking hand over hers—it covered them both out of sight—and he leaned a little nearer as he said:

"I can see I shall have to take the ordering of it all. You have done worlds for me. Now I shall have to take you in hand."

A harsh expression crossed her face for a moment, thinking of what his mother had written her.

"And go straight to perdition!" she said bitterly.

He winced a little.

"I'm sure you wouldn't want me to make excuses for my own mother," he remarked, with the quiet dignity that was already winning his name in the Law Courts, side by side with his gift for light satire. "You cannot but know in your heart just how far removed her outlook on the world is from ours."

She wanted to ask him if any outlook gave one woman the right to insult another at her pleasure, but she remembered Mrs. Hermon probably did not realise that she would have the fineness to see the insult, and was not even aware that she had been insulting.

"I should like you to know my father," he went on. "He is a very understanding man."

"But surely he…"

"No; he knew nothing about it. When my mother spoke to him he asked her not to interfere."

"Ah!"

For a few swift moments the generous treatment called to her own generosity, and for the sake of the understanding father she was almost ready to let go the straw. Only then again came the recollection of the uncle, and his impudent offer to substitute himself, and make amends at the same time; and again the smouldering fires leaped up, fed by the strong, protecting touch of the hand upon hers.

"I think Hal was right," Alymer was saying. "If my companionship, just to run down and see how you are, wherever you may be, will help to cheer you up and amuse you, there is no reason why I shouldn't manage it."

She knew he was making a concession of which he was half-afraid, because of what he owed her, and while one half of her longed to be self-sacrificing and release him, the other half fiercely demanded the straw that yet might save. And still she said nothing, gazing, gazing, into the flames.

"What do you think?" he asked.

"I hardly know," with a tired smile. "Of course I want you, but if—"

"Never mind the 'if'," cheerfully. "If I promise to run down and see you, will you go away at once, and try to get well again quickly?"

"It would make a lot of difference."

"Then that settles it. Can you start tomorrow?"

"I think I could."

Her pulses were leaping fitfully now—leaping and bounding with a swift delight. Perhaps he felt it, for he withdrew his hand, and gave himself a little shake, as if warding off something dangerous.

"Where will you go?" in a matter-of-fact voice.

"I hardly know, but I like the sea. Any little place that is warm in the spring. I might as well motor down, so it doesn't matter about trains, and the motor can come back for you."

"Shall I bring any one else?" his eyes searched her face.

"Just as you like." She leant forward and casually stirred the fire. "Anyhow, there is sure to be plenty of room at this time of year."

"Plenty of room, but not plenty of available companion chaperones," with a little laugh.

"Then we should have to make Sydney serve," naming her chauffeur. She got up from her seat.

"I suppose I must think about dinner," glancing at the clock. "Are you joining me this evening?"

"I can't; I have to go to Morrison's."

"How gay you are!"

"It is diplomatic. Morrison could get me a brief tomorrow if he liked."

"There is a very pretty daughter, just out; isn't there?"

"Yes."

"And is she so strikingly lovely?"

"I suppose she is; but she is so full of airs and graces she irritates one almost past endurance."

"I'm afraid you are a severe critic. The way is made too smooth for you."

She had moved near to him again, and stood beside him with one hand resting lightly on the mantelpiece, and one foot on the fender. He was standing as usual with his back to the fire. He looked down into her upturned face, fascinating now from a touch of roguishness.

"The splendid knight is hard to please; mere beauty is too commonplace."

"Isn't it sure to be?" a little smile played round his lips as he made his gallant retort. "How can mere beauty ever appeal to me, who have been accustomed to all you have besides?"

"Ah, flatterer!..." she said softly, and smiled into the fire.

There was a tense moment in which he longed to bend down and kiss her as he had done when the room was full of violets, but instead he pulled himself up sharply and moved away.

"Well, I must be off. Perhaps tonight I shall have the luck to be able to look at her from a distance, and not strike the jarring note. I'll try to come in tomorrow to see what you have decided, and then I'll run down on Friday afternoon for a long weekend, to see that you are taking decent care of yourself." As an afterthought he added: "I suppose Hal couldn't get off?"

"I'll ask her if you like. She would love it, if she could."

"And keep us amused too. I should get my head bitten off, but you could put it on again for me. Good-bye. Anyhow, it is a promise that you will go"; and with rather a hurried farewell, he was gone.

Lorraine remained some moments gazing into the fire, and there was a softness in her eyes. She knew perfectly well that he had hurried at the last moment because when they stood together on the hearth he had wanted to kiss her.

And she could not help comparing his strength in refraining with what would have been the action of most of the men she had known, who would have professed more, and meant less. She leaned her head down on her hand, and wondered a little pitifully:

"Why had the best she had ever known come to her too late?"

And then followed the dangerous thought: "Is it indeed too late?"

CHAPTER XXXV

Lorraine was not able to see Hal, but she talked to her on the telephone, and told her she was going into the country at once, and Alymer was coming down for the weekend. "We wondered if you could get off too. Do try," she said.

Hal answered at once that she could not manage it this week, but possibly the next, if Lorraine were still away.

"I've only arranged for a week's holiday," Lorr aine replied. "What a nuisance you should be unable to come this week."

As a matter of fact, Hal was only going out for the day with her cousin on Sunday, but an urgent little note from Sir Edwin had begged her to keep Saturday free for him; and because the suspense was becoming unendurable, she granted his request, determined to know the truth.

So it happened that Lorraine motored down alone to a quaint little fishing-village on the south coast, where there was a charming, old-fashioned, creeper-decked hotel, too far from the railway for the ordinary weekend tourists, and patronised mainly by motorists in the summer.

And on Friday the motor went back to town to fetch Alymer, bringing him down about four o'clock, unaccompanied.

"So Sydney will have to be chaperone after all," Lorraine said lightly. "Now, what should you like to do tomorrow?"

"Is there any chance of fishing?"

He asked the question with some diffidence, fearing that it might only bore her.

Lorraine clapped her hands.

"Exactly what I thought. We're going to have the jolliest little fishing-smack imaginable for the whole day; and Sunday too, if you like; and take our lunch with us, and fish until we are tired."

A glad light leapt to Alymer's eyes.

"By gad! You are a trump," he said.

In the meantime Hal waited a little feverishly for Saturday. They were to have one of their long outings. Meet at twelve, motor for two hours, lunch at two, then a walk; back to town to dine, without changing, in some grill room.

Sir Edwin had mapped it all out beforehand, sitting at his desk, with an anxious, unhappy expression, unrelieved by the evidences all around him of what he had achieved—of the proud position that was his. Indeed he almost wished he could will it all away, and be just an independent, moderately successful solicitor, able to please himself in all things; instead of bound by the demands of party and position.

And those demands just now were very exacting. It was not an easy party to serve, and the less so in that its ranks numbered many soldiers of fortune of the swashbuckler type, who meant to hold the power they had attained partly on the exploitation of a lie, by fair means or otherwise; even if necessary by further lies—lies upon lies—but clever, carefully manipulated ones; not bald, childish, outspoken ones.

One of their most prominent office-holders had recently perpetrated a lie of the latter type. Such a barefaced, impudent, obvious lie, that there was no possibility of covering it up, and the whole country talked of it. Music halls laughed at it, comic papers and comic songs rang with it, election platforms bristled with it.

Naturally the party was very annoyed. One could imagine them saying indignantly to the offender: "Lie as much as you like, but for goodness' sake have the common sense to lie cleverly. If you can't do that, better confine yourself to merely distorting facts."

The official in question held a post in the same department as Sir Edwin—which meant that quite enough opprobrium had been recently hurled at the Law without risk of any further scandal.

The party was not sufficiently strong for that. They had fright enough over a paragraph in the *Church Gazette*, hinting at a lady in connection with one of their Ministers—where there should be no lady; but prompt action had steered the ship through those shoals in safety.

But all the same, this business of The Right Honourable Sir Edwin Crathie and the Stock Exchange had got to be attended to at once. Under no possible consideration must it leak out that a Cabinet Minister had been speculating so heavily, and lost to such an extent, that nothing but an immense sum of money could save him from disgrace, bankruptcy, and ruin.

One friend and another had tided him over for some little time, but he had continued to be reckless and incautious, relying with an unpleasant sneer upon his title.

"Oh well!" had been his conclusion; "if the worst comes to the worst, I can always sell my name to an heiress."

Finally, that unhappy condition had arrived. It had further chosen the worst possible moment—the moment when the music halls and comic papers were waxing hilarious over the badly executed lie.

Sir Edwin had been summoned to a consultation that had been the reverse of pleasant. The only thing was that the way of escape had been thoughtfully planned for him. He had no need to hunt up the heiress for himself. She was considerately provided.

Miss Bootes' father was a wealthy Liberal, who had more than once generously supplied funds to the party, in return for some small favour he craved. Now he wanted a celebrity, with a title, for his daughter. Sir Edwin hardly came up to the required standard, but Mr. Bootes was easily persuaded that there was absolutely no limit to his possibilities, were he once set on his feet as far as money was concerned.

The Prime Ministership, followed by a Peerage, were in his certain grasp, had he but the necessary money to back him.

Papa Bootes said over an over to himself: "My daughter, Lady Elizabeth Crathie" (it was really Eliza, but had been discreetly changed to suit the fashion), and came to the conclusion that a Cabinet Minister for a son-in-law sufficiently banished the odorous flavour patent manures had given to his fortune.

Finally he inquired the amount of Sir Edwin's debts, and promised a cheque if the delicate little matter were settled.

Hence the consultation, and the polite but firm intimation that Sir Edwin must close with the offer—that he had not even the right to choose ruin instead, because of its effect on the party.

And of course, now the crisis had come, Sir Edwin did not want to close with the offer. In his own mind he consigned the party, and all belonging to it, to the very worst hell of Dante's Inferno.

But, beyond relieving his mind a little, their imaginary exodus did not help him in the least. He found himself in the very undesirable position of furnishing a telling example of the utter impossibility of serving two masters.

To do his common sense justice he had never had the least intention of attempting to. Without any prevarication as far as his own feelings were concerned, he had quite honestly chosen to serve Mammon. Having decided thus far, he banished the very memory of any other possible master. He did not exist for him. Mammon, in that it meant place, and power, and money, was the only god he wanted to serve.

And now?—

Well, of course, the Little Girl must go. At first he said it harshly, shrugging his shoulders and pursing his lips. It had only been a pastime all through, and, thanks to her own pluck and sense, it had been one of those rare, delightful pastimes that, ended suddenly, might leave only a gracious, enjoyable memory behind. He was glad of that.

Somewhere in his heart, that was mostly impressionless India rubber, there had proved to be a healthy, flesh-and-blood spot after all. She had found it quickly—gone straight to it with the unerring directness of a little child. It existed still—would always exist for her.

But in future the India rubber would have to close over it, and hide it from all chance of discovery. In future he must not even remember it himself. For that way lay weakness. No serving of Mammon could be achieved, whichever way he turned, with the frank, candid, clever Little Girl.

And so she must go; and since it was inevitable, the sooner the better.

Then had come the afternoon's golf; and, without asking himself why, he had hidden from her that there was any change. Afterwards, because the impending finale made him desire her as he had never desired her before, he went into the pretty little sitting-room and kissed her.

When he hurriedly departed, he remembered only that the kiss had been sweet. Also that evidently no rumour had reached her yet. But of course it would. Any moment of any day her newspaper office might get the news and publish it.

He spent a wretched week, torn mercilessly by his desire to serve two masters. In the end, because he was a man who hated to be thwarted, he swore a violent oath, and said that he would.

Then he sent Hal the urgent little note, and made his plans for the day. They all hinged largely upon his hope to get her to go to his flat in Jermyn Street, after that grill-room dinner. That was why when they met he cleverly took the bull by the horns directly he saw in her eyes that she had heard the news. He appealed, with insight, to her sense of humour.

"If you look at me like that," he said, "I shall punish you by sitting down here, in St. James's Park, on the curbstone, and giving you an explanation before all London that lasts an hour."

"I've a great mind to keep you to it," with her low, musical laugh, "and send Peter to bring a phonograph man with a blank record to take it down."

"And a dozen journalists with snap-shot cameras, and biograph apparatus, to link us in notorious publicity to all eternity."

"No; I couldn't stand that. What is your alternative?"

"A long, perfect day in this heavenly sunshine, pretending anything in the world you like that will make us forget the stale, boresome, old week-day world. Then, at the end of it, the unfolding of a glorious plan that is an explanation in itself."

Hal looked doubtful, and seemed to cogitate. He waited in an anxiety he could scarce conceal, watching her mobile, sensitive face. Finally the sunshine and the light-hearted carelessness made the strongest appeal, and she gave in.

"Very well. If it had been dull and cloudy I would not have agreed. But one daren't trifle with sunshine. We'll take our fill of it while it lasts."

So it happened that their last long day was one of the best they had known—each being clever enough to carry out the suggested programme and banish the following cloud for the time.

Hal was a little feverish—a little gayer than usual, with some hidden strain; a little pathetically anxious to act an indifference she could not possibly feel, concerning that rumour, and throw herself heart and soul into their compact of forgetting everything for a little while except the sunshine and the exhilarating dash through a spring-decked England.

In some places the hedges were white with hawthorn; and in sheltered nooks they sped past primroses, like pale stars in the grass. There were plantations of feathery, exquisite larch trees, their lovely green enhanced by tall dark pines, standing among them like sentinels. In gay gardens joyous daffodils nodded and laughed to them as they whirled past. Sir Edwin ventured an appreciative remark.

"Don't talk," Hal said. "Pretend you are in a worldwide cathedral, and it is the great annual festival of spring."

"May I sing?" he asked humorously.

"No; not as you value your life. We have only to listen to the choir. Hush, don't you hear the birds singing the grand spring 'Te Deum'!"

But after a time she spoke herself.

"Was it all like this on Thursday night—all these delicious scents and sights and sounds cast broadcast, for all who passed to enjoy?"

"I expect so. Why?"

The kindliness in the quizzical grey eyes was amazing, as he sat back, watching her with covert insistence, instead of the spring glories. How the divine spark changes a man for the brief moments when it reigns! Banishing utterly Stock Exchange scandals, convenient heiresses, exacting parties, the merciless claims of the god Mammon. He might have looked just so, years and years ago, before he entered that hard service, and buried all his best under layer upon layer of harsh, deadening, world-wise grasping. Pity that the best is so frail to withstand the onslaught of the demons of power and place—so easily overcome and thrust away probably for ever.

"I was up in Holloway. I suppose you know it? And there was a strong man dying a helpless invalid, and his sister breaking her heart, and a woman from the opposite flat, who said she stood for nothing in the world but a letter of the alphabet. And all round was gloom, and murk, and shabbiness, and hard, pitiless facts. I came home in the tube, and all the passengers seemed to look like lifeless, starved, white-faced mummies. They made me feel frightened. I wondered where joy had fled to.

"And here, was it just like this all the time?... flowers, and sweet scents, and spring, and hopefulness?... And scarcely any one to enjoy it all; while those white-faced, vacant mummies were journeying foolishly to and fro in that stuffy, detestable tube."

"You shouldn't go to such places. What have you to do with Holloway, and shabbiness, and starving people? If you belonged to me, I wouldn't let you go."

"Of course I have to do with them. We all have. But I don't know what. And it frightens me. I don't think I've ever felt frightened before. It was like being brought up sharp against a stone wall."

His lips were suddenly a little stern. Stone walls had to be broken down. That was the use of being strong. One was not frightened; one just got a battering-ram, and forced a passage through. He would tell her soon, but not out here. Not just yet.

"You are forgetting our compact. I'm surprised at you, Hal. I call it a slight on the sunshine."

"Why, so it is!... Avaunt, and leave my mind, Holloway! This day belongs to the spring."

And until they drew up outside the Criterion Grill, she kept her spirits high, and gave herself to the joy of the hour.

CHAPTER XXXVI

When they were half-way through dinner Hal asked, a trifle abruptly:

"Now, what about this piece of news? What does it mean?"

He looked away, unable to meet her candid eyes, and said:

"I will tell you presently."

"Where? Why not now? Why all this secrecy?"

"Because it is rather a big matter. You have sometimes said you would like to see the horns and trophies I brought back from my shooting-trip in Canada. Come and see them this evening."

"At your flat?" doubtfully.

"Yes. Why not?"

Hal knit her forehead and looked perplexed. She had so insistently declined to go hitherto, that she was loath now to change her mind. Yet she felt it was rather silly to have any fear of him now.

In the end she went.

It was only eight o'clock, and he promised to take her home about nine. Besides, something in his manner was baffling her, and she wanted to understand how they stood.

Once in the sumptuous, beautifully furnished flat, however, he seemed to change. He came up to her suddenly, put his arms round her, and kissed her.

"At last," he breathed. "At last I've got you absolutely to myself."

"Don't do that."

Hal disengaged herself and held him at arm's length. For a moment she looked steadily into his eyes, and then she asked:

"How has this report of your engagement got into the papers?" Her lips curled a little. "I presume you would hardly act to me like this if it is true."

"It is true in one sense, and not another."

"Oh..." She seemed a little taken aback. "In what way is it true. Are you engaged to Miss Bootes?"

"Yes."

"Indeed!"

She lifted her eyebrows, and moved a pace or two farther away.

"Don't move away from me," he said a little thickly. "It isn't the part that's true which matters, but the part that is not true."

"I don't understand."

"I brought you here to explain. I can do so very quickly. I am in a tight corner. The tightest corner I ever was in my life. Only one thing can save me. I must have money. Miss Bootes, or at any rate her father, wants a title. I haven't the shadow of a choice. I have got to sell her mine."

Again Hal's lips curled, and a little spark of fire shone in her eyes.

"Oh, I can understand all that!" She tossed her head half-unconsciously. "But why" — her lips quivered a little — "did you think it necessary to insult both of us by, at the same time, becoming lover-like to me?"

"I told you why; because I love you."

He stepped up to her, and caught both her hands in an iron grip.

"Now, listen to me, Hal. Don't try to break away, for I won't let you go. I tell you it's a matter of life and death. In your heart you know quite well that I love you. You knew it when I kissed you last Saturday, and you were glad. I don't know when you read that announcement, but whenever it was, your heart said to you 'Whether it's true or not, he loves *me*'. Probably you didn't believe it was true, because you knew nothing whatever about the devilish mess I was in. But in any case, your heart told you right. I do love you. I love you with every bit of me that knows how to love. If I have to be hers in name, I am at any rate yours at heart, and shall be all my life. Now, what have you to say?"

She tried to drag her hands away, but he gripped them tightly, forcing her to feel his strength, his resolve, and his masterfulness.

"I have nothing to say. What should I have? You have elected to sell yourself, to let a woman" — with swift scorn — "buy you out of a tight corner. I... I..." in a low tense voice, "am sorry we ever met."

"Why? —"

He hurled the monosyllable at her, now almost crushing her hands in his grasp, as he waited, silently compelling her to reply.

"Because the friendship was pleasant. It has meant a good deal. And now for it to end like this!... for me to have to scorn you."

"Why need it end?... Why should you scorn me?... Wouldn't every second man you know in my place act exactly as I am acting? I have no choice. I ought not to tell you, but my political chiefs have issued an ultimatum to me, and I have got to obey it. Do you suppose I would consider it for a moment if I could find any other way out? Do you suppose I would risk losing you, would even dream of giving you up, if I were not driven to it by the very hell-hounds of circumstance?

"To have felt love at all is the most wonderful thing in my life: I, who have always mocked and jeered and disbelieved. Well, anyhow it is there now. Listen, Hal. I love you. I love you? *I love you.*"

He tried again to kiss her, but she wrenched at her hands, held in his grip.

"Let me go. You... you... to talk of love. You don't know what it is. Let me go... let me go—"

"I won't. By God, you shan't speak to me like that. I won't endure it."

He was evidently losing control of himself a little, and the sight of it steadied her. Behind all her bravado and pluck there was a terrible ache. Caught in a mesh of circumstances, she knew she could not struggle out without being grievously hurt at heart. She knew that, however she loathed his action now, she could not unlove him all in a moment.

When he scorched and seared her with his passionate declaration, her heart cried out that she wanted him to love her, that she wanted to be his. And yet stronger and higher and better than all, was that woman's instinct in her soul which loathed his action and clung wildly in the stress of the moment to its own best ideal.

In the swift sense of hopelessness that followed, great tears gathered in her eyes, and welled over onto her cheeks. They had an immediate effect upon him. He let go her hands.

"Don't cry, Hal, don't cry," he said a little huskily.

"I can't stand that."

She brushed the tears away almost angrily, but, ignoring his motion to draw up an arm chair, remained standing, straight and slim beside the hearth, trying to recover her composure.

Sir Edwin commenced to pace the room. He had succeeded in his scheme so far as to get Hal to the flat to discuss the projects in his mind, but now that she was there he felt at a loss to proceed. He wished she would sit down; he changed his mind and almost wished she would cry; standing there, like a soldier on guard, with that direct, fearless expression, she disconcerted him, by making him feel mean and paltry and small.

And all the time he could not choose but admire her more and more. He wished with all his heart in those moments that he could throw his position and his party overboard, and go to her with a clean slate, and say:

"I have done with serving Mammon. Come to me as my wife, and I will serve you instead."

And instead he had brought her there to say:

"I cannot give up serving Mammon. I must marry the heiress, but let me be your lover and I will serve you as well."

And all the time Hal stood there with those resolute, set lips, as erect as a young grenadier.

But all the same he meant to have her if he could, and he remembered of old how often he had found a swift, bold attack won. So he stopped short beside her, and said:

"You know that whatever circumstances compel me to do, all my heart is yours, Hal, and you care a little bit about me. You know you do. Don't condemn me to outer darkness. Come to me like the sensible little woman you are. No one will ever know, and I can make your life gayer and happier just as long as ever you like."

She looked at him with a startled, perplexed expression.

"What do you mean?" she asked slowly.

"Now, don't get angry."

He laid his hand on her arm, with a caressing touch.

"You've knocked about the world too much not to know what I mean. You know perfectly well half the girls you know would let themselves be persuaded. But that isn't what I want. I've too much respect for your strength of character. Come to me because you can be strong enough to rise above conventions and because you dare to be a law unto yourself. It is the courage I expect of you. Hal, my darling, who is ever to be any the wiser if you and I are lovers? Think what I can do for you to make life gay and interesting and fresh. Don't decide in a hurry. If no one ever knows, no one need be hurt."

She moved away from him, and went and stood by the window, looking down at the passing lights in St. James's Street; looking at the lights in the windows opposite, looking at the faint light of the stars overhead.

It was characteristic of her that she did not grow angry and indignant; nor, in a theatrical spirit, immediately attempt to impress him with the fact that she was a good, virtuous woman, and that his suggestion filled her with horror. Her knowledge of life was too wide, her understanding too deep.

She knew that to such a man as he a proposal of this kind did not present any shocking aspect whatever. When he said, "Be a sensible little woman," he meant it to the letter. He actually believed she would show common sense in yielding to him, and taking what joy out of life she could.

But, unfortunately for the world in general, it is not only the horror-struck, conventional, shocked women who resolutely turn their eyes from the primrose path. There are plenty of large-hearted, broad-minded women, who, seeing the world as it is, instead of how the idealists would have it, are content to go on their own strong way, fighting their own battle for themselves without saying anything, and without judging the actions of others, content in striving to live up to their own best selves.

Hal was one of these. If another girl in her place had yielded to the alluring prospect of possessing such an interesting lover as Sir Edwin, to brighten the commonplace, daily round, she would not have blamed her, she would have tried not to judge her.

But she would have been sorry for her in many ways, knowing how apt the primrose path is to turn suddenly to thorns and stones; and in an hour of need she would have stood by her if she could.

But the fact of possessing these wide sympathies did not lessen any obligation she felt to herself. It was her creed to "play the game" as far as in her lay, and according to her own definition.

That definition did not admit of any irregularity of this kind. It called, instead, sternly and insistently for absolute denial. It told her now, without the smallest shadow of doubt, that from tonight she must never see Sir

Edwin again. She must take whatever interest he had brought out of her life, and go back to the old, monotonous round.

It was useless to question or reason. The decree was there in her own heart. The insistent call to keep her colours flying high, as she fought her way through the pitfalls of life to the Highest and Best.

As she paced the room behind her, disclosing a carefully thought-out plan, now pleading, now expostulating, she heard him rather as one afar off.

The plan did not matter one way or another. If she could have let herself go at all she would not have troubled about plans. His pleading and expostulating she scarcely heard.

She was looking out at all the lights, and her mind was grappling with problems. How harsh the glare of the streets appeared tonight. How far, far away the pin points that were stars. Hal liked a city.

Constellations hanging like great lamps in wonderful, wilderness skies would have wearied her quickly. She loved people, and she liked them all about her. But tonight she felt suddenly very near to the dark, shadowy side of life—very far from the stars of light.

She glanced up at the pin points a little wistfully. If perhaps they were nearer with their message of high striving; if perhaps the glare at hand were less harsh, there might be so much more steadfast courage in the world; so much less weak acceptance of conditions that led to pain and misery and disaster.

At last he stood beside her, and implored her to tell him, once for all, that she would yield and come.

But when he saw into the clear depths of her eyes, he knew his hopes were vain.

Suddenly, with swift self-distrust, his mood softened.

"I suppose I've shocked you past forgiveness now," he said miserably. "You'll think I've been a brute to you, and you'll never forget it."

"No; I shan't think that; but I should like to go home at once."

"But surely that is not your last word!"

"What else is there so say? I... I... can't do that sort of thing. That is all. From today you must go your way, and I must go mine. It is useless to discuss it. Let me go home."

"But you can't mean it," he cried. "Surely we are not to part like this."

She had moved back into the room now, and was pulling on her gloves.

"What else can we do?"

"But you care for me, Hal. You can't deny it. You do care a little; don't you?"

She looked into his eyes without a tremor, but with a pain at the back of hers that made him flinch.

"Yes, I care," she said very quietly.

"Ah!"

Suddenly he sat down, and buried his face in his arms on the table. Every good, honest trait he possessed called to him to throw "Mammon" to the winds, and make her happy. Let the party take care of itself. It was not for his nobility of character they had taken him into the Cabinet. Let his creditors do their worst—a strong man could win through anything. But the mood did not last. There was not enough room in that India rubber heart for it to expand and grow. It died for want of breathing-space.

"If you care, why can't you have the courage to come to me?" he asked a little fiercely.

"Because I have the courage to stay away."

And he knew—hardened sinner that he was—that she named the greater courage.

But his goaded feelings called to him, and drove him, making him mad with the knowledge he must lose her.

"Heroics!..." he said—"heroics!... Don't talk like a bread-and-butter miss, Hal. It is unthinkable of you."

He got up from his chair and took a step towards her, but stood irresolute—daunted by the calm strength in her face.

"The world is too old for heroics any more. Every one laughs at them. Where is the politician today who cares tuppence for anything but the main chance? We blazon our way into office, and we blazon louder still to keep there. It is the spirit of the age. The strong man takes what he wants, and holds it by right of his strength. In primeval times we used fists and clubs. Now we hit with brains and words or hard cash. That is all the difference. The strong man is still the one who takes what he wants, and keeps it. And I want you, Hal. It is mere feebleness—childishness—to be thwarted by convention and circumstance. Hoodwink convention, and stamp on circumstance. Go through stone walls with a battering-ram. As long as the world doesn't know—who cares? Those are my sentiments. They have been for years. When I want a thing, I go for it bald-headed, and take it."

He drew nearer boldly, refusing to be daunted, putting all his strength and determination against hers.

"And I want you, Hal. Do you understand? Don't be a little fool. Come."

She backed away from him towards the door.

"I understand well enough," she said quietly, "and I shall never see you again if I can help it. All that you say does not appeal to me in the least. I am not a politician—thank God—and I am still old-fashioned enough to possess an ideal. I am going now. Good-bye."

But when he saw she was already in the little hall, a wave of fierce desire seemed to catch him by the throat.

"Not yet," he exclaimed hoarsely: "Not yet... I care and you care—you cannot go yet—"

But before he reached her, she had slipped through the front door, and shut it behind her, and run down the stairs out into the street.

CHAPTER XXXVII

All through the next day, while motoring with her cousin Dick Bruce, Hal made a valiant effort to appear exactly as usual; but all the fresh spring countryside now seemed to mock her with its sudden emptiness, and the very engine of the motor throbbed out to her that something had gone from her life which would not come back any more.

She chatted away to Dick manfully, about all manner of things, but in the pauses of their chatter she was silent and still in a manner quite unlike her old self—reattending with a start, and sometimes so distrait she did not hear when he spoke to her.

After a time Dick began to notice, and then purposely to watch, and finally he perceived all her gaiety was forced, and sometimes was weighing heavily on her mind.

It was useless to say anything while they motored, so he gave all his attention to his driving, and purposely allowed the conversation to drop.

When they returned to Bloomsbury he went in to supper with her, as was his habit, and, as he hoped, Dudley was away up at Holloway. It was not until they had finished their meal, and the landlady had cleared away, that he attacked the subject; then, with characteristic directness, he said:

"Now, Hal, what's the matter?"

"The matter?..." in surprise. "What can you mean, Dick? Why should anything be the matter?"

She tried to meet his eyes frankly, but before the searching inquiry in them her gaze dropped to the fire.

"Something is the matter, Hal. Just as if I shouldn't know."

She was thoughtful a moment or two, thinking how best to put him off the right scent; then with overpowering suddenness came the recollection of all the pleasure and interest and delight the lost friendship had stood for, and her eyes filled with tears. It was useless to attempt to hide them, so she contrived to say as steadily as possible:

"I am a bit down on my luck about something; but it's nothing to worry about. Don't take any notice; there's a dear boy. I shall soon forget."

"But why shouldn't I take any notice? Don't be a goose, Hal. Tell me what's the matter."

She was silent, and after a pause he added:

"I suppose it is Sir Edwin?"

Hal felt it useless to prevaricate, and so she said, with assumed lightness:

"Well, it has been a little sudden, and we had some jolly times together."

"Then he is engaged?"

"Yes."

She told him briefly why. Dick watched her with a question in his eyes.

"Did he deliberately get engaged to the other girl, knowing he cared for you?" he asked.

Hal tried to lie.

"Oh, there was nothing of that sort between him and me. We were just good pals. But of course it can't go on the same."

"You're not a clever liar, Hal," he said, with a little smile.

She coloured and bit her lip, with an uneasy laugh. Then the tears shone again.

"Better tell me about it. Perhaps I can lend a hand to get through with."

Hal placed her hands on the mantelshelf, and leaned her forehead down on them.

"Tell me something funny, Dick, or I shall howl in a few seconds. Don't be serious. Be idiotic. Have the carrots and turnips decided which take precedence yet? Is her ladyship, the onion, weeping upon the cabbage's lordly bosom? Are the babies talking philosophy over their bottles? For Heaven's sake, Dick, be idiotic, and make me laugh." .

"I think it would do you more good to cry."

"Oh, no, no: I hate to cry. Do help me not to."

But Dick understood the relief it was to a woman to have it out, and he just sat down in Dudley's big arm chair, and reached the favourite footstool for Hal.

"Sit on the stool of confessional, and I'll make you laugh later on. If you don't cry now, you will when I've gone."

Hal sat on the footstool, and leaning against his knee, cried quietly for several minutes. He played with an unruly strand of hair until she dried her eyes, and then said:

"When we were kids, you always told me when things went wrong with you. Tell me all about it now."

"I left off being a kid about a month ago. I'm ancient history now"; and she tried to smile through her tears.

"Why?"

"Oh, just because—" and then her voice broke suddenly.

"I suppose Sir Edwin was in love with you?"

She did not reply.

"And he was obliged to marry the other woman for the money."

He was thoughtful for some moments, and then added:

"All the same, when a man like that goes so far as to love a woman, which must be a pretty novel experience for him, he doesn't let her go lightly. He won't let you go lightly, Hal."

"I shall not see him again."

"Has it come to that already?"

"It had to. There was no other course."

"It sounds rather sudden and drastic." He watched her keenly. "A man like that would try to get both of you. Did he try, Hal?"

The hot blood rushed to her face, and she turned her head away.

"Well, he would think it the obvious, sensible course, I suppose, and perhaps a good many women would, too. What did you think, Hal?"

"I didn't think. I hurried away. I shall not see him any more at all."

He looked at her with a light in his eyes.

"Bravo," he said; and there was a low thrill in his voice. "He'll think the world more of you, Hal."

"I'm not sure; anyhow, it doesn't help very much."

"Then you wanted to go."

She stared into the fire and was silent.

"I see," he said simply. "You are one of the women who would have dared, only... of course I knew you wouldn't, Hal. And, if you had, I shouldn't have been the one to blame you."

"Yes," she told him, still staring at the fire. "I could have dared under some circumstance. But not these. Never under pretty, ignoble ones. I think that all makes it worse. There were two Sir Edwins. There was one I knew, and another the world knew. It was the other that triumphed. Mine will never come back. It is all finished."

She bowed her head down on her arms.

"Oh, Dick," she said. "I shall miss him badly."

"But I'm glad you let him go, Hal." He spoke in a quiet voice full of feeling. "Most men are pretty casual and indifferent nowadays, and we often say we like a woman to be broad-minded, and daring, and all that; but, by Jove! when we know she's straight as a die, without being a prude, we're ready to kneel down to her.

"Stand to your guns, Hal. I... I... want to go on knowing that you are among those one wants to kneel down to. If he is very persistent and persevering, and it gets harder, I dare say I can help. You can always 'phone me at a moment's notice, and I shall consider myself at your beck and call."

"You are a dear, Dick, but I shall not see him. He can only wait for me at the office, and I shall go out the back way."

"Still, if you're rather lost there are lots of things we might do to fill up the time. I've been going down East with Quin lately. It's awfully interesting. Especially with him—he's so splendid with the most hopeless characters. There's a sing-song at one of the clubs on Wednesday eve. Come down with us. You'll see Quin at his very best."

"I'd love to come. Will you fetch me?"

"I'll fetch you from the office, and we'll have a sort of meat-tea meal at the Cheshire Cheese. Perhaps Quin will join us."

So they sat on and talked in the firelight till it was time for Dick to go; and all the time Hal was unconsciously drawing strength and resolution from him for the fight that lay ahead of her.

Many years ago when she broke her dolls he had tried to mend them and comfort her. And now, because he was a simple, manly gentleman, blessed with the precious gift of understanding—when she was feeling heart-broken he tried with all the old, generous affection to help to heal the wound, and bring her consolation.

And away on the southern shore, where a little fishing-village nestled in the cliffs, and a creeper-covered hotel awaited sleepily the coming of the summer and the summer visitors, Lorraine came to what she deemed her hour—the one great hour left—and, as a drowning man, caught at her straw. Two long perfect days they had spent on the sea, with an old fisherman, full of anecdote, and his young grandson to sail the boat.

Then came the dreamy twilight hour, and their utter loneness; and Alymer, with the strong, swift blood in his veins, and the strong lust of life in his heart, lost himself, as she meant that he should, in the intoxicating atmosphere of her charm and fascination.

CHAPTER XXXVIII

When Hal and her cousin emerged from the office the following Wednesday evening, the first thing Hal saw was Sir Edwin's motor, and Sir Edwin himself standing waiting for her. A disengaged taxi was just moving off, having deposited a fare, and instantly, without a word to Dick, she sprang into it. Dick gave a sharp glance round and followed her.

"Tell him where to go," she said.

He directed the chauffeur, and then looked anxiously into her face. She had turned very pale, and seemed for the moment overcome.

"Sir Edwin's motor?" he asked, and she nodded.

"Shall I call for you every day?" he said at once.

"No. He can't possibly see me if I go out the other way." Then she added: "He won't go on for long. He was there yesterday, but he did not see me; and after today I dare say he will give it up."

Finally she added, with an effort:

"I heard this morning the wedding is already fixed for June. It's to be one of the weddings of the season"; and her lips curled somewhat.

"I'm more sorry for her than for you, Hal," he said quietly. "You've a lot of splendid years before you yet. Heaven only knows what's ahead of her. I doubt he'll not give her much beside his name for his share of the bargain."

She made no comment, leaning back in her corner, white and tired. It was difficult to imagine anything ever being splendid again just then; or any man ever seeming other than tame, after Sir Edwin's clever, virile, interesting personality.

But Dick had judged wisely in suggesting the trip down East. Anything West would merely have recalled painful memories. The East of London was new to her, and could not fail to be interesting to any one with Hal's love of her fellows.

They went to a large parish hall, where Quin was in charge for a social evening of dancing and music. Factory girls were there in all their tawdry finery to dance; rough, boisterous youths mostly made fun of them; tired, white-faced, over-worked middle-aged women sat round the walls, laughing weakly, but forgetting the drudgery for a little while. At one end of the room older men sat and smoked, and looked at illustrated periodicals.

Hal entered with Quin and Dick on either side of her, and was immediately accosted by a young lady, with a longer and straighter feather than most of them, with the remark:

"Hullo, miss!... which of 'em's yer sweet'eart?"

A burst of laughter greeted this sally, but Hal, not in the least disconcerted, replied:

"Why, both, of course... I'll be bound you've had two at a time often enough."

The repartee delighted all within hearing, and from that moment Hal was a brilliant succes at the social evenings. She only wondered she had never thought to go before; but perhaps no other moment would have been just so propitious.

The sudden blank in her life craved some interest that was entirely new, and made her more ready to receive fresh impressions and create fresh occupations. She quickly found real pleasure in teaching the girls to dance properly, in listening to their outspoken humour, and soon developed an interest in their varied and vigorous personalities.

As she and Dick went home together that evening he noted joyfully that a little colour had come back to her face, and there was once more a genuine gleam in her eyes.

"You liked it?" he asked.

"Immensely."

"It grows on one. You'll like it better still yet. Alymer and I have always rather laughed at Quin, and regarded him as a crank. But he's not. It's just that he loves humanity, and he gets quite close up to the core of it down there, even if it is half-smothered in vice and dirt. I don't believe he'll ever take orders. It's partly because he's not a clergyman, and they know it, he's such a success. Tonight, for instance, there was a big bullying chap trying to spoil all the fun for the men who wanted to smoke peacefully and look at the books. Quin remonstrated, and he turned round and swore violently at him. To my surprise, Quin, if anything, outdid him. I wouldn't have believed

Quin could swear like that. I'm sure I couldn't myself. The chap just looked at him, and tried another oath or two doubtfully. And Quin said:

"Go on if you like, I'm not nearly through yet. I can't be a blank, blank, blank bully, and I don't want to be—it's nothing to be proud of; but I'm as much of a man as you any day."

"The other chaps laughed then, and the brute slunk off to the other side of the room."

"I asked Quin about it later, and he said:

"'Oh well, you've got to talk to them in their own language, or they don't listen. That's the best of not being a clergyman. Of course one couldn't very well curse and swear then. But it's the way to manage them. That chap will come to heel in an evening or two, and be reasonably quiet.'

"You hit the right note straight off, Hal. Quin was awfully pleased. Talk to them on their own level first, and presently you'll be getting them struggling up to yours almost without knowing it. He's frightfully keen for you to go again."

"I'm going every Wednesday," she said, "and other times as well."

They parted at the door, and Hal went in alone.

The moment she stood in the sitting-room she knew that something had happened. Dudley was sitting in his big chair by the fire, holding neither book nor paper, gazing silently at the flames.

At the table she stood still.

"What's the matter, Dudley?... What has happened?"

There were a few moments' silence, then, scarcely looking round, he replied:

"She's gone. Run away with another man."

"Gone!..." she echoed. "Gone... with another man! ... Do you mean Doris?"

"Yes. She was married at a Registry Office this morning. A messenger boy took the letter up this evening, after they had left for the Continent."

Hal sat down. It was so violently sudden she felt stunned. After a moment Dudley got up and moved aimlessly about the room.

"It's no use attempting to say anything, Hal. There's nothing to say. Of course I know you're sorry, and all that, but I'd rather you didn't say it. You never liked the engagement, and you never liked Doris. Probably you were justified, but it doesn't make it any easier for me now."

"Who has she gone with?"

"I believe he's a South African millionaire."

"Ah!—"

"You had heard of him?..." sharply.

"Only last week, from the tenant opposite. She did not know I was your sister, and said something about Doris having two young men, and one of them was a South African millionaire."

He made no comment, but continued his aimless walk.

"What about Ethel and Basil?" she could not help asking.

"They are terribly upset. As soon as I had been shown the letter I went out to make inquiries. Ethel could not rest for fear everything was not square. She wanted to go off after her at once. But it's all correct. I saw the Registrar. They were properly married, and they left for Dover at eleven, bound for Paris."

"What in the world will become of Basil?"

He winced visibly. Doris's flagrant selfishness to Basil hurt almost more than her faithlessness to himself.

"She stated in the letter that her husband was allowing her a thousand a year for herself, and she was prepared to pay a housekeeper to look after Basil and the flat."

"Little beast," Hal breathed under her breath. "What are they going to do?" she said aloud.

"The tenant opposite insists upon taking Doris's place. She was sitting with him when Ethel got home, and the letter arrived about the same time. Nothing else will satisfy her. She is going to be with him all day, and only teach in the evenings after Ethel has got back."

"How splendid of her!" involuntarily.

"She hardly seems the kind of person Basil would like, but he appeared quite pleased. It may have been a little quixotism. All he said was:

"What in the world should we have done without you, G; and there! only a few weeks ago you were wishing you had not been born."

"How like Basil. All gratitude and understanding as usual. But it must have hit him rather hard, Dudley. Is he all right?"

"I don't know." The gloom on Dudley's face deepened. "I thought he looked very ill, but I could not get Ethel to say much. She seemed rather to avoid me. I don't think she likes me."

Hal was conscious of a little inward smile of gladness. She had guessed Ethel's secret long enough ago, and she knew the power of uncertainty and a little thwarting. Dudley would naturally try to break down Ethel's dislike; and perhaps in doing so he would grow to know her better.

"I think I must try and get up tomorrow," was all she said. "Ethel is so reserved. She will get ill herself if she broods and frets on the top of all her work and anxiety."

"Will you?" he asked, with some eagerness. "Basil loves to see you; and if he is really worse, I shall get Sir John Maitland to go up and see him again."

"Of course I'll go. We may be able to help them between us."

She was just going away upstairs to bed, when the forlorness of Dudley's attitude, and the thought of her own sore heart before Dick comforted her, made her lay down her hat again and cross the room to him.

"Dudley, don't forget you've got me still. I know I'm very trying sometimes, but I love you so much more than Doris ever could have."

She sat on the arm of his chair, and played with the lapel of his coat.

"Don't forget about me, Dudley. If you are just only miserable, I shall be miserable too."

He looked at her with a sudden greater depth of affection than she had ever seen.

"I don't forget, Hal. If it weren't for you, what in the world should I do now?... It's no use talking about it, is it? You will understand that; but thank God you're still here with me, and we can go on the same again."

She stooped and kissed him hurriedly, and then left the room, that he might not see the tears brimming over in her eyes.

The next morning she rang up Lorraine's flat, to know if she had come back yet. She was rather surprised when Jean her maid answered. It was not like Lorraine to go away without her maid.

"You don't know when to expect her?..." she repeated uncertainly.

"No; Miss Vivian said she might come any day, or she might stay over another Sunday. She has the motor with her."

"Is she far from a station?" Hal asked, contemplating the possibility of joining her on Saturday if she had not returned.

"About seven miles, I think. She went down in the car, and is coming back in it. I have had one letter, in which she says she is having lovely weather, and absolute rest, and feeling much better."

"That's good. Well, if she comes back suddenly will you ask her to 'phone me? I want to see her."

But neither the next day nor the one after was there any call, and in reply to a second query on Saturday, Jean said she had only received a wire that morning saying she was staying until Tuesday.

Hal was a little puzzled that she had not been invited down for the second weekend, but decided Lorraine must have meant to return and changed her mind at the last moment, leaving no time to get a message to her.

A later encounter with Dick, however, puzzled her more than ever.

"Old Alymer is taking quite a long holiday," he said. "We were expecting him on Tuesday or Wednesday, but he never turned up. He was at the Temple on Thursday, but went away again in the evening."

"I hope Lorraine isn't ill?" she said anxiously; "but of course if she is, she would have sent for Jean."

"Is he away with Miss Vivian?" Dick asked in some surprise.

"Yes; I made him go," loyally. "He had scruples, but really they seemed too silly, and Lorraine looked so ill, and he always has the knack of cheering her up and doing her good."

Dick looked at her doubtfully.

"I hope you were wise," he said; "but they are rather fascinating people, you know."

"Oh, nonsense! Lorraine is quite eleven years older than Alymer, and she only likes to look at him."

Dick had it in his mind to suggest there had been a far greater disparity between her and Sir Edwin, but he only said:

"Well, he is good to look at, isn't he?... and such a dear old chap. Nothing seems to spoil him. And of course Miss Vivian has done an awful lot for him. If she wanted him to go, he could hardly refuse."

"That's just what I said," with a little note of triumph. "And Jean told me Lorraine had said in a letter she was having absolute rest, and feeling much better."

Yet, when Hal was alone she wondered a little again why Lorraine, after inviting her for the first Sunday, had said nothing about the second. It was quite unusual for her not to go for a weekend when Lorraine was at the sea.

She felt suddenly that they wanted to be alone, yet persuaded herself it was only because Lorraine had been so tired.

CHAPTER XXXIX

Hal's uneasiness concerning Lorraine and Alymer Hermon was swallowed up almost immediately on Lorraine's return, by a sudden alarming change in Basil Hayward. The first time she went to Holloway after Doris's elopement, she saw the decided symptoms of change, and her report to Dudley caused the latter once more, on his own responsibility, to request Sir John Maitland to pay a visit to the little flat.

Sir John's report was the reverse of reassuring, and they all felt the end was at hand. Dudley went to Holloway nearly every evening, and sometimes stayed until the middle of the night, to sit up with the sick man.

Hal went from the office in the afternoons, two or three days each week. When she was there the tenant from Flat G went home to snatch a short rest, in case a bad night lay ahead.

Ethel went quietly on her way, looking as if already a sorrow had wrapped her round before which human aid and human sympathy were powerless.

She went to the office as usual, and did her usual work, in nervous dread from hour to hour lest a telephone call should summon her in haste. She scarcely spoke to any one but Hal; and not very much to her; but it was evident in a thousand little ways that she liked to have her near.

With Dudley a new sort of coldness seemed to have sprung up. He was self-conscious ill at ease with her now; anxious to show his sympathy, yet made awkward by his self-sown notion that he was antagonistic to her. Ethel did not notice it very much. All her thoughts were with Basil.

Hal saw it and was troubled. She was afraid the slight misunderstanding might grow into a barrier that it would be extremely difficult to break down later on. However, she could only watch anxiously at present, and try in small ways to smooth out the growing difficulty.

Basil himself was the most consistently cheerful of all. He believed that he was near the end of his long martyrdom, and that in another sphere he would be given back his health and strength.

He had seemed very worried at first about Doris and Dudley, but gradually he became philosophical over it, and hoped the future would bring united happiness to Dudley and Ethel. He consigned her to Dudley's care and Hal's.

To Dudley he merely said:

"I know you'll always be a good friend to chum. I'm thankful she will at least have you."

Dudley did not say much in reply, but he looked sufficiently unhappy, and withal so glad of the service, that it spoke volumes.

To Hal he said:

"Chum is very fond of you, Hal. You'll keep an eye on her, won't you? Perhaps there is no one else but you who can."

Quick tears shone in Hal's eyes.

"Of course I will… two eyes.. I don't know that I shall let her out of my sight at all."

Other evening, because Dudley was so often at Holloway, Hal went to dinner with the Three Graces. Dick often fetched her from the office, and they went back together. Now that she had become interested in the East End, they had schemes to talk over, and she and Quin were never weary of discussing odd characters there, and odd histories, and plans for different amusements.

Dick joined in a times, but was very busy with his new book.

Alymer Hermon had grown strangely quiet. At intervals, for the sake of old times, he and Hal had sparring matches, but if, as was not very usual, he happened to be at home, he was inclined to do little else but lounge and smoke, and watch her while presumably reading a paper.

Hal did not notice it particularly. She had many other things on her mind just then, and Alymer only filled a very small corner. She was glad he was progressing so satisfactorily. He was well started up the ladder now, and though he had had no single big chance to distinguish himself once for all, it was generally regarded as merely a matter of time. She fancied she did not meet him so much at Lorraine's, but as she did not go nearly so often herself, on account of the Holloway visits, she could not really know.

But she noticed that Lorraine also was a little different—a little more reserved and likewise quieter. She seemed still to be ailing a good deal, and to have lost interest in her profession.

Yet she did not seem unhappy. On the contrary, Hal thought her happier than usual in an undemonstrative, dreamy sort of way. She was interested in the East End social evenings, and on one occasion went herself.

She was also interested in Basil Hayward, and motored up with lovely flowers for him; but she talked far less of the theatre, and seemed indisposed to consider a new part.

"I want a real long rest this summer," she had said, "free from rehearsals and everything."

In mid-June Sir Edwin was married, with a great deal of display, and much paragraphing of newspapers. The day before the wedding, Hal received a beautiful gold watch and chain from him.

"Do not be angry, and do not send it back," he wrote. "Keep it and wear it in memory of some one who was known to you only, and who has since died. To me, it is like honouring the memory of my best self if I can persuade you thus to perpetuate it. Good-bye, Little Girl; and God bless you."

Hal kept the watch and wore it, and the only one who demurred was Alymer Hermon. It was spoken of at the Cromwell Road flat one evening, when he was present but taking no part in the conversation. Dick admired it, and she told him it had been given to her recently.

Quin was not there, and a moment later Dick was called away to speak to some one at the telephone. Alymer looked up at Hal suddenly, with a very direct gaze.

"Lorraine told me Sir Edwin gave you the watch the other day. I don't know how you can keep it, much less wear it. You ought to throw it into the Thames."

Hal flushed up angrily.

"Of course I'm interested in your opinion on the matter," she said, "but I had not thought of asking for it."

Hermon flushed too, but he stood his ground.

"It would be the opinion of most men."

"'Most men' don't appeal to me in the least. I am quite satisfied with my own opinion in this matter."

"Still, I wish you wouldn't wear it," he urged, a little boyishly. "The man has shown himself a cad. He was in a tight corner, and he let a woman buy him out."

"And don't most men take help from a woman at some time or other?"

He winced, but answered sturdily:

"Not monetary help. Besides, he didn't worry much about getting you talked of, did he?"

Hal was just going to make a sarcastic retort, when Dick reappeared, and the matter was dropped.

But when she came to think of it afterwards, she could not but be a little struck at Alymer's attitude, and wondered why he had taken so much interest in her action.

A few days later Basil Hayward died.

Hal was not there at the time, but Dudley had not come home at all the previous night, and she was afraid that his friend was worse. In the afternoon she had been detained at the office, and she hardly liked to go up to Holloway in the evening without knowing if she was wanted.

So she sat anxiously waiting for Dudley. When at last he arrived he looked haggard and worn and ill. Hal stood up when he came in, and waited for him to speak.

"It's all over," he said, and sank into his chair as if he were dead-beat.

Hal's hart ached with sympathy. She felt instinctively there was more here than grief for a friend whose death could only be regarded as a merciful release.

She was right. For the last three weeks Dudley and Ethel had been in almost daily contact beside the dying man's bed. Silently, devotedly they had served him together.

But while Ethel was occupied only with the sufferer, Dudley, in the long night-watches, had seen at last what manner of woman it was he had passed by for the pretty, shallow, selfish little sister.

Ever since the elopement, three months ago, he had been changing. It had been the bitter blow that had stabbed him awake. In some mysterious way new aspects, new ideas, new understanding, began to develop, where before had been chiefly a narrow outlook and rigid conformity.

It was though in the fulfilling of her work, Life had harrowed his soul with a bitter harrowing, that it might bring forth the better fruit in its season. The harrowing had seared and scarred, but already the new richness was showing, the new promise of a nobler future.

The All-wise Mother works very much in human life as she does in nature—topping off a hope here, and a hope there; ploughing, pruning, harrowing the soil and branches of the mind and spirit, that they may bring forth rich fruit in due season.

The life that she passes by unheeded, leaving it only to the sunshine and wind and rain, often grows little else but rank vegetation, and develops rust and mould—never the crops that are life-giving and life-sustaining to the world; never the great thoughts, great deeds, wide sympathies, that raise mankind to the skies.

But for Dudley the harrowing was not yet finished. Perhaps, indeed, no moment of all had been quite so bitter as the sense of his utter unworthiness and utter incapability to help Ethel in her hour of direst need.

The mere thought unnerved him for the little he might have done. He was so imbued with the idea of his helplessness, that he could only stammer a few broken sentences she seemed scarcely capable of hearing.

He had but one consolation. Towards the end, the sick man, suddenly opening his eyes, looked round for his sister, and seeing she was absent, had regarded Dudley with his whole face full of a question.

Dudley leant down to him.

"Yes, old chap," he asked tenderly. "What is it?"

"Ethel... chum... you will try and help her?"

Then Dudley, with his new understanding, had grasped all that the dying man hoped.

"I love her," he said very simply. "I have been a blind fool, but I am awake now. I shall give my life to trying to win her."

"Oh! thank God... thank God," Basil whispered. "It is certain to come right some day—don't lose heart. You have made me very happy."

He sank into stupor after that, and spoke no more, except for a whispered "Chum", just before he died.

Then it was that the full flood of Dudley's bitterness seemed to close in upon him, for his tortured mind translated Ethel's stunned grief into veiled antipathy to his presence; and when there was nothing left for him to see to, he went home for Hal.

In his chair, with his head bowed on his hands, Hal thought he had aged years in the last three months.

"What shall I do?" she asked. "Shall I go to Ethel?"

"Yes—will you? She doesn't want me. I feel as if she hated my being there now. But if you would go—?"

"It is your imagination, Dudley. Things have all got a little topsy-turvy since Doris went, but presently you will see you were mistaken. Don't lose heart too quickly."

But he refused to be comforted, and merely shook his head in silent desolation.

"You'll stay with her if she wants you?" he asked.

"Yes, I'll stay"; and she went away to get her hat.

As she mounted the stairs in Holloway, the door of Flat G opened as if some one within had been listening for her, and a stealthy head peeped out. Then a hand beckoned.

Hal crossed the landing and went inside the door. The poor music-teacher's face was swollen almost past recognition with crying.

"What am I to do?... what am I to do?" she moaned, rocking herself backwards and forwards. "There was only one thing in all the world that made my life worth living, and now it is gone."

She sobbed bitterly for a few minutes, softened by Hal's sympathetic presence, then she told her brokenly:

"They're all mourning. Every single soul in this dreary building. Considering he never left the flat, it's wonderful—wonderful; but he knew all the children, and they all knew him. And if you know the children you know the fathers and mothers.

"Little Splodgkins, as we always called him, has been sitting like a small stone effigy on the stairs outside his door. He has patrolled the whole staircase for days, keeping the other children quiet. I told Mr. Hayward, and he sent him a message. He said, 'Tell him to grow up a fine man, and fight for his country, and not to forget me before we meet again.' The little chap fought back his tears when I gave him the message, and he said: 'Tell him, I thaid dammit, tho I will.'

"But they're young, and they've got each other, most of the other folks here, and I've got nothing—nothing. Miss Pritchard, I can't go on again the same—I can't—I can't."

"You must help Miss Hayward, at any rate for a time," Hal told her; "if you didn't you would be failing him now; and even little Splodgkins doesn't mean to do that."

"No, of course you're right. I can light the fire for her in the afternoon and put the kettle on. It isn't much to be alive for, but he'd say it was worth while. He'd say, 'What would she do without a G in the alphabet?' wouldn't he? I must remember. And now you must go to her. It's worse for her than me, only that she's still got all her life before her, and she's very attractive, while I never seemed to please any one in my life but him."

"Yes; I must go now," Hal said; "but I'll come and see you again. Come down east with me next Wednesdayn evening, to a social evening in the slums, will you? They're so interesting. We'll have tea together first. I'll arrange to take you, and then you'll meet Dick."

"Good-bye for the present."

Then she crossed the landing, wondering with a sinking heart how she could ever hope to comfort Ethel.

CHAPTER XL

It was not until a spell of exhaustingly hot weather set in in early July that Hal saw a still more noticeable frailty in Lorraine.

She was quite unable to act, and spent a great deal of time on her sofa near the window, where she could just distinguish the river through the trees. It seemed to have a growing fascination for her.

"I've always thought," she told Hal one day, "how I'd like to go away from the fret and worry of London, smoothly down the river to a haven of sunshine and sea."

"Why don't you go, Lorry. Why not go at once, before you get any weaker?"

"I think I must. This sultry heat is too much for me, and I'm very tired of London and everything belonging to it. I should like to have gone to my old haven on the Italian Riviera, but it would be too hot."

"Why so far?"

Lorraine glanced at Hal with a strange expression in her eyes, as she said:

"It is a greater rest to get right away. I shall try some little place in Brittany. Switzerland is so overrun with tourists in the summer."

When she was alone, some of the quiet went out of Lorraine's face and a restless look of pain crept in. She shaded her eyes and gazed long at the river.

That old spirit of recklessness, which had caused her to hurl scorn and defiance at Mrs. Hermon's emissary, and afterwards allow Alymer to visit her at the little fishing-village, against his wiser judgment, had passed away now, and given place to one of poignant questioning—a spirit of questioning concerning that mad action of hers, and its results. She could not find it in her heart to regret it, not for one moment; but nevertheless her mind was sore troubled concerning the future for Alymer and herself.

And at the back of all the questioning there sounded ever an insistent call to renounce—something above and beyond all desire and all seeming, which told her she must not remain in his life, that, as far as she was concerned, he must be free for the great work of his future.

And yet how hard it was to go! Ever and anon her longing whispered, "Why seek a crisis yet? Why not go on the same a little longer?"

But since, before long, she would be compelled to go, and since the nausea of London was gaining upon her, she began to feel it would certainly be wiser to start at once, and find some homely, quiet spot where she could remain in privacy, with her identity unknown for some months.

And always that quiet voice in the background insisted that she must cut herself off from Alymer Hermon.

Soon after Hal had left her he came in, and, standing as usual upon the hearth, regarded her with grave eyes. He was nearly always grave now, as with some recollection that weighed heavily on his mind.

Lorraine tried to rally him, but without much success; and a pitiless thought that had sometimes assailed her of late—that he regretted their friendship and everything connected with it, struck icily on her heart.

He was too loyal to show it, and yet, that strong instinct of womanhood, which reads closed books as if they were spread open to the light, sounded its warning note. He would never blame her openly, but in his heart he was already beginning to find it a little difficult not to do so secretly.

"You can't go away alone, Lorry," he said unhappily, "and I can't possibly come with you."

"Of course you can't," cheerfully. "It isn't to be thought of for a moment. I don't know whether you can even come and see me. You certainly mustn't run any risks just now. Flip tells me Hall is interested, and you may get your big chance shortly through him."

"Still, I shall feel rather a beast."

"You mustn't do anything so silly."

She got up and came and stood near him, leaning her face against his arm.

"If you will write to me often, dearie, I shall be all right. If you worry I shall be miserable. Try to understand that you have done nothing to make me unhappy. A little while ago I had a dream of how I longed to go away with a little one of my own, to some quiet spot far removed from all I have ever known. If I am to realise my dream, how should I not be happy? It is what I asked life to give me."

But his eyes lost none of their gravity. It was evident, in the midst of his dawning success, some cloud had descended upon his horizon, and shrouded much of the sunlight.

Lorraine's sensitive temperament read it quickly, and she decided, for his sake, to hasten her departure. She thought her continued presence in London under the circumstances was a continual anxiety to him, and that he would only breathe freely when she was safe in Brittany.

She did not know—how should she—that after that week's madness on the southern coast there had come rather a terrible revelation to the man whom fortune seemed to be smothering with favours.

It had not come all at once. It had been there, or at any rate the gist of it, for some time. But when it was present in full force, it had the power to make all the adulation, triumph, and hopefulness of his career seem but a small thing and of little account, because of one great desire beyond his reach.

It came definitely into being during those many evenings Hal spent at the Cromwell Road flat, when Dudley was away in Holloway with his friend.

It reached a climax of realisation when she openly wore the watch and chain Sir Edwin had sent to her. The night he asked her not to wear it, and she tautingly refused, saw him, with all his success and favours, one of the most perplexed and unhappy men in London.

It was just the waywardness of the little god Love. The fair débutantes with money and influence had left him untouched. No older woman but Lorraine had disturbed his peace, or appealed to his deepest affections.

It was left to Hal, the mocker, the outspoken, the impatient of giant inches and splendid head, to awaken his heart to all its richness of strong, enduring love.

And what did it mean to her?

The sunshine and the joy might go out of all he was winning and achieving, if it might not be won and achieved for her—but what did she care—what was she ever likely to care?

Had she not always dealt him laughter and careless scorn where other women bowed down? Had she not, over and over, weighed him in the balance, in that quiet, direct way of hers, and seen the weak strain that had always been there? First the lack of purpose, the idle indifference, which, in a different guise, had led up to a memory which now tortured his mind—the memory of a mad week; of love that was not love, because his whole soul was not given with it—nay, worse, was actually given in unconsciousness elsewhere. If she ever knew of that, what must her indignation and scorn be then?... Would it not indeed separate them for ever?

And even if it did, could it make him unlove her?... Why should it, since he had waited no encouragement before he gave her all? If he knew why he loved her, it might.

But he did not even know that. It was a thing outside questioning; something he seemed to have had no free will about. It was just there—a strong, undeniable fact.

Why reason? It did not *need* reasoning. He loved her. He would always love her—simply because she was Hal—and as Hal, to him, was the one woman who filled his heart.

No; Lorraine did not know just what fire of repentance and self-condemnation and hopeless aching her recklessness had lit for him; but it was enough that his gravity grew and deepened, and she believed she could lighten it.

She made immediate plans; cancelled her present engagement at considerable monetary loss to herself, and almost before any of them realised it, had vanished to a little out-of-the-way spot in Brittany, alone with Jean.

Hal was quite unhappy that she could not go to her for her own summer holiday, but Dick Bruce's people were taking her to Norway with them, and she would not have a day to spare.

She made Alymer promise to run across and see how she was, if possible, and then departed without any suspicions or forebodings, with Dudley and Dick to join the rest of the party at Hull, whence they were to start for the Fiords.

When she returned early in September, Lorraine was still away, and her letters gave no hint of returning. Still a little anxious, she sought an interview with Alymer, asking him to meet her for tea the following day.

The instant they met, Hal saw the change in him, and exclaimed in surprise:

"Haven't you had a holiday? You don't look very grand."

Unable to meet her eyes, he turned away towards a small table.

"Oh yes, I've had a holiday. I've been in France studying the language. I can talk like a French froggy now."

"Then of course, you saw Lorraine?" .

"Yes."

"I wanted to see you about Lorry," with direct, straight gaze.

He steadied his features with an effort.

"I guessed so."

"Well, what is the matter with her?"

"Nothing very much. She got thoroughly low I think, and is not pulling up very quickly."

"I don't understand it," with puzzled, doubtful eyes. "Lorry is not like that. She is quite strong really. She has only once before gone under like this, and then it was a mental strain. I wonder if it is anything the same again? Did you see much of her?"

"I saw her four or five times."

"And she didn't tell you anything?"

"Anything about what?"

"Well—about her husband, for instance. He isn't worrying her again, is he?"

"She did not speak of him at all."

"Then what is it?... I wish she had not gone so far away. I wish I could get to her. Did she say when she might be coming back?"

"Not at present. She likes being there. She does not want to come back."

"That's what I can't understand. Something odd seems to have changed her. Have you thought so."

"I don't think it odd in Lorraine to fancy a long spell of country life. She was always loved the country."

"Not alone," with decision, "except for a good reason. I feel there is a reason now, and I do not know it."

Suddenly she gave him another direct look.

"You are changed too. You are years older. Is it your advancing success, or what? ... I don't say it isn't becoming," with a dash of her old banter— "but it seems sudden."

He raised his eyes slowly and looked into her face with an expression that in some way hurt her. It was the look of a devoted dog, craving forgiveness.

She pushed her cup away impatiently, half laughing and half serious.

"Don't look at me like that, Baby," striving blindly to rally him—"you make me feel as if I had smacked you."

He laughed to reassure her, and changed the subject to Norway, trying to keep her mind from further questioning concerning himself and Lorraine.

After tea she left him to go down to Shoreditch with Dick, first meeting him and the forlorn "G" at the Cheshire Cheese for their usual high tea.

It had become quite an institution now that "G" should join them, and, as Hal had predicted, she and Dick were firm friends. It was the brightest spot of the music-teacher's life since Basil Hayward died, and neither of them would have disappointed her for the world if they could help it.

Tonight Quin was there also, so Hal was able to get a few words privately with Dick.

"What in the world is the matter with Alymer?" she asked. "I had tea with him this afternoon. He seems awfully down on his luck."

"I don't know what it is," Dick answered. "He is certainly not very gay—yet that last case he won before the Law Courts closed should have put him in fine feather for the whole vacation. Did you ask him if anything was wrong?"

"Yes; but he would only prevaricate. He has been in France, you know, studying the language, and he saw Lorraine, but he says very little about her. I wish I had time to go over and see her. Why, in the name of goodness, is she not acting this winter?"

But Dick could not help her to any solution, and an accumulation of work kept her too busy to brood on the puzzle.

It was at the end of October the shock came.

Hal reached home before Dudley that evening, and found a foreign letter awaiting her, written in an unfamiliar handwriting, and bearing the post mark of the little village where Lorraine so obstinately remained. With an instant sense of apprehension, she tore open the envelope, and read its contents with incredulity, amazement, and anxiety struggling together in her face.

Then she sat down in the nearest chair with a gasp, and stared blankly at the window, as if she could not grasp the import of the bewildering news.

The letter was from Jean, partly in French, and partly in English. It informed Hal, in somewhat ambiguous phrases, that La Chère Madame was very ill, and daily growing weaker, and she, Jean, was very worried and unhappy about her. She thought if mademoiselle could possibly get away, she should come at once. It then went on to make a statement which took Hal's breath away.

"L'enfant!... l'enfant!..." she repeated in a gasping sort of undertone, and stared with bewildered eyes at the window.

What could have happened?... What did it all mean?

Then with a rush all the full significance seemed to come to her. Lorraine, ill and alone in that little far-away village, and this incomprehensible thing coming upon her; no one but a paid, though devoted maid to take care of her; no friend to help her in the inevitable hours of dread, and perhaps painful memories and apprehensions.

All her quick, warm-hearted sympathy welled up and filled her soul. Of course she must go at once, tonight if possible, or early tomorrow.

Yet as she struggled to collect her thoughts and form plans, she was conscious of a dumb, nervous cry: "What will Dudley say?... What in the world will Dudley say?"

CHAPTER XLI

He came in while she was still trying to compose herself for the struggle she anticipated; and because she had not yet made any headway, he saw at once that something alarming had happened.

He glanced at the envelope lying on the table, then at the open letter in her hand, and then at her face.

"What is the matter?... Have you had bad news?"

For one dreadful moment, observing the foreign stamp, he thought something might have happened to Ethel, who was taking her month's holiday on the Continent. When Hal looked blankly into his face, as if quite unable to tell him, he added hurriedly:

"Is your letter about Ethel?... Is she ill?"

"No, it is not Ethel," Hal answered, noticing, in spite of her distress, his unconcealed anxiety. "Some one is ill, but it is not Ethel."

"Is it Lorraine?"

He spoke with quiet, kindly concern now, being reassured concerning the swift dread that had sized him.

"Yes," Hal said nervously. "She is very ill. Dudley, I must go to her at once."

She got up as if she could not bear the strain seated, and moved away to the window.

"It's all rather terrible," speaking hurriedly; "but don't... don't... be upset about it. I can't bear it. I *must* go, whatever you say, and I want you to help me."

"What is the matter?" He came close to her and tried to see her face. "What has happened, Hal?"

"Lorry is in trouble." She was half crying now; "I have had a letter from Jean. She has told me something I did not know. I did not even suspect it. But I must go. You will surely see that I must go, Dudley."

"Tell me what it is," he said, in a voice so kind, she turned and looked into his face, almost in surprise. He met her eyes, and, reading all the distress there, he added:

"Don't be afraid, Hal. I know I was an awful prig a little while ago, but... but... it's not the same since Doris jilted me, and since Basil died. I see many things differently now. Tell me Lorraine's trouble."

"She is so ill, because if she lives until next December she will have a little one. Oh, do you understand, Dudley? She is there all alone, because she made a mess of her life and is obliged to hide. I must go to her. You will help me, won't you?"

She glanced at him doubtfully, and then a swift relief seemed to fill her face.

"Yes, certainly you must go," he said gravely; "if Jean says she is ill now, I think you should go at once, and see for yourself just how things are."

"Oh, how good of you. I was afraid you would be angry and object."

He smiled a little sadly.

"I've enough money in hand for your ticket. You can catch the early boat train, and I'll send some more by tomorrow's post. Had you better see Mr. Elliott about being absent from the office for a day or two, or shall I see him in the morning?"

"He won't mind. I've got everything straight since I came back, and Miss White will do my work for a day or two. If you would see him in the morning, and just tell him Miss Vivian is very ill and I was sent for. He knows what friends we are, and would understand."

"Very well. Now you must have some dinner, and get to bed, for you will have a long, anxious day tomorrow."

In a sudden rush of feeling, she put her hands on his shoulders and kissed him.

"I'm so grateful," she said, in a quivering voice. "I can't tell you. It has all come upon me as a shock. I had not the faintest suspicion."

It was not natural to him to be demonstrative, and he only turned away with a slight embarrassment, saying:

"I'm sure you hadn't. But I feel I can trust you now, Hal, to be discreet as well as quixotic. Your mission, if one can call it such, will need both."

Then he sought to distract her mind for the present, and while they dined he talked of many things to interest her.

"Do you know that Alymer Hermon has just got the chance of his life?" he told her, before they rose. "I heard today he is to appear with Hall in this big libel case. Sir James Jameson told me at the Club. He said Hall had taken a great fancy to him, and if he does really well over this case he's going to take him up. He is very fortunate. Not one man in a thousand would get such a chance at his age. I hope he will do well; I like him; and if he isn't a success over this he may never get such an opportunity again."

"When does the case come on?"

"Almost at once, I think, but it probably will not last more than two or three days."

When Hal said good-night to him, she remarked shyly:

"I heard from Ethel last night. She loves the Austrian Tyrol. She said she hoped you were better for your trip to Norway."

His forehead contracted a little, and he did not look up from the book he had just opened.

"Is she better herself? Is she any happier?"

Hal looked thoughtfully into the fire.

"I think she is very lonely. I don't think she will be much happier until... until... there is some one to take Basil's place."

"No one can do that." He spoke a little shortly. "Basil was a hero. I do not know how she is ever to love a lesser man."

"If she loved a man, she would easily see heroic qualities in him. She could not love a man who was without them; but that does not mean he need actually be a hero by any means."

She longed to say more, but was diffident of doing greater harm than good. At last she ventured:

"I have sometimes thought she has a warm corner in her heart for you, Dudley."

"For me!..." He gave a low, harsh laugh for very misery. "No; she despises me. She has done for some time. I'm sorry. I'd change it if I could, but it's too late now."

Hal moved towards the door.

"It is rather a slur on Ethel to suggest that she could possibly despise Basil's best friend. Don't let an idea like that take root, Dudley. 'Lookers on see most of the game,' you know, and what I have seen has suggested quite differently. Good-night."

"Good-night. Try to sleep. I'll take you to Charing Cross myself."

The next morning Hal started off alone, to find her way to Lorraine's hiding-place, and give her what comfort of friendship she could.

And all the time she asked herself with harried thoughts, "Who has brought this trouble into Lorraine's life?"

And at the back of her mind was the dread premonition "Was it indeed Alymer Hermon?"

CHAPTER XLII

When Hal first saw her old friend she was almost too shocked for words at the swift change in her. Lorraine tried hard to smile cheerfully, but she could not hide any longer from herself how seriously ill she had grown, and she felt it useless to try and hide it from Hal.

Jean had not told her of the letter, and she knew nothing of Hal's coming until she was actually in the house. When she saw her, she could have cried for gladness.

"How good of you, Hal... how good of you!" she breathed, and Hal, on her knees by the couch, in an unsteady voice replied:

"Oh, why didn't you send for me sooner? Why didn't you let me come here instead of going to Norway?"

An hour later she went out to the little post office, and wired to London to know if she might remain away for a week.

It was evident Lorraine was very ill indeed and needing the utmost care.

During the day she seemed to grow steadily worse, and she could not bear Hal out of her sight.

"I don't know whether you are shocked or not," she said to her once, "but if everything goes all right I shall not regret what I have done for one moment. I wanted something more real for the rest of my life than I have had in its beginning." Her voice dropped to a whisper. "I wanted his child to live for."

With a caressing hand on the sick woman's, Hal asked in a low voice:

"Why isn't he here taking care of you now? Where is your child's father?"

A swift surprise passed through Lorraine's eyes, as if it had not occured to her Hal would not know the truth. Then she said, very softly, "Alymer."

"Ah!"

The exclamation seemed wrung from Hal unconsciously, and after it her lips grew strangely rigid.

"Hal," Lorraine said weakly, "I've loved Alymer almost ever since I first saw him. I swore I would not harm his career, and I have not. I will not in future. But the child is his, and I thank God for it. I do not believe an illegitimate child with a devoted mother is any worse off than the legitimate child with a selfish, unloving one. That there is love enough matters the most. What can any child have better than a life's devotion?"

Later on she said:

"This is his great week, Hal. In his last letter he tells me his big chance has come at last through Sir Philip Hall. We always hoped it would. It is the big libel case, and if Sir Philip chooses he can let him take a very prominent part. He will, I am sure of it. He is very interested in him, and he has given him this chance on purpose. Flip thinks it will lead to a great deal; and of course if so it is splendid for him."

Hal said very little. She was overcome at the revelation Lorraine had made, and seemed quite unable to grasp it.

Meanwhile she waited fearfully for the crisis the doctor had told her was impending. She was expecting him to call again, and was relieved when at last he arrived bringing a pleasant-faced French nurse with him.

She relinquished her post then, and waited for him anxiously downstairs. When he came he told her he must have another opinion at once, and Hal knew that something serious was wrong, and that he feared the worst.

The next morning, when she saw Lorraine again, she understood that they had saved her life, but probably only for a few days at the most.

Lorraine was almost too weak to speak, but she looked into Hal's eyes, and in her own there was a dumb imploring. Hal leant down and murmured:

"What is it, Lorry?... Do you want Alymer?"

"Yes," was the faint whisper. "I feel it is the end. I want so much to see him once more."

"I will go to London myself, and fetch him," Hal said, and a look of rest crept into the dying woman's eyes.

So it happened that the day before the great libel case Hal stood in Hermon's chambers, and delivered her message.

It was a tense moment—a moment of warring instincts, warring inclinations, conflicting fates. It was surely the very irony of ironies, that within sight of his goal, with all this woman had manoeuvred to give him almost in his hands, she should be the one to step suddenly between him and the realisation of everything his life had striven for.

To fail Sir Philip Hall at the eleventh hour, under such circumstance, could only mean an irreparable disaster. He would lose, as far as his profession was concerned, in every single way. It would strike a blow at his progress, from which it might never wholly recover.

No wonder, confronted with the sudden demand life had flung at him, he stood stock still, with rigid face, almost overcome by the swift sword-thrust of fate, and made no reply.

Since Hal told him, in a few, rather abrupt words, her story, he had scarcely looked at her. When she first entered his room so unexpectedly, his eyes had searched her face as if he would read instantly what she had come for?... what she had learnt?... Before hers, his gaze fell.

"I have come from Lorraine," she said, and he understood that she knew all.

A dull red crept over his face and neck, and then died away, leaving him of an ashy paleness. He was standing by his desk, and he reached out one hand and rested it on some books, gripping the backs of them with a grip that made his knuckles stand out like white knots. He did not ask Hal to sit down. Commonplace amenities died in the stress of the moment.

She stood in the middle of the room, very straight and very still. In a close-fitting travelling-dress she looked unusually slim, almost boyish, and something about her attitude rather suggested a youthful knight, sword in hand, come with vengeance to the Transgressor. Yet, even in his shame and stunned perplexity, Hermon lost no shred of dignity.

He towered above her, with bend head, rigid, white face, grave, downcast eyes, and in spite of every reproach her attitude seemed to hurl at him, he yet wore the look of nobility that was his birthright.

"When do you think I should go?" he asked at last, with difficulty.

"We ought to cross tonight."

"Tonight!—I—I—have a very important case tomorrow. It will not last long. It matters a great deal."

"I know," was the short, uncompromising answer.

He looked up with a swift glance of inquiry. Then he said quietly:

"Do you know that it may wreck my future to leave London tonight?"

"Yes," said Hal. "I know."

"And after all Lorraine did not help me to this hour of success, am I to throw away my chance?"

"Lorraine is dying. Her dying wish is to see you once more. Is it necessary to discuss anything else?"

Again there was silence between them—silence so intense, so poignant, it was like a live thing present in the room. Through the double windows came a far-off, muffled sound of the traffic in the Strand, but it seemed to have nothing whatever to do with the life of that quiet room. It did not disturb the silence, in which one could almost hear pulse beats. It belonged to another world.

Once Alymer raised his head and looked hard into her face. In his eyes there was an expression of utter hopelessness. She had not spoken any word of reproach or scorn, yet everything about her as she stood there erect and passionless, and without one grain of sympathy for his struggle, told him that, just as far as her natural broadness allowed her to condemn any one, she condemned him.

For a moment a sort of savage recklessness seized him. He felt suddenly he was stranded high-and-dry on a barren rock, with nothing at all any more in his world but his profession. He had lost all hope of ever winning Hal, which seemed to be all hope of anything worth having. Nothing remained but the hollow interest of a great name, and the lust of power. He had it in his mind for those brief, passionate moments, because he had lost all else, to insist upon taking his chance.

Even one day's grace might save him. The trial would perhaps last not more than two, but in any case, a wire reaching him in the middle, which he could show to Sir Philip, might mean all the difference between success and failure. The wire could be worded to hide what was truly involved, and the plea of a life-and-death urgency would set him free without any awkward questioning.

He glanced up to speak, and once again Hal's attitude arrested him. She looked so young, so fresh, so true, so vaguely splendid, in spite of the rigid lips that seemed to have closed down tightly upon all she must have suffered in the last forty-eight hours.

She was not looking at him now, but, with her head thrown back a little, she gazed silently and fatefully at the clock on his mantelpiece.

And something about her called to him, with the calling of the great, mysterious things, a calling that shamed and scorned that spirit of savage recklessness; that swift, relentless lust of power.

"What is anything in the world," it seemed to cry, "compared to being true to one's friend; true to one's word; true to one's love?"

He saw suddenly that in any case success and triumph would bring him little enough to gladden his heart; that whichever way he turned was gloom and darkness; that in that gloom a possible ray of light might still linger, if he could keep always the consciousness that, at the most critical hour of his life, he had rung true.

He raised his eyes suddenly, and straightened himself.

"What time does the next train leave?" he said. "I am coming."

CHAPTER XLIII

After Hal had left, Lorraine sank into a stupor from weakness, and remained thus until towards evening. Then she revived, and seemed to comprehend better all that had happened; all that was happening still.

She knew that the child she had dreamed of would never lie in her arms and look up at her with Alymer's eyes. She knew that in the first awful moments of realisation, and deathly weakness, her whole soul had so craved to see Alymer again that she had asked for him.

A few moments later the stupor had come down upon her exhausted senses, and without any further word or thought from her, Hal had gone on her errand.

At first, in the darkened room where she had suffered so much, she remembered only that very soon Alymer might be with her. And the thought, while it quickened her pulses, yet made her feel almost faint with the longing for him to come quickly. What if they were delayed, and this terrible weakness took her away from him without a last meeting.

The thought that death was approaching did not frighten her. She rather welcomed it. When she left London in the summer, she had felt that she could never go back. She had already fixed in her mind the picture of the quiet haven, where she would live restfully with Alymer's child—far away from the turmoil that had marked her life almost from its earliest beginning, and safe from slander.

She did not mind for herself. The things that most women valued, no longer held much meaning for her. She had experienced more than most; learned more than most how empty success and triumph may become; sounded for herself the shallowness of many things that society regards as prizes.

She had been tired for a long time. Now the tiredness had reached a climax. If the quiet haven might not bless her life, it was, on the whole, better that she should die.

This quiet fatalism only increased her longing to see Alymer once more. It was the one thing in all existence left to long for. It merged every remaining faculty into one desire. And Hal would bring him. Hal never failed any one.

Then came the night, and instead of a quiet sleep, restlessness seized her. The recollection of the lawsuit which was to make Alymer's name once for all, came back again and again with merciless insistence, fighting like some desperate thing that last, one, great desire. Try as she would to smother it, after a little period of rest it came back stronger than ever.

In vain she told herself that when he knew she was dying he would have no wish but to hasten to her. In vain, she said also, that success would no longer mean all it had done; that with love crying to him from a death-bed, he would understand its emptiness and scorn it.

Another voice, the voice of her truest self, answered: "Ah! but he is young. Remember he is young—young—young—and you, when you were his age, cared terribly to succeed. You say now that success is empty, but at least you had the satisfaction of learning the fact for yourself. You did not have to take another's word for it, and let your chance pass you by, just at the moment of grasping it. If he is to be left without you, what will he have then to make up for the great moment lost?

"Nay, worse—what will he have left to spur him to try and regain his proud position, and go on up the heights of fame? And for you, of all people, to deal this blow to his future—the ambitious future which you yourself have fostered and nourished with such care."

The hours wore on, and still, in spite of the awful physical exhaustion, the mental battle raged, draining away strength that should have been carefully nursed for each bad hour of many days ahead. The nurse watched beside her with growing alarm, seeing the feverishness and restlessness, where absolute quiet was imperative.

At last she went to her softly, and said, in a sweet, low voice:

"Madame is in trouble. Madame is fretting. It is not good. Madame must try to rest."

Lorraine turned her feverish, pain-driven eyes to the kindly face, with a look of beseeching, but she made no reply.

The nurse laid her cool hand on the burning forehead.

"Madame is not a Catholic, but the priest brings healing to all. Shall I ask him to come and pray, that peace may be given to the sick mind?"

"I cannot confess," Lorraine breathed a little gaspingly. "I could not bring myself to it."

"It is not necessary. The priest will come to pray if madame wishes."

"Yes," was the low response; "please ask him."

The little old man who took care of the souls of the little old-world village, and had done for three parts of a century, came to her at once, with a womanly tenderness in his face. In a low voice he blessed her, and then knelt down and prayed quietly.

After a time, some of the anguish died out of Lorraine's eyes. She turned to him weakly and said:

"I am not a Catholic. I do not know if I am anything, but I want to ask you something. If one has sinned, and led another astray, might an act of renunciation perhaps save that other from the consequences of the sin that was not his?"

"Self-sacrifice and renunciation are ever pleasing to God," he told her simply. "He knows that whatever else there is in a heart, with self-sacrifice there is also purity and nobility."

"If I thought I alone need bear the consequences, I think I could do anything," she whispered—"bear anything, renounce anything."

Again the quiet soothing of a prayer fell on her ears. She listened, and heard the old priest praying God and the Holy Virgin to help her to find the courage for the sacrifice her heart called for, that if she were about to enter the presence of the Most High, she might take with her the cleansing of repentance and a self-sacrificing spirit.

She lay still for some little time listening to the soft cadence of his voice, and then she opened her eyes and looked at him with a full, sweet look.

"I will do it, Father," she said to him. "Perhaps, if God understands everything, He will let my anguish of renunciation absolve that other from all sin. It is the most I have to ask of all the powers in heaven and earth."

"The Holy Mother comfort you, my child," he said; and with an earnest benediction left her.

Then Lorraine motioned to the French nurse that she wanted her, and gathering all her remaining strength asked for a telegraph form and pencil. The nurse supported her in her arms, while with a trembling hand she traced faintly the words of her message. It ran:

"Marked change for the better. No need for haste. Come in a few days.—LORRAINE."

It was addressed to Alymer Hermon, at The Middle Temple.

"Please take it now at once," she said. She knew that the Frenchwoman could not read English, and that Jean was not yet awake.

CHAPTER XLIV

In Alymer's room at the Middle Temple he and Hal were making their arrangements to catch the next boat.

The moment he had spoken his decision she had turned to him with a swift expression of approval, but, for the rest, her manner was somewhat curt and business-like, and showed little of the old friendliness.

It made him feel that, as far as she was concerned, he had sinned past forgiveness; and he knew with that unerring instinct that sometimes illumines a wrong action, that she judged him harshly because she knew he had not loved Lorraine with all his strength. How then could he ever hope to tell her that one reason he had not loved Lorraine thus was because, unconsciously, another woman had won his heart; further, that that other woman was herself?

No; of course the day would never dawn when he would dare to tell her that. An eternity separated them.

But he tried not to think of it now; to remember only that Lorraine, his best friend and his benefactress, was dying, and that she had sent Hal to fetch him to her side.

His face was very grave, and he looked white and ill as Hal explained what time he must meet her at the station, but he gave no sign of flinching; no triumph in the world could now weaken his resolution.

"Very well, that is all arranged," said Hal, and at that moment there was a knock at the door. Alymer crossed the room and opened it himself, and was handed a telegram. He read it, looked for a moment as if he could not grasp it, then, telling the bearer there was no reply, closed the door, went back to Hal, and handed it to her without a word.

Hal read, half aloud:

> "Marked change for the better. No need for haste. Come in a
> few days.—LORRAINE."

For some moments there was only silence, and then she looked at him with troubled, perplexed eyes, and said:

"I don't quite know what to make of it."

"Doesn't it mean that she has passed some crisis and will live?" he suggested. "I think it must."

Hal still looked doubtful; and at that moment there was another knock at the door.

Again Alymer opened it himself. "Lord Denton particularly wishes to see you," he was told.

"Show him in at once," he replied, and turned to tell Hal who was coming.

Flip Denton had come to inquire for more detailed news of Lorraine than he could get from her letters. He gathered from them that she was remaining away for the whole winter theatrical season, because her health was bad; but any suggestion on his part to run over to Brittany and see her was persistently negatived. Finally he had come to Alymer.

The moment he saw them he knew that something serious was wrong, and that it concerned Lorraine. But when, after learning she was very ill, he asked Hal what was the matter, and saw the scarlet blood flame into her face, he said no more.

"I was with her yesterday," she told him, "and the doctor said he feared she would not live many days. She wanted Alymer, and I came over to fetch him."

"And you are going at once?" Denton asked him, with a curious expression in his eyes.

"I have arranged to."

"Doesn't your great case come on this afternoon, or tomorrow morning?"

"Yes."

Denton's grave face did not change. "I see," he said, and turned a little aside.

Then Hal, who had the telegram in her hand, held it out to him.

"This has just come."

He read it, and his face cleared joyously.

"Why, that is splendid news—don't you think so?" And he regarded Hal with a slightly puzzled air.

"I hardly know what to think," Hal said. "Yesterday she was very ill."

"Ah, but you had to leave early," reassuringly, "and she may have been gaining strength all the afternoon, and had a very good night. What are you going to do?" looking at Alymer.

Alymer looked at Hal, and waited for her decision.

Hal only looked doubtful and troubled.

"I think you should stay for the lawsuit," Denton said, to help her. "It is evident that Lorraine wished it, and she of all people would not have Hermon miss such a chance if possible. I understood Hall it was only likely to last two or three days. He has some clinching evidence, I think."

"That is so," Alymer answered gravely; but he still waited to take his cue from Hal.

"You think he should stay for it?" Hal asked Lord Denton.

"I certainly think that is what Lorraine would wish him to do."

"Very well."

Hal commenced to pull on her gloves as if there were no more to say, and then Denton asked her:

"Will you wait too?"

"No; I am going back by the next boat."

"I will come with you."

She glanced at him with slight alarm, and then at Alymer. Denton saw the look and seemed surprised. Hal's eyes asked Alymer what they were to do. He spoke with an effort.

"I expect Miss Vivian would be glad to see so old and great a friend as Lord Denton."

"Of course she would," he said decidedly—and to Hal:

"What time do we leave Charing Cross?"

Hal spoke very little on the journey. A nameless dread weighed on her spirit, and a haunting fear for Lorraine. She was oppressed by a sense of deep sadness for the brilliant, succesful woman she had loved since her school days, who was now, after all her triumphs, alone in that little foreign village, caught in a maze of tangles and perplexities which offered no peaceful solution.

She could not understand Alymer's part at all, but she was convinced Lorraine's absorbing devotion to him was not reciprocated in like manner.

If Lorraine learnt this as soon as she recovered, what did the future hold for her again but more vain dreams, and bitter hopes that could never see fulfilment?

She felt a little pitifully that life was very hard and difficult, even when one had a fine courage and will to face it; and a leaden pall of sorrow seemed to fold itself round her.

What of Dudley and his hopeless love? Ethel and her inconsolable grief? Sir Edwin, and his secret bitterness? the gaunt music-teacher and her barren, joyless life?

Across her mind passed some lines, that had a strong attraction for her:

"So many gods, so many creeds,
so many paths that wind and wind,
And just the art of being kind
Is all the sad world needs."

Ah! in truth it was a sad world first of all; a sad, sad world in need of kindness and comfort. One could but go on trying to be kind, trying to be strong.

It was the only thing in a life of pitfalls and easily made mistakes, to just march straight forward—eyes front—and not let anything daunt permanently. She felt, more profoundly than ever, it was not wise to turn aside, looking to right and left, questioning overmuch of right and wrong, probing into the actions of others.

Each human being was as a soldier in a vast army, and all were there under the same colours, led by the same general, to bear, with what courage they could, the fortunes of war. Two might be standing together, and one be wounded and the other untouched; many disabled, and many unhurt; some left on the field to die, others found and nursed back to life.

But the soldier was not there to question. If a comrade fell, it was no concern of his how he fell—his concern was to try and help him to safety, then go back and fight again, undismayed if his place was but a little insignificant one in the smoke and dust, unseen by any but a near neighbour perhaps as insignificant as himself.

That was the true spirit of the great soldier, whether he was in the ranks, lost in the smoke, or whether, on a magnificent charger, he led gloriously for all the world to see.

She remembered the change in Dudley, which had led him so quickly to respond to her cry, and refrain from judging. He was seeing things in that light also, learning to fight his own fight as pluckily as he could, and only to look upon the warfare of others as one ready to help them if it chanced that he was able—learning in place of rules and precepts, "just the art of being kind."

Well, together perhaps they could help Lorraine—if she came out of this last encounter bruised and broken.

Then they arrived, and she and Lord Denton hastened down the short road to the little green-shuttered house. At the sound of the latch on the gate the door opened quietly, and Jean, with tears streaming down her face, came towards them, choking back gasping sobs.

Hal stood still a second, and then ran forward blindly with outstretched hands.

"She is better, Jean—say she is better. Oh, she must be, she must; she wired yesterday to say there was great improveent."

Jean broke down into helpless weeping as she sobbed out:

"She died this morning at six o'clock."

For one moment Hal seemed too stunned to understand; then she swayed, and fell heavily into Denton's arms.

Later when she had recovered, Jean told them of the restless, nerve-racking night; of the priest's visit, and of the fast-ebbing strength gathered together to write some message the nurse had taken to the post office. After that extreme exhaustion had set in, greatly aggravated by the mental stress, and they could only watch her sinking from hour to hour.

"She only roused once more," Jean said, "and that was to try and write a message for you. I have it there," and she produced a little folded note.

In faint, tremulous words Hal read:

"Good-bye, darling Hal. It is hard to be without you now, but you will inderstand why I sent the message. I want to tell you it has never been Alymer's fault; do not blame him. I ask it of you. At the last hour I have made what reparation I could. Don't grieve for me. I have made so many mistakes, and now I am too tired to go on. Give my dear, dear love to Alymer, and say good-bye to Flip and mother. I am not unhappy now—only very, very tired.

"Your own
"LORRY."

For the first time since she had recovered from her faint, Hal broke down, and Jean and Denton went quietly away, knowing it would be better for her afterwards, and left her sobbing her heart out over her letter.

Two days later, flying the colours of a great victory, and flushed with the pleasure of warm congratulations poured upon him from all sides, Alymer Hermon stepped out upon the little station.

He had never doubted the truth of the message, and he carried his head a little higher and his shoulders a little squarer, proud and glad to come to Lorraine with the news of his greatest success, and tell her of the proud position he had won almost solely through her. For had she not first imbued him with ambition and the real desire to achieve, and then, at exactly the right moment, procured him the first little success that meant so much?

The instant he knew the great case was won, he had dashed out of the court, scribbled her a hurried wire, and driven frantically to Charing Cross, meditating a special train to Dover, if he were too late. He was not, though the guard was just about to give the signal for departure, and the boat-train bore him from the station, full of that glad consciousness of a great achievement, to carry the news instantly to her feet.

On the little station in Brittany Denton was waiting for him. And when Alymer saw him the light faded out of his eyes, and the smile from his lips.

"She died before we got there," Denton told him. "We daren't let you know, because she sent that message, on purpose to give you your chance in the case." Then, very kindly: "Sit down, old chap. There's no hurry. Wait and rest a while here."

Alymer sat down on the little wooden station bench, and buried his face in his hands.

CHAPTER XLV

It would seem sometimes that Life has a way of keeping the balance between joy and pain, by making that which is a source of deepest sorrow to one the unlooked-for instrument of great joy to another.

It was so with the sorrow that came down like a cloud upon Hal's spirit, while she was yet striving bravely not to allow herself to fret over Sir Edwin's perfidy.

It was not until after Hermon's arrival that the announcement of Lorraine's death was sent to the papers. After an anxious consultation, Hal and Denton had decided she would have expressly wished nothing to be done which might bring the news to Alymer before his case was over, and so, while making all preparations for the funeral, they refrained from any announcement in the home papers. Directly he arrived, the notice was dispatched.

Ethel Hayward, returning from her holiday to the dreary, empty Holloway flat, read it in the train as she journeyed. Instantly her mind was full of Hal. She felt that in losing the one great woman friend of her life Hal would seem to have lost mother, sister, and friend in one.

She went home to the emptiness of the flat, with her heart so full of aching sympathy that some of the bitterness of her own loss was softened. On her sitting-room table was a beautiful array of flowers. She looked at them with soft eyes, believing Hal had sent them, and her tenderness made her long to hold the girl in her arms and try to bring her a little comfort.

After a restless, troubled half-hour, she decided to go to her. She remembered it was the evening Dudley usually spent at the Imperial Institute, and she thought it almost certain Hal would be alone.

She dreaded going if Dudley was likely to be there, as the constraint between them was a misery to her, but she believed he was obliged to be out, remembering how he had always been engaged on Fridays during his engagement, and she took her courage in her hands for Hal's sake, and went to the Bloomsbury rooms for the first time.

The maid who opened the door was just going out, and being somewhat hurried, did not trouble to note whether she asked for Mr. Pritchard or Miss Pritchard, merely standing for her to come in, and then showing her into the sitting-room without properly announcing her, she hastened away.

So Ethel unexpectedly found herself face to face with Dudley, alone.

He was so astonished, that for a moment he seemed unable to rise, merely gazing at her with incredulous eyes, as if he thought he must be dreaming.

For the past hour he had sat with a book on his knee, without having read a line, for all the time his thoughts had been with her. He knew she had returned that night to her empty, desolate home. He had sent the flowers up himself, to try and mitigate the emptiness and lack of welcome.

He had longed to go to the station to meet her, if only to look after her luggage and see her safely into a cab. He hated to think of her arriving alone, and departing alone to that empty flat. His utter helplessness to do anything for her, when all his soul ached to do all, tore at his heart, and thrust mercilessly upon him again and again his blindness and folly in the past.

And then suddenly, in the midst of it, without any warning, she stood there in the room, looking at him with startled, abashed eyes.

No wonder, with a sense of non-comprehension, joy leapt to his own, transforming the white, unhappy gravity of his face to swift, questioning eagerness; while at the same time he breathed tensely, "Ethel!... you!"

It was the first time he had ever used her Christian name, and in spite of her confusion she could not fail to hear the ring of gladness, of intense, almost unbelievable joy.

It sent the blood rushing to her white cheeks, and made her heart beat wildly. She moved forward a little unsteadily.

"I saw about Miss Vivian's death today, and I was afraid Hal would be all alone fretting... so I came to see—"

She broke off. Something like a sudden appeal in his eyes was unnerving her.

Dudley only heard vaguely what she said.

As she came forward he had seen that she was rather overcome; he had seen the quick scarlet in her face, followed by a striking parlor, and the bewildered surprise in her eyes.

What was it Hal had said that evening before she left? He could not remember, but he knew it meant that she did not think Ethel indifferent to him as he believed.

He knew she had meant more, but he had not dared to dwell upon it.

He stood up, but did not move towards her. Instead, he just stood looking, looking into her eyes. Hers fell, and again the quick colour came and went.

"Hal is not here," he said simply; "she went to Miss Vivian last week."

"Oh, I am glad. I was afraid she had not had time. I thought, when I saw the flowers…" An idea seemed to strike her suddenly. She looked at him, and her eyes were full of a question she could not ask. "I thought only Hal knew I should be returning today."

"I knew," he said simply.

"Did you… did you…" she was at a loss to finish.

This hesitating nervousness was new to him. He had never seen her before other than calmly self-possessed. It called, with swift-calling, to his natural masculine strength and masculine protectiveness. It enabled him to grow sure of himself, and strong.

"Yes, I sent the flowers," he answered. "I wanted badly to come to the station to meet you, but I was afraid you might think it an impertinence." He came a little nearer. "Sould you have thought so?"

He seemed to be waiting for an answer, and she said shyly:

"I should have thought it very kind of you."

"I am always wanting to do things for you," he said, "and I am always afraid I shall only vex you. And I wouldn't vex you for the world," in a low, fervent voice.

Again she gave him a swift, shy, questioning glance, and he grew bolder still.

He came closer, and stood beside her.

"Most of all, I want to tell you that I love you with all my heart and soul and strength, and, until this moment, I have been afraid that that would vex you too."

She raised her eyes then, swimming in sudden tears of gladness.

"But it doesn't?…" he said eagerly, "you… you… Oh, Ethel! is it possible you would like me to say it?"

"It has been possible a long time, Dudley, but I did not think it would ever be said."

He took her hands in his and kissed first one and then the other. For the moment he was too overwhelmed at the suddenness of his joy to understand it.

"I thought you despised me," he breathed. "It did not seem possible you could do anything else; but Hal said I was wrong."

She smiled faintly.

"Yes; Hal knew," she told him. "I think she has known some time." Then she seemed to sway a little.

"You are tired out," he exclaimed in quick commiseration. "What a brute I am, letting you stand all this time, after your long journey too! I have told myself over and over how I would take care of you if I might, and this is how I begin! Forgive me—."

He gently pushed her towards his own big chair, and when she had sunk down in it, fetched a cushion and a footstool. She leaned back wearily, looking up at him with eyes that were full of deep joy, if not yet emancipated from their long, long vigil of sorrow.

"Is this all true, or am I dreaming? Yesterday—an hour ago—I thought it could never happen at all."

"I too."

He was kneeling on one knee beside her now, holding her hand against his face for the comfort of it.

"I was thinking of you when you came. I am always thinking of you. My whole life is like a long thought of you. I was afraid it would never become any more. Since I grew to know myself better, it has never seemed possible any one like you could care for such as I."

She gave him her other hand confidingly.

"I think I have always cared, Dudley. Beside Basil, there has never been any one else who counted very much at all."

It was good to be sitting there together by a fireside. So good indeed that it swept everything away that had stood between them, with swift, generous sweeping. There had been nothing real in the barrier, scarcely anything that needed explaining, only the foolish imaginings of two hearts that had become imbued with wrong impressions.

"I thought I loved Doris," he told her, still caressing her hand; "but afterwards it was like a pale fancy to my love for you."

"I was terrified lest she should wreck both your lives," She answered. "She cared so much for money, and the things money can buy. Without it, she might have grown bitter and hard and reckless. With it, she wil grow kinder, I think. She felt Basil's death very much. She shed the most genuine tears she has ever shed in her life. Dudley, if Basil had known that this was coming, it would have been a great comfort to him."

"He did know."

"He knew!..." in surprise. "How could he?"

"I told him. I saw he was fretting very much about you, and I guessed what was in his mind. I told him I loved you better than my life; and he said: 'Thank God, it will all come right some day.'"

"Ah, I am glad that he knew. Dear Basil, dear Basil. If he had been less splendid, Dudley, I think I should have taken my own life when he died and left me alone. But in the face of courage like his, one could not be a coward."

Later Dudley took her home. At the door he asked her pleadingly:

"May I came in for a moment? I want to see the flat as it looks now."

She led the way, and they stood together in the little sitting-room where Basil had lived and died, and where Dudley's flowers now shed a fragrance of welcome.

She buried her face in the delicate petals, with memories, and thoughts, and feelings too deep for words.

"It feels almost as if his spirit were here with us now," he said softly. "He was so sure he was only going to a grander and wider life. I think he must have been right; and that tonight he *knows*."

Tears were in her eyes again. The loss was so recent still—the memory so painful. He drew her to him, and kissed them away.

"That night, Ethel, that first, terrible night when you were alone, it nearly killed me to have to go away and leave you, to feel I could not do anything at all. You must let me comfort you doubly now to make up for it. You must come to me quickly." She smiled softly, and he added: "It would have been Basil's wish, too. He hated the office as much as I do. Tell them tomorrow that you're not coming any more."

Her smile deepened at his boyishness.

"There are certain hard-and-fast rules to be observed about leaving. I'm afraid they won't waive them for you."

"Well, tell them you are going to be married... You *are* going to be married, aren't you?..." for a moment he was almost like Hal. "Well, why don't you answer? I want to know."

"I haven't made up my mind sufficiently yet," with a low, happy laugh.

"Then I must make it up for you."

His manner changed again to one of wondering, absorbing tenderness. Hal had been right, as usual. Under the man's surface-narrowness and superiority was a deep, true heart that had only been waiting the hour of its great emancipation. He took her in his arms and kissed her again and again.

"Child," he breathed, "haven't I waited long enough? Every hour of the last few months, since I knew, has been like a year. Don't make me leave you here alone one moment longer than is necessary."

So it happened that when Hal came back to a dreary, empty, joyless London, an unexpected gladness was waiting for her.

The last few days had almost broken her spirit. The pathos of that lonely, far-off grave, in the little alien churchyard, where they tenderly left the remains of the beautiful, brilliant woman who had been so much in her life for so long, seemed more than she could bear.

They three had stood together, representing her richness in friendship, her poverty in blood ties. The wire to her mother had only brought the reply from some one in London that she was travelling in the South of Italy, and could not possibly arrive in time.

Alymer still seemed almost stunned. He had scarcely spoken since Danton told him what had happened. At first Hal had declined to see him at all, but in the end Denton, with his shrewd common sense, had talked her into a kindlier mood.

When they came back from the churchyard she had gone to him in the little sitting-room, where he sat alone, with bowed head. He stood up when she came in, but he did not speak. He waited for her to say what she would, with a look of quiet misery in his eyes that touched her heart.

For the first time she saw how changed he was. There seemed nothing of the old boyishness left. Only a quiet, grave, deeply suffering man.

She had no conception that she, personally, added every hour and every moment to that suffering. She did not know he was enduring a bitter sense of having lost her for ever, as well as the friend and benefactress he had undoubtedly loved very dearly, if not with the same passionate love that she had known for him.

But he only stood before her there, very straight and very still, and with that old, quiet, ineradicable dignity which never failed him.

"Lorraine left a little written message for me," she said to him.

She paused a moment, and her eyes wandered away out to the little garden, with its last fading summer beauty yielding already to autumn. And so she did not see the expression in his fine face when he ventured to look at her. She did not know that because of his hopeless love, and withal his quiet courage and quiet pain, at that moment he looked even more splendidly a man than perhaps he had ever done before.

Had life been kinder, he would have crossed the space between them in one step, and folded her in such an embrace as would have lost her slim form entirely in his enfolding bigness. He would have given her a love, and a lover, such as falls to the lot of but few women.

And she stood there, with her head half turned away; with sad eyes and drooping lips that went to his heart; her mind full of her dead friend, and scarcely a glance for him.

"She said I was not to blame you for anything, and she told me to give you her dear, dear love."

He winced visibly, but stood his ground.

"Thank you," he said, in a very low voice.

Then, with a sudden, longing triumphing over all:

"I prefer to take the blame upon myself, but even then I hope some day you will find it possible to forgive me."

"I shall never forget how much Lorraine loved you," was all the poor hope she gave him.

"Will that make it possible for us to remain friends?"

"Yes; I hope so." She gave him her hand with an old-fashioned solemnity. "For Lorraine's sake," she said very simply, and then left him.

He turned with a stifled groan, and, leaning his elbows on the mantelpiece, buried his face in his hands.

Yet in that painful hour, out of all the tragic mistakes of her life, Lorraine might have gleaned this gladness. In that hour he was nearer than he had ever been before to the man she had striven to make him; for, mercifully for all mankind, there is a "power outside ourselves," which out of wrong, and weakness, and pain can bring forth good.

The sad trio returned to London the following day, and Hal wondered forlornly if Dudley would leave his office early to come and meet her.

When she stepped out on the platform he and Ethel were standing together, looking for her. Then they saw her, and Ethel came forward first, holding out both hands, with a subdued light in her face, that made Hal pause and wonder.

"How did you know? It was nice of you to come," she said, with another question in her eyes.

"Dudley told me, dear. I have been thinking of you so much."

Then Dudley stepped up to them, and in his face, too, was this subdued gladness.

Hal looked from one to the other.

"Have you?..." she began, and paused uncertainly.

"Yes, dear"; and Ethel blushed charmingly. "I am going to be your sister, so I thought you would let me begin at once, and come to meet you, and try to comfort you a little."

"Oh," said Hal, drawing a deep breath; "and I thought I was never going to be glad about anything again."

CHAPTER XLVI

It is necessary to take but a cursory glance at the events that followed. Life flowed smoothly enough in its way, but it flowed towards higher and greater achievements for some, and that can only mean a story of obstacles, and drawbacks and difficulties sturdily overcome.

For the three inmates of the Cromwell Road flat it held many prizes.

Alymer Hermon's career continued to advance by leaps and bounds. The "taking up" by Sir Philip Hall became quickly an actual fact, and he was soon easily first among the juniors. What he lacked in years and experience his striking presence and personal charm supplied, and his calm gravity and self-possession went far to counteract his youthful appearance.

Dick Bruce finished his great novel, and though it was not quite the jumble about vegetables and babies he had prophesied, it was considered the most original book of the year, and brought him instantaneous recognition and fame.

Quin inherited some money, and built a wonderful East End Club House that is all his own, and is as the apple of his eye.

If the great solution of life is to find one's true environment, he has at any rate found his; and in finding it knows a happiness, even amid the squalid poverty of Shoreditch, such as is found by few.

In the meantime Hal continued to work and be independent. When Ethel and Dudley married, they tried hard to persuade her to live with them, but she had already bespoken a smaller sitting-room with her old landlady, Mrs. Carr, and made up her mind to live there.

Later, when Dudley began to add to his income, they begged her to give up her work, but she was obdurate, again expressing certain views on the boon of steady occupation they could not gainsay.

"It is so boring sometimes," Ethel remonstrated, and she answered:

"Not so boring as idleness in the long run, and having to make up your mind each day what you are going to do next. The girls who only enjoy themselves without work little know what they miss in never waking up in the morning to say, 'Hurray! this is a holiday.' No! give me my work and my play well balanced, and I'll turn them into happiness."

It was months before Alymer dared to speak to her of love. It had taken him long to win her to the old fooling again; and in a sudden gladness at some little remark or touch that seemed to show him he was truly forgiven for his own sake, he told her the story of his love, and his long waiting.

Hal was very taken aback, and a little unhappy, but when she had convinced him it was really quite hopeless, he forced himself back to the old comradeship, and took up his self-imposed burden of waiting once more.

Then followed a period of rapid successes, during which Hal told him seriously he must now make a choice among the bevy of beauty, wealth, and lineage at his disposal.

"You really ought, you know," she said, "out of consideration for all the poor things left hoping against hope, and the numbers that are yearly added to them!"

"I have made my choice," he answered; "it is not my fault about the vain hopes. It is the obstinacy of one woman, who is keeping the others in the unfortunate condition you describe."

But she only smiled lightly, and put him off again, concluding with:

"I should be frightened out of my life at possessing anything so beauteous and attractive in the way of a husband."

So Hermon worked on, and waited, believing in his star.

Yet there were times when the apparent hopelessness of it weighed heavily on his mind—times when the very lustre of his success seemed only to mock him, because of that one thing he craved in vain.

It was so when the greatest achievement of his life came to his hands.

It was given him to plead for a woman's life against a charge of poisoning her husband, pitting his youth and slender experience against the greatest advocate of the Crown. The case caused a great stir, and with a growing wonderment and pride she hardly dared to account for. Hal followed the newspaper reports day by day.

The evening before the speech for the defence he came to her. She greeted him as usual, saying little about his present notoriety, but she noticed that he looked careworn, as if the strain were becoming too much for him; and then suddenly he stated his errand.

"I want you to come to the court tomorrow, Hal. I—I—have a feeling I want you to be there when I am speaking. Will you come?"

She looked up doubtfully.

"Why do you want me?"

"I hardly know. I mean to save this woman if I can. She did not give the poison. I am quite certain of it; but we can't prove it absolutely. We can only appeal in such a way to the jury that they will feel the case is not merely not proven against her, but that she is innocent. I think it would inspire me more than anything if you were there." He paused, then added: "I love you so much, Hal, I feel as if I shall save her life if you are there."

Hal looked touched, and agreed to go if he would arrange everything, and telephone to her what time to arrive.

The next day she went to the court with the card he had given, and found herself received with the utmost deference, and ushered at once to a seat reserved for her.

A few minutes afterwards Alymer stood up to make his great speech, and then Hal heard a subdued murmur around her, and saw that the judge was watching him with some interest and expectancy.

It was the first time she had seen him in his wig and gown, in court, and her heart began to beat strangely. She felt suddenly and unaccountably incensed with the women all round, who whispered and gazed. "What was he to them anyway! How idiotic of them to murmur to each other how splendid he looked! What did he care for their approval?"

Her heart carried her a little farther. "What is he to you?..." it asked. She felt a sudden warm glow of pride, and her eyes grew very soft as she watched him.

Then he began to speak, and it seemed as if everything in heaven and earth has paused to listen. Surely there was no big thoroughfare with hurrying multitudes just outside, no continual stream of noisy, hurrying traffic; no busy newspaper offices awaiting each flying message—nothing anywhere but that crowded hall, that white-faced accused woman waiting for death or freedom, that man in his beauty of manhood and power straining every nerve to save her.

An hour passed. No one spoke, no one moved. Sometimes a sob, hastily stifled, broke the oppresive hush, sometimes a stifled cough.

Alymer rarely raised his voice, for his was no impassioned, heated declaration. It was a magnificent piece of quiet oratory, which carried every one along by its earnestness and convincing calm, and was intensified by the look upon his noble, resolute face.

After a time every one knew instinctively that he had won. The tension grew less taut and more emotional. Women began to weep softly and restrainedly. Men cleared their throats again and again. Some one sitting next to Hal apparently knew him, and knew her.

"My God," he breathed in her ear, "he's magnificent. He's saved her. I wouldn't have missed this for anything. I'm proud to be his friend."

Hal's eyes suddenly filled with tears. She began to feel dazed and faint. It had been too much for her, and the relief was overwhelming.

She thought of Lorraine, and her heart swelled to think he had so gloriously fulfilled her vast hopes, and crowned all she had done for him. She longed that she might have been there, and then felt mysteriously that she not only was there, but was speaking to her. In a vague, unreal, mystical way, Lorraine was pleading with her to give him his happiness.

She looked again, confusedly, at the big, strong, calm man; and something that had been growing in her heart for months took shape and form.

What did the other women matter? He was hers—hers—hers. Why stop to question or demur? What did anything matter but that he had loved her so long and faithfully; and that at last she loved him?

In a stress of unendurable emotion, she got up unsteadily, and left the court.

A quarter of an hour later, Alymer finished his speech, and sat down instantly turning his head to look for her. Instead of the familiar, eager face of the first hour, he saw the empty space, and his overwrought mind sank to a dull level of bitter disappointment.

She was not impressed, then—not even interested enough to stay until the end. Oh, what did it matter? She was hard—hard, he was a fool to love her so.

The jury went away and came back with their verdict of "Not guilty."

There was a rush and buzz of congratulations. He smiled, because he had to smile, and grasped outstretched hands because he had to grasp them. The moment it was possible to get away, he walked blindly and hurriedly to the entrance, and got into a taxi, before the waiting crowd had had time to recognise him.

"Where to?" a policeman asked him, and for a moment he was at a loss to know. Then he gave Hal's address. "Better have it out and done with," was his thought. Once for all he would make her tell him if it was hopeless, and if she said yes, he would go away and try to forget her in another country.

When he was shown into Hal's little sitting-room, he found her crouching on a footstool in the firelight, before the fire. He stood a moment or two and looked at her, and then he said in a slightly harsh voice:

"I suppose you hurried away because you were bored. I thought you would have stayed until the end. I was a fool. Nothing I do ever has interested you, or ever will."

Hal did not look round. She was staring into the flames, with her chin resting in her hands. When he paused she said calmly:

"I can't hear what you say so far away."

He moved across the room and stood on the hearth beside her, towering above her, with his eyes on the opposite wall.

"I don't know why I came here at all," he continued; "but it didn't seem any use going anywhere else. Why did you run away in the middle! Did you want to punish my presumption for wishing to try and distinguish myself before you, as well as save a woman's life and honour?"

A little smile shone in Hal's eyes, where the firelight caught them.

"I can't hear what you say, right up there, near the ceiling."

He looked down at the dark shapely head, and something in her poise and in her voice made his heart suddenly begin to thump rather wildly.

"I haven't got a beanstalk," she added.

He leaned a little towards her.

"And if you had?" he asked tensely.

"If I had, I would perhaps climb up it."

He leaned lower still, his heart thumping yet more wildly.

"If you climbed up a ladder like that, you would be bound to climb into my arms."

"Well—and what if I did?" she said.